KU-615-845

THE TOWER OF
LIVING AND DYING

Also by Anna Smith Spark

The Empires of Dust
The Court of Broken Knives

ANNA SMITH SPARK

The Tower of Living and Dying

Book Two of The Empires of Dust

HARPER
Voyager

HarperCollins*Publishers*
1 London Bridge Street,
London SE1 9GF

www.harpercollins.co.uk

Published by Harper*Voyager*
An imprint of HarperCollins*Publishers* 2018
1

Copyright © Anna Smith-Spark 2018

Map by Sophie E. Tallis

Anna Smith-Spark asserts the moral right to
be identified as the author of this work

A catalogue record for this book
is available from the British Library

HB ISBN: 978-0-00-820408-2
TPB ISBN: 978-0-00-820409-9

This novel is entirely a work of fiction.
The names, characters and incidents portrayed in it are
the work of the author's imagination. Any resemblance to
actual persons, living or dead, events or localities is
entirely coincidental.

Typeset in Sabon by
Palimpsest Book Production Ltd, Falkirk, Stirlingshire

Printed and bound by CPI Group (UK) Ltd, Croydon CR0 4YY

All rights reserved. No part of this publication may be
reproduced, stored in a retrieval system, or transmitted,
in any form or by any means, electronic, mechanical,
photocopying, recording or otherwise, without the prior
permission of the publishers.

MIX
Paper from
responsible sources
FSC™ C007454

This book is produced from independently certified FSC™ paper
to ensure responsible forest management.

For more information visit: www.harpercollins.co.uk/green

This book is dedicated to my family,
Jamie, Ianthe and Neirin.

PART ONE

SUNRISE

PART ONE

SUNRISE

Chapter One

In the tall house in Toreth Harbour, the High Priestess Thalia lay awake in the darkness, listening to her lover's breath. Faint noises outside the window: a woman's voice calling, drunken singing and a shriek and a crash. Laughter. The wind had risen again. She could hear the sea, the waves breaking on the shingle, the gulls.

I have seen a dragon, she thought. I have seen a dragon dancing on the wind. I have seen the sea. The sky. The cold of frost. The beauty of the world. I have felt the sun on my face as it rose over the desert. I have felt clear water running beneath my feet. I have known sorrow and pain and happiness and love.

She sat up and brought a candle to burning. The man beside her stirred at it, clawing roughly at his face. She smoothed her hand over his forehead, and he sighed and relaxed back deeper into sleep.

King Marith Altrersyr. Amrath returned to us. King Ruin. King of Shadows. King of Dust. King of Death.

Dragonlord. Dragon killer. Dragon kin. Demon born.

Parricide. Murderer. Hatha addict.

The most beautiful man in the world.

She went over to the wall where his sword hung, took it up, walked back to the bed. For a moment her hands shook.

A kindness, she thought.

The gulls screamed at the window. Shadows crawled on the walls.

She raised the sword over his heart.

Looked at him.

A kindness. To her. To him.

But he's so beautiful, she thought.

She put the sword down and curled back beside him.

Slept.

Chapter Two

Full morning. The green moors above the town of Toreth Harbour. Grass and wild flowers running down to the cliff top, dark rocks, weathered stone, the steep drop to the churning sea. Grey sky. Grey earth. Grey water. A rent in the world, a scar, a sore, where the tower of Malth Salene had stood proud above the town and the water, where a battle had been fought, where a young man had been crowned king.

Marith Altrersyr stood on the cliff top, looking at the ruins. In the light of day the battleground was a desolation. Rock and earth and flesh and blood that had cooled and set like poured glass. A sheen on it, also like glass. In places human faces stared up through the surface, drowned and entombed. A great fortress had stood here. Bedchambers, feasting halls, the chapel of Amrath the World Conqueror where Marith had knelt to receive his ancestor's blessing as king. Treasures, beautiful objects, silks, tapestries, gold, gems. In a few hours, the army of the *Ansikanderakesis Amrakane* had destroyed it utterly. His soldiers' horses snorted and shifted uneasily at the death stink. Even the gulls and the crows had flown.

I did this, Marith thought. So strange, to know that. I did this, I made this. This ruin, this triumph of ending: mine. The summation of my life, perhaps. I killed a man and razed a fortress to ashes and thus I must be a king.

Or nothing at all. A ruined building. A bit of burned ground, where men will rebuild the walls and the grass will regrow.

It was the most wonderful thing I have ever seen, he thought then. Seeing it fall. Destroying it. The most wondrous thing I have ever done.

The memory of it, burning: the walls had run with fire, liquid fire pouring over it; it had shone with fire like stones shine soaked in water, like rocks on the tideline washed with the incoming sea. Its walls had glowed, they had burned so brightly, the stone had been red hot and white hot. Banefire shot from trebuchets, hammering the walls to dust, eating the rocks and the dust and the ground beneath. The men fighting around it, over it, inside it: armed men of his father's army, his own pitiful host from Malth Salene, unarmed servants, old men, kitchen girls. Struggling with each other, killing each other. Tearing down the walls of the fortress. Killing the animals in the courtyards. Cutting down the trees in the orchard beside the south wall. Such utter destruction. He remembered the trees burning, their branches red with fire; they had looked like a glorious forest of autumn beech trees. Sparks rising. Filling the sky. Blotting out all the stars. The earth churned with mud, black in the firelight and the evening darkness. His men dancing and clashing their swords, shouting for him, singing out his name, their faces stained with blood and smoke.

Glorious. Astonishing. Beautiful beyond all things.

They did this at my bidding, he thought. For me. I killed so many of them. They killed, they destroyed, they followed me. I killed them, he thought. And still they followed me.

And the killing. The killing, the fighting, it had been . . . ah, gods, it had been sweet.

He had left this place once with his best friend's blood on his hands. Come back here bound and humiliated, a prisoner, contemplating his own death. And now here he was made king. I didn't used to think I wanted to be king, he thought.

A strange thing to think.

A voice called, loud in the still cold air. 'We've found it.'

Ah, gods. Marith turned, walked to where his soldiers were moving. He walked slowly. His heart beat very loud.

'My Lord King, we've found it.'

Marith rubbed at his eyes. Looked down. Looked away. Looked down.

His father's body was stretched on the earth before him. Face down in the dust. Broken apart. Torn into shreds by his son's blade, like hands devouring consuming him. I killed him, Marith thought again. I killed him. Ah, gods.

Marith bent, knelt by the body, stared. Dead eyes stared back at him. A look of astonishment on his father's face. Had not believed that Marith would do it, even as the sword came down and down and down.

'Talk to him,' Thalia had said to him, one night only a few days ago, standing on the walls of Malth Salene looking at his father's besieging campfires. 'Can you not talk to him?'

He killed my mother. He told everyone that I was dead. He hated me. He was ashamed of me. What could I say to him?

The air hissed and writhed around Marith. Darker, colder air. The sound of waves crashing on the rocks of the shore beneath. His own heartbeat, like the beating of a bird's wings or the thunder of horses' hooves.

'Bring the body down to Toreth,' he ordered the soldiers. 'Preserve it in honey. We will return it to Malth Elelane. Bury it with honour there.' Malth Elelane, the Tower of Joy and Despair, the seat of the Altrersyr kings. Home. My father's father's grave, he thought, and his father's before that . . . All the way back to Altrersys, and to Serelethe herself, the mother of Amrath. The mother of a god. She who began it all. Who doomed me to this. Dragon born. Demon kin. The bloodline of the Altrersyr, whose very name is a whisper of pain and hate.

The air hissed and writhed around him. His father's dead face. Flies were crawling on its open lips.

'Marith,' his father had cried out, as he killed him. He remembered that. Bringing his sword down, again, again, again, his father breaking, falling, shattered into pieces, crying out his name as he died. 'Marith. Please.'

Can you not talk to him? Killing and killing. His sword so bright. The crash of bronze, his sword blade on his father's armour; his father had tried to defend himself against him, tried to strike him back, the two of them hacking at each other, so close to each other, strike and strike and the ring of bronze. 'Marith. Marith,' his father had cried to him. And he'd struck his father so hard, feeling his father's body break beneath his sword blade, flesh and fat and bones and bloodshed, his father's body opening up red and ruined beneath his sword strokes. Tear him into pieces. Hurt him. Empty him. Blood and blood and blood.

A king, Father! Look at me! I am a king!

Marith thought: he must have hated me.

Marith turned away from the body. The soldiers were lifting it awkwardly, in pieces, falling, flopping about, the head flopping back, black dried blood crusted on its throat. He thought: don't run; in front of the soldiers, my soldiers, don't run. And there in the burned earth before him a pile of tumbled stone, smudged with colour beneath the smoke, the mark of carving still clearly visible, the smooth curve of polished stone. The head of the statue of Amrath from the chapel, perfect and unharmed, cleanly severed at the neck.

He thought: don't run. Not in front of the soldiers. My soldiers. Don't run.

He went back towards his horse, stopped, stared round him, walked across the ruined ground north towards the cliff edge and the sea. There on the headland the ground was undisturbed, grass still growing, purple heather, the last yellow flowers of gorse, all the petals ragged and browned from the recent snow. A man's body, a dagger clutched in a raised hand. A child's body, eyes open to the sky. A mound of dark earth, topped with a stone carved with the crude image of a horse.

Carin's grave. It had watched the battle, seen Carin's murderer wade through blood triumphant and victorious, seen Carin's family and Carin's home destroyed.

'I'm sorry.' There was a flask of wine at his belt: Marith poured a libation over the gravestone. 'You . . . perhaps you deserved this, Carin. That you did not have to see this. What I have done.'

The stone gave no answer. But they had always avoided speaking of what he was. Marith rubbed his eyes. All done here. All that had held anything for him here was dead and gone. He mounted his horse, rode down the golden paved road back to Toreth. The soldiers followed, carrying his father's body on a bier, the eyes still staring up astonished into the grey sky. The air hissed and writhed. On the sea, the shadows of clouds ran. The sea was as cold as iron and the light did not dance on the waves. At the gates of the town the cheer rang out to greet him.

'King Marith! *Ansikanderakesis Amrakane*! Death! Death! Death!'

A single ray of sunlight broke through the clouds. Shone on Marith's silver crown.

Chapter Three

A king? He wore a crown, men knelt at his feet, he was first-born heir to the White Isles and his father the last king was dead. But the house of the king was far away on another island, his younger brother sat there on the throne of Altrersys in his place, the men of the White Isles believed him dead. King of a single town, a fishing port, his seat a fish merchant's house with tall narrow rooms and worn floors. So glorious a place from which to reclaim his own.

Perhaps, Marith thought for a moment, it had been possibly foolish to raze the one fortress he had possessed to the ground. Burn the world and piss on the ashes and end up sleeping in a lumpy old bed with mildew stains on the wall. A triumph indeed.

There were sea-worn stones and bird feathers hanging on leather thongs beside the house's doorway. They rattled as he went past. The owner of the house, the future Lord Fishmonger, the wealthiest herring merchant in Toreth Harbour, knelt like the rest as Marith entered. His hair was greasy, dandruff caught on his shoulders, beneath the perfume Marith was certain he smelled of fish. But he'd handed his house over so happily, so gladly, his face had been all bright with eagerness to let a blood-soaked boy throw him out of his lumpy old bed. Surely the greatest honour a man could ever have, that.

Lord Fishmonger looked nervous. 'My Lord King,' Lord Fishmonger said nervously. Marith thought: I must find out his name, I suppose. 'My Lord King . . .'

Thalia came down the stairs. The sun came in through a window onto her face. She wore a white dress with pink and green flowers on it: in the golden light, with her brown skin and black hair, she looked like a may tree in bloom. Marith closed his eyes. Opened them. Too bright to look at. The sunlight was bright on her, and her face was nothing but light.

She was holding her cloak in her arms.

She looked at him for a very long time. Seemed about to speak.

He thought: she is leaving me.

He thought: I have made it safe for her to leave me. And now she will go. The realization struck him: she did not choose to come here with me. I rescued her from a stranger's violence; she came here with me as a prisoner; she was trapped with me in a fortress under siege. And now that I have broken the siege she will turn and walk away.

She's too good for me, he thought. Parricide. Vile thing. King of Death.

Lord Fishmonger, edging around beside him, said, 'My Lord King . . .'

A cloud passed over the sun. The light faded. Thalia's blue eyes dark and cautious. She did not speak. In the shadow, she looked like the stone on Carin's grave.

Marith said, 'Thalia?'

She looked at him. A very long time, she seemed to look at him.

'Marith,' she said. She seemed uncertain. I don't . . . I don't understand, he thought. Look what I've done for you. All of this, Thalia, all of this I did for you. To give you all that you deserve. To make you queen.

She was the High Priestess of the Lord of Living and Dying, Great Tanis Who Rules All Things, the One God of the Sekemleth Empire of the Asekemlene Emperor of the Eternal Golden City of

11

Sorlost. She who brings death to the dying and life to those who wait to be born.

She knew that he was lying, if he thought he had done any of it for her sake.

'Thalia,' he said again. 'Don't go. Please. I love you,' he said.

Her eyes narrowed. She held out her hand.

He said, 'Please stay.'

She smiled. 'For now,' she said. 'As you ask me so well.'

Hardly an answer. Yet his heart leapt.

But things to do, the ragged soldiers of his army must be addressed, some plan must be made. Very well, Marith, you are king of one town on one island, you have an army of fishermen and servant girls, you have a borrowed horse and a borrowed sword. Your father left his ships at Escral a day's march to the west of here, perhaps even now more of his men are coming for you. You can destroy a tower, yes, granted. Such a display of power, to break mortared stones and bring down a place of peace. But can you hold against warriors, in battle? Killer of babies, you are, Marith. Women. Old men. What can you really do?

The thoughts drumming in him. Horses' hooves again, thundering. Beating wings. His eyes itched like fire. He stared at the walls, trying to see. Thalia sat opposite him in silence. A room that smelled of mildew, and a lumpy bed. All this, for you!

I was going to take you to Ith, he thought. To my uncle's court there, to make you a princess, dress you in gold and diamonds, we could have spent our days riding in the forests, reading side-by-side by a warm fire, talking and dancing and drinking and fucking and doing nothing at all every day. That dream is over. And what have I got for it?

Again, he felt her about to speak.

A confusion in the corridor outside. Knocking on the door, urgent, timid. A relief, even, that someone had come to break the tension, make something happen, give him something to do. Lord Fishmonger, I really must find out his name, Marith thought, Lord

Fishmonger at the door with a message: one of the lords of Third Isle had come, Lord Fiolt, with thirty armed men. Said he wished to do homage to his king. Said indeed that he was the king's particular friend.

Well now. Thalia looked up, confused. Carin Relast was my only friend, he had once told her, my only friend, and he is dead.

Marith got up. 'Osen Fiolt? I will see him in the main chamber, then. Have wine brought for us.' He tried to look away from Thalia. 'I should see him alone.'

She frowned. Thinking.

'I need to be sure of him,' said Marith, 'before I risk anything.' Again, he knew that she knew that this was not true.

She nodded. All so fractured and strained. Perhaps she should have left him. He could give her a bag of gold and a horse and send her on her way somewhere.

He went down the stairs to meet this man who named himself his friend.

Osen Fiolt was a young man, only a few years older than Marith. Dark haired, dark eyed, handsome, with a clever face. He knelt at Marith's feet, his sword held out with the hilt toward Marith in offering. Had the sense at least not to look at the crudely carved chairs, the plastered walls, the pewter jug and clay cups.

Osen said, 'You have my loyalty and my life, My Lord King. My sword is yours.'

Osen's voice half frightened, half mocking. Marith Altrersyr, crowned 'king'.

'Your life and your loyalty. Your sword.' Marith raised his eyes, looked at the ceiling. A stain up there where the winter storms had got in. The king's own particular friend. 'Yet you did not come, My Lord Fiolt, when my father was besieging Malth Salene. One thousand men and seven trebuchets and a magelord, and you did not come to my aid. So should I not kill you? For abandoning me? For not coming to my aid? Where was your sword then? Your loyalty? Your life?'

Osen's face went white. 'I . . . Marith . . . My Lord King . . . Marith . . .' He blinked, his hands working on the blade of the sword. He'd cut himself in a moment, if he wasn't careful. 'I . . .' All the mockery gone out of his voice. Marith Altrersyr, crowned king.

Men's voices drifted in through the windows, soldiers being drilled into some pathetic semblance of order. The army of Amrath. Marith's army. Marith's loyal and beloved men. Osen raised his eyes to Marith's face and Marith could see the thoughts there moving.

Osen said slowly, 'I am the Lord of Malth Calien. I am sworn to Malth Elelane, to the throne of the White Isles, as a vassal of the king. I swore an oath to your father. While he lived, was I not bound to keep it? Whatever my true feelings might have been? Without loyalty, there is chaos. So where does a man's loyalty lie, then, if not to his king above all else?'

Marith thought: we were friends, once, I suppose. I killed Carin. I killed my father. I suppose I may need some friends. He looked down at Osen. Tried to smile. Sitting at a table once, him and Osen and Carin, talking, joking, Osen's half loving half mocking envious eyes. 'I don't trust him,' Carin often said.

'As far as I can remember, we decided it rather depended on the king.'

Osen tried to smile. 'And on the all else.' Pause. 'Though as far as I can remember, we never reached a definitive conclusion, since we had to break off discussing it for you to be sick.'

Young men drinking together. Drawing plans and dreams in spilled wine on the table top. 'I'll need some other lords around me,' Marith had reassured Carin, 'when I'm king. Irlast's a big place just for me and you.'

His eyes met Osen's eyes. The tension broke.

Friends.

Marith reached out and took the proffered sword. 'Indeed. Very well then, My Lord Fiolt. I take your loyalty and your life and your sword.' He laughed. 'Want to drink to the fact I'm still alive?'

Osen sheathed his sword. Laughed back. 'Like I drank to the fact you were dead?'

'You drank to my being dead?'

'Drowning my sorrows. It's what you would have wanted, I'd assumed. No?'

They grinned at each other and sat down by the fire, and Marith sloshed wine into two of the cups. 'It's utterly vile, of course. Half vinegar. But it was this or goat's milk . . . We'll be in Malth Elelane soon, and then we'll have a proper feast to celebrate.'

Osen looked around the room. The rough furniture, the crude wall hangings, the ugly bronze lamp. 'We can have a proper feast quicker than that, at Malth Calien. My loyalty, my life, my sword, and all the contents of my wine cellars, I'll pledge you.' Raised his cup. 'King Marith. May his sword never blunt and his enemies never cease to tremble and his cup never be empty of wine. May my sword never blunt and my life's blood be shed for him.'

'And your cellars hold better things than this muck.'

'That I can pledge you unfailingly. If we ride today, I'll have you drinking hippocras by my fires tomorrow evening.'

He had friends here. Of course he had friends here. He lived here. Friends and lovers and drinking companions and people who'd known him since he was born. A world.

Chapter Four

Thus in the pale afternoon sun they marched out of Toreth, a long thin column of men in armour, with their king and queen at their head. Marith made a speech praising the soldiers' valour, calling them the first, the truest of his warhost, the army of Amrath that would dazzle all the world. The soldiers beat their swords on their shields, shouting, cheering him. 'King Marith! Amrath returned to us! King Marith! Death! Death! Death!' The townspeople mourned to see them leave, the shining new young king who had been made before their walls.

Familiar to Thalia, marching and riding and the creak and clash of armour and men's voices grumbling and the tramp of boots. All she really knew of the world of men. She found some comfort in it, riding into the light and the wind. Marith's face too was brighter, at peace, eyes glittering, looking out over the high curve of the land and the vast sky. The bier carrying his father's body followed behind them, the horses drawing it stamped, tossed their heads.

She turned to look at the soldiers. The survivors of two battles against King Illyn, who had fought to make Marith king. She thought of them as like the priestesses in her Temple. They did as was required by Marith, as the priestesses had done as was required by the God. They died as was required, as the people of her city had volunteered themselves to die under her knife for the God. Life and death balanced. Those who need death dying, those who need life being born. She touched the scars on her left arm, where she had cut herself after every sacrifice. Rough scabbed skin that never fully healed.

She looked at them, and for a moment, a moment, she thought she saw a face she knew. Tobias, she thought. Tobias is here. And I thought, did I not, that I saw him last night. She closed her eyes. When she opened them, she could not see him. Men in armour, marching, helmets over their faces half covering their eyes. Tobias is probably on the other side of Irlast, she thought, with the money he made when he betrayed us. The men shifted position as the road widened coming down into a valley and yes, there was a man who looked a little like Tobias but was very clearly not him.

'Look,' said Marith, pointing. 'The woods we rode in.' Brilliant red leaves clung to the beech trees, but the snow had brought the other trees' leaves down.

Thalia smiled, remembering. They went through the wood for a while. The ground was soft and pleasant, their horses' hooves made a lovely sound in the dried leaves and the beech mast. Thala saw a rabbit, its white tail flashing as it ran from the soldiers, and squirrels in the trees. Rooks cawed overhead.

'I like woodland,' she said to Marith. 'I like this place very much.'

As he had done when they rode in the wood before, he turned his horse, rode to a beech tree in glory, brought back a spray of copper leaves. She placed them in the harness of her horse, like a posy of flowers. Soon after, they came to a river, forded it with the horses up to their knees. The river was very clear, the bottom smooth and sandy. Marith pointed out a place in the bank upstream where he said there was an otter's nest. There were yellow flowers still in bloom on the further side of the river, and a mass of brown seed heads covered in soft white down that caught on their clothes and on the horses' coats.

'This is a good place for fishing,' Marith said.

17

Then the land rose, the trees ended, they came out across the moors, riding into the wind. Thalia's hair whipped out behind her. Marith's vile blood-covered cloak billowed like a flag. In the last of the evening sun the hills were golden with sunlight, purple with heather flowers; a great number of birds turned and wheeled in the sky. This too, thought Thalia, this too is a beautiful place. They followed the banks of a stream for a while. In one place the water made a song as it rushed down over rocks.

I thought I could live here with him, Thalia thought. I don't know, I don't know . . . Why did I let him live? Not just for his beauty. For the beauty of this place?

They slept that night in a way house, built down in a valley between the sweep of two bare hills. The men set up the few tents they had or slept wrapped in their cloaks with fires against the cold. All so familiar. The god stone by the entrance made her shudder; she saw some of the men nod their heads to it, place little offerings of pebbles or a coin, a lock of their hair. But the things that walked on the lich roads were silent and afraid.

A crown, she thought. For that? Only for that?

A soldier came running, eager-eyed, with a dead hare still warm as a gift. They had brought food up from Toreth, bread and wine and meat, but Marith smiled in pleasure, ordered it prepared for cooking, thanked the man. You can keep the skin, he said cheerfully. Make yourself some good mittens out of it. You'll need them, on campaign. Gets cold guarding the king's tent at night. Guarding the king's tent? the man echoed, breathless and radiant. Oh, I think you've earned that, don't you? The man's face lit like a lover's. What's your name? Tal? A good name. Start tonight?

They are falling in love with him, Thalia realized. There was a light to Marith's face as he spoke to them, savouring the fact that they bowed to him, gazed at him with rapture, their beloved, they looked to him already as something fixed and certain, King Marith, Great Lord Amrath, *Ansikanderakesis Amrakane*. She remembered the people of Malth Salene hailing him as king, clapping their hands and chanting his name. The people of Toreth

Harbour, throwing flowers, cheering his entry through their gates with his sword still dripping his father's blood. A few months ago he was believed to be dead. But they followed him now as though they had done so for years. As though all this was natural and real.

A bed was made up for them, blankets piled up on the hard stone bench of the way house. Outside the soldiers fussed, talked, sang, cooked food. Tal proudly served them the hare, roasted whole on the blade of his knife. Marith and Osen Fiolt ate it off the bones, licking grease from their fingers, laughing as they ate.

'It's better than the ground,' Marith said cheerfully. 'And only for one night.' He would have pressed on, she thought, marched them through the dark, except that he had seen her tired face. 'When we get to Malth Calien we'll be able to arrange things properly.'

Unless you decide to burn that too, Thalia thought for a moment. The shadow of the godstone loomed in the firelight like it was burning. The fire rose up and the flames flickered on the thin silver band of Marith's crown. Osen and Marith passed a wineskin, laughing. Poked at the fire to send up showers of sparks. Outside Thalia could hear the men talking, the stamp of horses, the clatter of bronze. Some animal cry, off in the dark: she started fearfully, then heard the men laugh. This darkness, alive and heavy with life. There was a smear of fresh blood, a tiny pile of entrails, at the foot of the godstone. She tried to look away from it, up through the doorway at the stars. So many stars.

'Open another wineskin?' Marith said behind her, to Osen.

'It tastes like goat's piss,' Osen replied. 'And you need to get some sleep, My Lord King. Save yourself for tomorrow night.'

'Oh, dull. All right, it does.' Marith poured the last dregs of the wineskin onto the fire, sending up a cloud of acrid black smoke.

'Oi!' Osen shouted. Laughing. 'What—?'

'I didn't realize there was that much left,' said Marith. His eyes were watering. He poked at the fire with a stick, trying to make it burn up again. 'Sorry,' he said to everyone and no one. The man Tal came forward to rebuild the fire.

Yesterday he was at war killing his own father, Thalia thought.

The country grew wilder the next day, grey rocks clawing up out of the earth, coarse grass and a harsh wind. The mountain of Calen Mon rose up to the south. Its peak shone gold in the pale sun. They marched on fast, meeting no one, following the old straight track of the lich roads across the moor. No people. Where were the people? Thalia wondered. This land was emptier than the desert. An empty land and an empty king. Behind them, the bier of the old king Marith's father followed, drawn on a cart with a red cloth covering the barrel in which the body lay. A dead land and a dead king. She could see, though she had not seen it, the rotting crow-eaten face lying in the barrel, just visible through thick black-yellow honey, eyes open, drowned.

Did I let him live out of pity? she thought.

Around midday it began to rain, a fine grey damp that misted Marith's hair and the filth of his cloak. Rainwater glistened on the men's armour, blurred Thalia's vision, vile and cold. The peak of the mountain disappeared in cloud. They marched on and the rain ceased; she could see off in the distance where it fell on the hills behind them, like a great dark stain.

Coming on towards evening they crested a ridge. Lights below in the gloom: Osen pointed, shouting triumphant. The road fell away steeply; beneath in the shadow of the hill a town huddled, gathered around an inlet fringed with marsh. The sea beyond shone silver dark, a hump of land rising in the distance that must be another island off to the south. On a hummock of dry land out in the marshes, the high walls of a fortress keep.

'Malth Calien!' Osen shouted. 'The Tower of the Eagle! Malth Calien! I offer it to you, My Lord King!'

Another hour's hard marching and they were in the marshes, picking their way with care along the winding causeway that led through them up to the tower. It was made of wood, slippery underfoot, narrow enough that they could walk only two abreast. On either side the reeds grew up high as a man's shoulder, rustling in the wind. A strong, dank smell of salt. A heavy, pressing silence, save the whispering of the reeds. They cut the skin if you brushed against them. And then breaking the silence the honk of geese flying white over them, shaped like an arrow pointing out into the sea.

The causeway crossed a creek busy with wading birds. A few men, too, picked their way across the banks, lanterns bobbing, bending to poke in the mud with long sticks.

'Lugworm gatherers,' Marith explained to Thalia, seeing her look at them curiously, black with mud, bent over, filthy wet sacks over their backs. 'Razor clams. Samphire. Good eating, samphire.' Mud worms? Thalia felt her stomach turn.

Reed beds again, then the path broadened and rose and they were on dry land, a round hill rising clear of the marshes, bigger than it had looked from a distance, crowned with a stone tower, a dark palisade of sharp spikes. On the other side, the hill ran down into mud flats and the sea.

In through the wide wooden gates. A handful of men cheered their coming with a crash of bronze. They pulled up to a stop before the gates of the central tower, where a woman in a green gown stood waiting, a jewelled cup in her pale hands. She sank down to her knees as Marith dismounted.

'My Lord King. Be welcome here.' The woman's voice was thin and sweet, like the chatter of birds. She held out the cup to Marith, who drank deeply then passed it to Osen who also drank. A servant came to help Thalia dismount. After the muck and emptiness of the marshes, the sudden contrast was startling: the woman, young and rosy fair, her dress worked with silver, jewels at her throat; the doors thrown open to show a chamber hung with bright tapestries; servants with fireside warmth pouring from their coats in the cold outside air. Osen took Thalia's arm and led her in after Marith, an antechamber and then a great room with high carved beams, small narrow windows to keep out the wild of the marsh.

She stood gratefully by the fire while the men of the place knelt in turn to Marith, kissed his hand as king. Then up to a high-roofed bedroom at the top of a steep spiral stair. Gloomy, with a strong scent of beeswax candles that made Thalia shiver, more small narrow windows giving glimpses of dark sky.

She assumed they would sleep now, her head was spinning with tiredness after the long ride, but a maidservant laid out a dress of blue velvet for her, a shirt and leggings and jacket for Marith. They were ushered down into the main chamber, where a feast was spread, hot smoky air reeking of meat and alcohol and sweat and salt water, a huge fire casting flickering shadows, cheering faces livid in the flames. The king's soldiers, the men of Malth Calien, Lady Fiolt and her women, all rose and bowed their heads as Marith entered, and the cry went up hailing him. Lady Fiolt placed a cup in his hands, smiling; she was dressed now in scarlet, with red jewels in her hair and at her throat. Marith drained it, gave it back.

'King Marith,' Lady Fiolt said.

Chapter Five

I cannot leave him.

Cannot? Will not? Do not want to?

Who can tell?

But there is pleasure, is there not, in being loved by a king?

Chapter Six

Darkness. A narrow passage closing around her like a fist. For a long time now it had tunnelled downwards, creeping deep into the earth. Worm lair. Grave pit. She had felt, for a long time as she crawled, the anger and hate following her. The earth ringing with the crash of stones falling. The world being ruined.

The tunnel dipped again. Sobbing, she crawled on, the rough ground cutting her hands. Her family's death riding on her back. She was tired now. So tired. Her grief came quicker. Grief and guilt and rage. She was hungry, she began to realize. She had no idea how long she had been crawling. Hours. Minutes. Days. Her mouth was dry with thirst. Her head hurt, where the mage fire had struck her. She desperately needed to piss.

The tunnel flattened, then began to rise. A smell came into the air, damp and fresh. A ghost of light ahead of her. A sound. Her pace slowed to inching forward, desperately eager, terrified of what she would find. Get out, escape this. Stay here in the dark of the tunnel, where nothing is real. Out there everything is ashes. Everyone is dead and the world is burned. She came on slowly to the end, where the mouth of the tunnel opened as a hole in the cliffs, shielded by tumbled rocks. The sea beat on the beach below her, making the shingle sing and sigh. The last light of evening, a few stars being swallowed by rising cloud. She crawled out of the tunnel gasping, clawing at the air that smelled of the sea. Alive. The grief in her turned to laughter, that she had beaten him. Alive!

Landra Relast, the eldest daughter of the Lord of Third Isle, kin to the Altrersyr and the Calborides and the kings of Bakh, descendent of Amrath, a great high noble lady of the White Isles. Landra Relast, whose brother and sister and mother and father had been murdered, whose home had been destroyed, who had watched Marith Altrersyr her promised husband burn everything she had to dust. Landra Relast, who alone had escaped the power he had over them, the glamour of King Marith who was Amrath returned to them, the madness of their glorious hunger for killing and death. Landra Relast, who had fled from him, wormed her way through the old secret tunnels beneath Malth Salene, away from banefire and mage fire and sword strokes, to the safety of an empty stony beach.

Landra Relast, who had nothing left.

She pissed behind a rock, though there was no one about to see her. Rinsed her hands and face in the sea, the salt on her wounds searing pain. Her dress was torn to shreds, she must stink of smoke. Dreaded to think what had happened to her hair and scalp.

It was very cold. The wind was picking up, the waves pounding the shingle. Thin, bitter rain. Landra tipped her head back, licked the water from her face. Her head was aching.

There should be a village ahead of her. An hour's walk, perhaps. Her legs were shaking with hunger so she would go slower. The shingle was hard to walk on, slipping under her feet, after a while she took off her shoes thinking it might be easier, then put them on again when the stones cut her skin. So dark, the sea roaring half invisible beside her. Finally, ahead, the lights that must be the village, the creak and chatter and smell of human life.

Landra sat down on the shingle and began to think.

Lady Landra Relast. Someone would recognize her. Impossible that they would not. Even if they did not recognize her, it would be obvious where she came from, with her fine dress and her burned skin. Impossible to guess how they had taken all that had happened, or what side they might be on.

But there was nowhere else.

The first house was in utter darkness. At the next a light burned, thin lines through the gaps in the shutters. A string of stones hung from the doorpost. Hagstones, wards against the powers of dark. A good omen. Landra knocked. Through the shutters she could hear voices whispering, a clatter of metal and then a silence, and then the door opened a crack. A man stared out. In his hands a long rod of iron, black in the night.

'I'm unarmed,' Landra said urgently, showing her white lady's hands cut and bloodied and burned and rubbed raw. 'I need . . . I ask your help. Please. Shelter. Food. I can pay.'

'Help?' Pale eyes stared at her fearfully. Saw her burned hair and burned face. The door moved to close.

Not back out into the night. The dark. Her legs almost buckled. So hungry. So thirsty. So tired. Not back out into the night. 'Please.' She almost screamed it. 'Please. I am Landra Relast of Malth Salene, Lord Relast's daughter. There has been fighting . . . You will know, I suppose. Please, I beg you. Food and water. Help.'

'Lord Relast's dead,' the man said. 'They're all dead. Malth Salene's smoking ruins. The king's dead there. There's a new young king come.' He studied her doubtfully. 'Well, you've the look of him, the young lord that died in the springtime. Lord Carin, Lord Relast's son.' Turned his head back to the warmth of the house, muttered something to someone, then opened the door wide. 'You'd best come in, then, whoever you are. Not a good night to be outside stone walls.'

The house was tiny, one room for living and sleeping, a beaten earth floor beneath the rushes, the ceiling hung with fishing nets. In the light of the hearth fire Landra saw that the man was young, not yet thirty, fair haired and fair skinned. A woman sat by the fire, also young, darker haired. A cradle stood in the corner, painted with the image of a deer.

The man set the iron rod back beside the hearth. 'I'll get you something hot to eat. There's some stew left, Hana?'

The woman Hana nodded. She got up and helped her husband fetch a cup of water, a bowl of fish stew, a hunk of bread. Landra ate, frowning at the rough salty taste. Her hand shook exhausted on her spoon. The sound of wind and sea came loud through the shutters, over the sound of the fire and the calm soft rhythm of the child's sleeping breath. The man and woman watched her eat, fear in their eyes.

'My name's Ben,' the man said at last. 'This is my wife, Hana. My son, Saem. She says she's Lord Relast's daughter, Lady Landra.'

Hana stiffened, then nodded. Turned kind eyes on Landra. 'I'm sorry, then.'

'You saw it? The battle?'

Ben shook his head. 'We saw the light in the sky where it was burning. Men up on the moor with swords.'

'Some men from the village went to look,' Hana said. 'Five, there were, went up there. Two came back. Said the other three . . . the other three weren't coming back.' Frightened eyes. Blinked, looked away.

'We'll make you a bed up,' Ben said. 'Get Alli the Healer to look you over in the morning.'

Grief and guilt and rage. She'd never sleep, worms gnawed at her heart. The bed was heather branches covered with a wool cloth, probably infested with fleas, poking at her, smelling of fish. She fell asleep immediately she lay down.

Woke again with a start. Grey faint dawn, the first traces of light clawing their way through the shutters, the sound of the sea very loud. Disorientating, the room unfamiliar, full of the sound of others' breathing, the smell of damp. Earth smell from the floor. A great shriek of gulls came up suddenly, wild and angry, filled with pain. Something else behind it. Landra sat up, jerking her head around in fear. A roar like laughter. Silent out beyond the sky. The child whimpered in its sleep, the man and the woman stirred fretfully. Then quiet again. The rhythmic sounds of sea and seabirds and the world waking as the light came. The house waking, Hana making oaten porridge, the child awake singing, spilling its cup of watered milk down its clothes, Ben sitting down with a mug of weak ale to mend his nets. Does it not concern you? Landra kept thinking as she watched them. That the king is dead? My father is dead? That the world is changed?

A little before noon, a man from the village came calling. Ben told Landra to hide herself in the half-loft where they kept their stores while he stayed. The visitor and Ben and Hana spoke in low voices so that Landra could not hear what was said. But when it was safe again they told her, and she saw then that they were concerned. The king was dead indeed, they said. His son was king now in his stead. Marith, whom rumour had had it was dead. He was known on Third, Prince Marith, visited often, a friend of the Relasts, he'd be a king they knew, where Illyn his father had been a stranger. Almost an enemy, indeed, old King Illyn: the Murades, Queen Elayne's kin, were not loved on Third, being long the sworn enemies of Lord Relast. The fighting was over, for the meantime. That mattered most of all to Ben, that it had not spread beyond Malth Salene to encompass his tiny corner of the world.

Concerned, yes. They looked grave as they spoke of it. Fear in their eyes. But Landra understood with slow puzzlement that for them the world was not changed.

They would not let her stay another night. Too dangerous, Ben said sadly and shamefacedly, looking not at Landra but at his son playing on the shingle throwing stones. If the king's men came . . .

'I'm nothing,' Landra said, 'nothing. The Relasts are all dead.'

Ben shrugged. 'Riders are out on the road already, proclaiming the new king, calling troops. Can't risk anything.' He was young and strong enough to be a soldier, Landra realized then, looking at him. Any danger, however remote, however small, any voice mentioning there was a stranger at his house, his name being spoken to anyone, anywhere, must be avoided.

'We'll get your wounds looked to,' said Hana, 'but then you must go.' She too looked at the child. Landra heard in her voice both the kindness and the threat.

Alli the Healer was the village wise woman, witch woman, bone charms at her neck, hagstone beads over her breasts, the green of leaf juice ground into her skin. Kind face. Kind, thoughtful eyes. She smeared a greasy ointment on Landra's burns. It smelled meaty and fishy and bitter, stung her, shimmered on her arms like a slug's trail. But she had to admit it soothed the pain a little. The raw red wounds looked softer, afterwards. When this was done the woman rubbed a switch of green marsh hazel over Landra's scalp, muttering prayers and healing words. *Toth*, that is the cold of water. *Ran*, that is the peace of evening. *Palle*, that is smooth sheen of a calm sea. Broke the stick in two, gave one half to Landra. The other half Alli took herself to cast away into the waves. 'Keep it safe,' she bade Landra. 'Keep it safe and it will help your skin heal.'

Hana gave Landra a cloth to bind up her head, making her look like an old shy widow woman. A dress, also, far too tight at the chest and waist. Stocky plain-faced Lady Landra. Never been pretty and her appearance had never been anything to take pride in and she'd never cared. A great lady, trained to rule a great household, raise a lord's sons or the sons of a king. A beggar woman, half bald with no home and no name.

'What will you do?' Ben asked her. 'Where will you go?' he meant, encouraging her to leave. Or perhaps he feared she would throw herself into the sea.

She had tried to think of this. How can I live? Where can I go? What can I be? She said, 'I'll go to Seneth. To Morr Town.'

'Morr Town?' Ben looked at her sharply. Sadly. 'That's where the new king will go.'

Landra looked back sharply. Sadly. 'Yes. I know.'

Thoughts moved in his eyes. 'I can take you to Seneth. But not

Morr Town. The coast to the south, somewhere well out of sight. You can take the road across the moors.'

Honoured guests disembark from their ships at Toreth Harbour and ride the golden road to Malth Salene. Murderers and outcasts and dead men take the lich way, and come in through the back gates where the middens are piled. So she had told Marith, bound and filthy, her prisoner, when she brought him back to Malth Salene, sealing all their doom. Such scorn in her voice. Cruelty. It had been a cruel thing. And Marith had bowed his head with shame.

'Tonight, then?' she said slowly.

Ben nodded. 'Tonight.'

Hana gave her bread cakes, salt fish, a hard small round of goats' milk cheese. She gave them in return the gold bracelet she wore at her left wrist. In the dark Ben took her over to Seneth, seat of the kings of the White Isles, where her ancestors Serelethe and Eltheia and Altrersys had once come ashore seeking shelter after the death of Amrath the World Conqueror, the King of Shadows, the King of Dust, the King of Death. Dark and cold, the only sound for long hours the slap of water against the hull, the creak of the oars. No light, for fear another boat would see them. The water in the darkness looked solid like black stone. Had to drop anchor and wait a little, when the mass of Seneth appeared half visible before them, Ben would not risk the cliffs and rocks in the dark, though he seemed to know the water without needing to see.

The light was breaking. A faint lifting of the night. Landra could see the land ahead of them, details in the cliff line, the slump of rocks.

'You sure?' Ben asked.

Morr Town, where the new king will go. She almost laughed. 'Yes. No.'

The oars dipped again. Light enough to see the water churned up before Ben got into his rhythm again. The cliffs in front of them looked like faces. Vast grey stone, sheer up to the sky.

Ben rowed south along the coast, past the first beach they came

to, round a sheer point where seals slept. The cliff dipped, scrub-
land running down to meet the sea. As they rowed closer, Landra
saw a rough path scrambling up. Seabirds circling in the morning
air, riding the dawn wind. A few seals sat on the rocks and stared
at them as they came in. The boat crunched against the shingle.
Wave breaking round the sides.

'You sure?' Ben asked again. Landra clambered awkwardly out
into the water. Cold up to her waist. She gasped at the cold. Sting
of the salt on her legs. Ben handed her the bundle of food.

'Thank you,' Landra said awkwardly. Ben was already pushing
the boat off back into the sea with the oars. She dragged herself
over the shingle through the water, her dress clinging heavily
around her legs. Slipped stubbing her foot against a rock and
plunged her left arm into the water, the salt stinging her burns.
Got up onto the steep rise of the beach, climbing upwards like
climbing a hill. The pebbles moved down around her feet in a
landslide. A thick band of rotting seaweed, alive with hopping
flies. Cuttlefish bones and a dead jellyfish, glistening silvery red,
tentacles splayed out. Looked like bones and a dead heart. The
grey cliffs stared down like faces. Old gods watching. The old
things of the land. The gulls circled, screaming at her.

Landra turned to look out to where Ben's boat was already
disappearing into the sea. Raised her hand and waved. Pointless.
But he'd been a kind man.

Eltheia. Fairest one. Keep safe. Keep safe. Him, and Hana, and
the child.

She sat down on the shingle. The pebbles pressed uncomfortably
into her skin. She picked up the first pebble her hand rested on.
A hagstone, grey-greenish, the hole blocked by a smaller pale grey
stone. An omen? She threw it wide into the sea. Made a lovely
deep sound. She chewed a little bread, drank from the skin of
water. Nasty, fishy, stale taste.

She got up and began to walk stiffly up the cliff path, a weary
peasant woman in an ill-fitting dress, smelling of fish and tallow
and herbs.

Chapter Seven

A month, they stayed at Malth Calien.

'What are we doing here?' Thalia asked Marith, after a few long dull days.

'Waiting.' He smiled with terrible heavy sorrow. 'Calling in all who will come to me.'

'For what?' she asked, feeling her ignorance. The place bustled with men, soldiers, business; a ship had gone out at dawn the first morning and Marith chafed after its return, watched the sea every day.

Marith said slowly, 'To claim my throne.'

'But . . . you are crowned king.' A crown of silver in your shining black-red hair.

'King of what, exactly?' Irritation in his face, that she did not understand this world of his. 'Third Isle is one island of the White Isles. The seat of the king is Malth Elelane, on Seneth, the Tower of Joy and Despair, the tower raised for Eltheia, the tower from which Altrersys ruled as the first king. There is my throne. My crown. My home. I have told Ti that I am coming. That I am king, returning home. Ti and . . . and Queen Elayne. They do not answer. So I must come with swords and spears, and make them kneel to me as king.'

'They thought that you were dead,' said Thalia. 'They may not

32

even believe that it is really you. Tiothlyn only saw you so briefly.'
You killed your father, she thought. What else are they likely to
do?

'They never believed I was dead,' said Marith. 'That would have
been too much for them to hope for, that I was dead.'

So bitter. So bitter his voice. But what do I know, she thought,
of family? I who was given up at birth to the God. And yet . . .
the petty rivalries of the Temple, the little slights over nothing that
grew and festered over the years into mortal wounds. Yes, she
thought, perhaps I do know of these things.

She said after a while, 'And if they do not kneel?'

He laughed bitterly. 'What do you think? But they will.' His
eyes rolled in his head, he looked mad as he said it. She shivered.
So vile. So much hate in him. Kill him, she thought then. You are
wrong to feel for him anything but disgust. But he woke that night
sweating, whispering his father's name. Thalia gave him water,
stroked his face. His eyes burned like fever. 'But I had to do it. I
did. I did. He would have killed me. Killed you.'

'Yes. You did.'

He had been drinking heavily at dinner, as he did every night,
laughing and shouting with his lords in Malth Calien's great hall,
rough and violent, a thing she hated and thought from everything
he had said to her that he would hate, but he seemed so caught
up with them, a man among men, a king in his court, a warrior
boasting of his deeds. He sucked up their adoration, the envious
among them raised endless toasts to Marith the War Leader, Marith
the Conqueror, Marith who would outshine even Amrath; he
laughed about it to Thalia, mocking them, but it pleased him, his
pale flushed face shone; the next morning he would smile and tell
her they were empty craven fools and then in the evening he would
drink it up again with his wine and come stumbling to bed filled
with their praises, laughing with pride.

'He hated me.'

'Yes.' She thought: he did not hate you. I saw that, I who have
never known a father. He did not hate you, any more than you

hated him. But there is nothing else that can be said. If we repeat the lie, it is true, is it not? Without that lie . . . without that lie, we are nothing.

I could have stayed in my Temple, when the men came to kill me. Woken the other priestesses. Called the guards. I did not call for help. I ran. Two slaves died. I ran.

'I'll bury him with all honours.' Marith rubbed painfully at his eyes.

He is almost pitiful, Thalia thought. And I . . . I do pity him. So indeed we shall be happy. If pity and lust together can make love and happiness.

'All honours.' He was drifting back towards sleep. 'He would have killed you . . . He told everyone I was dead . . . King Illyn . . .' he muttered again, rubbing at his face, 'King Illyn Altrersyr . . .' The walls of the Great Temple rose up in Thalia's mind, high and huge, the faint glimpse of golden domes and silver towers, the sound of voices talking about things she had never seen. High great walls, shutting out the world.

The weather changed, becoming bitter cold, hard frosts, one morning a faint dusting of snow. The marshes froze over, a thin skin of ice that cracked beneath the weight of a man's foot. The reeds stood out bare and black. The birds fled with the ice, the last flocks of them gathering on the roofs of Malth Calien and flying into the west like long plumes of smoke. Lone deer picked their way through the frozen landscape. The trees bent furred under the frost. The last few lords of the furthest islands came, of those who would come, and the news ran down from Seneth that Tiothlyn was crowned king at Malth Elelane and was raising his own troops.

'Why does he hate him?' Thalia asked Matrina Fiolt, Osen's wife. At first Thalia had not liked her at first, golden haired with deep, heavy breasts and round cheeks, making eyes at Marith, smiling with him as a woman who had known him for longer, who knew how to say things that Thalia did not understand but that made him laugh. 'My Lady', she called Thalia, but with something in her voice that Thalia recognized from her Temple, meekness cutting like knives. But it was so dull, sitting in this cold place looking out at the marshes with nothing to think of but what was to come.

'Who? Hate who?'

'Marith. Why does he hate his brother? And the queen?'

Matrina put down her embroidery, a long fine girdle patterned with flowers. Frowned. 'I . . . Most brothers hate each other, a little bit, I think . . . And Marith and Ti . . . I don't know, I've never met Tiothlyn. But it must have been hard, I suppose, the two of them, with so much before them . . . Being Marith's brother . . . Did you not have brothers or sisters you were jealous of? Saw yourself less than or better than or different to, and thought your parents loved the more?'

No. Nothing. Only the God, Great Lord Tanis Who Rules All Things, whose power reached to a small dark room and a knife. Thalia thought: life and death I know. Light and dark. Killing. Nothing in between. Nothing that means anything in the living of a human life.

'I quarrelled with my brother all the time when I was a child,' Matrina went on, 'we fought like cats and dogs over everything. I love him, of course. But I was glad to leave and come here. And they are so close in age, and so similar, and Marith — and the king's birth mother—'

'She is dead,' Thalia said. 'His father killed her.'

Matrina coloured a little, then laughed. 'Look at me!' She shook her head. 'There's no reason not to talk about it, any more. She died when Marith was still only a baby, and the king, the old king, I mean, King Illyn married Queen Elayne so soon after that. These old things, they get forgotten. What does it matter? Twenty years, she'd been dead. But then Marith started talking about it, stood up before his father and accused him of having his mother killed. My father and brother were there, they saw. And Tiothlyn was so angry back. And the king too, of course. Marith had to apologize, say it was lies. Who knows? But young men quarrel with their fathers, and their brothers, and take against their step-mothers. My father and my brother quarrel. My father wasn't even sure he meant it.'

On and on. So far back, the shadows that ate at him . . . Thalia shuddered. Saw it all before her, and the old king again, eyes and mouth jutting open, golden with honey. Killers and murderers, all of them. Death and hate. On and on and on.

A clatter from the courtyard, a harsh voice shouting, 'Faster! Again! That slow and you'll be dead, the lot of you! Again!' A flurry of fine powdery snow blew in at the window. Sand and dust had blown in occasionally, long ago in the Temple when all things were different.

'Seneth is a beautiful island,' Matrina said. 'Perhaps Osen will take me to live there, if the king keeps him close to him.' She frowned again, took up her embroidery and set back to her work. 'I wish my father would come. It's so awkward like this.' Marith had explained it to Thalia: Matrina's father Lord Dair sat in his hall on Belen Island, torn between astonishment at his daughter's husband's good fortune and his own loyalty to the Murades and the queen. The complexities of it all made Thalia's head ache. Always, it came back to killing their own kin.

'This is war,' Marith said wearily later when she asked him. They stood together on the outer wall, watching a column of men march in under the gate. 'That is what war is.' His face was pale, following the soldiers' progress with hungry eyes. Scarlet armour and dark spears, white pennants fluttering with the great blaze of an orange sun, come up from ships beached on the mud flats, black timber and white sails and red painted eyes on the prow. Almost the last, he thought, Stansel of Belen with three hundred men and five ships. Not a huge host gathered, though enough to fill the halls of Malth Calien twice over, camped in the orchard and the horse yard, eating the castle and its villages out of everything in their stores, hunting and fishing the marshes bare. It would be a hard winter, for those left behind. The earth around the castle was fouled with sewage that would spread disease.

They must leave soon. Marith must know it. The men cooped up in the fortress grew restless, eager for war. Ghost lights flickered out on the marshes. Shadows circled the towers of Malth Calien. Bright dead screams in the evening. Kill and kill and kill and kill. Death! Death! Death! It would be better for him when they were moving, Thalia thought. Away into clean air. Away into doing. He sat in the hall at night and let them praise him and call him king and conqueror, and most times he laughed with them and believed it, but sometimes now he would mock them and curse them to their faces, and once he had broken down and wept. Get him away from these things. If they could be alone, themselves . . . He and she stood together alone on the walls and he smiled his sad smile and looked more what he had been, beautiful and desolate as the frost on the marsh. They would leave for Malth Elelane. They would bury his father, kill his brother and his step-mother. They would marry and he would crown her as his queen. And then perhaps he would have some kind of peace.

He turned with his beautiful dead eyes and his smile as the last men came under the gateway, a voice calling out the order to bar again the gates. 'That is the last of them. Soon. Very soon.'

Men's voices shouted from the courtyard, commands, greetings, cheers. They came down from the walls into the midst of it, men and horses and servants, Matrina Fiolt with an anxious face trying to order her household in the face of something almost like a siege.

Marith said, 'Let's go and look at the forge.' He liked to watch it, the ringing of the great hammer, the shattering showers of sparks, the white metal hissing and writhing and turning black as it cooled, the cauldron where the light of the sun blazed, pouring liquid fire more brilliant than the light itself. Almost something sacred, the way his eyes danced with the sparks, the noise of it so loud it blotted out thinking. They kept the old ways, the men of the Islands, brought gifts of ale and honeycomb and green willow leaves for the men of the forges, bowed their heads to them in reverence at their power of making and burning and raising up death things from the gleaming light. Half gods with their blackened hands pricked with scar tissue, glittering scales of metal embedded in their skin. Magicians. Death summoners. Dragon men.

'They've almost done,' Marith said happily as they came to the low doorway of the smithy. 'The sword.' The hammer started up with a stink of metal and his voice was lost. They stood and watched in silence as the master ironsmith beat out a long sword.

Drew the sword from the anvil, plunged it into a bucket of water with a great hiss of steam. Turned it in his hands, tossing it to feel the weight. Held it out to Marith. 'It still needs much work. But if My Lord King would like to try . . .?'

Marith took it carefully, looked it over, turned and moved it as the smith had. Brought it up and struck down at the hard stone of the floor. Ringing song of metal. Sparks. Dirty and unfinished. It gleamed in his hand.

'A good sword, I think. The weight seems good.' He passed it back to the smith. 'How long, do you think?'

The smith considered, shifting the sword again from hand to hand. 'A few days, perhaps . . . Three? Four? It must be retempered and beaten and retempered again. The final cooling in horses' blood. Sharpened, the jewels set, the runes made . . . Five days.' His face was anxious. 'Does that satisfy My Lord King?'

'There's not much I could do if it didn't, is there? I expect we can wait that long. Five more days in a soft bed, at least. Five more days Tiothlyn can pretend to be king.'

Five days. Two days and two nights of wild feasting, the men drinking themselves to dropping in the hall, fights breaking out over a woman or a slurred word or nothing at all, three men dead and one injured near enough to dying, the hall running with chaos and filth. Singing the paeans and the war ballads, wilder and angrier and with such perfect eager joy. A day and a night of calm, Malth Calien grey and silent, sleeping, servants creeping through the hallways scrubbing it clean. The snow came, white to cover the ruins, as it had snowed over Malth Salene to cover the dead.

Then a sudden great rush of activity, the place churning like a rats' nest, rushing, shouting, everywhere carts and armour and swords. Out of the chaos an army forming, eight thousand men armed and ready, horses, ships, supplies. Tearing its way to life like a child birthing. Coalescing like bronze in the forge. A night's rest, Marith restless, muttering in his sleep, finally in the dark before dawn settling a little, his face buried in Thalia's hair. The dawn of the fifth day, and servants come to wake them and dress them and bring them down to the Amrath chapel, to make the prayers asking blessing on their war.

The lords of Marith's army stood assembled in full armour. Outside in the courtyards the soldiers lined up in long rows. Still, strained silence. Marith alone beside the statue of Amrath, the stone face looking out beside him so like his own.

Osen came forward, knelt at Marith's feet holding up the sheathed sword. A scabbard of dark red leather, worked all over in silver lacework, dragons writhing to swallow their own tails. A hilt of dark silver, plain unworked metal with a single great ruby at the pommel. Marith drew it. The blade hissed in the air.

'I am Marith Altrersyr, Lord of the White Isles and of Illyr and of Immier and of the Wastes and of the Bitter Sea. The heir to Amrath and Serelethe. The Dragon Kin. The Demon Born.' He lowered the sword slowly, turned to face the statue. 'Amrath! I go now to reclaim my throne, that was Your son's before me, to restore the true line of Your children, to take my rightful place as Your heir, as lord and king. Where the people of the White Isles once welcomed Eltheia Your consort, I will stand and be welcomed as king. I will be king.'

The crowds in the chapel went down onto their knees in a clatter of armour and a sigh of heavy silk. A deep indrawn breath, held for a moment with the tension of breaking rain. And then a great roar: 'All hail Marith Altrersyr, *Ansikanderakesis Amrakane*! King Marith! King Marith!' White fire leaping and running the length of the blade, rushing like water, surging over Marith's hands, gilding him, covering him, tracing the lines of his bones and his hair, his fingers clenched on the hilt of the sword, white fire pouring down his skin, alight and liquid, brilliant as the dawn sun. He stood looking at them, his people, still as the statue beside him that did not burn but sat dark and silent with its face so like his own. Thalia wondered, even, if he knew he burned.

He sheathed the sword. The fire faded. Smiled across at Thalia. Joy in his eyes. *Look! Look! Look what I am! Look what I've done!*

The court rose to their feet, hailing him again as king. 'All hail Marith Altrersyr, *Ansikanderakesis Amrakane*! King Marith! King Marith!' Out of the chapel in procession, down to the shore where the ships bobbed at anchor or were drawn up on the mud. Marith held Thalia's arm, his eyes raised, not seeing. Somewhere far away, in the fire and the light. His hand was cold as cold metal. Behind them came the lords and ladies, breathless, still cheering his name. The soldiers followed, the servants, Malth Calien emptying of people, rushing out onto the mud flats where the ships waited, craning their necks to see the king. 'All hail Marith Altrersyr, *Ansikanderakesis Amrakane*! King Marith! King Marith!'

A bonfire burned on the shoreline. Men had sat all night watching, guarding the fleet from the powers of sky and sea. Now in the glitter of morning Thalia saw long shadows curl around the masts. Ghost lights flickered out on the marshes, visible even in the light of day.

Marith stopped on the sand near the bonfire, the furthest running of the waves touching at his boots. Again, he drew the sword.

A horse was led up, richly harnessed with ornaments of gold. It stepped high and proudly, the smooth movements of its flanks like water curving over stones. At the last, as it came up to Marith, it realized. Its nostrils flared, snorting, rolling its eyes. Marith reached out his hand for it and it stilled again, sank down on its haunches before him, head bowed. The cut was gentle. Blood pumping out onto the sand, running into the sea. Silence. Then from a thousand throats a great wordless shout of triumph, swords clashing against shields.

When the horse was dead it was raised up on wooden spikes set in the water, the men cheering as they worked. 'Amrath! Amrath and the Altrersyr! Victory to the king!' Gulls and crows came immediately, shrieking. Death drawn. Death things, like the swords. The hot stink of the blood made Thalia tremble. Memory. Grief. Pride. So many had she killed, in her Temple, to bring death to the dying, life to those who needed to live. She could feel blood on her skin. The horse flopped on its spike, bleeding into the water, black against the silver-black sea. The tendrils of blood in the water were like the curls of Marith's hair.

Trumpets sounded. The slow beat of drums. The men moved together, a churning mass on the shoreline, coloured tunics, coloured armour, the colours of their pennants. Iridescent beetles. Flowers blooming. Women dancing in swirls of cloth and gems. Trudging out to the ships, swords and shields and helmets, waiting faces, coming on in neat long lines beside the dead body of the luck horse, splashing out into the water boarding the black ships with their red gazing eyes and the water flowing with the tendrils of the horse's blood, mud and silt rising with the smell of salt and salt-rot, the bright fresh light on the waves.

Servants helped Thalia up onto the ship. Her feet slipping on the wet planks. Wet heavy skirts pulling around her legs. Cold and vile, like clinging dead skin. On another ship they were loading horses, kicking out and neighing, making their grooms curse. Her own fear like the horses' fear, even as Marith took her arm, smiled, called her queen. Blood on his hands that the seawater had not quite washed away. She could smell the fresh blood on him, over the scab filth of his cloak. Osen handed him a gold cup, he raised it, threw it out into the waves. It flashed in the sunlight, wine spilling out into the water with the blood.

'May the sea not spite us! May the sky not spite us! Victory!'

The wordless cheer back at him. The clash of swords on shields.

We may be going to war, Thalia thought. Such an absurdity. To

war! She had told him that she was going, she would not stay
here in the marshes sitting and waiting for him. She had ridden
away from the battle at Malth Salene, and men had died in pain
for her. She had been the High Priestess of the Lord of Living and
Dying, the holiest woman in the Sekemleth Empire. She would go
now as the army of Amrath's queen.

'Do you think,' she had asked him, 'do you think that I am
afraid?'

'Of course not.' He tried to smile. 'But I am afraid, for you.'

'You don't need to be.'

'No?'

'No.'

He said, 'It will all be well, anyway.'

On the shore men struggled with the barrel holding King Illyn's
corpse, loading it carefully onto the ship. The dead face still staring
with its eyes and mouth open, shocked. It had all honours now,
indeed, his father's corpse. Kill him and curse him and bury him
with gold and love.

The ships hung ready, troops lined up on the decks. Matrina
and her women on the shore beside the dead horse. Wind-blown
faces. Black mud on their fine skirts. From the king's ship flew the
deep red banner of the Altrersyr, white cloth soaked red with
blood. Bright sails, swollen and hard with the wind. The ship
juddered. Moving. Marith stood in the prow wide-eyed. Pink fever
flush in his cheeks.

A great wild scream cut the air like a sword drawn. A shadow
moving over them. An eagle. Black against the sun. It turned
overhead, circling the fleet. Men's eyes and the red painted eyes
of the ships and the dead eyes of the sacrifice, watching it. Screams.
Swooped low over the ships. High into the sky with the light
flashing on its wings. Something fell from its talons, spiralling in
the air, falling and twisting, landing at Marith's feet. Soft crumple
sound. The eagle screamed and was gone.

At Marith's feet was a foal, new born, matted with blood and
fluid, shimmering inside its caul.

A strange smell of birth and bloodshed. It twitched a moment, as though it were still alive.

'The luck horse! The luck horse!' Voices on the ship whispering, awed. Hands moving in signs of wonder, signs against great magic and god things. 'The luck horse!'

Marith stared down at the pitiful body, up at the sky, his eyes straight unblinking into the sun. 'The luck horse.' He took Thalia's hand. 'You see it? You understand?' The men on the ship bent to kneeling. Marith lifted the vile thing in his arms. 'Raise it up! Raise it on the mast!'

They tied it above the sail, sailors scrambling upwards like lizards, treasuring the burden one carried bound to his back with long fine legs flopping like he had grown some fragile leprous wings. Still it shimmered, black and rainbowed in the sun. Thalia tried to turn her head away but the only other place to look was the body of the sacrificed horse on the shore. She thought: do I understand? Any of these things?

Under a banner of dead horses the fleet sailed fast across the bright water, red painted eyes staring hungrily ahead.

Chapter Eight

'The isle of Third is a fine land,
Her corn rising high like maidens dancing,
Her fat flocks, her fat cattle,
Her green meadows and her green forests,
Her rivers sweet and clear.
But still I say nothing is more lovely,
More joyous, more worthy of praise,
Than a great host girded for battle,
Bronze swords bright in the sunlight,
Young men's faces raised and eager,
Red banners proud in the wind.'

The marsh and the banks of the estuary slipped away behind them. Ahead, the dark sea and the darker smudge of Seneth Isle. The wind blew fair in the sails. Scant hours, before they made land.

'That's the biggest load of cock I've heard in days,' said Tobias.

'I'm sorry?'

'That bloody song. A load of crap. Third's a shithole, and an army's a load of ugly sweaty buggers ready to rip someone's guts apart.'

'Watch your mouth,' said Brand. 'Third's his kingdom, and we're his army, and it's bloody glorious.'

44

'Oh, bloody glorious.'

'I said watch your mouth, Immishman.'

Fuckhead romantics. Tobias went back to looking at the water. Maerlk, the man who had started it by singing, went back to looking at his sword. He seemed quite astonished to be wearing one. Tobias kept feeling an itching need to tell him which end you held it by.

Back on a bloody ship. Spent years successfully avoiding ships. *Never get involved in amphibious warfare.* One of Skie's old maxims. Suddenly made a hell of a lot of sense. *Just never, Tobias. One thing this company'll never bloody do.*

Never do a lot of the things he'd somehow done in the last little while.

It was all cloudy in his mind, making him irritable. He'd hated the king, once. Before he realized something. Something. And now the great coming battle, to decide who got the crown and got to say he was better and everyone loved him more. He hadn't wanted the king to win, once. Had wanted . . . something else for him. Kind of hard to remember what. Just still a nagging sense of pointlessness, that there was no real reason for any of this. That he should just turn around. Run.

A little house and a girl to clean it and a pint of Immish gold of an evening and a fat soft gut. That had been . . . been a really good good idea he couldn't quite shake. He'd done a bad thing, hadn't he? Something bad. To the king. Hadn't wanted . . . something to happen.

He looked across the water and the king was there, standing at the prow of his ship, looking straight ahead. So tiny, a stick of black with a red cloak, maybe a flash of light where his crown was, but you knew him. They all knew him, even without seeing him. The ships moved slightly, changing formation; the figure was gone. Light snow furring the deck, making it slippery. Hands cold and raw on the hilts of their swords. He's the king. We'll make him king. His kingdom and his army.

Bloody glorious! Yeah!

Third was still an ugly freezing damp shithole, though. And his army was still a load of ugly sweaty buggers ready to rip someone's guts apart. Bloody wounds and oozing sores glorious.

Yeah.

Seneth was coming properly into sight, grey rocks and green hills rising up clear ahead of them, blurred in the snow. Huddles of houses down on the shoreline; you could even see the smoke of hearth fires. Didn't look any different to Third.

Tobias had kind of expected they'd be making land soonish, camp for the night and then march. Instead, the ships turned, moving north following the line of the coast, the king's ship taking position at the front. Another hour's sailing, slow in a weak wind. The snow had stopped, thank the gods. But still bloody cold. Rations of bread and meat and beer handed out, they ate crouched on the deck, eyes on the shore. Could feel people on the shore looking back. A couple of fishing boats sailing panicked before them, tacking and darting to get away. An army looks like a dragon to peasant men, Tobias thought watching them. Gods alone know what an army of ships must look like, when you're out on the dark pitiless sea. They sailed on, then a shout came from one of the ships ahead of them, orders relayed back whipping on the wind, voices calling like the gulls, the sound of the waves slapping against the hull, the men craning to hear.

'Furl the sails! To oars!'

A movement of men to the mast, a great creak of canvas and rope thrashing like snakes. A space in the sky where the sail had been, the mast standing useless like a dead winter tree, rough splintered wood with the bowsprit across it like wide-spread arms. Like that stupid sodding stake they stuck the stupid sodding dead horse on. Oars striking out into the water. The sound of the ship now the crunch and crack of men's bones.

'Strike the drums! To arms!'

So they were moving much more slowly now, crawling along with the land bedside them, a high rugged headland, harsh black rocks. Something looking from the top of the cliff a moment, a flash of white. And then the ships turned and the land fell away, and before them was a great bay with smooth clear water, the towers and roofs of a town rising up behind a thick harbour wall, a crowd of black ships.

The King of the White Isles said, 'We go straight to Morr Town. Land at harbour.'

Lord Bemann said, 'They'll be waiting for us. Closed the harbour. Have ships out. We need to land in the wilds, come to Malth Elelane overland. Somewhere they can't predict.'

The King of the White Isles said, 'I am their king. I am Lord of Malth Elelane. I will not creep into my own home. Morr Town will open her gates and her harbour to me gladly.'

Lord Fiolt said, 'My Lord King . . . Malth Elelane is indeed yours. But . . .'

Lord Stansel said, 'What he means, My Lord King, is that sailing straight into Morr Bay would be . . . unwise.'

Lord Fiolt said, 'What I mean, Marith, is that sailing straight into Morr Bay would be suicide.'

The King of the White Isles said, 'Malth Elelane is mine. Morr Town is mine. She will open her gates and her harbour to me. She will.'

Swords ready. The sound of the waves slapping against the hull. Drumming. Gulls.

Oh fuck, Tobias thought, watching the line of ships grow nearer.

Tiothlyn's ships were moving towards them, the same black ships with red painted staring eyes. The drums coming up from them also, the same dull beat to keep the oarsmen steady, loud over the water calling the oarsmen to their work. The only sound they could hear in the world. The dark water between the two lines narrowed. Trumpets began to blow in the ships and on the shore. Trying to frighten the other side off. But there was nowhere for either other side to go. The town, and the cliffs, and the sea.

In the sea things were beginning to move and surface, drawn by the drums.

'Archers: draw!'

'Archers: loose!'

A flurry of arrows from the leading ships. Beautiful, like the shuttle of a loom. But too early: they fell short, floating on the water, bobbing on the waves. Tiothlyn's men jeered. We meant that to happen, we're just doing this to taunt them. Aren't we? The figure of the king standing in the prow of the first ship with the sunlight on his silver crown. He is death. He is ruin. He is Amrath reborn. He will be victorious. The dead body of the luck horse, the sky's offering, hangs from the mast as a sign. The enemy's ships are fewer. Weaker. Bloody glorious. Bloody victorious. Kill and kill and kill until the water heaves with bleeding. Kill them all! But the arrows float on the water, bobbing on the waves. Sticks. Long green fingers reached and pulled one under, snapped it. Flaccid fucking sticks. We meant to do that. Miss everyone. Didn't we?

An enemy arrow clattered onto the deck of Tobias's ship. Hissing. Burning. Green. Fire. Green tendrils rushing across the planks, scouring channels as they went.

Oh gods and demons, not again. Not again. Not a-fucking-gain.

'Earth! Get earth on it! Now!' Men ran forward, throwing mud from a barrel. The flames died in a choking sputter, stinking wet smoke for a moment and then gone. Another arrow shot past, dripping flames. Then a rock. Dripping flames.

Salt-soaked pitch-soaked well-seasoned damp wood is . . . astonishing when it explodes.

Two more rocks: the ship jolted wildly as waves hit it from both sides. Boiling waves. Green waves. On fire waves. The ship's timbers smelled kind of funny, hot like singed wood. The hull was beginning to smoke.

So, what, King Marith just clean forgot Morr Town had two massive banefire shooting trebuchets set up on the harbour in the entirely unlikely event anyone ever decided to invade an island kingdom by sea?

Or never noticed them?

Thought they were purely decorative?

'Archers: draw!'

'Archers: loose!'

Patches of green twisted on the water, fighting with it, the sea churning and boiling at this unnatural thing searing into it, fire it cannot quench, steam rising with a hiss of clenched teeth. The ship the rock had hit was sinking almost to the mast top, spewing out steam and fire and dead men. The mast of another ship was burning, crackling and hissing, sparks of salt and the crack of old wood, green and blue flames. Gnawed apart, swaying as the banefire tunnelled into its veins.

'The oarsmen! Aim for the oarsmen!'

Another shower of banefire arrows. Another volley of burning rocks. More frantic scrabbling with mud until the flames died. The burning mast came down, shattering the side of its ship. Still burning. The stricken ship tilted down into the water. Long fine fingers like coiled skin reaching up for it, pulling. Men leapt screaming into the sea, then screamed louder and began frantically trying to crawl back onto the burning ship. The water was stirring. Thrashing about. Something down there. Screams. Men's arms trying to cling to anything to get out. A whirlpool, and for a moment maybe you saw eyes. A fountain of blood shot up from the water, bits of flesh and bone bobbing. Higher than the masts of the ships. A nasty crack that might be someone's spine breaking. A sound like the gnashing of giant teeth. A man with another man's innards floating round his neck, as though some kind soul had thrown him a rope. Actually he did seem to think some kind soul had thrown him a rope, from the way he hung on a moment before he realized what it was and screamed and let go and something pulled him under. Bubbles. Then no bubbles. Then another fountain of blood. Screams.

Still they were pressing slowly forward, another volley of arrows from each side crossing each other in the sky, the sea on fire, voices in the sea laughing. Long fine fingers probing the planks of the hull. The king in his silver crown.

More ships. We've still got more ships. Stronger men.

'Archers: draw!'

'Archers: loose!'

'The oarsmen! Aim for the oarsmen!'

The two fleets finally came together, the first ships meeting, men screamed and the voices in the water laughed. Ramming each other, swords clashing. Like a cavalry charge, really, Tobias saw then. Two big things driven straight at each other in the desperate hope one breaks. The red eyes of the ships staring at each other, and suddenly the eyes were alive, the ships were dragon things in the water, twisting and fighting, and he saw that the men didn't control them, the ships were fighting among themselves, taking their crews with them down into the water, enjoying it as they fought. The planks of Tobias's ship groaned as it surged forward. Came up alongside one of Tiothlyn's ships, rushing fast towards them, there was a channel between them in the water and then the ships met and men were fighting across the gap trying to board, lashing out with swords, the oars meshing and striking together, each shoving at the other ship, trying to pull it in and push it away. Like a beast with too many legs, scrabbling at itself.

Tobias swung his sword at the figures facing him. Very little art to this with the world moving and the men really too far away to hit. The deck tipped, suddenly he was near enough, got a man on the arm. Blood dripped into the water. A crash as the two ships collided. He was fencing for a moment with the man he'd just injured, up very close, got hit himself on the shoulder leaving a hard pain through his armour, then the ships moved apart again and he was looking across grey water at his opponent, their swords flailing at each other across the gap. Again like a thing with too many legs, like a louse on its back scrabbling.

Maerlk shouted as the ships moved, lost his balance, fell. His head was visible in the churning water. Blood in the water. Long fingers, curling around his legs. Screaming like someone might stop to throw him a rope. The ships came together. He was gone between them, wood closing over him like doors shutting, trying to claw his way up through the hull, buried alive in the dark as he drowned.

'In oars! Board her!' The men scrambling across the sides. A crack of wood as an oar was crushed between them, the rest pulled back up into the body of the ship. Tobias leapt and scrambled with the others, got across, picked up fighting again with the man he'd left off before Maerlk died. Brand was across too, pushing hard at an enemy soldier, blood on his face, smiling. Never get involved in amphibious warfare. Never. Never. Never. Just don't. The bloke Tobias was fighting almost got him in the neck and Tobias moved backwards and whacked his leg on an oar and suddenly he was up against the side of the ship and there really wasn't anywhere to go that wasn't either into a sword blade or into the sea. This was not fun fighting. This was fucking nightmare fighting. This was about the worst fighting Tobias could remember, possibly barring the dragon, or the Sorlostian Imperial Palace, or the first battle of Malth Salene, or . . .

Or pretty much anything involving King Marith. The sea was on fire. The ships were on fire. The ships were sinking. The trebuchets were slinging stones around not really caring which side they hit so long as they hit something so that it died. Men were thrashing about in the water, weighed down by their armour, and you could see the arms reaching round their necks to pull them down. Crunching teeth. Hot blood.

Pretty much anything involving King Marith . . .

The ship jerked and moved of its own accord, swinging round, the ship they had come from wedged into it locked by oars and ropes and dead men's bodies; for a moment he saw King Marith on his own ship, fighting, shining, his sword flashing silver-white.

Pretty much anything involving King Marith.

The snow was getting heavier, settling on the deck, making it slippery, hissing and steaming where patches of banefire still burned. Can't see. Snow and smoke and I can't bloody see. They shouldn't have engaged us, Tobias thought. Should have just stood back and shot green fire at us until we were all floating in the sea with our skin melting off our faces, nicely cooked. He fought on relentlessly with gritted teeth. Just survive. Just survive. He slipped on the wet wood of the deck, almost fell, got his balance back, killed someone.

The ships looked like wrestlers tussling together. It looked like a tavern brawl, these vast dark shapes gripping, moving, shoving, giving way, coming together again. Cheers and screams one against the other. Impossible to tell who was winning or losing, except that Tobias had a strong sudden feeling that they were losing on this one ship. Brand seemed to be fighting with the wrong hand and his right hand was a mass of blood. Maerlk had drowned lifetimes ago. Lots of other soldiers with them fighting but there seemed to be a lot more trying to fight them off. A bloke called Janis went over the side, one of the enemy's lot went down too, another two came at Tobias together seeing him as a good dangerous threat. Definitely seemed to be more of them.

This was hard. Getting really fucking hard. He was getting tired, the voyage wearing on him. Hacked and parried and the men he was up against were just better than he was. Maybe not on a good day. Maybe certainly not on a good day, rested and ready on dry land with the confidence of what he was doing at his back. But not after everything else. Not like this here.

Wasn't thinking all this, not really, not thinking anything except trying to stay alive and to kill the men trying to kill him, but it was squirming around burrowing at the back of his mind, some new kind of release and wondering. Why? Why? Why? Why am I here and why did I want Marith to be king, and why am I doing this? Echoing out to the rhythm of sword strokes, the creak of the ships, the hammer of iron on bronze. A sword got into his arm, bruised him and ripped his armour apart at the elbow, blunting the enemy's blade but now he was vulnerable in the sword arm that was weaker already from Sorlost. His leg was aching too, giving under the constant movement of the ship that made him slip and work. Not good. Not good. He lashed out, hit one bloke in the shoulder, the bloke went back with a groan looking hurt but the other came again at him seeing his damaged armour and the grey sweat on his face. Not good. Oh fuck. Fuck, fuck. I don't want to die, Tobias thought. I really don't want to die.

Wasn't anywhere else to go that wasn't either into a sword blade or into the sea.

Jumped.

Cold water tasting in his mouth like blood. Oh gods he couldn't see anything just churning dead water, salt and froth and waves, his eyes stinging, the cuts on his body stinging, the weight of his armour pulling him down, cold vile metal shifting against his skin in the water, wet leather dragging on his shoulders, arms and legs thrashing to keep afloat, fingers dancing around his ankles, images of great curving teeth closing, thrashing wildly, down under the surface where it was so dark and the water wormed at his mouth. He pulled his head back above into the air spluttering with salt burn, spitting, his eyes stinging, tugging at his legs and the weight of the armour carrying him down, the things with teeth fuck he could see them circling, the water's a maelstrom, patches of burning fire stinking, hissing, snow beating on the surface, where it lands on the fire it boils off into steam. He sank down again into the dark and pulled himself up again choking, kicked at something he maybe felt reaching for him, fuck I'm going to die, I don't want to die, I don't want to die, oh fuck. It was so dark beneath the surface like a fucking tomb, not just dying but being buried alive. I should have let them stab me. I'd rather die of a stab wound quick and bright with red blood. The bulk of a ship moved near him huge like a black wall curving outwards the red eyes staring at him, and it's more alive than anything he's ever seen and the water was in his mouth again worming through his lips and his clenched teeth and he felt something reaching pulling at his legs and long cold fingers curling at his arms.

Half an oar bobbed past him, smouldering at one end. It's on fire, he thought; then grabbed hold of it anyway desperate with a glorious wonderful feeling of victory. Kicked his legs a little and he could even move. Still very low, his head half underwater, the sea slashing at his mouth and nose, not really moving in any one direction to speak of and yeah, the thing he was holding on to was definitely on fire, but no longer actually drowned.

Someone's arm bobbed past him, blood spiralling out of the cut off end. Then a bit of planking, also on fire. Then a bit of something that could have been pretty much anything, red and black and white and pulpy-looking. Someone's head? Then another broken-off oar. A bit of rigging. Tobias looked up. Another of the ships was sinking, its prow and mast burning, a ragged great hole in its side that looked like a torn mouth. The red eyes still stared, hopeless. Men were scrabbling up the burning mast, clinging to the burning prow. It made a sucking noise like an old man drinking as it went down. The sea boiled. Still burning. Light flickered up from underwater. Bubbles of air, then nothing. Men floating clutching bits of wood. Another ship came towards them, the men shouted and waved and then arrows loosed and one of the men sank and disappeared, and the ship rowed over the men floating on straight towards a third ship, moving fast, the men on the third ship shouted and Tobias realized it was going to ram them. The crash made the water rush up in waves, slapping him in the face. He was spun round blinded and choking, clutching his burning oar. When he could see again the rammed ship was sinking and burning.

The swirls of the water pulled him round, caught in spiralling eddies of moving ships and sinking ships. The strength of the water astonished him. The snow still getting heavier, a wind getting up, whipping up the waves. White foam. Laughter in the water, long arms, long hair, long teeth. A ship sank in the water with the men on board screaming and the white horses rode over them and pounded them down to the depths where the other things waited for them. Two other ships charged each other, smashing planks and oars. Men fighting across decks slippery with blood and snow and banefire. The sky getting dark with the yellow and grey of a bruise.

If Tiothlyn wins, it occurred to Tobias, he may not be entirely magnanimous in victory.

If Tiothlyn wins, it occurred to Tobias, I'm probably pretty much entirely fucked.

If Marith wins, it occurred to Tobias, I'm also probably pretty much entirely fucked.

Seeing as I sold the boy out to Landra Relast and all.

Why the fuck am I fighting for him? I wanted to kill him. He almost certainly wants to kill me. I almost certainly would.

He'd say the thought hit him like a bucket of cold water, but given his current position that would be too much like a nasty joke.

That fucking poison bastard Marith. That sick, vile, diseased, degenerate fucking bastard. His head felt odd, like a weight lifting from it, like a cloud moving off and the air changing from cold to hot.

I wanted to kill him. I wanted him dead.

What am I doing fighting for him?

Began to kick in the water, trying to move himself along in one clear direction. Preferably the direction of something resembling land. Preferably not the town. Preferably not anywhere with the battle between it and him. Which kind of left as the only option some jagged black rocks on the headland cradling the bay, very sharp and very nasty looking and really, again, you couldn't help thinking about teeth. Like some huge fucking thing had sat down there and opened its mouth. Dragon rocks.

The thing about rocks, though, the thing about rocks, right, is that they're dry land. People very seldom drown on rocks. If they can get onto the rocks. If he could get onto the rocks. He kicked and thrashed about with his burning bit of wood sinking further under the water still glowing with fire. His armour was so, so heavy. Felt sick in his stomach from the salt water he'd swallowed. Getting cold, too. Cold as ice, the water. Where it wasn't boiling hot. The wind freezing on his wet hair. His teeth were beginning to chatter, a numb cold pain was jabbing at his legs. Squeezing his chest. His arm hurt. His leg hurt.

Shouts of triumph from a ship to his left, presumably captured by a boarding crew. Half Tiothlyn's men were on Marith's ships. Half Marith's men were on Tiothlyn's ships. Just somewhat unlucky perhaps that the other half were drowned. The shouts turned to yells as another ship bore down on it, drumming to get the oars going fast to ram. Splinter of wood as the two collided. The ramming ship moved to pull back but was stuck somehow, her prow locked into the shattered wound in her victim's side. Desperate voices, figures running and pushing, the crew of the stricken ship clambering over with swords. The wounded ship was sinking, pulling the other down with her. Hugging and refusing to let go.

The water moved. Tobias had to look away from the battle, kicking and panting, splashing to keep his head up, wrestling with waves cold and heavy as dead muscle, again that sheen on the water, the slickness like the slickness of a muscular body moving that made you think the sea was a creature flexing itself, the smooth roll of its flank and then the broken white of the waves and it was almost a shock that his head sank in it, the water flooding over his mouth and eyes and up his nose making him shudder and choke and almost sink again. He shouldn't be able to sink in it. He should be able to ride on its surface, glossy and moving like muscle and skin. Churning like a body convulsing in pain.

When he looked back the two ships had disengaged, the rammed ship was sinking, the ramming ship, her prow broken and letting in water, was moving back off in a judder of oars while men fought on her deck. Sailors scrambled up the mast, cutting at the ropes that held the sail furled. It opened, took the wind, the ship lurched forward with the oars flailing. The wind was blowing stronger. Blowing the ships away from the land. The snow covering them.

I'm freezing, Tobias thought. Freezing and drowning. He thought for a moment of trying to wave down the ship. But nobody would come. Nobody could see. Nobody cared. He kicked and wrestled and sank and got himself moving properly again, torn away from the magical spectacle of the black ships fighting, huge black dragons birds horses whales, fighting relentless. If I hadn't seen a dragon, he thought, if I hadn't seen a dragon, I'd think this the strangest and fiercest thing I ever saw. He kicked and wrestled, sank, floundered, suddenly a tide got him, pulling him moving in a rush of strength until the black toothed rocks were up gnashing towards him, the water white on them, their points like knives.

The waves took him. Dashed him towards the rocks. Oh gods and mercy and fuck. I should have been stabbed. I should have died by the knife. A soldier's death. A warm death. A death where someone might feel some pride that you're dead. Instead I'll be torn up on a rock by the sea and no one will ever know and by gods it will hurt and be cold and lonely and cruel.

The waves took him. Dashed him towards the rocks. Hands, lifting him. The water broke in a great jet of spume. A hollow beating like the sound of his heart. He spun around trembling, his ears roared with water. The rocks tore gashes in his legs. Long slippery tendrils of green stuff that whipped his face; he tried to cling on to it but it slid through his fingers feeling vile as raw meat. And then suddenly his face clear of the water, the rock pulling back under him, he clawed and pulled, dragged himself and he was out of the water on a little ledge of rock tilting away from the sea. Water slapped over it when the waves broke, but he rolled and crawled and the water seemed to be receding and he scrambled up rock rough with encrusted shells and collapsed gasping and panting to look back and see ships sailing fast out of the bay away to the south, some maimed and limping, some smouldering still on fire, others making their way fast back into the harbour of Morr Town similarly smashed and broken, others still sinking and dying in the water before him, spreading slicks of planks and oars and dead men.

The battle was over. Marith had lost. Knew him, still, felt the draw of him, a tiny figure on one of the last ships fleeing the harbour, the rage and shame in him radiating out like the beams of the sun, the way you could see light on far hills in the dusk.

Failed! Ha!

You're fucking delirious, Tobias thought to himself, and collapsed on the rocks of the headland soaking wet and wounded and still just sort of alive.

Chapter Nine

The ships pulled back raggedly, like crows flying up from a field when the farmer comes out with a sling and a pouch of stones. Moving fast, with a wind driving them. Sixty had departed from Malth Calien. Perhaps thirty remained. They straggled down along the coast, hugging tight to the line of the cliffs. Looked smaller, weaker, the planks of their sides crushed in like the flanks of a broken-down old horse.

The king's ship was the last, as was fitting. It sailed blindly, the king looking back staring blindly, the dead thing that was a portent of nothing flopping from the mast with the crows and gulls fighting over its unborn eyes and the blue tongue lolling in its unborn mouth.

There is no plan to get out. There never was. You didn't really think this bit through, did you?

Luminous creatures rose from the deep of the water, called up by the setting sun. The surface of the sea shimmered, solid as metal to a man's fooled gaze. Usually they only came in deep water: Marith had only seen them this close to the land a handful of times, and seldom this bright. They'd gone out in a little boat once, him and Carin, paid a fisherman to take them. Sat floating on the water pulling up pure colour hand over hand over hand. It ran through the fingers like milk curds. Smelled sweet as rotten fruit. Eltheia's tears, the shore people called them. The tears she wept for joy and for sorrow, that her husband was dead.

There is no plan to get out. There never was. Not for any of us.

But he hadn't thought he could fail. Everything had been so easy. The black ships dancing, the wind strong in their gleaming sails, coming in all together with the men's armour flashing in the light. The dead foal had seemed such an omen. He had seen them staring, calling it for luck, awed whispered voices as they pointed. Eagles. Horses. The old, old things of the White Isles, even before his ancestors came. Sacred things that knelt at the king's feet. The men in their coloured armour like a flock of birds on the decks of the ships, his men who would fight for him forever, onwards and onwards forever to be king. They would die for him. They would kill for him. Bright they raised up their voices and shouted the paean, drew their swords to take the enemy, certain in their faith in him. Two battles he had fought for his crown. Two battles he had won. All the men of his father's army had turned in their allegiance to come to him. They loved him. They knew him. Saw what he was. Ti's men should have loved him. Known him. Thrown down their swords to bring him joyously to harbour, cheering his name. Bid him welcome to his hall in clouds of dried flowers to place his crown on his head.

And then the fighting! His soldiers fierce and confident, Ti's ships meeting them in flights of arrows, the water lurching, the fire, but still he'd been so certain he would win. Kill them! Kill them all! So wondrous, fighting on the cramped confines of the deck, penned with nowhere to go, slaughtering. Sending a man crashing down into the cold water, bleeding into the water, the hungry sea claiming him, the white fingers taking him, his body too weak to keep himself afloat, the look of panic in his eyes as he bled and drowned. Wondrous. Fighting pure and without thought. Nowhere to go. No one who could come. One false step and the water beckoned. Nothing could be controlled; he could not even order his men. Maelstrom like the water. Death like the breaking waves. So certain he would win.

Thalia had seen him fighting. That would have been a good thing also, that she had been there and seen. Her kiss of welcome as he turned back to her, perfumed with his enemies' blood, raising her hand with his as they came into harbour, leading her up the roads of the town to his home, the people acclaiming him, her face bright with pride and desire; 'Be welcome to your home and the home of our children, my beloved,' he would have said as the doors were thrown open, the men and women and servants kneeling in the blare of silver trumpets, a victory feast and then up to his bedchamber with crimson hangings, the windows open to the sea, her eyes wide.

That was what it should have been. Not this. He could not even bear to look at her.

A splash, the iridescent colours of the water rippling. A body, thrown overboard from the next ship. It sank straight as a stone. Coated and covered in luminous colour. He remembered his own hands, out in the rowing boat, dipped in it, the tiny things sticky and shining, a thin film like dipping his hands in the honey in which his father's body lay. Carin's hands covered in it. Carin placing his hands sticky and shining over his heart. The water closed, the ripples stilled. They couldn't keep the dead on board the ships. Weren't going to take them with them to wherever they were headed for. A pile of corpses, lined up on the decks. A pile of the dying, needing water and aid. Throw them over into the deep. Forget them. The iridescent colours of the water. The red painted eyes of the ships. Kill them! Kill them all! Dead's dead.

He'd killed so many, fighting on the ships. Seen one of his brother's ships holed and sinking, sinking with men jumping screaming from its sides. Oh gods, that had been beautiful and worth seeing! The great crack as the wood shattered where two ships met, the water rushing in hungrily, the enemy's ship lurching and mawing and breaking, coming apart into pieces, disembowelled. An animal gutted, its life pouring out in thrashing bodies. Life spilling. Men as the entrails of some great blind beast.

Thalia had been in danger, then, Ti's soldiers coming over the sides with swords while he stared at the dying. He should never have taken her. Left her safe with Matrina to wait on her and teach her good eastern ways, had her brought over in triumph, crowned and robed in gold. But she had insisted. Said she would be safe. And he had so wanted her to see. And the fear in him, when Ti's men came at her, there were so many between him and her and the thought for one moment that she might die, her beautiful body sliding down into the water, lost to him, and the thought of what he'd do to the world if she died. He'd come running, killing as he came towards her, killing everything, Ti's men, his men, the things in the air, the things in the shadows calling him as king. All the blood coming down. She had saved herself, blazing up in light, the men falling back from her, falling into the water, screaming down on the planks of the deck with their eyes buried, so that he'd killed them where they lay, Ti's men and his men, until she was safe, and he knew then that he'd kill everything in the world that ever was and ever would be, apart from her.

Fighting. Killing. Nothing but killing. Perhaps that was when it had started to slip away from him. And his men had been fighting. And he had been fighting. And the ships had crashed and holed each other and fought as living things. And the swords had been bloody. And the water had been bloody. And his men had been fighting. And somehow, somehow the battle had been lost. The ships had turned in panic with Osen cursing him pointing out he'd been wrong, and he hadn't had a chance to kill anything more. And he'd lost his kingdom and his crown and his father and his mother and his brother, and everything in the world that had ever mattered, apart from her.

Chapter Ten

'Do you need anything else doing in the village, Ru?' the woman Lan asked. 'While I'm down that way?'

Ru thought. 'Not the village. But you could check on the goats. Saves doing it later.'

'I will, then.' Lan adjusted her headscarf and went out. Took a deep breath of air after the smoky tallow damp of the house, that was one more thing she could not get used to. Physical weariness. Hunger. Her skin itching, her hair itching, her clothes itching. She had a grim and certain horror that she had become infested with lice.

'If the young one's a bother, slap him on the nose and tell him "no",' Ru called after her. Lan called back yes. Her hands were rough and callused, broken nails, red scabbed raw knuckles. Slap him on the nose. She walked quickly down the track leading to the village, that ran out over the cliffs over Telorna Head.

A bed by the hearth and three meals a day and a clean dress. What Ru gave her, in exchange for work. She checked on the goats, did her errands in the village, went back to Ru by the fire to cook them an evening meal. Thought about walking on to Morr Town. Never did.

On the first day Lan had walked on shaking legs up the beach over the moorland of Seneth, following smoke from a village where she thought she might get directions to Morr Town. And the villagers had been kind enough, given her directions, if not to Morr Town then to a town called Ath west along the coast from where the road ran off towards Morr Town and the seat of the king. She knew the name, she thought. And that had been good and easy, along a well-made road banked with beech trees fiery with dried leaves, beech mast crunching pleasantly under her feet. On the second day her body shook and her mind screamed and she could not walk for seeing fires burning, and she had stumbled down the road off into the wilds, and there she had found a rundown house, and an old sickly woman, who was called Ru.

'Did the young one bother you?' Ru asked.

'Yes. But I hit it on the nose as you suggested.'

'He's the next to be slaughtered. When needs be. Difficult, that one.'

Lan served the food. They sat quietly to eat.

Ru said when they had finished eating, 'I'll teach you to spin, if you want. If you're staying here.'

'I can't stay,' Lan said.

'My husband died,' Ru said. Lan looked up at her, confused. 'A long time ago. Years. Years and years. Still young, he was. I was young. He died in a brawl in a tavern, the innkeep said he was attacked by thugs, but . . . He died and I stayed here, learnt all the things I needed to learn, did what needed doing, worked hard. It's not much of a life. But he had locked my skin away somewhere, you see, and I never found it. So I have to stay. I'll teach you to spin and cook and work if you want. If you're staying.'

This thin tired old woman bent double from her work. A selkie. A sea maiden. A god thing. She swam in the sea as a seal, shed her sealskin and danced on the shore as a woman, until a man came and stole away her skin. And while the man had her skin she must stay with him. Marry him.

Ru said, 'Always, for someone, the world is being broken, Lan, girl. I'm not so resigned to it. Still long to go back to the sea. Dream it. But it was a long time ago. So many years.'

They stared down at their empty plates. Lan said, 'My brother was murdered and I couldn't bear the grief of it. So I went far away to try to forget. And while I was far away I walked out of a shop doorway and saw my brother's murderer's face. And I dragged my brother's murderer all the way back here with me to punish him. And everyone I ever cared for died as a result. If I hadn't walked out of the doorway. If I hadn't seen his face.'

'If,' said Ru. 'If.'

'I could search the house for you. For your skin.'

'I've searched. You think I haven't? It's not here. Wherever he put it, it's hidden somewhere fast. Under a stone on the shore. Buried in a box in the cold earth.'

'Let me search. Please.'

Ru said, 'And what would I do, if you found it? Go back to the sea?'

This thin tired old woman bent double from her work, her hands gnarled and shaking, her eyes half blind. Seals swimming, lithe and glossy and beautiful, twisting and diving in the water, wild and nameless and free.

Ru said, 'Don't search for it.'

Ru said, 'There are a thousand cruelties in the world, Lan. Cruel dead things. Monsters. Chance. Tidy the plates away. Then I'll teach you to spin.'

The woman Lan nodded, took the plates away to the slops bucket and the bowl of water for washing she had been heating on the fire. Hot water, lye soap that made her hands dry and sore. The soap was a new thing, like the bread, got from the village where she had taken the wool Ru spun. Great massed coils of it, fine for weaving, thick for knitting blankets and mittens and caps for the winter cold. Ru had spun it and saved it, unable now to reach the village on the other side of Pelen Brook to trade. So some tiny good comes from my ruin, Lan thought. Someone's world kept alive. The cottage was filthy where Ru could not see the dirt. The goats were wild with uncombed coats where Ru could no longer walk to them. If I leave she will die, Lan thought.

They sat in the half-dark by the fire, and Ru taught her to spin.

'I will show you a special thing,' Ru said a few days later when Lan had returned from milking the goats. She went to a cupboard at the back of the house by her bed, brought out a bundle wrapped in leather. Unfolded it carefully and there on the leather was a piece of yellow cloth. Fragile as cobwebs, with a sheen like a child's hair. Ru held it up. It shone and glowed and blazed. Not just lit from the sun but lit from itself. Like mage glass. Like magic fires. Like laughing eyes.

'Oh!' Lan cried. One beautiful thing. Such a beautiful thing. 'Is it . . . Is it magic?' Mage cloth, worked from dreams. A princess shining in the light of her own gown. Eltheia herself must have worn such things.

'Smell it,' said Ru.

Lan bent towards it, carefully, fearful she might damage it by breathing, so delicate it seemed. It should smell of spices and honey and the petals of new flowers. It should smell, she thought with a pang of rage, like Thalia's hair. She breathed in the scent of leather, the worn skin smell of Ru's hands. And under it . . . Salt. Seaweed. Fish. She looked up, shocked.

'Sea silk,' said Ru. 'The threads of tiny sea creatures. In the sunlight it glows. If left in the sun it will glow at night. Touch it.' Soft as thistle down. So soft Lan could barely feel it. Glowing. But the smell of the sea. A dress for a mer princess, perhaps, a selkie to dance on the sands in the moon. No human woman would wear it, smelling like that.

'Is it yours?' Lan asked. She imagined Ru as a young beautiful sea maid, silvery haired and slender ankled. This the last precious fragment of her gown.

'I wove it,' said Ru. 'I gathered the silk. Wove it with my own hands.'

'But I've never heard of such a thing.' There would be a way to take the stink out, and all the lords and kings and queens of Irlast would want such a fabric. Eltheia and Amrath, shining like the sun. Landra Relast should have had wardrobes full of it.

'I made it,' Ru said again. 'The most beautiful fabric in the world. No one else knows how to make it. It took me forty years to make.' Held it to the sun again and again it glowed. 'If you stay, I can teach you.'

An image for a moment, the two of them, the sea witch and the burned woman, bent at their work, weaving dreams and light into cloth that would never be enough to use and that smelled of salt and sea and fish so that no one would wear it even if they ever made enough to wear. Bolts of shimmering, stinking gold falling through their hands. All the lords of Irlast could not conceive of such a treasure.

'I can't stay,' Lan said. Still mesmerized by the silk, but the silk made her think of other things. Silk gowns, gold bracelets, the glitter of drinking cups in her father's hall.

'No.' Ru wrapped up the leather again, placed the bundle back in the cupboard by her bed. I have just told her she will die this winter, Lan thought. Without me here she will die. 'I didn't think you would. You want to go. You want and you don't want. But you will.'

'I could stay here the winter. Find someone to take care of you. I could look for your skin.'

'I don't want my skin, Lan, girl. Not now. If you found my skin I'd ask you to burn it, and then I'd die. But you wouldn't burn it and you won't find it. And I won't die.'

'I'll stay a few weeks more. Get you supplies in. Make things easier for you. Find someone to help you, maybe.'

'I managed before you came without that. Daresay I can manage again. Though it's kind of you to think of it.' Ru's rheumy eyes flickered. 'Don't go looking for revenge, Lan.'

'Revenge?'

'The sea and the sky have blood in them. A great wrong was done to you. But don't go looking for revenge.'

Why not? Lan thought, and Ru looked at her hearing it in her face.

Ru picked up her spinning. 'Come and sit and we'll try the thick thread for knitting again.'

But what else have I got left, Lan thought, except revenge? That's why I left the rest of them to die, isn't it? So I could avenge them? She said in a rush, like water pouring out, 'I watched my sister dying. I watched my mother dying. I ran down into the dark and hid. Ran away. Left them dying. To be revenged.' In her mind the crash of breaking stonework, the roar of fire rushing in waves, the screams. More than men screaming. Claws in the sky. When she thought of it now she saw bloody eyes.

'I brought him back here for vengeance,' Lan said. 'That's why I brought him back here. To be revenged. To destroy him. And that's why all this came about. Because I brought him back.'

All this, because Lady Landra couldn't live knowing he was living. All this, because Lady Landra was filled with the need for revenge.

Silence.

Ru said, 'You hold it gentle, with a loose wrist. See? Careful. Get the softness in the thread as you turn it. Good soft cloth. A bone spindle's best. Gives the luck. Strong and supple as young limbs, we want it. Strong and supple and soft. Horse bone's best of all, of course, if you can get it. That's it, hold it loose, see? You feel the difference now?'

The spindle turned. A small worm of greyish thread. The woman Lan nodded.

'*Hel*, for warmth and comfort. *Benth*, that is safety from disease. *Anneth*, to ward off the lice. Say them as you spin. *Hel. Benth. Anneth. Hel. Beneth. Anneth.* Warm the cloth. Soft the cloth. Warm the wearer. Soft the cloth.'

Keeping someone warm and keeping them comfortable. Keeping them safe and free from lice. Worse things in the world, surely? And more useful than most things.

'*Hel. Benth. Anneth. Hel. Benth. Anneth.* A cloak to shelter in the winter. A blanket on a cold night. A bed to sleep and bear children. A winding sheet for an old man's corpse. *Hel. Benth. Anneth. Hel. Benth. Anneth.*'

Lady Landra had stepped out of a shop doorway in Sorlost and seen Marith's dead face walking past her. Not been able to look away. 'I'll kill you,' she'd screamed at him. He'd looked back at her and said, 'You're the ones who'll die.'

If she'd stepped out of the doorway a moment earlier. A moment later. Dismissed her glimpse of his face as an illusion. Looked the other way from him.

Left him alone.

Marith has to die, she thought.

Lan said, 'I have to leave, Ru.'

'So you said. Stay a few weeks to get some supplies in for me.' Ru broke off the spinning, set down the thread. 'Someone from the village to help me would be a kindness. To look after the goats, tend the field by Pelen Brook. But don't look for my skin.' Ru took up the spindle again. 'And don't go looking for revenge.'

So it was settled. A farmer in the village had a daughter who would go to Ru, live at the house, do the work, take the place as hers with Ru living there to spin wool and sleep in the corner where Lan had slept.

Ru gave Lan the stinking yellow gold cloth. 'There's no purpose to it,' she said to Lan. 'I can't go down to the shore now, even, to gather more of the threads.'

'You could teach Kova, when she comes.'

'I could.'

I did all I could do, thought Lan. Kova will work the farmstead better than I ever could. Manage the goats better, cook better food. Kova will maybe find a man to marry, has a man in the village already maybe, they'll have children and Ru will look after them like a grandmother. They'll bury her nicely on the seashore when she dies.

And gold and silver pieces will blossom over her grave and they'll all live happy in a marble palace, thought Lan, and the sun will always shine. Kill them all and burn them and spit on the ashes. The world's a cruel place.

'Have this too,' said Ru. She pressed a small bone spindle into Lan's hands. Lan looked at it. 'Horse bone,' said Ru. 'My husband's father made it.' Worn and yellowed. Old.

'How old are you, Ru?' Lan asked, while she thought of the tales of the sea folk she'd heard. Deathless. Ageless. Gods. Carin had been fascinated by them, but they'd never much interested her. Peasant people. Sea things. Men things, also. Rape and kidnap and desire. Keeping something you shouldn't.

Weak things.

'Old,' said Ru.

I don't need to worry she'll die, thought Lan suddenly then. Fool! She put the yellow cloth and the bone spindle away in her pack beside the willow wand. *Hel*, for warmth and comfort. *Palle*, that is smooth sheen of a calm sea.

Kova came next morning, strong and plain with strong green eyes. Seemed kind enough, Lan thought, judging her with a new way of judging that Landra Relast had not known. Her hands were strong, used to work. Her face was meek. She looked a little afraid of Ru. Maybe she knew what Ru was.

'There's soap and candles in the cupboard by your bed,' Lan told Ru. She did not say that she had traded the silver ring she had worn for them. To Kova she said, 'There's bread in the pantry, flour and butter in the crocks. I milked the goats this morning. They don't give much. There's a nice bank of winter mint on the path down to Pelen Brook, near the big ash tree. Ru likes it in the stew.' She took Kova out to the vegetable garden behind the house, all bare now apart from black kale ragged like leather. 'She tries to do more than she should,' Lan said to Kova. 'Thinks she's stronger than she is. Care for her and she'll be kind.' Kova looked at her with strong green eyes and strong hands used to work and a meek face. 'I've a sister who's marrying a fisherman, mistress,' Kova said.

Some, some in this world must be kind.

So that was that. Lan set off slowly down the path into the village.

There were rumours flying in the village of things happening in the lords' halls, ships and soldiers summoned to Malth Elelane, mutterings of war. Lan walked with slow steps along the coast road. Walking the road again alone was the worst thing. Without her name and her wealth she was nothing. How strange it was. This was how Marith had been, she thought dully as she walked. Nameless and powerless. She remembered Thalia on the moorland stumbling in the cold, the way Marith's eyes had been when he looked at her. Little wonder he felt so angry now. But this was also what he had wanted, she thought. To be nothing. To be the thing that was hurt, not the thing that did the hurting. 'I was happy,' he'd said. 'I didn't ask to come back. To be king.' Briefly, she thought, briefly he had escaped.

She walked on all day. She tried not to think of Ru in the damp dirty house that was warm. She stopped in the evening in a way house, huddled in the corner furthest from the doorway, frightened someone might come. Cold greasy trimmings of meat, bread, water: she placed some of each carefully before the godstone at the entrance, saw its gratitude in its blank faceless eyeless face. Before she tried to sleep she got out her pack and looked at the things she had. A horse-bone spindle. A scrap of yellow cloth. A broken twig that was bound to her skin. A gold ring stamped with a bird flying, her father's crest.

'Eltheia,' she prayed as she curled up on the stone ledge to sleep, 'Eltheia, fairest one, keep safe, keep safe.' She slept with the bone spindle in her hand, dry and smooth and chipped at the edge, old yellow bone riddled with tiny holes where it was chipped, carved from the shoulder bone of an old broken-down farm horse that she heard galloping in her dream. The things that walked the lich roads walked past her, and let her be.

'I am not going looking for revenge,' she said aloud when she woke to frost crisp white-silver on the dark ground. 'I am going to make him nothing. As he wanted to be.' A bird flew up cawing from the trees behind the way house. 'Not revenge.'

The things that walked the lich roads walked past her. Laughed.

Chapter Eleven

A body was lying on the beach in the sand, face up to the rain. It was lying in the tideline, the ebb and flow of the waves making its head roll back and forth. Its skin was very white.

Thalia watched it for a while. It shook its head and shook its head and there should be something meaningful in it. Just a dead thing, she thought. Just a dead thing bloated up and eaten by the water. Swollen and salt-filled. There was a jagged hole in its chest, where it had been dead before it drowned. The sea had taken its blood.

'Here's another!' a voice called across the beach. Two soldiers came down near her, took the body by the arms, dragging it away up to the pyres that burned on the shore where the sand was dry. Driftwood and reeds and dead flesh. The salt crackled, burned up a brilliant yellow; they fed the fire with pitch to keep the flames high even with the wet bodies in the rain. Thalia watched them drag the body up, its feet making ruts in the sand.

Osen Fiolt came down the beach towards her. He stopped, nodded his head to her.

'The raiding party has come back,' he said.

'And?'

'They've got some bread. Dried fish. Beer. We won't die hungry, at least.'

'We will not die,' Thalia said. We will not. We will not. I will not.

Osen's face flickered, looking across the beach where the men worked at the pyres, feeding the flames with pitch-soaked wood. The bones of the ships, consuming themselves. 'We can't sail, in this wind, and Tiothlyn can't sail either, and that's the only luck we have. But he'll come. And we'll all be dead.'

'We defeated' — she did not quite know how to say it, 'his father', 'his brother', what do I know, she thought again, what do I know of fathers and brothers, these foreign words, even in my own tongue I have never spoken them, meaningless words, and yet to say them, it hurts me, to say what it is he did — 'we defeated King Illyn. We can defeat Tiothlyn.'

'Whatever happened at Malth Salene . . .' Osen shook his head. 'I wasn't there, of course. So perhaps you could ask him to do whatever he did again? I'm surprised Ti hasn't come already, in all honesty. King Illyn would have marched the men overnight immediately we turned tail on him, followed the ships along the coast. We're less than a day's march from Morr Town.' He gestured at the smoke from the pyres. 'It's not exactly like he can't know where we are.'

'So we will destroy him.' Thalia thought: I saw what Marith did, at Malth Salene. I saw every man who opposed him die. I know what he is. What is in him. I will not die here. I will not.

'Destroy Tiothlyn? He'll cut the men's throats like dogs, Thalia. Those that haven't already fled. But no – that will be why he's waiting. Why kill us himself when our men can do it for him?'

The men were slumped in ragged shelters frozen in the wind, breathing in the smoke of dead flesh. But they would fight. She knew, looking at their faces, she who had seen Malth Salene fall. They would fight for him. Or she would make them fight, if she must. But perhaps they would die, even so. More broken bones on the shoreline, buried in the sand like the wreck of the ships. She looked across at the litter of shelters, like plague sores on the grass beyond the sedge. No one, she thought then, no one thinks that they will die. I do not suppose that his father thought that he would die. His father, his brother – they must have thought, also, that they would win. Remembered the eyes of the sacrifices bound to her altar, staring up at her, she stood before them with the knife in her hands, the High Priestess of Great Tanis, and still, in their eyes, the certainty there somehow that they would not die, that her knife would not truly kill them, even as she killed them.

But I will not die here, she thought. I will not.

'Why are you still here, then, Lord Fiolt?' Thalia asked. 'Why have you not already fled? Or killed him?' Some little of the dignity game in the Temple, drawing her old status as the God's hand and the God's knife. If this is ended, if I am broken and dying here, I can at least have that.

'Because . . .' He rubbed his eyes. 'I could ask that same question of you, High Priestess Thalia.'

You could. They looked at one another. Each pitying the other, perhaps, Thalia thought. For being caught in this. Not able to leave. Drawn to what was offered. Kingship! Victory! Glory! The promise in Marith's face.

Osen looked away from her. Looked again at the bodies burning in sparks of salt and pitch. Breathed in deep, and Thalia could see his nostrils flare, breathing in the smell of the smoke. Put his hand on the hilt of his sword. Caressing it.

'Anyway. Here we are. The raiding party has come back,' said Osen again. 'There's food, at least, now. That's all I came to tell you. I'll have something brought to you. And to him. Our Lord King. I'll have watches set tonight. Hopefully we won't be slaughtered in our sleep, at least.' He rubbed his face again. 'Bread and beer and dried fish. Some of the men might even stay here to die with us, if we feed them.'

'Thank you, Lord Fiolt.'

I will not die, she thought. I spared Marith's life, only a little time ago.

The promise in Marith's face . . .

She went back to the shelter they had built for him as king. Sail cloth, ship's timbers, branches. The sand was soft under her feet, then the crunch of pebbles, up over the dunes, down though the sedge to the coarse bare flat grass. Men's faces followed her as she walked. The man Tal sat before the ragged flap of the tent doorway, wrapped in his cloak, his sword on his knees. He bowed his head as Thalia entered.

'Marith?'

He was sitting staring at the wall, where the canvas was ripped to let in a beam of half-light.

'Thalia?'

'The men took some food in the village. Osen Fiolt is having something prepared for us.'

No answer. She sat down next to him.

'I'm sorry,' he said.

'Yes.'

'I thought . . . I thought . . . They should have welcomed me. They were there. My brother. My mother — my stepmother. They should have . . . they should . . . I'm sorry. Ah, gods.' Spat out a laugh. 'I told you I was afraid for you to come. But I really thought . . . She's my mother. How could she not welcome me back?'

Memories: his face in the desert, his eyes soft and sad and filled with light like stars; his face in the golden morning, bright and living and filled with joy and love and pride. And she remembered also Ausa, the priestess in the Temple, her friend, whom she had punished and maimed and ruined, and who had asked after her in friendship when it was done.

Perhaps, she thought. Perhaps they would have welcomed him back, even despite everything, if he had been able to see them. Perhaps they still would.

Marith said, 'Hilanis the Young skinned his brother alive, you know? His wife wore a gown made of the skin on the day he was crowned. My great-great-grandfather. Skinned his older brother alive. I found an old leather robe once, tucked away in a cupboard, I thought for years it was Tareneth's skin. There was a mark on it I even thought was a bloodstain. Until Ti pointed out he would have had to be five feet wide and four feet high.'

Or not.

Pain like knives stabbing. The filth of these people. The filth of this world.

Marith closed his eyes. 'Let Ti have it. Have all of this. I'll go down to the beach and die there. You should go back to Sorlost. To your God. Be free.'

Pain like knives stabbing.

The walls of the Temple closing around them. Blotting out the light. I ran from that, she thought. I will not go back.

'You should be sorry,' she said.

The doorcloth of the shelter jerked open. Osen stood there, the man Tal behind him, frightened and elated both at once.

'Marith — My Lord King — Ships. There are ships in the bay.'

Marith's eyes blinked slowly open. 'Ships . . . how . . . how many?'

'Ten. War ships. Large. But they're not Ti's ships. Not from the Whites.'

'Not Ti's . . . Whose, then?'

'I . . . I'm not sure. It's hard to tell, in this gloom. And they're coming . . . They're sailing against the wind. Not oared. Sailing.'

Marith got up, rubbed at his face. 'Against the wind?' He frowned. 'Get the men drawn up.'

He raked his fingers through his hair, did not wait to put on his armour but belted on his sword, fastened his bloodsoaked cloak at his neck. Thalia followed him out, Osen and Tal following behind. The camp around them was an ants' nest, men scrabbling to arms, meals abandoned, dice and drink scattered beneath their feet, voices shouting for order and discipline. The chaos trying to pull into something like the army of a king as they passed. On the beach the sedge whispered and shivered. A group of men stood watching the sea. Lights on the water, the ships coming in. Black shapes like clots of shadows. Silent. No oars indeed, sailing with sails swelling the wrong way to the wind.

A shout from the first ship, the splash of an anchor. A rowing boat came across, the oars making flashes as the water caught the light. It met the breakers on the tideline: men leapt out, ran it forward up the sand, beaching it clear of the waves. A man got out carefully, flanked by servants. Came across the sand to Marith, and Marith came across the sand to him.

The man smiled, his face livid in the torches. 'King Marith.'

Marith tried to smile back. 'Uncle Selerie. Welcome.'

Chapter Twelve

Once upon a time, a long, long time ago now, there was a young king who needed a wife. And the wife he chose was called Marissa, and she was the sister of Selerie Calboride the King of Ith. She had yellow hair and grey eyes and she was sweet natured and gentle, kind and fair and wise and good. The young king, King Illyn, his name was, he sailed over the wine dark sea to her, and he married her in great splendour in her brother's fortress, and he brought her back with him to his own kingdom, and crowned her queen with a circlet of diamonds and silver on her beautiful head.

So, nine months after the wedding, Queen Marissa gave birth to a baby boy. The boy was beautiful, a shining child, strong and healthy, with bright clever eyes. The whole kingdom rejoiced, that their king had an heir, and such a beautiful baby at that. The queen was filled with joy, she loved her son, doted on him, cherished him. Oh, such a loving mother! Oh, such a happy child she had!

But the king her husband was a bad man. Or, better, perhaps, say that he was a cruel man, for he did not love his wife Queen Marissa, for all that she was so fair and so gentle and so wise and so good. He was a bitter man, and a harsh one, and before he ever married Marissa he had had a mistress, Elayne of the Golden Hair, who was as hard and harsh and selfish as he himself. And

Elayne was filled with jealousy against Queen Marissa, who was queen and mother and so bright with happiness.

And Elayne and King Illyn between them killed poor Marissa. They poisoned her. And King Illyn married Elayne and made her queen.

But no matter how she tried, Elayne could never manage to harm Marissa's son, the prince, the heir to the kingdom, left motherless when still a baby before he could even speak his mother's name. Though Elayne longed for his death with all her heart, to make her own son king. Though King Illyn longed also for this.

Marissa's brother Selerie had loved his sister. He had rejoiced when she bore her child. Thus when the boy was grown into a fine youth, strong and clever and healthy and beautiful to look upon, King Selerie invited him to visit him in Ith. And this is the story which he told him.

Chapter Thirteen

Selerie Calboride's war tent was blue and silver leather, the colours of Ith, gold leaf round the doorway, a standard capping it in the shape of a golden stag with antlers shifting into eagles' heads. Fur rugs on the floor, two light folding chairs, a table in silver gilt, a brazier beneath the smoke hole, the dividing curtain to the sleeping place beyond drawn back to show a bed made up. Even a woman, dressed in shimmering green velvet, her hair braided with gold, holding a tray with a jug of mulled wine on it, steam rising to fog the light of her eyes.

'Nephew.' Selerie rose from his chair. 'Would you care to sit?'

'Uncle.' The beautiful backdrop, the king in his jewelled robe, the girl. Utter humiliation. But a flush of pride crept into Marith also, that his uncle felt him worth enough to want to humiliate. He sat down and stretched out his hands to the fire.

A strange man, Selerie Calboride, King of Ith. Some people said he was mad. Though they said most Calborides were mad. Tall, reddish fair, with pale grey wide bulbous eyes. It was the eyes that made the madness convincing. Nothing like Marith's father's eyes, and he did not remember his mother to whom he had been told there was a close resemblance. But Marith felt self-consciously as though it was his father who looked at him.

The girl stepped forward to offer him a drink. Marith took it.

Felt his hands shake. Very good wine, naturally. The warmth spread pleasantly through his fingers. The cup was almost empty suddenly. His hands were shaking and he almost dropped it. Tried to keep himself from staring at the girl with the jug.

Selerie raised his own cup. 'As one king to another, then, Marith of the White Isles.'

'One king to another, Uncle.' Tried to look at his uncle speaking to him. 'You've come, I'm sure, to congratulate me on my success. Such a triumph! But of course you always knew what I had in me to do.'

Selerie shifted in his chair. I hate you, Marith thought. I hate you. I am a man, a king. 'I came to offer you my aid,' Selerie said slowly. 'Hail you as a fellow king. Promise alliance. The old sacred bonds between Calboride and the Altrersyr, back even to Amrath and Eltheri, that your father spurned. Help you kill the whore's son who claims to be heir in your stead. I came to confirm with my own eyes that my only sister's only child was still alive. My sister would weep with shame, were she to see you now.'

So it's lucky then my father killed her. You think I don't weep with shame myself? Marith said, 'It was your decision to come, uncle. I was perfectly happy sitting in my tent in the filth. My soldiers had just found something alcoholic for me to drink, I'm told.'

Selerie said crisply, 'Happy, were you? Perhaps I'll leave you be, then.' They looked away from each other, both caught. Can't leave. Can't tell you to leave. Can't ask you to stay. Can't ask you to ask me.

'Your brother the whore's son has claimed the throne,' Selerie said at last. 'That is why I have come. There are some things I will not permit. The whore's son wearing the crown of Altrersys is one of them.'

I . . .

'My brother the whore's son is claiming the throne,' Marith said dully back.

'And you seem to have done a most wonderful job of opposing him.'

Marith looked away at the walls. Shadows. Hate. Pain. Leave me alone, he thought. Just leave me alone.

Selerie said, 'Don't fret, dear Nephew. War's a difficult game at which you've had very little practice. I'm sure even Amrath himself made mistakes occasionally. You'll learn.'

'I'm sure I will.' His cup was empty again. Held it out to the girl for more. Her eyes flicked to Selerie. Selerie's eyes flicked back. She stepped backwards away from them, leaving Marith's cup hanging.

'It's a very fine rug you're sitting on,' Selerie said kindly. 'I wouldn't want it spoilt by you vomiting on it.'

Felt like being back being raged at by his father for turning up falling-down-dead drunk at some important event. Felt like being laughed at by Skie for killing a dragon and it somehow being embarrassing that he had. 'I'm the king, Uncle. Not Ti. A greater king than you are, indeed. King of the White Isles and Illyr and Immier and the Wastes and the Bitter Sea. *Ansikanderakesis Amrakane*. You're only king at all because my ancestor spared yours. I should make you kneel at my feet.'

Selerie said nothing. Looked around him with his bulbous mad eyes. The gilded leather. The fine furnishings. The furs and the wine and the jewels and the girl. Marith twirled the empty cup in his fingers. Gold. Don't pretend you didn't want this, Uncle. You sit in your tower drinking quicksilver and seeing the same things I do. Days, it takes, to get from Ith to the White Isles, even with magic in your sails: you sailed well before my failure at Malth Elelane, to join me, secure me as king. You must have been read-ying your troops since first you heard I was still alive. Look at this tent, these fittings, the men with bright bronze spears outside the door. Why else did you come, if not for this?

Selerie looked away at the walls, seeing something there in the leather in the corner where the light from the brazier hardly reached. 'And what would you do, King Marith of the White Isles and Illyr and Immier and the Wastes and the Bitter Sea, *Ansikanderakesis Amrakane*, parricide and dragonlord and dragon killer and despoiler of the holiest woman in Irlast, if I knelt at your feet?'

Tell you my father was right to kill my mother. Tell you it's lucky indeed neither of them are alive to see what I've become. Tell you to kill me and bury me beside Carin in one grave. You might even do it, I think, perhaps, Uncle, you who once gave me an old sword with a ruby in its hilt like a clot of blood.

Marith said, 'You know what I'd do.'

Selerie gestured to the girl to refill Marith's cup. 'Do I? Do you?'

'I'd ask you to give me your ships, and your men, and your allegiance.'

'And why would you do that, then, Nephew?'

Marith looked at him. 'You know why.'

Selerie smiled back. 'I remember you when you were a child, Nephew. You seemed so very bright. Full of laughter. Yet one might have guessed, even then, that this would be where you'd come to in the end. King Ruin, I hear they have named you. King of Death. Very well then. I'll give you my ships. And my men. And my allegiance.' Sipped his wine. 'But I do not think that you will thank me for doing so.'

Marith thought: no. I do not think perhaps that I will. I told you, I was perfectly happy sitting in my tent.

Selerie rose to his feet, placed his cup back on the tray the woman held. 'I have another ten ships riding at anchor around the next cape. Twenty ships in all. Two thousand men. We'll meet again this evening, then, to discuss. You'll bring your woman to dinner afterwards, perhaps? I would be most interested to meet her, this holy and incomparable creature who gave up god and empire for you. For this.'

Hateful old man. Selerie's eyes like his father's eyes again. Yes, I failed. Yes. I know. But next time . . . Marith tried to think of other things. Thalia. Dinner. Plans. There'd be better fare for her here than whatever his soldiers had managed to hunt up in the marsh and the village huts. A few hours' warmth in a dry tent. A pretty dress and some jewels and a chance for her to be treated as she deserved. Oh, she'd looked so perfect, seated beside him in the high seats of honour at Malth Calien, radiant by firelight with the men all eying her with jealous desire in their hearts.

Selerie said, 'I have a man with me whom you may I think be interested to meet, given your current circumstances.'

'A hatha merchant, is he?'

Selerie's face went dark with anger. 'A weather hand.'

'A weather hand?' Marith started. Never met one. Half convinced they didn't exist. Just lucky men. And not loved, on the Whites. Storm-bringers, death-dealers, things you scared fisher children with. But he'd seen the ships last night, sails swelling against the wind. 'Really? That might be . . . handy.'

Selerie snorted. 'So I thought when I found him. Handy. Though lacking his right hand.'

Marith got to his feet. 'At sunset, then. Osen had better come as well; a couple of the other lords. There's a fishmonger some-where here who lent me his house and everything in it after I tore apart his liege lord's fortress. I said I'd give him some high post somewhere.'

Selerie said nothing. Looked away at the gold and the furs and the girl.

Hateful old man.

He stopped outside his uncle's tent watching the Ithish soldiers raise the last section of a scrubby palisade. All neat and efficient. One thousand Ithish men here. Another thousand coming in. And then they were ready. Done and sealed and too late. I wish Carin was here, he thought suddenly. He hadn't thought about Carin so much recently. Getting weaker in his mind. Harder to remember his face, the exact colour of his hair and eyes. Carin would have stopped all this. Dragged him off for a drink so he forgot all about it. King Marith the Unmemorable, who did absolutely nothing at all. King Marith the Incapable, too stupe-fied to pick up a sword. Hard to think really properly seriously about killing people when you're slumped in the gutter covered in puke and piss and drool.

Gods, you were good to me, Carin, he thought.

But this time I won't fail.

The man with the weather hand was called Ranene. A middle-aged man with a wart on his nose, who could call the wind and make the sea change and bring a ship safe to harbour in any storm. Black skin and hair, the accent of Allene. He spoke in a hoarse whisper like a rustling of dead leaves, where his throat had once been cut. Wore a collar hung with seed pearls to hide the scar. He had brought ships to safety and ships to drowning for hire, trading a ship's fate to the highest bidder, before Selerie found him and made him his man. Safer that way, at Selerie's court guiding the king's ships. Sailors feared and hated a weather hand, knowing what they could bring a ship if their mood turned. Marith found him rather agreeable. He grinned cheerfully back at Marith when Selerie introduced them.

'I'll bring you across the sea as my king, My Lord,' he said in his quiet scratched voice. 'What comes when you come to shore . . . I don't even have a hand.' He paused: Marith had to strain to hear him. 'But if your brother comes out to meet you with his ships . . . High winds and high waves might be handy. Does your brother have a weather hand, My Lord?'

'No.' King Illyn had never had one. Rare. Almost a myth. Hated. Feared. 'No.' Marith shut his eyes at the thought of the sea in storm. The greatest storm he had seen as a child, he had been ten years old, watching from his window awed as the waves shattered the rocks of Morr Head and the roofs of Morr Town. Ships smashed on the headland, bodies washed up far inland as the water rose over the streets of the town, trees and walls ripped away. Like the fire at Malth Salene, scouring the coastline clear. The air had stunk of seaweed and dead bodies, pallid puffy fish things dragged up from the depths, the broken stones of old cities far out beneath the sea. Sand and salt had been blown even onto the high balconies of Malth Elelane.

A ship out in that. A ship out in that . . .

'You could do it?'

'I could.'

'How?'

Ranene said, 'I feel the waves. I feel the water. I feel the sky.' Pause. 'I have no idea how I do it, My Lord. Especially as I was born a month's walk from the sea.'

Well, that was disappointing. But then he'd asked Thalia how she made the light and she could only say 'I do'. 'Magic's a subtle thing'. 'Magic's a complex thing'. 'Buggered if I know' had at least the virtue of honesty.

'Do it, then.' Destroy them. Shatter them to pieces, smash them, break them. They had refused him. They should have opened the city to him. Welcomed him in. His brother! His mother! His home!

Destroy them. Break them. Drown them. Curse them.

Ranene bowed his head. 'As My Lord commands.' Looked happy as anything. Couldn't imagine a weather hand got the chance that often to really let himself go.

'The whore's son's ships will be broken, then,' said Selerie. 'Well and good. You will have command of the sea. But you will need to take Malth Elelane. Morr Town.' He looked pointedly at Marith. 'Ideally without either of them being entirely reduced to smoking ashes. Unless you think otherwise, Nephew, of course?'

'We bring the ships in at night down the coast,' said Lord Bemann. 'March on Malth Elelane with the dawn. Order them to open the gates.'

'No.' Lord Stansel. A poor man, who held a poor island with few men to fight. A cripple, bound to his wheeled chair. But a clever man, with a reputation for good sense. 'If we were taking a foreign city, even any other town on the Whites . . . But Malth Elelane . . . We are not coming as invaders. We are coming to bring our rightful king to his throne. We are coming to bury the last king in the tomb of his ancestors, where Altrersys himself lies. We do not sneak in the darkness like outlaws. We do not threaten. We do not cajole. Tiothlyn's ships need to be destroyed. Yes. We send storms in the night to shatter the ships, frighten the people. We come into harbour with the dawn, beneath the banners of Amrath and King Marith His heir. Where Tiothlyn the Usurper has brought the sea's anger, Marith the true king will bring strength and a favourable wind. The town and Malth Elelane will yield graciously to us as is our right.'

'And if Morr Town doesn't yield graciously to us? If Morr Town starts chucking banefire at us again? If Master Handy here somehow can't whistle up a storm?'

Somewhere in the barrel of honey the dead king stirred, moving. Shadows beating on the walls of the tent. Selerie looked about, almost seeing them. Fear in his eyes for what he'd begun. Marith took a breath. Say it. Say what must be done. 'Lord Stansel is right. We sail straight into Morr Town harbour. And this time they will welcome me as they ought. Malth Elelane will yield. It was built for the kings of the line of Amrath. It is mine. Thus it will yield to me. Morr Town will yield or it will resist. If it resists, it will be destroyed. Morr Town is nothing. It can be rebuilt. Or I will build a new city elsewhere, leave the ruins as a warning.' He looked at his uncle. 'Morr Town has banefire. Very well then. It is only a liquid that burns. Morr Town has defenders. Very well then. They are only men with swords. We have an army. If half of that army falls, they also are only men. Men die. We need only enough left alive that the gates of the city are opened and my brother's body hung above them in chains.'

The men shifted. The lords of the White Isles. The king's captains, the chosen companions of the *Ansikanderakesis Amrakane*. Thugs and chancers, men with younger brothers themselves, men who hungered for chaos and bloodshed, men who clung blindly to the right of the eldest born son as heir. Faces smiling. Rictus grins of terror. What did you think, Marith thought, what did you think it was we were to do? Osen shivered, looking from Marith to Selerie to Ranene. Fear in all their eyes. Seemed also to realize, suddenly, at last, what it was they were about.

'Master Handy here can certainly whistle up a storm,' said Ranene. His voice piped like a hollow reed blown between a boy's hands. Profoundly irritating. But you could hear something in it. This one has power, Marith thought, looking at the man's lumpy, warty nose. 'The greatest storm you island men have ever seen. My Lord Selerie has seen some small amount of my powers. But for the king here, this king who is lord of death and shadows and ruined things . . . For him, I will raise such a storm as will never be forgotten. I will raise a storm that will shake the island of Seneth to its roots. The men of Morr Town will open their gates to him with joy and rejoicing. Those few that are not drowned.'

Eyes watched him weak with horror. The shadows blinked and laughed in the corners of the tent.

'A storm, then,' said Selerie lightly. 'Then I think we are dismissed for the night. Dinner is I think prepared and waiting. My Lords of the White Isles. Master Weather Hand. Till tomorrow.' Selerie got to his feet. 'A drink, Nephew, while we await your lady?'

Selerie had somehow brought white bread and sweetmeats and cured venison over with him on campaign as well as wine and gilt chairs and a girl.

'Amrath campaigned rough with his men,' Marith said defensively when Thalia raised her eyebrows at it all. 'You can't move fast, with all this lot to lug around. We keep the proper ways of war here on the Whites.' He thought of Skie's bare tent, where the fact that it didn't stink of mildew had been sign enough of power. A bedroll. A cloak. A change of shirt. A day's ration of bread. Nothing else had seemed necessary. Nothing else had been necessary. 'Yes, well, yes, I could, possibly, have put some more thought into the logistics.' First course was apples baked in honey. The smell of the honey was making him nauseous. The spoon dug into the fruit and he couldn't not think of his father's head. Folds and folds of skin, the soft brown dapples like winking eyes; his father floating like an unborn baby, all soft and unformed . . . 'Any thought into the logistics. But Osen didn't think about it either. And he was almost sober some nights.'

'I have something for you,' Selerie said to Thalia. 'Here.' He gestured; the girl stepped forward, held out a little wooden box. Cedar wood, carved with a delicate pattern of flowers, a few last fragments of gold leaf. The more beautiful, for being old and use-worn, the wood smoothed and darkened by careful, loving hands. Thalia opened it slowly. In her perfect fingers a short chain of silver, set with sapphires almost the same colour as her eyes.

'Oh!' She held it to the candle flame to make it glitter. Blue stars. Blue fire. Blue lights shining in the sea.

'I am the nearest kin my nephew has,' Selerie said. 'It seemed apt therefore to welcome you as such.'

Thalia smiled at Selerie kindly. The girl disappeared with the empty box. Servants brought cold cured meat and hot bread. Spiced greens. Cimma cakes. Hippocras. Even keleth seeds in a silver bowl. It was a pleasant enough evening. They wandered back afterwards in the light of a torch flickering on Tal's armour. Stopped a little while to look at the sea. Again before their tent to look at the stars. Clear and cold, their breath puffing out white. A hard frost.

Till tomorrow, then.

A child, a youth of thirteen, when he sailed to Ith, to visit his uncle. A child, strong and happy, climbing trees in the orchard, scrumping sour apples, running and running through the wild country of his kingdom, running into the sun with the wind in his hair. Even then, he knew, the shadows followed him. Felt them. Knew them. Shadow eyes that watched him. Longed for him. A child, a youth of thirteen. Dreaming such dreams. His brother was less than two years younger; he loved him so dearly, looked after him, his best friend, 'when I am king', he would say, 'and you are my closest adviser, my second in command, the captain of my armies – you and I, we'll conqueror the world, won't we? I'll win you a kingdom too, Ti. A really big one. Rich and grand. We'll share out the world.'

He went to visit Ith.
Selerie told him things.
He came home.
His brother was waiting there for him.

Chapter Fourteen

On the sand of the beach His wonder worker raises his arm. Speaks words that mean nothing. Empty sounds. His face is calm, still like the smooth water. His eyes are closed. Sweat trickles slowly down the line of his jaw. The wonder worker, the weather hand, the vessel of His hopes. The weather hand grasps at the sky before him. Lowers his arms. Speaks meaningless words.

He opens his eyes. Looks at the calm clear water, the calm clear sky, the pale liquid light. Birds dance on the horizon. The marsh reeds whisper behind him in a soft breeze. His weather hand speaks. Shouts.

The air shimmers. The storm comes. Vast black clouds pile on the horizon, rushing in on a warm, strange, savage wind. He watches the rain coming, a wall of black water, the sea churned and shattered with the weight of it, so heavy it rips the canvas of His army's tents, breaks down branches, bruises the skin. The ships dragged up on the beaches tremble in it. Like iron falling from the sky. Like the stars are falling. Like there are no stars left in the dark.

Hours. Days.

Waves batter the rocks high as buildings. Their crests are furious white with foam. Sea bulls, His men call them. As the storm goes on He begins to see things floating on them. Tree limbs. Bits of boats. Bits of houses. Dead things. In a lull in the storm some of His men find the bloated carcass of a horse, its hooves painted in gold. They eat it raw, the wind being too strong to kindle fires. Two men die of it. Should not take that which belongs to the old gods. Sea and sky and earth and stone. And it's bad meat, being drowned.

He sends men over the cliffs of the headland, to spy out the land nearer to the storm's heart. For they are only on the edge of it. Shielded. The men go on hands and knees in the darkness, heads wrapped in leather against the rain and the earth blown by the wind. He has promised them their own bodyweight in gemstones if they bring back news of His enemies. They cannot get far, in the storm, the first stream they come to is a raging torrent, the path up the high steep cliff is a knife blade, three of the ten slip and fall. The sea at the cliff's foot boils like a cauldron. They are hurled around in the water and the rocks show briefly red. Three go back, shaking. Four go onwards, reach the top of the climb where the land sweeps down to a wide golden valley and a river mouth. A long view across the lowlands, before the sea-girt hills and then the forests that rise slowly to the north. They cannot see beyond the length of a spear thrust, in the wind and the rain and the whipped-up spray. The waves are tall as battlements, their white caps huge as drifts of snow. When they break on the fields they shatter rocks and tear the earth. Lightning rolls and roars and hangs as cracks in the world through which another light burns. Stormspirits shrieking, dancing with long teeth and long nails. His troops cower in their shelters. He stands on the shore with His face in the rain.

The sky is boiling. The sea is boiling. There is no sky. No sea. No earth. All that exists howls in the wind.

Days. Nights. No sun. No dawn. No dusk. Men drown standing on the cliff top, from breathing in the rain. The waves are huge as towers. Sea dragons. Harder than stone. The air is screaming. A man's mouth opens, pleading, and he cannot hear his own voice. The rain is rock and metal, crushing, shattering down the world. There is nothing left.

And then calm.

The storm fades to stillness. Slow, heavy beat of the wind. A heart slowing. The rain stops and the air is fresh and sweet. Cold. Pure. Washed clean. The land is transformed by wind and water, raw holes in the land, broken stone where the earth is ripped open like a miscarried womb. Piled mounds of muck and filth. Scar tissue across the landscape. Pus. Timber and flesh litter the beaches, stranded by the outrunning tide. The sky and the earth are silver, shining water that laughs musically as it runs back down into the sea.

The shattered remains of ships begin to float in at the mouths of the marsh channels. Black wood. Red painted eyes. Dead men in armour, heads and limbs. Ripped metal, its surface pitted by the rain. Dead women. Dead babies. Broken walls.

He walks the tideline, wondering. Bids His men ready their own ships for sailing. Today He will come into His own.

The sea is choked with rubble. Dead people. Dead animals. Broken trees. Broken houses. Broken ships. They sail slowly, prows brushing through the bobbing ruins of lives. The wind is against them, but the sails fill and they sail.

They come again around the headland. A flash of white on the high cliff. The smooth waters of the bay open before Him. Winter sunlight. The sea welcoming Him home. His fortress rises before Him. The harbour is broken, its wall shattered into pebbles, not a single ship remaining whole. The war engines are missing. The houses and taverns of the lower town have been swept away like sand.

On the broken stones of the harbour His people are waiting. They cheer Him, receive Him kneeling, throw open every door and window of their town as a sign. He walks up the high road to His fortress, the whalebone gates that were raised for Him a thousand years before He was born. The grey towers of Joy. The golden tower of Despair. His fortress. The stones bid Him welcome. His fortress, built for Him and Him alone. His servants kneel before Him in a blare of silver trumpets, holding bloody offerings in outstretched hands. They spread the victory feast before Him. Wine and honey and plates of gold. His soldiers raise the paean, shout His name. Victory! Victory and triumph! Rejoice! Rejoice! And then His bedchamber, with the crimson hangings and the windows open to the sea, and the woman with her eyes wide.

And He is home.

PART TWO

A WEDDING PARTY

IN SORLOST

Chapter Fifteen

A wedding party in Sorlost.

It was painfully hot. Yellow dust piled in the streets, thick with dead insects, dead leaves. The skin felt grimy, gritted by the heat, eyes stinging, bodies sticky and overripe; people clung to the shadows, poured lemon scented water on the parched flagstones, drank tea under wilting trees. Birds hung in cages from heat cracked branches, singing out notes to cool the ear. The street sellers sat by the fountains, kohl stained faces rank as peaches; at dusk the knife-fighters grappled, sodden with each other's sweat, warm metal slipping over warm bone. In the corners bodies mounted: firewine drunks and hatha eaters and beggar children, mummified and wet lipped. The air moved sluggishly. Dust in the shafts of light. *Curse this city in her burning. Her body and her soul are silver mirrors, heated with solipsistic lust. Like a dog she pants and scratches, the sweat of her lovers coalescing on her azure tiles. In her dust is her voice harsh as trumpets. Her dust chokes me as it fondles my mouth. Hot dry air of the furnace, drawing out all of my waters, salt fingers sucking me dry. In her desiccation her stones drip perfume. In her desiccation I am entombed in ecstasies of rain. Her rough stones enfold me, the arid depths of her passion, her kisses an abrasion dry as desert sand. Oh city of shit and sunlight! Oh city of dawn and the setting sun! In your embrace I dream of water. In your embrace I am withered to broken straw. Curse you, and yet I will lie forever in your burning, my body wracked with the heat of your love.*

Serenet Vikale, *The Book of Sand*. New and popular, much quoted, certainly caught the sensation of the current heat. But, if one were feeling uncharitable, one might be inclined to ask questions about the state of the man's private life.

Anyway. A wedding party in Sorlost. The meeting of two great families, a symbol of peace and stability in an uncertain time. That the two great families concerned were the cause of that instability is to be ignored. Get some money moving around the city, largesse distributed, gifts and jewels and silks bought. Demonstrate to the masses that all is secure and perfect. There is no reason to be concerned. Why should anyone in Sorlost be concerned?

Whisper it: there is discord in the Sekemleth Empire of the Asekemlene Emperor of the Eternal Golden City of Sorlost. Two high lords, Orhan Emmereth and Darath Vorley, conspired against their Emperor, hired assassins to kill him and all his court. The Emperor survived their manoeuvrings. The assassins all died in the attempt. But Orhan is now Nithque to the Emperor. The Emperor's hands and eyes and mouth. He has the power to rebuild the Empire's armies, restore its glory, rehouse its starving poor. Inevitably, such power has brought opposition. Enemies. For a brief few days, there was fighting in the city streets. The price of Orhan's power is the sacrifice of Darath's brother Elis to a rival nobleman, March Verneth. The weapon of choice is March's daughter Leada's wedding veil.

Thus, a wedding party in Sorlost.

Elis Vorley wore an ivory silk shirt fastened with diamond buttons, a long cloak trimmed with seed pearls, an arm-ring of wrought gold. Sweat trickled down his forehead, matting his hair beneath a garland of hyacinths and copperstem leaves. Darath and Orhan, similarly garlanded, stood and watched while a body servant made the last careful adjustments to the groom's clothes.

'Are you finally ready?' asked Darath.

Elis gestured hopelessly at the body servant. 'Ask him.'

'He's fine,' Darath told the body servant. 'He'll do. We need to leave.'

Another delicate sweep of the man's hands over folds of red and gold silk fine as breathing, an iridescent sheen on it like wet stone. 'He is ready, My Lord.'

'Good. The bride will have run off with one of the flute players before we get there at this rate.'

Elis started to speak. Darath held up his hand. 'Don't say it, dear brother. Peace and concord and all that, remember? We all make sacrifices. I have a scar on my stomach the length of my hand; Orhan has the job of Nithque. You just need to poke a not unattractive young woman a couple of times.'

Another servant brought forward a dish of salt and honey. All three ate a mouthful. Salt and sweet: the grief and pleasure of this brief, pitiful life. Before battle. Before marriage. Before death. Before birth. The Emperor ate of it every morning and evening, to remind him that immortal as he was he was but a man. Outside the door a new litter waited, built of whale bone and silver lace. All things done as they ought.

'Come on then.' They climbed into the litter. A procession formed up around them, guardsmen and servants and hired celebrants crowned in copperstem, shaking rattles made of walnut shells. At the front of the procession a man danced in gold ribbons, life and light and the joy of the rising sun. Crowds had gathered to watch, shouted out luck songs to the groom. So hot, sweat seemed to rise from the flagstones. Everything shimmered in the heat, luminously unreal as the sheen on Elis' cloak. A flute piped tunelessly. A street woman swayed on bound ankles in a tinkle of tiny bells.

Orhan thought of his own wedding procession, the bitter irony of the singing, the cold, sad sorrow in Darath's eyes. The two of them in the litter, hands clutching, knowing it would all be different, saying it didn't matter but it did matter, trying to see how beautiful

101

each looked in his wreath of flowers, fiddling with the clasps and folds of their cloaks. It had been hot that day too.

The curtains of the litter were open to display the groom but there was still no air. Under incense and perfume bodies were already rank with sweat. Orhan wiped his forehead, damp and clammy, a smear of pollen coming away on his hand. Some petty magery kept the flowers from collapsing into mush. Save safe charms: useful for preserving meat and keeping dead things in bloom. The petals had an odd crusted feel to them like they'd been coated in broken glass. Darath smiled at him, deep blue hyacinths and pale pink roses against his gold-black hair and copper-black skin, sweat on his forehead like drops of honey, glints of longing in his silver-black eyes. Remembering the same thing.

'Nice comfy litter,' said Darath. 'But whale bone? Somewhat eccentric for you, I'd have thought?'

Elis groaned. 'Eloise insisted on it. Said it had more cachet. Certain people's sisters have set the stakes in litter fashions remarkably high. I keep thinking I can smell bloody fish when I look at it. And as for the cost . . . do you have any idea how much people charge to carry a dead whale for a month through high desert? But Eloise went on and on. I have no particular objection to marrying Leada. It's the fact I seem to be marrying her grandmother as well that's going to cripple me.'

'You should be filled with gratitude Eloise judges her granddaughter such a jewel. You wouldn't want a wife whose own family thought her only worth a cheap knock-off job.' Darath said, 'You've got something on your face, Orhan. Come here. No, stay still . . . Pollen. Stop poking at your garland or you'll be yellow by the time we get there.'

'It itches.' A stem of something, rubbing arhythmically against his left temple. Sure to be there nagging at him all day.

They reached the gates of the House of Silver. More crowds, gathered to peer at the brilliance of the spectacle. Also March had probably paid them. Shouts of 'hurrah' as the litter swept past.

'Here we are then,' said Darath with an encouraging smile at Elis. 'Marital bliss.'

'Taking one for the team,' Elis muttered. 'I expect some very good New Year gifts from you two.'

'Oh come on. She was meant for you. If she takes after her father, there can't be two people in the city better matched. Stupid, venal, fat arsed, terrible taste in clothing . . . Who else were you planning to marry, anyway? That bath girl you like with the wonky nose?'

Litter servants came to hand them down carefully, stepping them onto a man's broad thick back. Another final rearrangement of clothing; Orhan pushed at the garland in the hope it would stop digging into his head. Then looking up at the House of Silver that glittered before them, its doorways crowned with orange blossom, walls suppurating in the heat.

So here is the man who wants to kill me, Orhan thought. The last time he'd been here . . . the last time he'd been here had been the night of Eloise Verneth's party, when Tam Rhyl had mocked him and Darath had begged to be involved in the conspiracy to kill the Emperor. Such complex patternings. Orhan thought: I think maybe I sealed your death that night, March.

Inside the first atrium the air was thick with perfume. Rose. Jasmine. Cinnamon. Mint. Paper blossoms floated in silver bowls. Outside in the courtyard shouts and the jangle of rattles. A murmur of voices from the room beyond. Elis tossed his head. Darath and Orhan led him through into the wedding chamber, where all the great families of the Sekemleth Empire were gathered. Hot, sweaty stink beneath their oils, reeking of life and the glories of human flesh. A mass of light and colour. Shifted as the guests turned. Fluttering of silk sleeves, jewelled feathers nodding, painted faces opening in panting smiles.

Leada Verneth was sitting on a high golden chair at the very end of the room, swathed in a silver bridal veil. Black skin and hair showed through vaguely, like a shadow of a woman, very still but if you looked you could see her head moving, her gaze shifting from guest to guest and then to her bridegroom as he walked down towards her. She stood awkwardly; Elis lifted her veil and folded it back. Not an unattractive young woman, indeed, and could carry her wedding splendour, swirls of gold paint over her cheek bones, diamonds on her forehead, pearls the size of pigeon eggs hanging from her ears. She looked at Elis and smiled.

Darath as the groom's kinsman was given a dish of bread and oil, came up to them, broke the loaf in half, dipped each half in the oil, gave a piece to each. Bride and groom solemnly ate a small mouthful, put the rest back on the dish. March as bride's kin repeated the same with a sweet cake dipped in wine. The couple sat on their matched chairs and the women of the house sprinkled them with water. Sighs. Muttered cheers. They stood and clasped hands and walked together back down to the perfumed atrium, out and into the lace and bone litter with its dancers and flurries of noise.

The sacrifice is made. Married.

Orhan travelled back to the House of Flowers with Bil in their own litter. Rather have gone with Darath, but . . . He felt himself more accommodating towards Bil. Less pitiful in her pride, perhaps, now he and she, Lord and Lady Emmereth, the Nithque and the Nithque's wife, were the centre of the Sekemleth Empire, the most powerful of all the inhabitants of Sorlost. Ten guardsmen with drawn knives marched around them. It had been a horrible scrum of bodies as the cream of high society scrambled for their litters. Jamming the streets as they processed to the groom's house for the bridal feast. The litter kept having to stop: Orhan shuddered each time, feeling Bil on edge too beside him. Vulnerable, prostrate within their silk curtains. Not that long at all since a mage had brought down fire in an attempt to destroy Orhan. Killed several of his guards. The litter curtains would go up in streams of white silent burning. Knives and swords and magery tearing around Orhan and Bil as they sat . . .

'March didn't want to kill you, Orhan,' Darath had reassured him. 'He only wanted to humiliate you.'

'I'll tell that to the bereaved families.'

'He'll hardly likely try anything on his own daughter's wedding day, will he?'

'No,' Orhan had agreed. Of course not. Carried entombed in silk through slow crowded streets, Bil's swollen body beside him, he thought: of course not, of course not.

Darath had excelled himself arranging the wedding banquet, decking the walls with silk ribbons, finding some wonderworker to make the ceilings swirl with coloured lights. A soft murmuring sound like the fluttering of wing beats or the drumming of heavy rain.

'Not . . . not . . .?'

'No, of course it's not the same mage, Orhan! March sacked him and drummed him out of Sorlost.'

Low couches spread with green brocade clothes were arranged in intimate groups of four or five diners, each with its own sweet-faced young table servants to attend: they would be dining in the old high style, reclining, titbits eaten with fingers, small shallow bowls for the drink.

Behind the newly-weds, Elis' bridegifts were arranged on a canopied dais. March should be well content there, at least. Stacked up four deep with so much carved gem work they seemed to be giving off sunlight but carefully judged to indicate that the Verneths were the wealthier. Bil flared her nostrils daintily as she looked at them.

'Tasteless.'

'Most of them, yes. It's meant to be something of a joke.'

'How?'

'Because March won't see how tasteless they are.'

They were led to their couches, very close to Elis and Leada, in a group of four with Darath and a friend of Bil's. Orhan squirmed a moment. Waiting for Bil to say something bitter. She frowned then smiled at Darath. The bright carapace she had drawn up around herself, hard and polished and silent, unreadable as glass. Or no, let us be charitable, thought Orhan: a child coming, and such power and status in her hands. It was like this a long time ago, Orhan thought, the three of us, and I hoped it would work then, and perhaps it can work now. Ameretha Ventuel said words praising the beauty of Bil's dress, got on to asking about the preparations for the nursery, had Bil decided on clout cloths yet, who was making the Naming Dress, what about filling for the bedding, lilac petals or rose? Bil smiled more sweetly and relaxed herself, though Orhan could see Darath next to her burning into her and her nerves edgy underneath; but he would not give up sitting next to Darath any more now for her so she would have to manage, the three of them would have to manage, because love and pride and honour and happiness; he would not break his heart again after what he had done and made Darath do.

'They make a charming couple,' said Ameretha, twisting a long white neck towards the bride and groom on their couch. 'Look almost as though they're enjoying themselves.'

'Elis protests too much,' said Darath, 'they'll be fine.'

The sweet faced servants brought them dishes of candied dogs' hearts, green lotus roots stewed in red vinegar, cold boiled doves' eggs three days off hatching, cimma fruit with sandfish cutlets, unborn goats' tongues in jellied hot sauce, iced wine (as the heat mounted Darath had toyed with the idea of scrapping the prepared menu and serving only roast meats and hot punch). March made a long rambling speech about marital harmony, visibly licking his lips at his daughter's new home. Elis toasted his bride and managed to get her name right. The dogs' hearts in particular were superb.

'I want to go home now,' said Bil. She was getting more and more tired in the hot weather, but complained every morning about being unable to sleep. The swell of her body seemed to be sucking at her like a stone drawing up heat.

'If you like.' Darath was drinking too much and rolling his eyes at the speeches, and the wreath was still poking Orhan in the side of the head. A good time being had by most and sundry, so yes, fine, time to go home.

'We've only just finished eating,' said Darath as Orhan got to his feet. 'You can't slip off before the bride and groom.'

'Bil's exhausted.'

'Oh, Bil can leave.' Darath gestured to a server to refill his cup. 'No, go. Virtuous as you are, escorting your wife home. Such a good man, isn't he, Bilale? I'm sure Elis will be the same.' His face changed, the same endless strained weariness Orhan felt. Concern in his eyes. 'Take care, going home.'

The heat dust was almost obscuring the stars, so that for a moment Orhan hoped it had clouded over and might rain. If the heat breaks, he had begun to find himself thinking, things will settle again. It seemed some kind of wager with himself: if I can just get through until this . . . until that . . . Beneath the closed drapes of the litter, with Bil's pregnant body, after several cups of drink, it was stifling. Sweat ran down Bil's forehead, gathered in the hollow between her breasts. In the darkness, her scars were less visible: many men, Orhan supposed, would find the traceries of her body attractive, there in the hot dark. She seemed heavier, graver, like an old statue, her skin so white and her hair so beautifully gloriously red. She blew air onto her face in an attempt to cool it, smiled wanly at him.

'Did you enjoy it, then?'

'I suppose so. As these things go.'

'Darath did well with the food, I thought. I should get the recipe for the goat's tongue.'

'Yes.'

'Retha says rose petals, for the bedding. Better for calm temperament.'

'Oh? Yes, I suppose they would be.'

Bil said, 'Is March really our enemy, Orhan? Was he really conspiring with the Immish against Sorlost?'

'Who told you that?'

'Celyse.'

Naturally. Why even bother to ask? Orhan said, 'Celyse shouldn't be telling anyone.'

'That's not an answer.'

'I don't know,' Orhan said. That's not an answer either, he thought. His head was hurting. He thought: I need another drink.

Such slow going, with the swarm of guards around them with knives out. Bizarre and absurd, that they could possibly need that many. Orhan had a knife, too, tucked quietly beneath the litter cushions, his hand resting on the hilt. Patterned metal slick with sweat. Yet it still felt . . . absurd, to need so many guards. Orhan shoved off the wreath; the flowers were sagging despite the enchantments on them, petals crushed and brown. They felt grainy, like they'd been crystallized and left to go rotten, unpleasant, like rotting ice. A funny smell to them now. It filled the litter. Maybe cover the scents of sweat and wine and two people's bellies overstuffed with food. Bil sighed and stared out through the green curtain, giving up attempting to talk. I wonder if she'll take one of the new guards as a lover? Orhan thought. Or already has? The gates of the House of the East swung open before them, the litter passed through, the gates shutting again noiselessly, sealing themselves. Relative safety, unless an assassin could climb a wall. The litter servants helped them carefully down, guards still flanking them, watching, torches raised to check for shadows that might be men with drawn blades. Elis might be taking Leada up to bed by now, Orhan thought. Darath no doubt cheering as he followed behind. He handed Bil carefully in through the pearl doorway.

'Good night, Bil.'

She frowned. 'You're going back out?'

'I am.'

'Where?'

None of your business. Where do you think? We agreed, once, that we wouldn't ask these things, either of us. She sighed, walked away. She wasn't sleeping with any of the new guards, Orhan thought.

'Be careful, Orhan.'

'I'll go in the litter. With half the guards. Order the rose blossom tomorrow, then, if you like.' His head was aching. The litter was foetid with sweat and flatulence. Candied dogs' hearts gave a man truly terrible wind.

The litter bearers went slowly. Tired out, like everything. The streets still swam with people. In the heat sleep was painful, so they wandered endlessly around the city day and night. At the House of Flowers the wedding feast was ending. Feathers and sequins and gemstones and flakes of paint and flower petals were scattered over marble floors. The detritus of beautiful wealth. Servants smiled in the corners, had probably made bets on whether he'd come back. Darath smiled in his bedroom doorway, held out his arms.

The bride and groom went the next morning to pray and light candles at the Temple; Orhan and Darath and March and Eloise went with them as bride and groom's kin. The mad-eyed child High Priestess knelt ragged before the altar as she did now even on days when there was no sacrifice waiting, chewing on long fingers red ragged bloody at the tips. Glorious omen! But people tried now not to care. Days passed: Darath hung around Orhan's bedroom complaining of the strangeness of having a woman living in his house; Bil slunk in her chambers, brittlely restless, swollen like a bluebottle in the heat. The hot weather continued, the world red and sweat-sticky, dust in heaps on the pavements, trees withering in the heat. Stone walls too hot to put a hand on. Plaster and gilding crumbling into more dust. Orhan stared dully at old ledgers in the palace offices, dictated letters, tried to govern an empire of one decaying city in a desert of yellow sand.

And then ten days after the wedding Darath came to Orhan's study to tell him in triumph that March was dead.

'How did he die?' Orhan asked. He hadn't heard anything. Must have been sudden. Or his spies were even more useless than he'd thought. But it still must have been sudden. Celyse would have been round to tell him otherwise. She'd already passed on the news that Elis had bedded Leada four times so far and the girl had very much enjoyed every moment of it. So that was something else Orhan would now go to his grave unable to forget.

'He technically hasn't. Yet. Soon. Tomorrow, maybe the day after. By Lansday, anyway, or I'll sue the man who sold it me for false trade.'

'That's—' Orhan looked up at Darath's glittering eyes. 'God's knives, Darath, what did you use?'

'I told you I'd take care of it. I have. You really want to know?'

'No! No. Yes.' Dear Lord. Dear Lord. Great Tanis have mercy.

'Deadgold leaves and sysius root and beetle's wings and bear's gall and powdered lead.' It sounded like a lullaby. 'Poured in his wine with his lunch today. He complained of the sour taste but the man who gave it to him told him it was the heat affecting his tongue.'

'I . . .' God's knives, Darath. 'I mean . . .'

'You mean: "thank you, beloved of my heart, for killing the man who tried to kill me so I don't have to do it myself".'

'I . . . Yes . . . But . . . I mean . . .' But, I mean: it's such a horrible, horrible way to die.

'This way everyone will think it's heat flux. You would have done it all nicely with something cool and sleep-inducing and obvious like sana fruit? Would that have made you feel better about it?'

'I . . .' Silence. The ox heavy on Orhan's tongue.

'Your plans, Orhan my love, have led to my brother saddling himself with an unwanted wife. Your plans have led to me being stuck with said wife strolling round my house like she owns the place. Your plans have cost me a great deal of money and almost seen both of us fucking killed. If I want to do something to help you the way I want to, you should thank me.'

And there's nothing to say to that. Orhan looked at Darath and Darath looked at Orhan.

'Thank you.'

'Oh, your gratitude is like music.'

'Thank you.' Orhan took Darath's hand, held it to his cheek.

Hot and angry. His face and Darath's hand. Long drawn silence, where they could hear the click of a house servant somewhere going about the house with a bucket and broom. The drapery at the windows fanned out with a snap. The air changing. A hot wind. In the central gardens the birds in the lilac trees felt it, rose up a moment all together in a puff like a skein of silk unravelling then came back to roost.

'You're welcome.' A grunt. Grudging. Darath sat down again, leaning back in his chair. Orhan sat again also. The wind banged at the windows again, the open shutters creaking, hiss of sand blowing onto the marble floor. *In her desiccation I am entombed in ecstasies of rain.* Doesn't some poet say somewhere that life is like the sand wind, blasting heat teetering on the edge of a storm from which one will never get relief? A house servant came hurrying in to close the shutters, the room dark for a moment before the candles were lit.

'We hired a troop of sellswords to assassinate the Emperor,' said Darath. 'We killed hundreds of people, we killed Tam Rhyl, we almost burned the palace down. We desecrated the Great Temple. We've told so many lies I can barely keep up. We did all that because you told me March Verneth was conspiring with the Immish, that the Immish would invade the city, that the world would be over if we didn't do something. Remember? Remember, Orhan? All those things you told me? *"The city's dying, Darath. The Empire's a joke. The Immish will come with twenty thousand men and a mage, and we'll fall in days." "We're too weak, the way we are, sitting on our piles of gold pretending nothing exists beyond our walls. We need to be ready. And yes, that does mean blood."* Remember?' Pause. Cold eyes. 'And now you're getting squeamish about March dying?' Slammed his fist down, hard, on the arm of his chair. 'I could have died that night, Orhan. Stop claiming morality at me.'

God's knives, thought Orhan, God's knives, Darath, what have I done to you?

'I—'

Darath shouted, 'Stop bleating "I" like a bloody goat.'

They sat and looked at each other. The wind smashing on the shutters. Flickering candlelight.

A tap on the door, an anxious-faced door keep. Orhan snapped at him, 'What?'

Poor wretch. Hardly his fault, he'd had to come up this moment, hear this. Terrified fear in the man he'd be punished. Dismissed. 'Excuse me, My Lord. My Lords. Lady Amdelle is waiting downstairs.'

Celyse. Dear sister. Thank her and curse her for turning up now. Orhan rubbed at his eyes, wiping away tears. Celyse came in in a sweep of satin, rearranging dusty hair.

'Lord of Living and Dying, it's horrible out there. My bearers were being blown around like flagpoles and the curtains were almost ripped off. I should have gone back home, sent a note.' She stopped when she saw Darath and Orhan's faces. 'Shall I leave again?'

Darath got up with a crisp, angry smile. 'No need. I was just leaving myself anyway.'

Her face changed. Recognized Orhan so very much wanted Darath to stay, perhaps. A clever woman, his sister. Even sometimes a kind one. 'You'll want to hear this too, Darath. March is sick. Took to his bed this hour past with a fever. Very sudden, it came on.'

Darath said, 'Do they know what it is?'

'The rumour among the servants is heat flux.' Celyse said after a moment, 'But you two know exactly what it is and so I've come to ask you.'

And there's nothing to say to that. Orhan looked at Darath and Darath looked at Orhan.

They sat and looked at each other. Wind smashing on the shutters. Flickering candlelight.

'You really think people aren't going to guess?'

'It's heat flux,' said Darath.

'You could at least act like you're surprised.'

'There's nothing particularly surprising about a man getting heat flux in this heat.'

'Does it matter what people think?' said Orhan. 'Nothing can be proved.' Darath shot him a look that was part confusion, part sneer. Why are you pretending you did it, Orhan my love? his face said. Just to be even more superior and make me feel even more ashamed? Orhan made a movement with his lips, turned his head away. Why am I pretending I did it? But in the end which is more shameful: killing someone, or asking my lover to kill someone for me because I'm a better person than him and too good to do it myself?

I'm the thing at the centre of this, he thought. The knife. But I'm only trying to build a better world. Make things safe. Make us good again.

And so does Marian Gyste compare love to the storm that is the soul of those few who suffer damnation. Raging heat and noise and madness, not for them the cool eternity of death. Not for me. God lives in His house of waters; Tam and March are dead and gone and damp rot. We who live: we're the ones who'll burn.

'He got to see one of his daughters married,' said Darath. 'It would have been very sad if he'd sickened before that.'

'Is that supposed to be a consolation?'

'Oh come on, Celyse. You know how this works. Such things were done once without anyone raising an eyebrow. Them or us. You know that.'

'Them or us because my brother was stupid enough to start this.'

Orhan said, 'Them or us because things would have gone to pieces in fire if I hadn't. Them or us to save Sorlost.'

Celyse opened her mouth, closed it again. Wind smashing against the shutters. Hot dry storm without rain or relief. The sky outside would be so dark now like the death of the sun. Sand clouds black-golden like Darath's hair.

Celyse laughed. 'My dear fastidious brother. Even you can't keep your hands clean any longer. You killed people so you could get power. That's all you did. Kill people. For power.'

Darath laughed.

A tap on the door and Bil came in, heavy and tired and her scars standing out on her face. The heat still sickened her, she spent long hours floating in the cool bathing chamber where her body blurred into the oily water. The skin on her hands was wrinkled, odd white.

'News,' she said. 'March Verneth is sick. Heat flux, they say, or that Lord Emmereth poisoned him at Leada's wedding feast.'

Celyse clapped her hands to her mouth.

Chapter Sixteen

When they had all left, Orhan went to his books, tried to work.
The ancient tomes of the Imperial ledgers. Give himself something
else to worry about.

Any fool could assassinate someone, if they really put their mind
to it, as the history of Irlast so often proved. Making things better.
That took effort. That was the work. March Verneth is dying. So
what? The weary business of remaking the world, that must still
go on. This city is dying, the richest empire the world has ever
known, her beggars wear silk and satin, eat rotting scraps off plates
of gold. Immish and Chathe and the other great powers laugh at
us and do not bother to cover their mouths. Sorlost is a dead man's
dreaming. A useless heap of crumbled rock. Weak and defenceless
and worn down. But I, Orhan lied to himself every night in the
dark, I am a capable man, a learned man, I can change that.

Several streets had been destroyed in the rioting that had followed
the attack on the palace. Fine, lofty shops and town houses, and,
behind them, tenement buildings with broken-down walls and
ceilings, floors running with human sewage, whole families
crammed into single windowless rooms. 'Tear them all down,'
Orhan had ordered, 'rebuild them, clean them up.'

'And the cost, My Lord Nithque?' Secretary Gallus had asked
him.

'Levy a tax on something. Appeal to the goodwill of the high families. Borrow it.'

'And the cost of expanding the Imperial army, My Lord Nithque?'

'Levy a tax on something. Appeal to the goodwill of the high families. Borrow it.'

'We do not need an expanded army. We do not need to rebuild a few ruined houses. This is Sorlost!' the Emperor and the Emperor's High Lords told him curtly, when he suggested any of these things.

The outbreak of deeping fever in Chathe had flared up again. Worse than before. The gates must be closed again to Chathean travellers, trade would suffer, everyone from the hatha addicts in the gutters to the High Lords who refused to fund his army would complain.

The Immish were outraged by the accusations made against them concerning the attack on the Emperor, demanded compensation for their people's losses in the riots, had expelled several hundred Sorlostian merchants from Alborn as tit-for-tat. Some of them spoke little if any Literan. Most of them were now destitute. All of them blamed the Emperor and the Emperor's Nithque for their plight.

The rains had failed in Mar and the grain harvest this year would be poor, raising prices. Even if one ignored the fact that Chathe acted as the middle man for the Empire's grain trade with Mar. Those who didn't riot for lack of hatha might well riot for lack of cake.

The guard house at the Maskers' Gate to the east of the city had finally fallen down. A family of exiles from Alborn had been killed when it collapsed. The merchants had gnashed their teeth at the tax levied to pay for repairs. Nobody now knew where the tax levied to pay for repairs had been spent.

Futile. Great Tanis: Lord Emmereth and Lord Rhyl and Lord Verneth had locked themselves in the death struggle, for this?

Charge your guards' upkeep to the palace and award yourself a new stipend or two, Orhan. You can do that.

Gold ink and old leather, all the words blurred. Here, look, on the cover of one ledger: a smear of honey, where Darath had sat reading it and stuffing himself with candied apricots. Would it be too symbolic, Orhan thought, to note the dirt now stuck to the honey, on the leather that was said to be human skin? But 'stipend' reminded him: Orhan turned the pages, found the list of March Verneth's Imperial stipends. 'First Lord and Viceroy of Riva'. 'Protector of Maun'. Comic, absurd, empty lies. Orhan crossed them savagely out. A whole six talents saved with one pen stroke!

At the bottom of the page a human hair was stuck to a smear of honey. Bile rose in Orhan's throat.

He threw up his hands. Slammed the book shut.

Watched the dusk come. The bell rang for the twilight. *Seserenthelae aus perhalish*. Night comes. We survive. The little girl in the Temple, killing. Bringing death for those who are dying, life for those waiting to be born. From Bil's rooms came the sound of a boy singing, Bil listening to songs and music to nourish the child in her womb.

I'll go out, Orhan thought. Go for a walk. Get out of this house.

Foolish, he thought, to go out alone. March and Eloise will be wanting vengeance.

I don't care, he thought. If it's dangerous. He dressed simply; simple to disappear by removing a few gems, donning a cheaper cut of coat. An anonymous man walking the streets.

The wind had dropped, leaving sand piled everywhere, the leaves of trees and bushes ripped to shreds. The city was slowly working to right itself, sweeping off the dust, setting awnings and scaffolds back where they had fallen, clearing up broken glass and damaged stone. Still very hot, but the air felt cleaner, after the wind.

He walked towards the palace. Habit, the path he so often now walked. At the gates to the palace Orhan stopped and looked at it. The golden dome haunting in the moonlight. The silver towers. The white porcelain walls. But the palace windows were dead and empty. No longer glowed with mage glass. There were dark streaks on the white and the gold and the silver, where no man could reach to scrub it clean. I did that, Orhan thought. My shame. My guilt. Incomparable, irreplaceable, the mage glass windows of the Imperial Palace of the Asekemlene Emperor: by which, of course, he meant that there was no money to spend on getting them replaced.

He went back away from the palace, into the Street of Closed Eyes where people were moving, sliding through the shadows, shimmering in flickers of torchlight. Flash of jewels, the rustle of silk, the chime of women's bells. Onwards into the Court of the Fountain, where the knife-fighters circled. One had been fighting, lay dying with his hand still closed on the hilt of his knife, bleeding wounds turning the dust of the flagstones to mud. Orhan flicked a silver dhol onto his chest. Burial fees. The dying man blinked back weakly, moved his lips. I could, I suppose, kill him, Orhan thought. End his suffering. But I won't. We don't. Not even a drink of water from the fountain he's dying beside.

He stopped his walking at a street corner off the Street of Yellow Roses. The noise of a wine shop caught him, a man's voice singing, the music of a flute. Stood and watched the light moving through the thin curtain covering the door. The poet sang of the desert hills of the east where the sun rose over golden sand, ending in a long wordless ululation of sorrow in imitation of a bird. His audience applauded; the flute picked up again, calm and soft. Good taste, these musicians. The listeners too. Orhan pushed the door curtain aside, went in. A small, crowded place, clean and well kept, mostly old men sitting over tiny cups of spirits, lined faces nodding to each other silently, listening to the song. In the corner a man and a woman played yenthes, clattering ivory tiles. A few of the others watched them, murmuring quietly as the game flowed. A faint smell of keleth seeds.

People turned to look at him, saw nothing of especial interest, turned back away. A woman looked him over with greater interest. She was not attractive and was aging, her hair streaked with silver, her body sagging to parched fat, but she moved elegantly, a calm soft tone to her like the flute. Orhan shook his head at her. He bought wine and a plate of cinnamon sweets, sat down to listen to the flute then found his attention drawn to the yenthes game. The tiles rattled past. Chance, as much as skill. A game of luck. Not something Orhan really had much interest in playing, but he liked the sound the tiles made. The woman drew green, spread green and blue tiles in a spiral on the table top. The man sucked his teeth. The man drew blue, set out a square of blue over the woman's spiral. Their audience nodded approvingly.

The game went on for a while, patterns moving across the table, the clatter of tiles, the quiet of the old men content to sit, the music of the flute. Then the poet rose to his feet again to sing. Older than his voice sounded, his black skin had an ashy grey tint, his hair was white. Wearing a woman's coat of pink and silver peonies, threadbare. Oh, but his voice was beautiful. He sang unaccompanied this time, a slight waver at the end of each line, deep and clear like a bronze bowl.

> 'Oh golden Sorlost, from whose embrace I
>   am exiled,
> The beautiful, the ever shining,
> The bride of all the cities of the earth.
> Her high towers of cedar wood, her high
>   turrets,
> Her bronze walls strong as lovers,
> Her gardens where the penthe birds fly.
> Sweet evenings of grief and love and music,
> Long afternoons beneath the lilac branches,
> The wet scent of her streets in the morning
>   warmth.
> How can one live, away from her?
> I am like a wife forsaken,
> A child motherless, a house empty and
>   closed.
> I am like a man thirsting, forsworn in the
>   desert,

119

Lips dry with dust.
Oh Sorlost, most perfect, most beautiful.
My words are as ashes, my heart as grave-
*   soil.*
Oh city of gold and sorrow—
Better to die,
Than to think of you standing
Without my feet on your stones.'

The last tremor of the voice died away. Orhan shivered. A few of the men wiped tears from their eyes. The lament for the city. The secret fear of all who lived in Sorlost, that they would waken from their shared illusion and never see her again. The bronze walls, the golden light, the corridors of the Great Temple: the perfection of this place in which we live that is a memory of a memory of a dream. To live in the sublimity of ruins, the eternity of never quite dying, dust and dust and dust gilding the beat of our hearts. Thus how can any other place in all the world compare?

Really, of course, the grief of exile is only a metaphor for the inevitability of death. Why we sing these songs. Mourn the city we will never leave. A reminder that all is futility, and yet we go on.

Tam Rhyl's family were exiled somewhere. In Immish, living hand to mouth. Abandoned and alone there.

A desperate desire in Orhan to speak to someone about something normal. Outside himself. He turned to the person nearest him: 'He's very good, the singer.'

The woman who had been playing yenthes. She was chewing keleth seeds, her breath smelled milky sweet. Flakes of dead skin clung in her hair.

'Would he be insulted if I offered him silver?'

The woman laughed. 'No. But he'd be best off without.'

The poet had returned to his corner, drinking from a cup from which tendrils of smoke seemed to rise. A firewine drinker. Older than most survived to be. Orhan could see, now he knew, the tremor in the man's hands, like the tremor in his voice. The same note of slow poignant decay.

'He sang for the Emperor once, in his youth,' the woman said. 'The Emperor gave him an arm-ring of pearls. "The Pearl Singer", he was called, after that.'

'The Pearl Singer? But I have a book of his poems! That's him?' He it had been who compared life to the sand wind, teetering on the edge of never achieved relief. God's knives, Orhan thought, he must be ancient. Not this lifetime of the Emperor, or even the one before.

'That's him.'

Orhan gave the woman a handful of silver dhol. 'Would you give these to him slowly? Or, no, see that the owner gets them, gives him food?' She took the coins with a smile. She might, of course, keep them. Spend them herself on keleth seed.

'I'll see to it.'

'Thank you.'

The poet sang again a little later, another song of exile. His voice was more tremulous, slurring, losing the note; several times he forgot his words. Orhan left when the song was over, began walking home in the thick hot night. The wind rose again, scattering dust, banging shutters, showering Orhan with dead leaves. His skin prickled in case a knifeman or a blast of mage fire was waiting for him. It had been very foolish to go out alone. For a moment, passing the Street of All Sorrows, he thought of turning up at Darath's, throwing himself at Darath's feet. Or perhaps he should go to the House of Silver and throw himself at March's feet. Forgive. Forgive. Forgive.

The streets still ran with people, whores wrapped in bells creeping across the marble, street sellers offering cool drinks rank with dust, a knife-fighter in white with the hatha scars was circling, looking for someone to kill him and let him feel again for a moment a man. From a dark alleyway a child's voice called. One of the women stopped staring down into the dark. Things moving. She took a few steps, cried out something, fled away into the lights of a square where a conjurer made coloured birds race on the wind. The voice turned to laughter. Something there best left unknown.

I should go to the Temple, Orhan thought. Pray. Remind myself of the mercy of the God.

I should go home, he thought. So March is dying. What of it? I knew from the beginning that he would end up dead. Him or me. I should have told Darath I was grateful. I should have told him about the child. I'm a fool. It's late. Go home.

Instead, he stopped again to watch the conjurer. Afraid of returning to his house and his life: if I stay walking forever none of this will come to be real. An eternal dream. The man wasn't a bad performer; a small crowd clapped in applause. The woman was watching. Beside her, a young man, turning to look at Orhan, feeling him see him back. Orhan caught his breath.

A young man in the flower of his manhood. Glossy deep black skin, long black silky curls. Lips as red as the juice of pomegranates. Eyes as big as the night sky. A narrow waist, fine smooth muscled arms and legs. Like an antique statue. Like a painting on ivory. Too beautiful to be real. Men did not look like this in the living world.

The young man's mouth opened, smiling. Orhan shuddered. Smiled back. Go home. Go to the Temple. Go home. Go home. The young man moved over towards him, graceful, lilting like the music had been. The same fine slurred tremor in his movements as in the poet's voice. The same cause. Rotten teeth in the perfect mouth, stained with firewine, fragments of keleth seeds on his lips. Sweet drugged desperate breath. His fingers drummed on the cloth of Orhan's sleeve. 'Five dhol.' Go home. Go home. As beautiful a waste as the poet. Too beautiful for this. 'Five dhol. Or for you, amber eyes, four dhol.' Go home. Go home. 'Who sent you?' Orhan almost asked, 'just kill me, please don't do this. Not this first.' 'Four dhol.' Orhan's hand went to his purse. 'Four dhol.'

It was dawn when Orhan returned home. The house was silent. A few early house servants scurrying across the hallways with cloths bound to their feet to damp any noise. Birds were singing in the gardens. He had had to knock, of course, to rouse the door keep; the door keep stared yawning, looked mortified that he had been asleep. Orhan went down to the cold bathing rooms and scrubbed at himself. Dirty. Cheap heavy perfume was smeared on his skin and clothes. Sweet and sensual and rancid, like the smell between a man's legs. He rubbed himself with salt and oil to try to cover it. Abrade it away. A bathgirl, woken in a panic by the door keep, came in to take over; there were distant footsteps as others ran to stoke the fires, get the water hot. Orhan sent the girl to bring him tea.

His eyes were gritty with tiredness, his head aching. Do I feel guilt? he thought. Do I? I should. Did I enjoy it? he thought then slowly. I don't know.

The cold water was beginning to wash some sense into him. By the time the girl came back with the tea jug he was shaking. After his bath he sat in his bedroom and stared at his hands.

God's knives, he thought. God's knives. Why?

Bil came in without knocking, dressed in a night robe. Showed her breasts very white. The huge curve of her belly. She'd agreed never to come into his bedroom. She sat down on a couch and stared at him.

'Orhan . . . Are you all right?'

'I'm fine.'

'You don't look fine.'

'I'm fine.'

'Do you want me to send a messenger for Darath?'

'No!' Far louder than he meant. Bil flinched. 'No. Just leave me alone.'

'One of the bathgirls woke Nilesh. She woke me. They were frightened for you.'

'Just go away. Tell Nilesh and the bathgirls to mind their own business.' I will not, Orhan thought wretchedly, be an object of pity in my own home.

'It's not Darath, is it?' Her scars coloured, real fear in her face. 'Lord of Living and Dying! Nothing's happened to him?'

'No! It's nothing! Just go away. Leave me alone.'

'I'm your wife, Orhan. I do care about what happens to you.' Bil got to her feet with a sigh. 'I'll go, then.'

As she moved towards the door Orhan almost cried out to her to stay. To tell her. Ask her what to do. She stopped in the doorway, like she was waiting for him to speak. A pause held between them. Both waiting for the other to speak. But he didn't speak.

Chapter Seventeen

Couldn't sleep either. Kept thinking about March and Darath. The young man in his squalid room opening onto an alley soaked with piss. Hands on his hands, a mouth on his mouth, fucking and gasping and collapsing with a cry of triumph on top of the perfect rotten body, oozing firewine sweat from its luscious luminous radiant skin. Sharp, bitter desire. Different from anything he'd felt for Darath or anyone else. I think I did enjoy it, then, he thought. And still he did not feel guilty. Perhaps it was just too unreal. Couldn't have happened. He'd been at home asleep all night, dreaming. The man was a memory of a dream.

He lay with his eyes closed seeing black hair and black skin and March thrashing in fever until March sweating and rolling in pain was all muddled and merged with the young man twisting and sweating in fake ecstasy under Orhan's weight. He felt sick with fever himself. Sleep starved. As sleep wasn't going to come he got up and dressed.

Bil was awake, sitting in the garden listening to the girl Nilesh read. A stab of guilt towards her, seeing her, her belly, her child there. She ignored him. She knew he had done something terrible. He stood in the hall of his own house, lost.

He should go to the palace. Do something, while he waited for Darath to find out what he'd done and come looking for him.

Please come looking, a part of him whispered. He had a sudden, chilling horror that Darath would ignore him. Wouldn't come. Wouldn't care. Would fuck the man himself, longer and harder and better, and pay him more.

Would tell everyone and anyone the truth about that night and his plans and March and Tam . . . Well done, Orhan! You just did the one thing you're classically never supposed to do when intriguing for power. But maybe he'll forgive you, you just need to tell him he's still the better lover, yes?

Bil came into the hall. She looked very tired, shadows under her eyes. She smoothed her hands over her belly.

'We should get a food taster,' Bil said.

'A food taster? What? Where in the God's name are we supposed to get a food taster from?'

Bil gestured towards the doorway. 'There are enough hungry people in Sorlost.'

'That's vile!'

She flushed scarlet. 'But do you want to die?'

We should get a food taster, he thought. March is probably regretting that too.

Go back to the palace. Pretend everything was normal. Bury himself in work. Serious, dull, calm things. So very effective that had been, after all, yesterday. He took the full complement of guards with him, leaving only the four for the house and two to watch. They trooped through the streets he'd walked last night. People drew back out of the way as they passed. Still, occasionally, looks of respect and admiration, Lord Emmereth who had saved the city from despair. But mostly now whispers and fearful glances. Lord Verneth's murderer. A gang of men with swords.

'He's dying of heat flux!' Orhan wanted to shout to the crowds. 'Heat flux!' If he said it enough times it might somehow come true.

When he got to his rooms in the palace, Secretary Gallus was arranging letters on the desk. Looked at Orhan a moment with the same nervousness as the people in the street. Perhaps I should throw a huge party, Orhan thought. Watch them all finding reasons not to eat or drink. We should have done it before the wedding, Darath could have saved a fortune in catering costs.

He said, 'Good morning, Gallus.' Heard his voice weak at the edges. A new, harsh, grating tone to it.

Gallus said formally, 'Good morning, My Lord Nithque.'

Orhan looked wearily at the pile of papers. 'Anything of any interest?'

Pause. 'Another letter from the Immish Great Council, demanding recompense for the Immish merchants attacked during the . . . the Immish invasion. Another petition from the money lenders, demanding reparations for the destruction of their property during the, uh, the same.'

Pause. 'Court gossip from Chathe: Prince Heldan seems sensibly reluctant to consider an Ithish wife. Court gossip from Allene: Queen Amnaia is pregnant again, father unknown. Her older children are piqued at it. As one might expect.'

Pause. 'And this.'

He handed Orhan a piece of parchment.

Court gossip, this time from Malth Tyrenae, the Ithish court. The Ithish equally reluctant to consider Prince Heldan as an Ithish princess's husband, and thus putting the Chathean delegation's disdainfully wrinkled noses very much out of joint. *They are leaving in a hurry, threatening dire things for the insult to their prince. Yes. But all this has been of little notice, for the king and all the court are very preoccupied with the news from the White Isles, indeed talk of little else. There has been great disorder there, the old king is reported dead. Both of his sons are claiming the throne in his place. There is likely to be war between them, all think. This despite the fact, as I told you before, that it was said openly only a few months ago that the elder boy, the Princess Marissa's child, was dead.* Orhan stared at it in astonishment. 'Civil war. Great Tanis. The stupidity of these people. But it might tie up the Ithish, I suppose. Even Immish, it might distract them. Two boys.

The Immish might feel duty bound to back the younger against Ith. Or . . .' But I can't see why you're so nervous, he thought, looking at Gallus's face. You're afraid, Gallus. Why in Great Tanis's name should you be afraid of this?

'No, My Lord Nithque.' Gallus pointed to a passage halfway down the page. 'I . . . Read from . . . this part here. "The elder prince, Marith, the Princess Marissa's child, has a woman with him . . . "'

The elder prince, Marith, the Princess Marissa's child, has a woman with him, and concerning this woman some very strange tales are told. She is claimed to be the High Priestess of Great Tanis the Lord of Living and Dying, He Who Rules All Things, the One God of your Empire of Sorlost. It is said that the prince himself has been heard to boast of this. You will know, of course, that he does indeed claim to have been in Sorlost, and even to have led an attack on the Imperial Palace. Of this also some very strange tales are told, but I myself do not now believe them. For I had gathered from you yourself that the Immish attacked the palace. Though the Immish deny it. But they would. But to return to my story: the woman is said to be young, barely out of her girlhood, and very beautiful, with dark skin and black hair, and her eyes are blue. The High Priestess, I believe, is described as such? All here are uncertain regarding this, for another story is circulating that both the High Priestess of Sorlost and the Emperor himself are dead. Of this, too, there is much uncertainty; that the Emperor is dead I know for a lie, as you yourself told me. However, whoever she is, the prince is said to be besotted with her and has ordered her to be called 'Queen' and plans to marry her — although you will remember that last year he was said to be equally besotted with a young nobleman, who is now certainly dead—

Dead.

Dead.

Gallus said, 'You see, My Lord?

Orhan put the paper down. His hands trembling. The sudden

choking stink of burned flesh and spreading blood. I'm going to be sick, he thought. The world was spinning, the ground lurched away into unsteady shifting dark. It's not true. It's stories. Delusions. Dreams. Lies. A great terrible weight clung on his shoulders, he felt a thousand years old, sick from his bowels to his head. I'm going to be sick, he thought. I'm going to be sick.

'My Lord?' Gallus was looking at him. Terrified.

'Who . . . who else knows about this? Has seen this?'

Gallus said, 'No one but you and myself, My Lord Nithque.'

Gallus said, 'As yet.'

The stories started in the wine shops the same day. A friend of a friend had met a merchant who traded with a man from Reneneth or Skerneheh who traded with a man from Ith or Illyr who'd met a man from the White Isles who'd had a strange tale to tell. The Altrersyr were stirring, fighting among themselves, planning war. A new king had been proclaimed there who was Amrath come again. He was as tall as a mountain, as beautiful as the sunrise, his sword dripped fire, his watch words were ruin and death and pain. At his side was a witch woman sworn to Great Tanis the Lord of Living and Dying, who had abandoned her god for his love. For her sake, he had burned the Great Temple, razed the Summer Palace, battled dragons, killed the Emperor's own guard. He was King of the White Isles and every man on the White Isles loved him. He was King of the White Isles and any man who did not fall down and worship him, he killed. His face shone with light. His eyes were too terrible to look at. His lady was the most beautiful woman in the history of the world.

'Lies.' 'Absurdities.' 'Blasphemy.' 'The High Priestess Thalia is dead.' 'The heir to the White Isles is dead.' 'The heir to the White Isles was a notorious hatha addict and a drunk.' 'The heir to the White Isles was insane.' 'The High Priestess Thalia is dead.'

Thus the first day of the rumours. The friend of the friend

had met a merchant who'd met a man who was himself drunk or hatha-addled or mad. If one person could at least name their informant, give some proof. There was that incident ten years ago, the siege of Telea, when the Immish had dressed up that poor young girl, claimed she was the ringleader's daughter, killed her. The last King of Tarboran died two hundred years ago, and still people appeared claiming to be his heir. These strange bizarre things. Impossible to conceive of, isn't it, that a beautiful young girl of twenty who has lived her whole life in the confines of one building should run off with a glamorous young foreign king?

The second day of the rumours, the Emperor and the High Lords his advisers met in council. *The Emperor comes! The Emperor comes! Kneel for the Emperor, the Eternal Ruler of the Golden City of Sorlost!* The crash of bronze doors opening and closing. The hard tread of guards' feet.

Orhan sat at the opposite end of the table to the Emperor.

Hostile faces looking at him.

'You told us she was dead,' said Cammor Tardein, the Lord of the Dry Sea, Dweller in the House of Breaking Waves.

'You showed us her body, made a speech over it,' said Aris Ventuel, the Lord of Empty Mirrors, Dweller in the House of Glass. 'That we must ensure her death was not in vain.'

'You told us the invaders were from Immish,' said Samneon Magreth, the Lord of the Southern Sky, Dweller in the House of Mists. 'And that they were all dead.'

Dead. Everyone, everyone looked at the empty chairs where March Verneth and Tam Rhyl should be sitting. Darath and Elis, sitting beside each other, away from Orhan, Elis sitting next to the chair in which his goodfather should be sat.

Dead. All dead.

Orhan opened his mouth to speak. Memories. Eyes staring at him. Eyes like knife blades. A voice shouting. A boy, soaked in blood to his eyeballs, blazing like a star.

Dead.

'Dead.' His voice was coming through thick dry dust. His mouth tasted of blood. 'The invaders are all dead.'

'Lord Emmereth?' Cammor Tardein said.

'The High Priestess Thalia is dead and the invaders were from Immish,' said Orhan. 'Whatever is happening on the White Isles is madness and lies.'

A boy. A beautiful shining screaming blood-soaked boy. Dead. Dead. Dead.

'The High Priestess Demerele drew the red lot,' said Darath. 'The High Priestess Demerele, the High Priestess-that-is, drew the red lot. Barely days before the High Priestess Thalia's untimely death. If Demerele was not chosen by Great Tanis, she would not have drawn the red lot.'

Orhan said, very slowly, his voice dry and cracked, 'That, surely, must mean something, must it not?'

'The Altrersyr are liars and deceivers. Accursed demons,' said Darath. 'But the Asekemlene Emperor cannot be deceived. The Emperor saw the High Priestess Thalia's body. The God Himself, Great Tanis, the Lord of Living and Dying, ensured that we had a new High Priestess waiting, that we would not be abandoned after the High Priestess Thalia's death. Who would dare to argue with the Asekemlene Emperor and the God?'

A rational man, Orhan Emmereth. Fifteen thalers, it had cost him, for Demerele to draw the red lot. Yes, he thought, yes, that's it.

The Emperor stirred himself. Spoke. A weak, pale man, the Emperor, neither clever nor good looking, puffy in his face and belly, red broken veins on his nose. A fishmonger's son in a desert city. A raven had landed at the child's feet to caw out 'Emperor', and the High Priestess Caleste had sighed when she confirmed that the child was indeed the Asekemlene Emperor reborn to them, the Ever Living, the Eternal, the Husband of the City, the Blessed Golden Light of the Sun's Dawn.

'I saw her body in a silver casket,' said the Emperor. 'I presided over her burial. I saw the Immish assassins. I sent a letter to the

Immish Great Council, protesting their attack on me. Was I deceived? Was what I said a lie?'

Silence.

The Emperor said, 'The Emperor cannot be deceived.'

'If anyone repeats these lies,' said Darath, 'they should be executed for blasphemy against the God and treason against the Emperor.'

The wrong words, there. Eyes flickered sideways. Back to March Verneth and Tam Rhyl's empty chairs. Orhan felt himself flinch. A terrible fear that he would be sick.

'And then, perhaps, the city can recover itself from bloodshed,' said the Emperor.

'We all pray as much,' said Cammor Tardein. Looking at Orhan.

The Emperor rose to his feet. The High Lords of the Sekemleth Empire rose and knelt before him. The doors of the council room swung closed with a crash of new forged bronze.

Orhan got slowly to his feet. Try not to look at the other lords' faces.

A boy with eyes like knife blades. Beautiful. Shining. But they were all dead. They were from Immish, a hired troop, rough mercenaries from Immish, they were all dead. And the memory, Great Tanis, the memory of the woman's body, stabbed and broken, and his sword coming down on her, cutting up her face into an unrecognizable pulp of blood. Not even the worst thing he'd ever done.

'The High Priestess Thalia is dead and the invaders were from Immish and they are all dead.'

'Orhan.' Darath caught his arm. 'I need a word with you.' Darath had dark, terrible hateful eyes. He knows I was unfaithful to him, thought Orhan. They hadn't spoken since the day of March's poisoning. Would have pleaded illness himself, despite everything, to avoid seeing Darath here; his heart had leapt, despite everything, at the thought of seeing Darath here. An excuse to talk to him. This new catastrophe that has struck us: perhaps a bridge between us, to smooth what we have done. We are beset by further chaos: and you were right to kill March, Darath, I see that now. For what would March have made of this new way to attack us?

'A word,' Darath said. 'Now.'

They travelled all the way to the House of the East in silence. Darath trying not to meet Orhan's eyes or touch his hand.

'You betrayed me,' Darath said when they were alone in Orhan's bedroom. His voice was bitingly cold.

'I — I can't explain it. I don't know what to say. What came over me.' Just tell him you're sorry. Tell him—

Darath struck him in the face, a ring scratching and drawing blood.

'You manipulative, vile, evil, lying bastard! You used me! All those lovely speeches about saving the city, about making us great again, about the poor and starving, about needing to protect us from an Immish threat. And you sold us to the thrice-damned fucking Altrersyr! I paid for it! I fought for it! The Altrersyr! What in God's name did they offer you? How much can possibly have been enough for that?'

Shock. Astonishment. Horror. For a moment Orhan didn't even understand.

'I told Elis I believed in you! That him marrying Leada was a part of remaking the Empire! My brother! I made my brother poison his own goodfather in his own house!'

'Elis? You made Elis do it?'

Darath's face went almost purple. 'Yes, I made Elis do it! I made Elis kill his wife's father! For you! How else did you think I managed it?'

'I . . . I don't know. I tried not to think. I . . . I'm sorry. I—'

Darath hit him again, on the face, stinging his eyes. 'Sorry! You sold us to the fucking Altrersyr! What the fuck did they offer you? How can anything have been enough for that? You know what they did to Tam's daughter. You know what they fucking are. A thousand thousand years our enemies! Death and ruin! And you sold us to them!' Spittle clustered on Darath's lips. Weeping. Never seen him so angry. 'Monsters! You sold us to them, Orhan!'

'No! Darath, no, please.'

'You sold me! You made me help you! I gave them money!'

'No . . .'

Darath's face like a dog's bared teeth. 'You bastard. You lying, poisonous, hateful bastard.'

'I don't understand. Any of it.' Orhan himself like a man without sword or armour, crouching trying to ward off the death blow with his outstretched hand.

'What the fuck is there to understand, Orhan? You arranged for the new King of the White Isles to burn the palace, despoil the Temple, carry off the High Priestess. So he can brag about it to his drinking friends! Why, in God's name? Why? Why? Did he promise you something? Land? Titles? Gold? His love? Are you running away to the Whites to be something at his court? How long were you planning this?' A horrible light came into Darath's eyes. 'Is this why you took me back to bed? To win me over? Help you make your pretty boyfriend king?'

'But they . . . they were a hired troop from Immish. I didn't know they had any connection to the Whites. How could I know? Why would I do that? Why would . . . why would this man, this king, why would he have done that, even? And they're dead. They're all dead. I saw them. The High Priestess Thalia is dead and the invaders were from Immish and they are all dead.'

Dead. Dead.

It sounded so pitiful. His voice whispered like leaves. Eyes like knife blades staring at him. A voice shouting, 'I'll kill you, then.' A boy, soaked in blood to his eyeballs, falling backwards in a crash of brilliant glass. We were too frightened to search for him, Orhan thought. No one would have gone to search for him. Not out there into the dark. His eyes, seeing you, out there in the dark . . . The boy raising his sword and Tam shaking, screaming, losing control of his bowels. Tam rasping out 'Alive' as he died.

'What have we done? What have you done? He'll kill us, Orhan!'

We paid for the men who attacked the palace to die. We killed them. We killed them all. I remember. I thought I did. Killed them. Dead.

Dead. Dead. Dead. Dead.

'They are everything they say they are. And worse,' Tam Rhyl had said, when he came back from the White Isles. Sailing away thinking Tiothlyn Altrersyr would marry his daughter. Sailing back with his daughter's womb rotting out of her body, his daughter crippled with pain. 'He did it by his own hand,' Tam Rhyl had screamed. 'He sent her a letter. Telling her. If Great Tanis were merciful he would wipe Malth Elelane from the face of the earth.'

'I didn't know! God's knives, I swear, I didn't know.'

'Liar! Fucking lies! Lies, Orhan!'

'I swear it! I didn't know! I swear by Great Tanis—'

'Liar!'

'No . . . Please, Darath. Please.'

'I'll kill you! I swear it! I'll see you and everything that's yours die in agony! I swear!'

And that, that is the most terrible thing he has ever heard and ever will hear.

They stopped, the words hanging visible in the air between them, bright as sunbeams, too terrible to be unsaid. Both breathing hard, weeping, grief running out of them from their souls, fear in their eyes.

Orhan got down slowly onto his knees at Darath's feet. 'I swear to you on my life and my love and the day of my death that I didn't know.'

Darath stared down at him for what seemed like lifetimes. Rigid. Bent as stone.

'Truly?'

'Truly. On my life and my death and my love for you. I didn't know.'

Darath sighed, a ragged, shuddering sound that ran through his body and Orhan's. '"On your love for me"? You fuck some filthy whore in the streets and you swear on your love for me?'

'Yes. Yes. I fucked some filthy whore in the streets and I swear on my love for you.'

A long silence. Then Darath laughed like a man dying of disease. 'And you're sorry for that, too, I suppose?' And he was laughing and weeping and hitting at Orhan's chest. 'And I suppose he'll turn out to be the Last True King of Tarboran, will he, your whore?' And Orhan was clutching at him so tight it hurt, almost fighting him, sobbing out 'I'm sorry', while the tears ran down his cheeks.

And then a servant came running, terrified to interrupt them, to tell them that Bil's labour had begun.

Chapter Eighteen

Hours, it must be, Orhan sitting and listening to the screams. March Verneth dying. Bil's baby being born. Felt like the screams were March's, as well as Bil's. Maybe his own heart.

Darath left. Hurriedly. Couldn't blame him. Orhan would have left himself, if he could. Janush the doctor rushed around looking anxious. The servant girl Nilesh, banished from Bil's bedroom, slunk wide-eyed outside the door. Mannelin Aviced, Bil's father, was summoned, slunk wide-eyed around Orhan's library. Doting future grandfather. Chewing his knuckles raw.

You told us the High Priestess Thalia was dead, and you told us the invaders were from Immish, and now my daughter is screaming giving birth to your heir. Orhan fled from Mannelin back to his own bedroom.

Janush the doctor ordered they burn lemon peel and mint leaves. Fill Bil's room with candles. Light candles in the gardens and before the house's gates. Bright clear light to welcome the new life.

Let her live, thought Orhan. Dear Lord, Great Tanis who rules all things, from the fear of life and the fear of death, release us. Let her live.

Bil screamed.

Orhan sent servants out to buy more lemons. Sent a message to Celyse, confirming what she would already know.

Let it live, thought Orhan. Dear Lord, Great Tanis who rules all things, from the fear of life and the fear of death, release us. Let it live.

I wonder what Sterne would be feeling? he thought. Would he be happy? Rejoice at the birth of his child? I wonder if she told him, before he died.

Bil stopped screaming. A long, terrible empty waiting silence. A strange high-pitched wail. Like nothing Orhan had ever heard. Painful. Heart rending. But also something filled with hope.

The baby. Screaming. Raging and rejoicing at being born.

We are grateful. God's knives. For these things, we are grateful.

Janush the doctor entered, threw himself at Orhan's feet. 'A boy! Great Tanis be praised! A boy! The heir to the House of the East! The next Lord of the Rising Sun!'

Celyse will be disappointed, Orhan thought dryly. Her son is now no longer my heir. He smiled at Janush, who must know that the baby was heir to a dead guardsman called Sterne. 'A boy! Great Tanis be praised indeed.'

'Will you see it, My Lord?' Janush gestured towards the doorway. A servant girl entered, carrying a bundle of shining white cloth. She knelt awkwardly before Orhan, holding out the bundle. From the silk, a tiny thing thrashed its hands. It reminded Orhan of the unhatched dove chicks he'd been gorging on at the wedding feast. Disgusting. Raw looking. He reached out and touched it. Fingers closed around his fingers. The strangest thing he'd ever seen.

'Great Tanis be praised.' It smelled odd, like blood and bread and fruit mould. Crusted and streaked with blood. 'The heir to the House of the East. The next Lord of the Rising Sun,' he said loudly. If any of them survived. Dead. Dead.

The baby whimpered. Orhan raised it to his face. My heir. Its tiny hands brushed at his face. Wrinkled like old, old man hands, webbed skeletal hands. It did not look like a human being, but its hands looked like human hands. Tiny nails. Its hands caught his face. Scratched him. He kissed its forehead. Up so close the smell was sweeter. A good strange smell. Its skin was waxy. Bil's body fluids. Bil's blood. So astonishing.

'And Bilale?'

'Lady Emmereth is well, My Lord,' said Janush.

Good. Such deep relief: I do care for her, he thought, you see, I am not a monster. 'Good.'

He kissed the boy again. This strange raw looking tiny thing.

My son, he thought slowly then. My son.

The girl took the baby out back to its mother. Orhan almost winced watching her rise awkwardly to her feet and walk out backwards with the baby in her arms. It made a shrill cry as it was carried out. Made him shudder with guilt.

Names, he thought wearily. Names. Name day ceremony. Offerings at the Great Temple. Telling Darath. Confirming the news to Celyse. The Emperor would have to be informed of the birth of an heir to the Lord of the Rising Sun his Nithque. He summoned a messenger, started composing a formal letter to Celyse.

And then a servant came running, terrified to interrupt him, to tell him that March Verneth had died.

PART THREE

FIRES

Chapter Nineteen

The Great Feast of Sunreturn had been going for six days now, and seemed in no danger of stopping. Amazing anyone had the stamina. Amazing anyone had the stomach capacity. Amazing anyone was still conscious. The people of Morr Town danced in the streets, kissed strangers like they were old lost loves. A huge bonfire had been raised in the main square, the wood treated with something so that it burned green. Gangs of men wandered the town, masked in leather, branches hung with bones and bells and ribbons fastened to their heads to resemble the antlers of stags. They carried buckets of pitch. Torches, long leather paddles, knives. Daubed pitch on doorways and window ledges, set it burning then beat out the flames. Shouted 'Luck! Luck! Luck!' as they danced. On the crag above the city, the high towers of Malth Elelane were hung with golden banners, sewn with golden bells that chimed night and day. Huge wreaths of branches and horse skulls had been raised over the open gates. Bonfires were lit in the courtyards, on the walkways at the tops of the great outer walls. There too the smoke was greasy, the flames green and too bright.

The whole effect was striking. Especially the centrepiece. Difficult not to be struck by a load of corpses, chains ringing out louder than the bloody bells when the wind got up. Very bright and festive looking, hanging there on the wall like wreaths, Queen Elayne's hair was almost the same colour as the banners, where it wasn't covered with blood and bird shit, and several of the women had been wearing jewelled dresses that still sparkled fetchingly in the sun.

Tobias didn't as a general rule approve of hanging people from buildings. They'd done it at Telea, in high summer, after the city fell for the third and final time. All the noble lords and ladies, a couple of higher ranking mercenaries, the richest of the merchants, some bloke who'd claimed to be a mage. Very impressive, put the fear of all the gods into the rest of the surviving Teleans and anyone else stupid enough not to think the Immish a model of reason and good governance, a pleasingly large number of people had rushed forward immediately afterwards to surrender up big piles of buried silverware and decide their wives' and daughters' virtue was in fact an eminently overrated quality easily tradable for an absence of rope. But gods and demons, it had been a bugger marching in and out of the citadel and having maggots and bits of rotting flesh shower down on you every single sodding time. Really hard to get the stink out of your hair.

That wasn't a problem here, of course, seeing as it was freezing cold and snowing. But when you looked up at some of those blue lips and blue faces . . . Kind of worse than rotting quickly, that they were so well preserved, like they might sort themselves out and be up and walking if you gave them a hot bath and a good rub down and a stiff drink. Queen Elayne had a mass of frozen blood blooming like flowers over her belly; Prince Ti was in pieces so small some of them had had to be tied up in little bags. But even their faces were sweet and perfect, delicately frosted with frozen tears.

Tobias looked at them thoughtfully. Seen the young prince a couple of times at a distance, not been overly impressed with him then. The queen you could tell must have been stunning, for a woman of her age. Lord Gaeve the queen's cousin had seemed a normal enough kind of bloke, for a nobleman, although you had to admit what Tobias assumed had been his wife had a face like an ill-favoured horse.

Funny, how things went.

People were hanging round the bodies, staring up at them like he often did. He'd assumed they were mourning them, at first. Loyal and heartbroken. Possibly even refuseniks of the new regime. Then the birds' pecking had dislodged some of Elayne's jewellery, and he'd realized his mistake.

The town had been snow-bound since the first day of Sunreturn, twinkling pretty and clean. People went out on sleds or skated down the frozen waterways; the court had ridden out, the second night of the feasting, to hold a dance on the ice. Not much of a man for ice and snow himself, Tobias, being Immish born and bred and feeling the cold more than he liked now, but gods it was beautiful. He'd watched some girls out skating on the river and that had been a very fine sight.

The ice could break any moment and kill you. Sharp as knives and cold as death and brittle as the bones of a man's skull. The girls skating so fresh and pretty and innocent. They knew. All of them.

'Stop looking at them.'

Tobias turned around. A woman. Familiar looking. He blinked. 'Raeta?'

Well, she was from the Whites. And everyone and their dog seemed to have turned up in Morr Town for Sunreturn, to drink, fuck and try to catch a glimpse of the new king.

'Five times, you've come up here to have a stare at them. Not that I've been counting. They're dead, Tobias. They're of no interest to you anyway.' She stepped towards him. Looking better than she had on the ship where he'd last seen her, when he was sailing merrily into Morr Town to tell old Illyn his son was still alive, mainly because she'd been able to wash her hair and change her clothes sometime in the last month. Wearing the nice thick warm cloak she'd got off the merchant they'd neither of them ever heard of or met.

'I told you your future's a nasty thing, Tobias. Told you you're bloody lucky, too.'

'Oh, I'm lucky. I only got two ribs broken and my left arm twisted and half the skin ripped off my bloody legs.'

'Better than drowning.' She gestured at the gateway. 'Better than that.'

'He'd do worse than that to me.'

'"He"?'

'Don't act all arch and innocent to me, woman.' What am I even doing talking to you like this? And I can't just — Came out unstoppably anyway, like sneezing: 'How about I buy you some lunch?'

'You want to buy me some lunch?'

'Oh, I'm lucky all right. You remember that bag of gold thalers you could smell on me? Can't you smell them still?'

'I can't smell anything beyond burning.' Smiled a cold smile. 'I gather our new king rather likes the scent of smoke.'

'Oh, yeah. Smells better than whale shit and salt water, though. Just about. Anyway: lunch?'

A moment's thought. Her eyes actually twinkled. 'My inn or yours?'

They walked slowly back down into the town. The masked-horned-pitch-wielding-setting-fire-to-things blokes were already out in force, staggering around threatening to set fire to passing women if they didn't give them a kiss. A glare from Raeta and they lurched off across the street. 'Kissies or flames, girls! Kissies or flames! My good big stick to keep the demons away!'

'Everyone in this bloody place seems to like the smell of smoke.'

'So he'll be a good king, then.'

Tobias's inn was near the Thealeth Gate, pleasantly far from the sea. A poorer bit of the richer bit of the town, away from the harbour, looking out onto the wheat fields and woods of Thealan Vale, a good long hike off the bulk of Malth Elelane that you could almost pretend you couldn't see it if you kept your eyes fixed the right way. Not a rich inn, but not a particularly bad one either. Needed somewhere decent with decent food and a decent bed when you had stab wounds, burn wounds, crushed by rocks wounds and a lungful of bloody burning salt water to recover from. Gods knew what he'd swallowed while nearly drowning. He was certainly pretending he didn't.

Something on top of it all that was oddly, painfully akin to a broken heart. All my life and all I've done with it, and I'm here and the world's fucked itself and the boy's a frigging king.

Outside the inn, more masked men were prancing about, seemed to have managed to set fire to someone's front window and were frantically trying to beat it out. Kept falling over, having to haul each other up again, the buckets slopping burning pitch about. A woman stood and screamed at them. A man who might have been the householder sat half naked on the opposite side of the road laughing, snowflakes settling on his fat bare chest. Heavy flakes swirling downwards while the sparks swirled up. Soot stained faces. Sweat smell. The shadows of horns and talons lurching back and forward. Someone shouting 'kissies or flames!' Inside the inn, a woman was crawling across the common room floor with her skirts over her head showing off her arse. Two men wrestled until one fell over with a crack. Voices roared out a song about the king and his big big sword. Nice, respectable place.

It's barely past midday, thought Tobias. I haven't even had lunch yet.

'Very nice,' Raeta said. Sounded genuine. They went up to Tobias's room, Tobias ordering a jug of hot beer and two bowls of stew to be sent to follow them. Let the innkeep think what he liked about Raeta. He'd crapped himself in front of her. She could probably cope with sitting on his bed.

'You think? Had a room in an inn right out on the other side of town near the sea for a while. Stayed for free the first night and all after I limped there dripping wet with bloody seaweed in my hair. Until being a hero of Morr Bay suddenly stopped being something to tell people about. Stroke of luck they kicked me out, actually, seeing as the storm dismantled the place two days later and everybody staying there died.'

Raeta laughed. 'You're lucky, see?'

A girl entered with a tray. She gave Raeta a quick look, grinned at her feet, left. Way too classy for him, the girl was probably thinking. Unless he pays damned well. Downstairs, a burst of enthusiasm for the king's peerless ability to disembowel people. His cloak was red as widows' eyes, apparently. And his subjects sang like crows.

'What do you want, then, Raeta? Been following me. Been hanging around Malth Elelane looking at me looking at dead things.'

'You smell of guilt, now, too, Tobias. Blood and gold and guilt.'

'Anyone who smells of blood and gold smells of guilt, Raeta. Stop pretending to be some witch thing.'

'You feel like you killed them. The queen. Prince Tiothlyn. The king even, maybe. The old king. The dead one.' Not even a question. Tobias shut his eyes. Tiothlyn had screamed so loud people had heard it through the walls of Malth Elelane. They'd looked kind of alike, Ti and Marith.

He'd seen King Marith a few days before, from a distance, pulled himself back into the crowds with a panicked fear he'd be seen. Riding down Sceal Street to the harbour to see the storm damage, mounted on a huge white horse the size of a fucking bull with that horrible stinking vomit-inducing cloak waving behind him that everyone else seemed to think was terribly dramatic and kind of stylish if you were that way inclined. The people had cheered their heads off but there'd been an undercurrent, a frightened thing underneath. The shadows had crawled around the boy and over his eyes. I fought for him, Tobias had thought dazedly. I marched in his army. I seem to remember jumping around shouting 'Hail to the king!'

I mean . . . what the fucking bloody fucking fucking fuck happened back there on Third?

'I feel like I killed, them, yeah,' he said.

148

'I won't ask why. Got the oddest feeling I somehow know. Lots of good new stories going round, the Deed of the New King what killed a dragon and sacked a palace and carried off the most beautiful woman what ever lived to spread her legs for him five times a night. Some Immish blokes in the background there somewhere, looking on applauding him.'

'So much my hands bloody ached. They mention the time he puked on my boots?'

'Not in the version I heard. Hardly noteworthy, either. He's puked on the boots of half the innkeeps of Morr Town.' She sipped her beer. Bitter, tang of herbs that the heating made worse: Tobias saw her mouth pucker slightly, then a slight smile that she liked the taste. 'Medicinal' might be a good word for it. 'Cleaned the palate'. They seemed to like bitterness here too. The steam softened her face. I don't desire you in the slightest, he thought, but I think I kind of trust you more than anyone I ever met apart from Skie.

Worse luck for you, then, Raeta, woman.

'How's your ma?' Tobias asked. Try to talk about something more pleasant than kingly vomit while we eat.

'She died. That's why I was visiting her.'

Good one, Tobias. 'I'm sorry.'

'No you're not.'

'Look, a bloke can be a right fucking bastard sword for hire and still feel sorry someone's ma died, yes?'

Raeta barked out a laugh. 'Yes.'

'So how's your brother?' Not dead too, oh please, he thought, the moment he'd said it.

'Well enough. Sailed off back to Immish just before all this blew up. Got a nice new ship cheap as cheap to go sailing off in too.'

'Yeah? Lucky for him.'

'He thought so. Called the ship *Another's Luck*, in fact.' She spooned a mouthful of stew, didn't look as pleased with it as with the beer. No accounting for taste. It had salt pig and beans and lumps of stale bread in it and was about the only good thing he'd come across since setting out for Sorlost. Looked up at him. 'You're, what, forty, Tobias?'

'Something like that.'

'You've been a sword for hire for, what, your whole man's life? Twenty years and more? Twenty-five?'

'Something like that.'

'So how many years you got left, you think, before you can't do it any more and some younger man spills your guts out in the dust?'

Bitch. 'Not long. Not the state I've been left in by things recently. Five years, maybe. Maybe less. Maybe more.' Two years tops, he thought, with his aches and the way everything was turning to shit. Then I'm dead meat chunks, like the whale at Skerneheh docks.

'Not much else you can do with your life, I'm guessing, except kill.'

Bitch, bitch, bitch, bitch. 'I'm a bloody good weaver, actually, I'll have you know. Lovely silk velvets, I could make you.'

'Yeah?'

Looked down at his calloused weather-bitten scarred fingers, the thumb of the left mangled flat somewhere, shaped so they curved mostly to fit the hilt of a sword, ached all the time. 'Yeah.'

'You want to do something more with your life than dying, Tobias?'

'Is there anything to life apart from dying, Raeta?'

She sipped her beer and spooned up her stew and smiled at him. Lumps of pig meat. Smoke. Dead dragons and dead soldiers and dead babies and dead whales. Prince Ti in lots of little soggy bags.

'You want to help me kill the king, Tobias?'

Chapter Twenty

Happiness. Sorrow. Hope. Despair.

Lan stood in the snow at the gates of Morr Town, looking up at the walls.

She who had seen Sorlost in the golden desert, the White City of Alborn rising on five hills above the Iannet marsh, she should not now find Morr Town imposing. And the last time she had been here, they had all been alive. But still it caught in her heart, to see the high stone walls, the open gateway, the red cloaks of the guards, the central tower of Malth Elelane shining, Eltheia's diamond blazing at its height to call the ships of the Altrersyr kings to their home. The Tower of Joy and Despair indeed. Unchanging. Unchanged.

The snow was heavy, thick piled against the city walls. The guards stamped in the snow. A blue tinge to their faces. At least they had furs. Looked bored, also, stamping and eying the road. Very few people about, in heavy snow, a day after the end of Sunreturn. No reason to be coming or going. Nothing grew. Nothing was alive. One of the guards yawned, showing a red mouth. Steam on his breath huffing out. He stamped again, shaking his head. The snow at his feet was trampled down brown hard muddy ice. The same men who had been there yesterday, and the day before.

Three days, she'd come to the gate, steeled herself to go through, failed. She was sleeping in a broken-down barn an hour's walk outside the town. The snow had come two days after she left Ru, blowing up out of nowhere, such a long walk ahead of her, icy fingers and frozen toes, crawling on through the cold. She should have turned back. Gone back to shelter, and she worried about Ru in the snow with the village girl supposed to be tending her. The winter was a cruel mother, devouring her own children; the poor folk left out offerings, in the hope she would be contented in her hunger and let them and theirs be. Lan had stopped in a farmstead where they had let her sleep in a hayloft and eat their bread in exchange for scrubbing the floors of the place clean, until she could bear the work no longer, set out again. So cold. Such slow going, step after painful step. Bent double sometimes, like an old crippled woman, snow stabbing her face. A battle. She could have gone back to Ru, and she worried about Ru. But if she went back, she would never leave. It was horribly cold in the barn, snow blowing in through the broken walls, frost creeping up the floor and the walls, Lan burned the timbers of the barn for warmth, starved in the cold, her hands shook. Red open sores on her hands with the cold. She could not go back. But she could not go into the town. She reached the gates and could not enter. She began to walk back again towards the barn. I am dying, she thought. She thought of Ru without her skin. Proud.

The guards moved aside as a party came out through the gateway. Great beautiful horses, rich furs, armed men around a woman on a cream and gold horse. They came closer. Lan stopped. Without thinking she stepped up towards the horses. Thalia in black furs stared down. A guardsman shouted at her to get out of the queen's way. Kneel in the snow. The horses came on. Lan stepped backwards again, afraid of the horses and the guardsmen.

For the first time, afraid of horses and armed men. She began to edge back off the road into the snow.

Thalia said, 'Halt.' The horses stopped. Lan sighed with relief, began walking again back to her barn.

A man's voice shouted, 'Halt, the queen says! You! Halt. Kneel.' Lan started. Held still and rigid, then went down on her knees in the snow. Cold. Oh, so cold. She began to shake.

Thalia rode the horse up carefully. Looked down with her sad, lovely face, white snow in the dark tendrils of hair. Some kind of joke in it, remembering the first time they met, Lady Landra on horseback looking down at this desperate pitiful thing. Saw and felt that Thalia remembered too.

'Get up.'

Lan rose, trembling. I broke you, she thought. I hurt you. I took your skin away.

But he loved you. He shouldn't love you. He loved Carin.

Thalia said, 'She's frozen. Garet, give her your cloak.'

Confusion. Someone not particularly happy at the order. But a thick fur was folded round her, warm and soft as weeping, fragrant with wood smoke. She stood staring. Thalia stared back. All this a reversal of how things had once been.

'We cannot stay standing here,' said Thalia. She looked around at the guardsmen. 'Someone take her up on their horse. You, Brychan.' The man nodded, unhappy and confused. They rode on, turned the horses off onto a track leading down to woodland white with snow. Lan sat wallowing in the smell of horse and fur. So very painfully, afraid. But impossible to her mind that Thalia should harm her. All this is a dream, she thought. Nothing real. Nothing had been real since Malth Salene burned. Or since her brother died. The smell of horse and fur and the movement of the horse's shoulders was real.

They came into a little clearing in the woods. Very still and silent: the woods all around Morr Town were king's land where no one came. A bower of beech limbs had been built in the centre of the clearing. Young trees, brilliant copper leaves still clinging to the branches, rimed in silver-white frost. The trees around the clearing were white birches, trunks whiter than the white snow, white enough to make the skin on Lan's hands itch they looked so dry. Painful as bone.

'Here.' A man helped Thalia dismount. Went to help Lan too. Lan slid off easily with a snort of disdain she knew was foolish.

Thalia said, 'Take the horses. Wait on the track.' Brychan looked at her, uncertain; he is half in love and in lust with her, Lan thought, he worships her. The blue eyes widened. Brychan nodded. The men left them alone. Thalia gestured to the bower.

Warmer, for a moment, relief at being out of the wind. The strange metallic rustle of the leaves. Shadows. White snow light on the fur of Thalia's cloak.

'You survived,' said Thalia.

'Will you tell him?'

A sigh. 'No. I will not tell him.'

'He killed Tiothlyn.' The rumours had run along the roads, the prince and the queen dead after torture, nailed up alive on Malth Elelane's walls, sacrificed like horses on the old king's grave. Even without the rumours, Lan would have been certain. If Marith was alive, Ti must now be dead.

Thalia's face narrowed. Cold sad fear. Grief. A faint, ghost smell of blood.

'He . . . That was Selerie's doing. He . . . He did not want that to happen. Not as it did.'

'He got drunk and cried about it, I suppose?' A harsh attempt at mockery in Lan's voice croaking out strangled. Lan thought: I do not fear you, woman, whatever you are, any more than I fear him, whatever he is. See how much I scorn him? But she shivered. The blue eyes flickered, all the hairs on the back of Lan's neck rose up like she heard a hawk scream.

'He calls their names sometimes, in his sleep. Tiothlyn's. Illyn's. Your brother's.' A pause, Lan went to speak, then Thalia sighed and said, 'He did get drunk and cry about it.' She seemed almost to laugh.

'And Queen Elayne?'

'She . . . He calls her name also. "Mother", he calls her. Then he tries to correct himself. But she . . . she was dying anyway. She tried to kill herself when she knew it was lost.'

A pause. Thalia said in the voice of the priestess of the death god of Sorlost, 'She killed his real mother.'

Ah, gods. Not that. Lan said hotly, 'No, she didn't.'

The blue eyes flickered again. 'She made his father do it, then.'

'No, she didn't.'

'Everyone knows it.'

'Everyone knows it's not true!' The old rumour, that had so quickly soured King Illyn's marriage to Queen Elayne. Flickered up, was silenced, flickered up again. Then Marith had stood up and screamed it at his father's face. Drunk out of his mind, Carin had said afterwards he'd been taking hatha for three days beforehand, crawling in and out of consciousness, weeping, swaying on his feet, spitting out the words. The king his father had struck him. Would have killed him, Carin had said, had Queen Elayne not grabbed hold of the drawn sword with her bare hand.

Landra had watched the penance King Illyn had ordered the next morning, Marith white and shaking, swearing he had no memory of what he'd said, knew it to be lies. So it had been settled again. Silenced. They all knew it was lies. They all knew Marith was mad. A friend of Ti's had set up a game shortly after, betting on how long before he either died or completely lost his mind. His white shaking hands and his red-ringed empty eyes.

'He told me himself. And Selerie. That was why they did it. For vengeance. Elayne killed his mother so that she could be queen in her stead.'

'His mother died of a baby gone wrong inside her. Of course people talked of poison. They always do, when a king or queen dies. But she died of a baby. As Altrersyr women often do.'

Thalia stood silent. They built this place for her, Lan thought. For him and her to be king and queen in the snow. He loves the snow.

'My father was at court when it happened. She bled. Died. The king brought every healer on Seneth to try to help her. Old selkie wise women, a mage, village witches with god charms who'd saved peasant girls from dying the same way. But she died. Too soon after her first child, they said, her body was too weak. The king was close to my father then. He would have known, he said, if anything had been wrong. It is common. Queen Elayne almost died, birthing Ti. King Illyn's own mother died.'

No answer. Thalia's hands danced birds' wings, folding over her stomach as if she was clutching a stab wound, the long fingers weaving into the fur.

'My father told me all this. The Relasts and the Murades, the queen's family, we are old enemies: my father had no reason to love Queen Elayne.'

'I—' The radiance in Thalia's face seemed lessened. Looked around the bower, her hands still folded over her stomach kneading the fur. 'It does not matter. It is over now. He is king and I am queen and his father and mother and all are dead and gone.'

'He killed them,' Lan said.

Thalia said, 'He did.'

'Come away,' Lan said. Found herself saying. 'Come away now with me. We can get away, there are people who can help us, we can go to Immish, to Alborn, or take you back to Sorlost. You can leave him.' She thought: you are more alone even than I am, Queen Thalia of the White Isles, is that why you cling to him? You know nothing and are nothing, without him. But I can help you. She thought, madly, bitterly, of taking Thalia to Ru's cottage, the two women weaving stinking gold cloth together the long dull skein of their lives. 'I can help you,' Lan said.

Cold sad fear. Grief. A faint, ghost smell of blood. The snow outside came more heavily. Thalia shivered and pulled at her cloak.

'Is that what you think? That I want to be free of him?'

How can you not want it? Lan thought. Look at you! Look at him!

'Free of him!' Blue eyes huge as worlds. Lan felt her body shake. So much light in the bower, rainbows thrown in Lan's vision, bronze leaves and white snow too vivid, the white trees beyond lit like mage glass, dry as bone. Thalia standing in her furs, remorseless, endless grief leeching out from her, beautiful as a beating heart. 'I would have wished it to be different. But it is too late.' The blue eyes closed a moment. A swirl of snow. White fire danced on the bronze beech leaves, white as the bark of the white trees.

Nothing, Landra had thought this woman. A whore or a hatha eater Marith had picked up somewhere. Then, learning what she was, she had seemed pitiful. Marith's victim, trapped beneath some yoke. Haltered. Hobbled. Maimed.

White light flickered on the dried leaves and the bare branches. Poured like water from the beautiful face.

This woman was not pitiful.

'I hold his life in my keeping. His life or his death. He lives because I chose it. Better perhaps to ask him if he wishes to be free of me.' The terrible voice softened. 'For fifteen years, I killed men and women and children for the sake of a city I barely saw. A prisoner in a bronze cage. My only purpose to kill, so that others might live. Life for the living, death for the dead. A holy calling. Needful. Necessary. I do not regret. But . . . Out in the city, the city I shed blood for, there was nothing. Cruelty. Pain. Men who wanted to harm me. And you. And Tobias. Rate. Your father. All of you, you were cruel. You wanted things from us. Used us. Bought and sold us. Marith, alone, of all the people I have ever met in the world, Marith alone has been kind to me, for no reason, except that he cares for me.

'So yes, I choose to spare him. Despite knowing what he is. He will do terrible things,' said Thalia, 'I know that. It would perhaps have been better if I were to choose to let him die. But I do not. And that is his grief, and mine. It is nothing to you.'

Gods. Gods. Eltheia, fairest one, keep safe.

'Leave us in peace,' said Thalia. 'Leave me in peace. You and your family have done enough to him. To me.' She reached out, talking Lan's hands, helping her up. 'You are cold. Hungry.' A sudden thought seemed to strike her. 'Where have you been living? You have no home. You must have come such a long way, did

157

you walk all this way? You must be worn out. And here we are standing in the cold . . .'

Thalia called her guards back. The man who had given Lan his cloak looked blue-lipped and wretched. Lan mounted up with Brychan again; Thalia rode the honey-coloured horse Lan recognized now from Malth Elelane. She had, Lan saw, become a fair enough horsewoman in the few short months since she had screamed with fear on Jaerl's horse. They rode back towards the town, stopped just beyond sight of the gates. Lan saw clearly that Brychan and the other two men looked unhappy at all that had occurred.

'I cannot take you into the town with me,' Thalia said. 'I cannot give you any money, either: I went for a pleasure ride, the men have no coin with them.' Her face furrowed. 'Wait . . .' She drew off her riding gloves, unfastened the necklace she wore. Gold flosswork, lace fine, set with amber. 'Will this be enough? I do not . . . I do not know these things. The cost of things. But Garet will need his cloak back.'

'Won't he . . . the king, won't he see you've lost it?' Thalia had said she would not tell, but she would, she might, the guards would tell, Marith would come with vengeance, hang them both from Malth Elelane's walls . . .

'He has given me more jewels than I could wear in a thousand years of living.' A sad inward smile, remembering something. 'All the gold in his kingdom, he has laid at my feet. No one will miss this small thing.'

'And your guards—'

'They will not tell.' That Lan doubted, thinking of her father's men. But Thalia seemed so very certain.

The horses started.

She was gone.

Back here again, Lan thought. What did she want with me? Why didn't she kill me? What did she mean by any of this? She looked at the necklace in her hand. Warm metal, the amber warm rich deep orange, flower blossoms encased in its depths. She thinks I can go into the market and trade the queen's jewels for a better cloak? Then Lan remembered giving the fisherman Ben her gold bracelet to buy bread.

Well, then. She steadied herself. This time she must go through the gates. She braced herself, walked around the bend in the road, there they were. Open. The guards stamping bored in the snow, a procession of sheep being herded through, a man on horseback waiting behind them. She took a deep breath, like a swimmer, followed the horseman in. Her steps through the gateway were heavy, as though she walked through thick mud or the beating snow-filled wind. A physical thing, a pressing on her, her body shaking.

Unchanging. Unchanged.

Sorrow and joy.

And then she was through, into the gatehouse square, surrounded by milling sheep.

It felt very strange walking there, knowing herself unknown. She went through the town up to the gates of Malth Elelane, to see what Marith and she herself had done. It was very silent, the banners and ribbons of Sunreturn were gone packed away in waxed cloth for another year, the snow had mounted up on the roofs. The narrow windows were almost all dark. Grey and cold, the stone of its walls, towers like bare trees, at its heart the golden tower of Eltheia rising, its jewel hidden in clouds. A thin, still beam of light reflected on the sea beyond.

A woman's voice said, 'Stop looking at them.'

Chapter Twenty-One

He killed his brother and his mother. Marith. My husband. He killed them.

He blames his uncle Selerie. Says Selerie did it. Perhaps Selerie encouraged him. But he killed them. His brother. His mother.

And then I married him.

The storm calmed and we sailed. We entered Morr Town harbour to a thousand voices raised in joy. The town was ruined. Storm-soaked. We rode through the town. 'My home,' Marith kept whispering. 'My home.' He looked ahead of him, so eager, he had to keep himself from urging his horse into a run. We came into the fortress of Malth Elelane. The storm had blown all the banners of the towers down, washed the gold from the roof of the Tower of Despair. The diamond set at the top of the tower flashed for us, shone like a star, shone with every colour like a rainbow. 'Eltheia's diamond,' Marith said when he saw me looking. 'And you, now, come here as the new Eltheia.'

Ah, yes.

The doors were thrown open for us, lords and servants kneeling; half the soldiers there had killed the rest, showed the bodies proudly as though we should be glad. Marith paled, halted. His home,

160

running with blood he has caused to be spilled. His eyes went very bright. Glittering. His face was flushed.

There was a pause then, a silence. Embarrassed. Afraid. All of us, the lords, the servants, all waiting. Knowing. He is come home, and he is waiting for them to come to him, his family, welcome him, and he knows, he knows . . .

'Where is she?' he said. 'The queen? And my brother?' He stepped forward, looked around him, held out his hands, as though he expected them to come and embrace him.

A stir in the people there kneeling. Servants looking at each other, nervous, trying not to be the ones to speak.

He said, 'Bring them.'

It was like the time I had to punish Ausa, in my Temple. Like the way the priestesses looked at me then. She sinned against the God, Lord Tanis. I punished her, and it must be done, and they all looked at me, and knew.

You will say that he is monstrous.

You will say that I am monstrous.

I chose to spare him. Remember that. I chose to let him live.

They brought them in to us. His brother and his mother, bound and under guard. His mother was injured. Her dress was wet with blood. Marith's face went white as ashes, when he saw the blood.

'She tried to kill herself, My Lord King,' one of the men holding her said. 'When she saw that it was lost.'

Marith put out his hand. Stepped forward and touched the blood on her dress. Touched his bloody right hand with his scarred left hand.

'Marith,' his mother whispered. 'Marith. Please.'

His brother spat at him. 'Filth and murderer!' his brother screamed. 'They were right! You were right! You should have died long ago! Father should have killed you!'

They looked so alike, Marith and Ti.

'I can't do it,' Marith said. His eyes were like his mother's wounds. The whole room was screaming, running with shadows. He paced round and round, staring at them. His mother's blood on his hand. He rubbed at his eyes and cried out as the blood was rubbed onto his face.

His mother said, 'Please. Marith.'

'What else will you do, then?' Selerie asked him.

Marith looked at me. Looked at Selerie. Looked at the walls. At the blood.

'Get out,' he said. 'Everyone.'

'Stay,' he said to me then. 'Please, Thalia, no, you stay.'

I pitied his mother, his brother.

I stayed.

I did not stop him doing it.

It took a long time to do it. His uncle Selerie helped him to do it. His uncle Selerie made it take longer. That much is true.

And now it is done.

Hilanis the Young skinned his older brother alive. Such are the stories of his family. The customs of his kingdom. What is done. What it is, to be a king.

His father abandoned him. His mother hated him. His brother replaced him. They all three wanted him dead.

What do you expect him to do? Forgive?

He got drunk and cried about it afterwards. Sat in the hall where he had done it, with his sword in his hand. Screamed as loudly as Tiothlyn did as he died. And I thought of Ausa, and the way that she had screamed. All night, he sat there. In their blood, with their bodies at his feet. I hoped and feared, dreaded, that he would kill himself.

The next morning he came out as though nothing had happened. Did not speak of it.

I did not speak of it.

'I love you,' he said to me.

The next morning again we were married.

Our hands were bound together with silver ribbons, in the great hall of Malth Elelane we stood before a blazing fire and cast grain and fruits and oil into the flames. Burning. Oh how much they like to make things burn. Do you worship the fire? I asked him once, watching the way he watched the flames in the desert night in the dark that is not like the dark here. He laughed and said no, not worship, only that they find it beautiful. Perhaps, he said, it is only because it is so damned cold on the Whites. But everything here is on fire. We cast offerings into the fire for our wedding. We burn the dark away with bonfires. We burn the town clean. What comes of burning? But I thought then of my Temple, filled with light where the candles burn. We went for blessing to the Amrath chapel, carried on litters of bare white branches, our hands still bound together so that we were pulled together and twisted apart. It made me think of the long slow walk down the corridors of my Temple on the day I was consecrated, half carried in high copper shoes to keep me from touching the ground. Such strange rituals, I have had done to me. And all to the same end. If he stared at the walls where the bodies are hanging, if he closed his eyes in pain, if he stared at his uncle Selerie with hatred, we ignored these things. If he jerked and cried out when a voice shouted that we be blessed with many children, we ignored these things.

Days pass. Selerie praises him, embraces him, hails him as king, departs. Marith's eyes are perhaps easier. He stares less often towards the bodies hanging in the gates. A sudden joy bursts over us all. Wild and mad and bright. We hold the fest of Sunreturn. We celebrate our victory. We do not stop. The hall runs with music and dancing, we go out on the ice to race horses, feast all night and into the next morning, dance by torchlight in the snow. I am enthroned by his side in ice palaces or fur lined tents or under bare trees hung with silver stars. I am dressed in cloth of silver, crowned with winter leaves brown and pale golden and skeletal, fragile as silk net. Gold and gems and treasures shower down on me, more jewels than I can wear in a lifetime, gifts from Marith and from all the lords and ladies of the White Isles. He goes out riding with Osen, comes back laughing to order a feast laid, finally collapses into sleep then orders another feast laid as soon as he wakes. Our hearts are filled with wonder. Time and order are lost, no one cares whether it is day or night, the days are so brief here in the heart of winter that all time is lost in the snow. So long ago it seems, already, what we had to do to reach this. We do not think now of the dead.

I try not to think of the dead.

I try not to think of killing him.

Of not killing him.

So now I am a second Eltheia. I have so many glorious things. Power. Pleasure. Wealth. Love.

At fifteen I was dedicated to Great Tanis the Lord of Living and Dying, the One God of the Sekemleth Empire of the Golden City of Sorlost. I was veiled so heavily my vision was blurred and buried, wrapped in gold and silver like a burial cloth. I knelt before the High Altar. I walked into the Small Chamber and killed the High-Priestess-that-was with a holy knife. My life then was pleasant enough, I suppose. I could have lived in my Temple, stepped out the rituals, said the words, sung the songs, served the God, done what must be done. I had some little power: in my hands, in the knife; I was the Chosen of God.

To give that up, it must be for something glorious.

I have something glorious. You cannot say I do not.

Power. Wealth. Worship. Pleasure. Love. Living.

Desire.

Disgust.

I have so many glorious things.

Of course I married him. What else do you think I would do?

Chapter Twenty-Two

Once upon a time, a long, long time ago now, there was a young king who needed a wife. And the wife chosen for him was called Marissa, and she was the sister of the King of Ith. She had yellow hair and grey eyes and she was sweet natured and gentle, kind and fair and wise and good. The young king, King Illyn, his name was, he sailed over the wine dark sea to her, and he married her in great splendour in her brother's fortress, and he brought her back with him to his own kingdom, and crowned her queen with a circlet of diamonds and silver on her beautiful head.

King Illyn did not want to marry her. He had never met her. Did not love her. There was a woman at his court whom he loved, and he thought perhaps that had he been free to choose he would have married her. But he was young and his father had died and his father had lost a battle, and he needed strong allies to help him keep his throne. And so he married an Ithish princess, whose brother was his ally, whose family had always been allied with his own. And they were happy enough, as such things go. Marissa bore him a child, a son, strong, healthy, radiant with beauty. She was a good and fine mother. Illyn was delighted. Loved the child. Sent the woman Elayne away, albeit with grief.

Marissa became pregnant again. The child miscarried. Marissa died.

Well, now, the king's heart was broken, as anyone's would be to lose a wife in such a way. But after a few months had passed, his advisers said to him that the child needed a mother, and he needed a queen, and the kingdom needed more than one heir. And he thought again of the woman he had loved, Elayne Murade, Elayne of the Golden Hair. He married her. And he was happier, married to her, than he had been married to the Ithish princess, because he loved Elayne and she loved him.

And Elayne loved Marissa's son. He was beautiful and strong and charming: how could anyone not love such a child? Perhaps she loved her own son more. Perhaps. She was his own mother. Is that so very hard to understand? But she watched the boys grow and she loved them both, and Illyn loved and cherished them.

But they were afraid of Marissa's son, also. Watched him sometimes with fearful, wary eyes. For he was so bright. So radiant. And there was something in him that terrified them. Shadows gathered around him. His hands seemed red with blood. And one day he stood up before them, mad-eyed, ruined, broken, all they had done, all they had tried, begged him, pleaded with him, wept, screamed, comforted him in his sorrow, hated him for his hate, he was mad and ruined, sunk into himself, filled with self-loathing, there was nothing they had not tried, to help him, and they could not help him, and one day he stood up before them and told them that they had killed his mother and he knew they wanted to kill him and that he hated them and wanted to kill them too.

What do you say, when your child hates you? What can you do?

A beautiful child, and his shadow stinks of bloodshed.

What do you do?

Chapter Twenty-Three

'Kill him'.

'Well . . . yes. That's pretty much established. As a life goal, I can't really disagree with you there, Raeta.'

The boy's face killing a house full of people, back in Sorlost. Killing everything. They'd almost had to stop him killing the rats in the pantry walls. He'd wept as he did it. This man is alive. Now this man is dead. It's my fault. This child is alive. Now this child is dead. It's my fault. This woman is alive. Now this woman is dead. It's my fault. This man is alive. Now this man is dead. It's my fault. That horrible blank grief and the blade coming down and down and down. That had to die. That face. 'I can't let you go to Ith, boy,' he'd told Marith, when he betrayed the boy to Landra Relast. 'You know that. Can't let you have power and command. I know what you are. What you'd do. Think of this as a kindness, like. 'Cause it is.' And Marith had looked up at him, defeated. Known Tobias was right. That poor boy with puke in his hair and wild mad sad eyes, jumping out of his skin if someone farted too loudly, staring about him like he was haunted, sobbing in the night, whispering for his mum.

'But, you know . . . how?' And don't, Tobias thought, just don't say 'with a knife'.

Tobias thought: I've seen the boy fight. Although 'fight' is possibly the wrong word. I am not ever, ever, ever going up against him with a blade, not for all the gold in his kingdom, and that's that.

'How we kill him,' said Raeta, 'is why I'm here and what we need to plan out. Obviously. Although I'd have to say with a knife might be a good starting point.'

There was a knock at Tobias's door. The innkeep's daughter, or whatever she was. 'There's a woman downstairs says she's here to see you,' she said.

'To see me?' He wasn't even using his right name. Also, pretty much everyone he'd met while on the White Isles was dead.

'Tobe, from Immish, she said. Staying in the room under the eaves with the chimney that smokes, she said.'

'Show her up, please,' said Raeta. She handed the girl an iron penny. The girl glared again at Tobias and went out.

'Something to do with you?'

'Someone who might help us. Possibly.'

'Possibly?'

'It does smoke,' said Raeta. 'The amount they're charging you, they should get it sorted out without having to be told. Did you a favour.'

'Any number of favours, you've done me. All worked out so bloody well. Don't change the subject. So who in gods' names is this possibly helpful woman and how does she know me?'

'I met her in the same place I met you. Underneath the queen's corpse. Invited her here to see us, gave her the name you go by. You'll know her. Wait and see.'

Actually, was he imagining it, or did Raeta look . . . uncomfortable? Embarrassed, even.

Thalia, he thought, for a very brief moment, like the sun on his face and a knife in his gut. Thalia. She'd come sweeping up the stairs in a gown of gold and moonlight.

The door opened. 'Here you are, then,' said the innkeep's daughter. 'Tobe of Immish, who's staying in the room under the eaves with the chimney that smokes.'

168

Footsteps in the hall. Hesitant. The woman came in. Who the fuck is this? thought Tobias. A woman with a burned face and her hair covered up in a cloth. Looking terrified.

Looking kind of familiar, too, weirdly. You'd think he'd remember meeting a woman with a burned face like that. Not something he was going to forget. Sadly for him.

The woman was staring at him. Looked puzzled herself, on top of the terror. Like maybe she thought she knew him. Her eyes opened wide. 'What—?'

'You have met, I believe,' said Raeta. 'Briefly. Though more than once. Landra Relast: Tobias, formerly of the absurdly named Free Company of the Sword and briefly squad commander to a certain young man you know. Tobias: Lady Landra Relast.'

Lady Landra Relast? The woman who paid him a king's ransom for Marith's head on a platter? Her? Lady High and Mighty? What in gods' names happened to—?

Oh. Yes.

The most awkward silence since the awkward silence that had followed Tobias kneeling before King Illyn to tell him that he was indeed absolutely certain dear Marith was back on the White Isles, and, um, well, he knew this because, um, well, uh, he, uh, might have had some hand in getting dear Marith back there. Gods, I have absolutely no idea in the world what to say right now, thought Tobias. 'Shouldn't have shafted me on the deal, should you, woman?' not seeming entirely appropriate, in the circumstances.

'I'm really sorry for the loss of your entire family, your face, your childhood home and everything you've ever known or cared for?'

'Well, gee, that didn't quite work out the way we'd planned, did it?'

'Want a refund?'

'I'm sorry,' he said at last.

Lady Landra Relast sat down on the chair.

'I didn't think you'd come,' said Raeta.

Lady Landra was holding a funny scrap of yellow cloth in her hand. Squeezing it. She looked blankly at Raeta. 'What else could I do?' She poked at the cloth around what must until recently have been her hair, itching at it. I don't, Tobias thought, I don't want to think what your head looks like under that. Not if I ever want to eat pork scratchings again, anyway.

'I'm not looking for vengeance,' Lady Landra said. Her eyes were red where she'd been crying.

Okay. Really?

Well, that's unfortunate, because I certainly bloody well am.

'I'll go and get us all some beer and some stew,' said Tobias.

They all sat around in further awkward silence until the innkeep's daughter had been and gone with bean soup and the speciality herb flavoured beer. The soup was noticeably thinner and less meaty than it had been when he first arrived at the inn. The girl glared at the chimney and then at Tobias before she left.

'Good soup,' said Raeta after a long pause.

'You are planning to kill him?' asked Lady Landra.

'That's why you're here, isn't it?' said Raeta. 'Otherwise Tobias has just wasted a penny buying you a meal.'

'I can pay you for it,' said Lady Landra. She grabbed at a purse round her neck. She looked at Tobias and her eyes shrank away.

Remembered hating her as a bitch queen, when they met before. When she shafted him over Marith and Thalia.

'She's joking,' said Tobias.

'Oh, yeah. Soup's way more than a penny a bowl, now, what with the cost of rebuilding half Morr Town and meeting the king's drinks bill.' Raeta took a long gulp of her beer. 'Good beer, though, still.'

They ate and drank in silence. Tried not to notice Lady Landra was crying into her bowl.

'So,' said Raeta. 'We were discussing how to kill him.' She turned to Lady Landra. 'You know him. You've been thinking about how to kill him. For a long time. Any thoughts?'

'I'm not looking for vengeance,' Lady Landra said again.

'No,' said Raeta. 'Of course not.'

'Do it publicly. Shame him, as he dies. Everyone in Morr Town should see him die.' Lady Landra's eyes flashed. Looked for a brief moment like Tobias remembered her. Fierce. Cold. 'We could bribe his guards. Ambush him in the street. Cut him down. Leave him in the gutter, with the filth.'

Tobias snorted. 'Ambush him in the streets? Me and whose army? If you can find me a hundred heavily armed men and an inside contact . . . I'd still tell you you were mad. There is no sellsword company in the world, anywhere, who'd take that job, knowing what I know.'

'I know my way around Malth Elelane,' Lady Landra said. 'I know where he sleeps, everything. I've been in his rooms.'

'I don't care if you know where he shits. Which you probably do, I'm sure. But it's too dangerous. We'd never make it in and out in one piece.'

Lady Landra widened her eyes. 'You're a sellsword. A hard tough man, the leader of a troop of hired killers, you destroyed the Summer Palace of the Asekemlene Emperor of Sorlost.' All the strength seemed to run out of her then, as she spoke the word 'destroyed'. Her voice choked off. 'You . . . He is one man. You go into his bedchamber at night and stab him. Cut his throat, cut out his heart. I will . . . I will pay you well, when it's done, if that's what you're worrying about.' Her voice shook, her hands were shaking. Her voice was small as dry dust.

'Pay me?' She was wearing a cheap, badly made dress. Too big leather boots with scuffed-up toes. There was a lot of grime under her fingernails. Looked like she'd been sleeping in a barn. 'Not for all the gold in Irlast,' Tobias said.

'We go into Malth Elelane in the night and stab him in his sleep,' said Lady Landra again. 'I'll do it.' She was crying again. Hunched in on herself. Like snapped thread. 'Just give me a knife and I'll do it. What else am I still alive to do?' Lady Landra said.

Raeta laughed.

'I'm not looking for vengeance,' Lady Landra said.

'Yeah. You said. Look: you're both thinking too personal. Assuming we do it ourselves. Up until a few months ago he was dead and buried. Now there are corpses hanging off his fortress walls. There must be some other people around here who want to see him dead.' Turned to Landra. 'You, Lady Landra, must have some friends left among the rich and powerful you could talk to.'

'Lady Landra is dead,' Lady Landra said.

'Someone? Anyone?' Gods, come on! Lady High and Mighty Landra – taken over a whole lodging house in Sorlost she was so rich, *'kneel, Tobias', 'the Relasts are the most powerful noble family on the White Isles, Tobias', 'my family are connected by blood to all the great families of Irlast, Tobias', 'I have Altrersyr blood myself, Tobias', 'just give me word, Tobias, and we will take him and destroy him and give you such a reward and your name will be celebrated across the Whites'* – Relast? No powerful friends?

But her voice was like something that was already dead, yeah.

'His friends, then. What are they like? Any of them for turning? This bloke Lord Fiolt his new best mate? I'm guessing he's not exactly unambitious.'

'Osen Fiolt?' A dead laugh. 'Osen's spent his whole life trying to thrust himself into Marith's affections. Osen was so jealous of Carin. Carin used to talk about killing him. Gods, I wish Carin had killed him.'

'I'll go and get some more beer,' said Tobias at last. 'If anyone wants some.'

In the common room a bunch of early drinkers were getting all over-excited. Roared out singing: *His cloak is red as widows' eyes. His big big sword he thrusts hard and wide.* The innkeep's daughter broke off from clapping time to give Tobias three more cups of beer. He took them upstairs in silence.

'Death! Death! Death!' a drunken voice shouted outside the window. Lady Landra jumped and whimpered.

'You just pissed on my foot, you arse.'

'Look, Lady — Landra, you got anywhere to stay?' said Tobias. 'Anywhere, uh, better than this?'

'I was sleeping in a barn,' Landra said after a long silence. 'I . . . I spent last night outside the gates of Malth Elelane. Walking through Morr Town. There is a woman I know, somewhere, I could . . . I thought I might go back to her.'

'But I can't,' Landra said.

'The room next door to this one's free,' said Tobias. 'As far as I know.'

'I . . .' Her hands went to the purse round her neck.

'He'll pay for you,' said Raeta.

It was your money, some of it, anyway, Tobias thought. Blood price for Marith Altrersyr. I can't bring myself to spend it on anything. Left his hands feeling tainted. Slithered through his fingers like raw meat. If he gave it to a shopkeeper to buy something . . . like it was cursed, or something equally bloody stupid.

One of the richest men in Morr Town, was old Tobias. Laugh or weep so hard you'd bloody piss yourself.

'You need a bath and a sleep,' said Tobias. 'Some new clothes, all of that.' Gods, he sounded like someone's mum.

'And then tomorrow, when you're feeling . . . slightly better, possibly,' said Tobias, 'we'll start planning how to kill him.'

Landra nodded dully.

'Good,' said Raeta. 'I'll leave you two friends alone, then.' She got up. Went out.

Come back . . .

So. The two of them. Alone. Kind of awkward, yes?

'I'm sorry,' Tobias said.

Landra said nothing. Twisted the cloth in her hands.

'I'm sorry. Honestly.' Gods, he thought suddenly, what if she'd noticed my face, when I was there at Malth Salene? She'll kill me.

'I thought it might hurt him, at least, to see Carin's grave.' She took a long sip of her beer. 'Such a little time he spent grieving. That creature, that woman he's married. Married! If you'd told

173

me who she was . . . And heaping Osen Fiolt with honours. His dearest friend, they say he calls him!'

She said, 'Osen Fiolt wanted to marry me too, once. A long time ago, when we were all still really children. He tried to charm me, brought me flowers, whispered things. My hand in marriage, and only Carin's death between us and all my father's power and wealth. I had him thrown out. But it gave us the idea, Carin and me. And now Carin is dead, and Osen is Marith's beloved friend.' She stood up and bowed her head to Tobias. An odd gesture, not a sign of deference but . . . some attempt at her pride? 'I'm sorry. This means nothing to you. You just wanted to make some money out of my pain. Couldn't know what it was that you did. I'll go downstairs. Take the room.' She blinked. 'Thank you, Tobias.'

Poor woman. The tangled wreck of her life. He watched her go, heard her come back up, the innkeep's daughter showing her the room. Her voice shiny and ladylike thanking the girl. Then the horrible muffled sound of her crying. On and on. Idiot, he thought. For offering her the room. Her and me . . . every time we look at each other, nothing but guilt.

He went down to the common room to drink, to get away from it, but they'd moved on to a song about Amrath's conquest of Mar.

'*Now the King of Mar, his lady wife was a god:*
She had horns and a tail, the dirty old sod.
But that didn't stop Amrath.
He cut off her tail,
Even though she turned pale,
And He cut off her horns with His knife!'

Went back upstairs and stuffed his head under the pillow to try to sleep.

Chapter Twenty-Four

Sat bolt upright in bed.

He wanted to kill Marith because he'd seen what Marith could do to people – no, scrub that, he wanted to kill Marith because he'd seen what there was in Marith's eyes – no, scrub that, let's be honest here, Tobias, shall we, he wanted to kill Marith because Marith was rich and beautiful and brilliant and a total evil poison shit.

Landra Relast wanted to kill Marith because fairly bleeding obvious.

Why in all gods' names did Raeta want to kill Marith? Raeta was a woman Tobias had chatted to on a boat. The way she talked about it, she'd been dreaming about killing Marith her whole life. Her eyes, when she talked about killing him, they lit up. She strolled up to him when he was standing underneath a load of dead bodies, suggested he help her kill someone she'd never met, and it all seemed perfectly natural?

Lay staring at the ceiling, all his thoughts tangled up. Raeta's eyes lit up like a starved wolf when she talked about killing the boy. Raeta was some woman he'd met on a boat.

Moonlight and torchlight in through the shutters. Drunken yells of 'The king! The king!'

* * *

The next morning, he woke up feeling refreshed and peaceful, and his leg didn't hurt quite so much. A weight off his mind.

He had some idea, then, that he'd been worried about something in the night. Couldn't for the life of him remember what.

The goal of all our lives now, he thought. Killing him. I will kill him, he thought. Evil vile poisonous little shit. His life or my life. A knife, or a sword, or an arrow, or poison? Plans already starting forming in his head.

Chapter Twenty-Five

Spring came. The first white flowers pressing up through the dark earth. The snow melting. The world unfurling. Green haze on the trees, the first buds, the first tiny leaves. The air smelled warmer, even in the cold biting north wind. The light changing. The sea and the sky also somehow changed.

It delighted Marith, to see Thalia see it.

'I did not know,' she said, her voice filled with wonder. They rode out of Malth Elelane into the woods where they had built themselves a frozen ice bower. Green things pushed up everywhere, putting out blue and yellow flowers. The beech trees were all in bud.

'Listen.'

She closed her eyes.

'A greywing,' Marith said. Sound of pure joy. It hung in the air above them, beating its wings frantically, black against the sun.

'They are coming back for the summer. From the south, from Maun, to nest on the cliffs.' They were coming early: a good sign. Meant a warm, early spring.

'All the way from Maun?' said Thalia, astonished. 'They fly across the sea?'

'They've come even further than you, beloved.'

Another greywing came to join the first. A flock of them, swirling in the sky on the horizon, a smudge like smoke.

So much that needed doing, a kingdom to rule. But ignore it: they rode out alone into the country around Malth Elelane; the beauty of the land opened itself to Thalia like a new language. He saw it in her, the sky with its ever changing clouds, so different from the golden blue dust of Sorlost, the pine groves sweet with resin, the fast white rivers, the cliffs falling dark into the sea. They rode out and she drank in it, filled herself with it. Wonderful to watch. He himself saw it anew, more beautiful even than he remembered it.

'Shall we go on?' The woods opened into a meadow, sheltered and south facing, almost warm already, carpeted with white and purple clover. The meadow grass grew up as high as the horses' knees, they rode through it as if they were riding through a shallow sea. There were small brown cattle in the meadow, shaggy coated with long twisting horns. These raised their heads lazily, grass and clover hanging from their mouths, watched them with big liquid dark eyes. They always looked rather sorrowful, cattle, Marith thought.

'It's so alive,' said Thalia.

'Well . . . yes.'

'I didn't realize.'

But of course, she wouldn't have realized. She must have thought all of the White Isles was just ice and frost. It astonished him again, her ignorance, the closed nature of her world. She lived her whole life within the walls of a temple in a city in the desert, where there were no seasons, no change. She had seen such things: life; death; the single act of chance, of a lot drawn, that had made the difference between the two. She had been sacred to a god, chosen, hallowed, almost herself a goddess. But she had never seen running water, until he showed her a stream; she had never seen the spring coming until here, now, looking at the trees and the meadow.

'Ah. Wait. This will please you.' Marith steered the horses through the woodlands upwards, onto the higher slopes of the Tremorn hills. The landscape here became wilder, more like the moorlands of Third Isle that she had seen already, but she gasped still as she saw it, for the gorse had all come into flower. The melting snow had watered the high ground and the earth shone green with grasses and yellow with gorse flowers.

'And see here.' They dismounted, walked across spring turf that was soft as furs underfoot. Thalia stepped and almost jumped, delighted.

There were hares on the high hills, and hawks hunting the greywings.

'Oh,' she whispered. 'Oh. Oh.' The yellow gorse flowers made her skin golden. 'Thank you,' she said.

Marith sighed. 'We need to go back now.'

'Already?'

'I'm afraid so. Things that must be done'

They passed a way house, riding home again. Marith left an offering of a few coins at the godstone at its entrance. A ruined house, out in the woods, tumbled into shapeless piles of mossy stone. Humps and hollows in the ground beneath a copse of ancient apple trees that Carin had said were the remains of an ancient village.

'Look!' Thalia said suddenly, pointing. Marith saw a flash of white, in the trees.

'What was it?'

'I'm not sure. I didn't see it properly. I think perhaps it was a deer.' Her face changed. 'No, not a deer. Just a bird, I think, moving in the trees.'

She looked suddenly, oddly frightened.

'There are no wolves on the White Islands,' said Marith. 'Nothing to be frightened of. And I have a sword.'

'It was a bird,' said Thalia. Her hands were shaking, holding the horse's reins.

Fear. Fear on him. Something that had made her so afraid.

'Let us go back,' said Thalia. She made her horse go quickly. 'I'm tired,' she said, 'I want to get home.'

Ah gods. Fear. What was it? Marith thought. But he found that he could not ask her what it was that she had seen.

They rode back quickly. And there were indeed things that must be done.

The burial of the dead. Finally, with the snow melting, the spring coming, at last now it must be done. The rancid vat of honey, pus stink, oil-thick sweetness around decaying flesh and bones. The bodies on the gatehouse, ragged, crow food. Black meat. White skulls. His mother's hair still yellow. Ti's hair. Could have been his own.

Bury them first, his stepmother, his brother, take them down from the walls where they hung. The rest, Elayne's family, let them hang there forever, rust stains on old bones nailed to the stonework. Bone charms. Like charms against ill luck. Stay there, until no one remembered what they meant. But his mother – his stepmother – and his brother, they must be buried.

I will not march off to wonders, Marith thought, with their eyes watching from the walls of my home.

The bones were taken down at night. Osen supervised the work. Offered to do it.

'Some things no one should have to do,' Osen said. Osen had buried his own mother, two years past.

He ordered a Queen's Mound raised, for Elayne. White white heaped stones. She was buried wrapped in silver cloth, what was left of her, her body garlanded with yellow flowers. Ti was buried next to her, a prince's grave, a child's grave. He was a prince and he died. That is what they would say of him. Who lived, now, that could say he had ever claimed to be king? They were buried in the dusk, the evening light falling, the sky was filled with clouds and the dying sun came through them death-wound red. They were buried beside Marith's own mother Marissa, who had lain for twenty years beneath a cairn of blue stones. The rocks of their grave were carved with flowers and patterns. Rune words: *hel, henket, mai, bel*. For comfort, for death, for grief, for love.

* * *

The next day, he took Thalia out riding again. They went up the bank of the river Heale, that ran fast and clear down from the hills. Marith took her to the Leaping Stones in the woods where the river fell over rocks in white rapids; there was a pool beneath the rapids where he had swum in summer. It was too cold to swim, of course, but she dangled her feet in the water, giggled at the cold. There were big fish in the river, they saw them in the depths, moving like shadows. Pike, with sharp teeth. A single, very early dragonfly. Thalia had never seen a dragonfly before. It landed, for a single moment, on the sleeve of her silver gown.

The sun was setting, when they returned to Malth Elelane.

Deep, sweet sleep. And then he woke in the dark, sick and frightened, and things were crawling and whispering on his bedchamber walls.

And then his father's burial.

In the dawn Marith went up to the Hill of Altrersys. It was a bare, barren place, grey stones tearing up through the soil of Thealan Vale, black earth. The sea was visible from its height, a thin line of silver, Morr Town and Malth Elelane lay before it, between the hill and the sea. It looked already like a grave and had always been the grave site of kings. The one place on the White Isles where the lich roads did not go.

At the summit were the grave mounds of Altrersys and Serelethe and Eltheia. Small, low mounds, half covered in soil, weathered, slipping away. Their stone still crusted, if one looked closely, with bronze and gold. The tombs of the Altrersyr clung around them, sliding down the hillside. Hilanis. Fylinn Dragonlord. Tareneth Whole Skin. All of them lay there, the great lords, the legendary kings of the past, Marith's kin. His grandfather Nevethyn lay there – if you went up there to his grave on the evening of his defeat in Illyr, the folk of Morr Town claimed, you could hear him moaning in pain. 'Nonsense,' Marith had said when Ti had asked him about it, terrified, when they were children. 'Nonsense.' The maid who had told Ti the story had been whipped. Years later,

Marith had suggested to Carin that they go up there to listen, both of them dead drunk. They had got to the foot of the hill and turned back.

'So now your father will lie there,' said Osen. 'And it's done. So let's get it done.'

'I have some hatha', said Osen. 'If you want some. It might actually do you some good, today.'

Ah, gods. Marith rubbed his eyes. Ah, yes. He said slowly, 'No.'

'Sensible, possibly.'

'Ask me again when it's done.'

'Even more sensible.'

Lord Stansel led up the horses and the bier. A long column of soldiers marching behind, sarrissmen with their long spears, bronze helmets over their faces; archers with ceremonial bows of horn and sweetwood. The barrel containing his father's body. Wrapped and wrapped in scarlet cloth, and he could see it, rotting and oozing into the honey it swam in, the grim face still staring out balefully, the shocked open eyes in the darkness, the hands moving, coming up to its chest to ward off the blows of a sword.

He said to Osen, 'I'll have some hatha, yes. Just a bit.'

Drifted up the hill behind the cart, his head aching, the land and the sky blurred and blurring together into one. Effort to move his head, lift his legs. The colours of the world were all wrong. Thank you, Osen. Gods, thank you.

He'd asked Thalia not to come with him. Not to this, or his mother and Ti's burial. 'I don't want you to see,' he'd begged her. 'Please. Please, Thalia, I don't want you to see it. See me.'

'I saw you kill them,' she'd said.

'Please.'

'Bury her,' Thalia had said. 'Bury him. Then it will be over. But yes, I will not come.'

A great pit had been dug into the side of the Hill of Altrersys. Men lowered the barrel into the pit. It rocked, unstable, one of the men shouted, stifled a curse. Marith's head was spinning. Ill omened, the man shouting, he thought. He stumbled, Osen had to catch him to stop him falling.

'Kill the man responsible,' he muttered to Osen. His voice sounded heavy. Slurred. Hard to get the words out.

Osen's face swam in his vision, shrugging at him. 'You don't mean that.'

'I don't. I . . . don't.' No. Yes. I—' He closed his eyes. Saw colours flickering. Shapes in the dark in his head. What were we, were we talking about? He swayed. Osen was holding him. We're burying my father, he thought.

Osen said, 'Marith.'

A servant led up a horse. Again. Another of his father's horses. Chestnut. Gilded hooves and gold on its head and forelegs. It whinnied, recognizing Marith, pricked its ears, trotted towards him.

'Good horse. Good horse.' It came to him dimly that he had to kill it. He drew his sword. It felt so odd in his hand. Too light. Too heavy. Soft, like it was made of something other than metal. Don't take hatha when you're fighting, Marith, maybe, he thought.

The horse whinnied. Marith killed it. Again the stink of blood. The horse screamed as it died. Servants swarmed over it, flayed it, butchered it, its bones and skin were built up into a tent over the grave pit, earth and stones placed over the top.

It took a long time. The hatha was wearing off horribly. The morning light was too bright. We're burying my father, Marith thought.

'Look.' Osen pointed. 'Look there. Eagles!'

Eagles. They came circling up from the mountains to the north. The sky was very light; Marith squinted. The morning sun flashed on their wings.

'A good omen,' said Lord Stansel. 'They should always come, at the death of kings.'

Marith looked up into the sun to stare at them. Thought of other things flying overhead. The crows and gulls that had gathered wheeled off, shrieking.

Lord Stansel shouted to the archers: 'Loose! Shoot them!' The horn and sweetwood bows were drawn, bronze arrows went flying upwards.

One of the eagles fell. Spiralling downwards. It crashed down with a scream onto one of the kings' mounds. Another came down falling to the south of the hill, into the wheat fields between the hill and Morr Town. The surviving eagles screamed and flew off back into the mountains.

'Two!' Osen said. 'Two shot down. A good omen indeed.'

Marith went up the hill to where the first eagle lay. It was dead. It was dark golden, streaked brown and black, it looked so soft lying on the raw ground dead. Its beak was bone white, splashed with blood. The stones of the grave mound were disturbed, where it had come down.

'Like the last omen was, you mean?' he said to Osen. 'The luck horse? Like that?'

Osen shook his head. 'You've buried him and it's over, it's turned out fine. Good omens and all. Hail King Illyn, dead and buried with his forefathers. Now let's go and get you drunk.'

> No *man can say of him,*
> *That he did not fight his share or give it.*
> No *man can say of him,*
> *That he did not deserve his renown.*

Marith rubbed his eyes. 'You wouldn't happen to have any more hatha left, would you?'

That night they poured oil over the cairn, burned it; the flames burned very high and blue. The dead eagles, burning, the dead horse, burning, all piled high on the tomb of the dead king. The soldiers danced around it, beat out the sword dance. Swords crashing, striking, sword blades beating against shields. The ringing music of the bronze. All night, they danced by the fire. Drank and feasted up there on the Hill of Altrersys, the burial ground of the Altrersyr kings.

'I'm ready now,' Marith said to Osen.

Osen looked up from his cup. 'Ready?'

'Your sword and your life, you swore to me?'

'Yes.' Osen's eyes, dancing. The swords clashed and voices screamed out the paean. The flames on the grave burned up blue, lit Osen's face.

'You meant it?'

'Of course I meant it, Marith.'

The crash of bronze rang out, louder. There were more than just men dancing by the funeral fire. More than just men shouting and laughing at the flames.

Marith said, 'Good.'

The ground rang with the stamping of feet like horses charging. Swords clashed. Men were beginning not to dance but to fight.

Yellow dawn in the east. A new day coming. New things. I buried my father, Marith thought. It's done. He stumbled to his feet. 'Your sword and your life. The captain of my armies. It's time. Come on, then.'

Chapter Twenty-Six

The world. The world is waiting. The *Ansikanderakesis Amrakane* and his Army: the world awaits them. Wonders and glories and triumphs, heartbreak, joy beyond imagining. All of it, it waits, it calls to him.

Morr Town's forges burned night and day and the air smelled of hot metal, fires flickering working their holy magic of change. The bright blaze of liquid bronze. The ringing of gleaming iron. Swords and helms and sarriss points being made. Men came from the mountains behind Thealan Vale bringing the ore to be smelted; deep in the mountains they mined it, bodies soiled with soot and sweat and earth. Thalia saw in her mind their bodies hacking at the roots of the mountains. Boring into the island's bones. Holy and apart like the metalsmiths, the mine men, who knew the secrets of rock and metal run through the earth like veins of blood. The smiths took it, shaped it in the furnace, wrought it with their hammers, the ringing of it came night and day. The living metal glowing like fire sprites. Gods who shouted and laughed as the hammer fell. Trees were felled for charcoal, green wood in the flames. Smoke smell. Death smell. Charms of making. The final tempering must be done in the blood of a war horse. A man's blood, once, Marith said. A growing pile of bronze and iron, gleaming sharp as winter winds, waiting. Each day new soldiers marched in under the gates of the fortress, hearts rejoicing at the lovely sound of the forging, peasant boys and fisher boys with a few days' stale bread in their packs, eager for killing, bright they waited in the courtyards to be given sword and spear and turned out into the camps built on the wheat fields of Seneth. The soil was trampled by their feet and the feet of horses, the air thick with ash and smoke. The spearmen, the servants, the great lords, the young boys practising to swing a sword . . . they were so filled with the joy of it, so bursting and eager. Rushing filled with joy like the green things growing up through the wet earth.

Thalia sat with Marith, helping him draw up his plans. Supplies must be brought in, food for men and horses, they must have tents for the soldiers, camp servants, baggage carts. Great long lists of things. It made him groan.

'Putting more thought to the logistics?'

'Something like that. This is making my head ache. Am I allowed to say it was more fun not putting any thought to it?'

'No. You're not.'

'No. It'll be hard going, Thalia. A fast march, horse pace, no time to rest. Mud and rain and cold, I should think. We need to march light, keep the baggage to a minimum, but we'll need to bring so much with us. If the reports are even half accurate . . .' He looked at his lists again. 'Which is why it's making my head hurt so much. But I'll have some kind of wagon made up for you. A little queenly palace on wheels. Books and blankets and thick furs, servants, a bath tub.'

It was odd, hearing him talk like this, Thalia thought. He had been trained in these things, he knew them. He was a king. Still strange. 'I will be fine,' she said. 'Stop worrying.'

He grinned at her, no longer looking kingly. 'I'm not worrying. I'm putting more thought to the logistics. Also, I might like the occasional bath and fur blanket myself. It's such a wretchedly long way.' A thought seemed to strike him. 'You haven't even asked me where we're going yet.'

'I don't need to ask.' Amusing that it hadn't occurred to him already. Marith and Osen and Lord Stansel, they made war plans, counted off horses and ships and soldiers, thought they were being so secretive.

'Where are we going, then? Tell me.'

'Oh, I wonder. I wonder . . . Where in all the world would he who is called the *Ansikanderakesis Amrakane* go? He refuses to sit at rest by his hearth in his new won kingdom, enjoy his throne for a while, he wants to drag his new wedded wife through freezing cold mud at a fast hard pace. So where is it he is going, so urgently, so impatiently, that he cannot wait even a little while but must be rushing off to? Where is he going? Shall I tell you?'

His face was glowing. He looked like a wide-eyed boy. Wriggling in his chair with excitement as she spoke. 'Tell me.'

Thalia said, 'He is going to Illyr. He is going to win back Amrath's kingdom. Amrath's city. Ethalden. The Tower of Life and Death. Yes?'

'Illyr. Ethalden, Amrath's fortress, His temple, the seat of His power, the mustering place of His armies, the place where Eltheia was crowned queen, where Altrersys was born. The most beautiful building that was ever raised, the most glorious, it shone like a star, men fell down and wept at its beauty.'

Thalia smiled. 'I have read of it, Marith. The people of Sorlost, however, refuse to believe it could have been as beautiful as they say.'

'The people of Sorlost are barbarians. And wrong. As you will see.' He leapt to his feet, almost dancing around the room. 'Even its ruins are beautiful beyond imagining . . .' His eyes closed: he was seeing it, Thalia saw, seeing it as he spoke, as he had dreamed it. 'Its walls were gold and mage glass. Its towers rose shining in the sun. Its gates were carved of white marble. Its chambers were adorned with silk and fur and gems. Throne rooms, banqueting halls, pleasure gardens, crystal fountains, orchards sweet with ripe fruit. A spire of pearl and silver like a knife blade, reflecting the fast running waters of the river Haliakmon and the breaking waves of the Bitter Sea. The city around it was razed to dust, so that not one stone of it now stands. But the ruins of the fortress itself remain. And somewhere in the ruins is Amrath's body. To see Him! To bury Him, finally, after all this time, in a fitting tomb! Always, we have dreamed of it. Every child of the Altrersyr line. To rule in Ethalden, to raise again Amrath's walls, Amrath's throne . . . Oh, Thalia! To do it! Actually to do it!' His eyes opened joyfully, he pulled her to her feet also. 'We will do it. You and I!'

Five times, the Altrersyr kings had tried to retake Illyr. Nevethyn Marith's grandfather's failure just the last in a long series of defeats. Hilanis the Young raised a fleet of two hundred ships. A few planks of timber had been found floating far out in the Bitter Sea by Ithish fishermen. Something that might have been the mast of a ship. The wood was an odd colour. Spongy. Bad smelling. Unpleasantly broken up. Tareneth Whole Skin marched across the Wastes on foot. A hundred thousand men, he had with him. Three thousand at last came back. Did not speak of what they had seen.

On the first day of the second moon after the last night of Sunreturn, the first day of the month called in Pernish *Ianarm*, the month of beginnings, in Literan *Semerenthest*, the month of the unchanged, Marith was crowned again at Malth Elelane with the crown of Altrersys, a fine plain band of silver like a ribbon around his head. Every lord of the White Isles came to do him fealty; Selerie came again from Ith, accompanied this time by his wife, thin and sour, heaped with gemstones, gold bullion crusted on the hem of her dress. She drank a cup of quicksilver every night and every morning: it turned her skin pallid, sparkling, her hair white and crisp as frost.

Feasting after, three days of it, the fortress and the city running wild, fires lit again in the streets and in the courtyards of Malth Elelane, fires burning blue and smokeless on the grave mounds of the kings.

On the dawn of the fourth they rode down to the ships at Morr Town harbour, to sail west to the coast of Ith.

As before at Malth Calien, they sacrificed a horse, raised its body up on wooden stakes. Marith's face was brilliant with fresh blood. The lords marched beneath it to the ships. Thalia as she passed with her guardsmen felt the metal of a knife hilt hard in her hand. The gulls screamed as they circled. A memory of utter darkness and utter cold.

An ill omen, she thought, remembering the last time.

'What is done,' said Osen Fiolt. 'What is always done. It worked out well enough in the end, did it not?'

Marith had given Osen everything Tiothlyn had owned, as well as all the lands that had belonged to the Relasts.

'Yes,' she said, 'it worked out well enough in the end.'

Thirty ships jostled in the sweep of Morr Bay, riding white foam breakers. Low and fast, thin in the water, whipping like snakes. War ships, without shelters: even the king and queen and the great lords of the White Isles must sit all day uncovered around the oarsmen's benches. The sails were the black-red of their king's hair. More ships would come to meet them from the islands as they passed them. Two hundred, in total, promised to the king.

Their masts made a forest. The water sang where their prows cut the waves.

They sailed quickly, borne on Ranene the weather hand's magic. Very soon they were clear of Seneth, racing past Third Isle. When they rounded Toreth Head, the scar of Malth Salene was visible in the earth, the land opened and bleeding. Thalia turned away from it. From Marith staring. She looked instead at the peak of Calen Mon, imagined she saw eagles dancing there on the wind.

A seal head appeared in the water, watching them. Thalia thought: a selkie?

'I'm glad I got to see it again,' Marith said softly, half to himself. 'I gave him a great funeral pyre, in the end, didn't I? Enough to satisfy anyone. Raised a mound such as will be remembered for a thousand years. If I should die, I used to want—' He blinked, ran his fingers through his hair, smiled. '*Seserenthelae aus perhalish.*

190

Night comes. We survive. No matter. Let's go to the prow instead. See what's coming, not what's gone.'

Third disappeared beneath the horizon. A shout went up from the sailors, that they were in landless waters. No more land, now, until they reached Ith. They would disembark there and march on Illyr across the mountains. Even with a weather hand, Marith had told her shortly, no one sailed to Illyr. No one. The very sea itself was cursed. In Ith Selerie would give them further troops, more horses, supplies. Five days sailing, once they left Third, even with Master Ranene's wind. Landfall north of Tyrenae, ten days across the mountains, another thirty perhaps across the Wastes.

'Hail to the sea!' the sailors shouted. 'Sea and sky, have mercy! Sea and sky and wave and wind!' The ship's captain threw a cup of sweet water into the sea from the prow. 'Have mercy!'

A wooden cage was brought up to Marith. Within it, a hawk. Its taloned feet and its beak were bound with leather thongs.

'What is it?' Thalia asked.

'Sacrifices.' Osen laughed. 'Good omens.'

Marith opened the cage, drew out the hawk. It beat its wings, struggled violently, tried to bite and tear at his hands. Osen passed him a bronze knife.

'Sea and sky and wind and wave,' said Marith. The hawk stopped struggling. Lay still in Marith's hands. Marith cut its throat like the horse; Osen caught the blood in a gold cup. The blood was poured into the sea. A sailor scaled the mast and hung up the bird's corpse.

Thalia looked back again a moment towards the White Isles and there was bright light behind them on the water, golden and warm.

A night at sea.

Tents were rigged up across the decks, but there was little comfort to be had, packed in so tightly, the work of the ship to be kept to, lights on the water, cold as there could be no fires, and the ships and the tents and the men smelled. Even the king and queen must sleep rough with the men. Selerie of Ith and his wife had their comforts, on board their ship that was not a ship of war. But Thalia lay awake a long time listening to the creak of timbers, the voices giving watch, the sounds of the water, the sense of things moving under the ship. For a little while at first darkness the phosphorescence had come to the water in a thousand colours. A thousand colours too the light of the stars. These tiny ships on the vastness of the ocean. Things beneath the skin of the water of which men could not dream. A thousand years of darkness, sinking down. Some said the seas had no bottom, went on for ever into the depths. Thalia sat up suddenly, stifled. Marith lay sleeping, breathing slowly, his hands moving to his face. She made a little light.

His sword lay beside him, the jewel in its hilt winking in the light. *Joy*, he had named it. She touched it. Cold. He had drawn it at his crowning and she had seen it glowing in her mind.

She only need raise it. Plunge it into his heart. Roll his body over the side of the ship into the endless water. His beautiful hair streaming out in the currents. Down and down and down. It was not too late.

She lay down again beside him, pressed her arms around him, felt him stir and smile at her touch.

Five days sailing. The empty sea. The empty sky. The creak of the sails. The taste of salt spray.

Eight days sailing. The mountains of Ith to the west small as a painting, rich in quicksilver and copper and gold and tin. Thick and darkly forested. White snow on the highest peaks. Dragons danced once between their summits, wild in the wind. The old kings of Ith tried to tame them, bind them to their will as the Godkings of Caltath their forefathers had once tried. Undyl Silver Eyes tamed the dragon Aesthel by feeding it the flesh of his own children, until his sister killed both man and dragon with a golden sword. Canenoth the Fool thought to do likewise, but the beast was wild and would not be broken, and half of Tyrenae burned.

On the flanks of Mount Pelelion are riven great gorges, that are said to have been made by its body as it finally fell and died.

Ten days sailing. The rich wooded hills of Ith. They made land towards evening in a wide bay six days' hard march north of Malth Tyrenae. A village, half cut off from the land around it by marsh and a deep channel running out to a spithead of shingle, a long beach of pale muddy sand. At the very tip of the shingle, caught against the sea and the sky, a roofless building of white stone, a shrine place to the god powers of the sea. The black ships were drawn up on the beach well clear of the tideline; only Selerie's few ships, smaller but deeper bellied, rode at anchor in the bay. Selerie came ashore with them; a troop of Ithish horsemen were waiting, camped close by the village, to be handed over to Marith for the campaign. These had drawn up in full formation on the spithead, flying the green and crimson standard of Ith and the red banner of the Altrersyr besides.

'Palmest. It was a big town, once,' Thalia heard one of the Ithish tell one of the White Isles men. 'Careful with that barrel there! That's banefire, you fools! Careful! That's better, that's it. Anyway. A big town. Trade. Fishing. Whales. But the currents changed, the harbour silted . . .' He gestured at the channel. 'That's all that's left. Mud choked. Careful, I said! Gods and demons, you all want to be burned? What was I saying? Ah, yes, mud choked. Like everything else in Ith. Why your marvellous lodestar of a king wants to come here . . .'

The White Isles man shrugged. '*The isle of Third is a fine land.* *'Cause everywhere else is mud and ash and shit.* Doesn't really matter where we start from, does it? It's where we're going that matters. And that'll be worth the wait. Won't be mud we're choking on then. You're blessed and lucky that we started here. Show some gratitude. Careful with that barrel there!'

They noticed Thalia watching them, paled, hurried away.

* * *

The tents were set up half an hour's walk inland of the village, on a good flat spur of heath running down into boggy forests, rising again to the north up towards the distant mountain peaks. The air smelled strongly of leaf mould and green stuff growing, spring was coming fast and early, the trees putting out the first tiny budding leaves or covered with drifts of blossom or hung with yellow catkins that danced in the breeze. On the edge of the heath near the king's tent a clump of birches shone pure white. Some of the men made offerings there, water poured around the trunks, a coin buried in the soil, a hair from their head tied to a branch. Osen tried to stop them, said they were coming too near the king and the queen, but Lord Stansel brushed him away. 'Move the king's tent, then, if you must.'

'Let them stay,' said Thalia. She went up herself to the white trees, hung a silver chain from a branch. Her hand touched the wood and it felt cool and alive. Yes, indeed, she thought, a sacred thing. A holy thing.

Servants were setting up, preparing hot water, fussing over furnishings for the tent. She was looking forward to a bath more than anything. Filthy and salt grimed after the days at sea, her hair all knots. Then a hot meal, and hot wine. Sleep in something resembling a proper bed. Then tomorrow there was the wagon for her to travel in, with cushions, braziers, screened windows, books. A very long way, very boring, a dull journey, Marith kept warning her, to reach the pain and wonder of Illyr. The maidservant poured sweet oil into the bathwater. Perfume of roses. Thalia began to unbind her hair ready to wash it.

Suddenly there was a stir in the camp. A voice said something, quiet but firm. Men were getting to their feet, moving. Marith was there, his vile cloak over full armour, holding his sword. Her guards: Brychan; Garet; Tal, leading the pretty cream and gold horse. Osen moving over to Marith, smiling, drawing on his helm.

'Marith? Marith, what's–?'

Marith said easily, 'It's all right. Your guards will take you down into the woods. There's another clump of white trees, I think, about a half hour's ride. Wait there. If I'm not back by nightfall, they're to take you across country towards Immish, then back to Sorlost, if you wish. Or anywhere. There's gold in the saddlebags, enough for you to live well.' He helped her up himself into the saddle, ran his fingers through her hair. 'We're not going to Illyr, beloved. Not yet.'

A groom came up with his horse, the white stallion, its hooves gilded, its head plumed and armoured in red and gold. He swung up in the saddle, arranged his cloak behind him, the horse snorting eagerly at the scent of blood. 'Not until I've taken Ith.'

Chapter Twenty-Seven

His horse comes over the water flying, He feels the water on His legs and then they're across on the opposite bank, throwing themselves into the camp, the others are behind Him, can't keep up, for a few glorious heart beats He's alone going forward at them, His horse rears and comes down with blood on its hooves, the camp is in confusion, men running, shouting, they don't know what to think, what to do, He hears, incredulous, the words 'treachery', 'traitor', He almost wants to laugh at what they're saying.

Now His men are across. He feels the shock of the horses meeting the unarmed men, the shock of pleasure uncoiling as the swords come down. Pleasure at the killing. Pleasure at being killed. He takes a man at a run, drives His sword through; it's so easy, back to this cutting of unarmed flesh, severing it, taking a man apart into pieces and showing him look, that's you, that's what you are, stinking meat and bone. There's no glory, no wonder in the human form. Men are not gods. Look at your shit filled entrails spilling out on the ground: that's you, that's all you are. Meat and shit and it'll be gone, all gone, your life nothing, worth nothing, nothing to remember, a fool's lie.

There. Gone.

He aims higher next time, gets His man in the face. He likes cutting faces. The man's alive for a moment after the sword peels his skin back, flays him open, showing him red and white down to the bones of skull. Noseless mouthless lump. The jaws work gurgling before the man falls. He rides on past, going so fast He's come to the bounds of the camp already, the washing place they've dug, the latrine pit downriver, the horse lines. Shit again, stinking in the wet air. And memories: digging latrine pits for Skie and Tobias, nothing man, boy they laugh at, piss weak butt of their jokes. Men are running, struggling down into the water, He cuts one down through the back of the neck, cuts another's head right off. It's almost a shame there aren't more of them, He thinks, it'll all be over so quickly, He can hear the roar of the fighting behind him, His men killing. Only a hundred of them, the enemy has five times that, but they cut them all down. They will. They must.

His men reach the horse lines and wheel back, more of a fight now, a few are even mounted coming on towards them. He meets one fighting, the white plumes on the bronze of his helm show he's a commander, his sword has a curved blade like a hook. It crashes down hard on His arm, the curve of it pulls Him, drags His sword arm so He has no control. It has tiny, serrated teeth at the tip that sting. He twists and jerks His arm away, there's blood on Him, the plumed helmet hisses out 'Traitor! Betrayer!' as His own stroke is parried wide. Something crashes hard into the flank of His horse, making it stumble, He wards off the curved blade, another sword smashes into Him. Feels the blade tear at His armour and His skin. He whirls round again, brings His sword round hard into the weak area of the neck where the bronze helmet doesn't quite meet the bronze plated coat. The impact jars His arm. A glorious, wet-sand crunch of flesh. Hot blood in the rain. He licks His lips and it tastes iron and lovely, the taint underneath of quicksilver: they drink quicksilver, the Ithish, the nobles, the gods alone know why.

But He can't enjoy it, the other batters at Him, He feels pain in His left shoulder, throws Himself round twisting like storm water, His horse shrieks finally reaching the point almost beyond

His controlling, the dead man's horse tries to bite at Him before it flees. He makes His horse turn and turn, fighting with it too for a moment, gets His sword up and down, parries, hacks, smashes hard into His opponent's right arm. The plated cloth gives, it feels strange the softness of it, thick wadding yielding almost like the feel half forgotten of killing a child. A scream.

He feels almost guilt. But it had to happen like this: it surprises Him, wounds Him, that they call Him 'traitor' as He kills them. Couldn't they see, clear and plainly, that this had to happen? He is king. Amrath returned to them. He will not have allies and alliances and aid.

What did Amrath do?

He killed things.

He kills another couple of them. On foot, stupid ones who never made it to their horses. Gods, He wouldn't have wanted these men anyway, not if they couldn't even make it to their horses in time to defend themselves. He kills another who is mounted, already wounded, the man fighting left-handed with his right hand a glossy mass of red. His horse crashes through one of the cook fires they have burning, wood and ash scatters with a cloud of sparks, the hot charred smell where a body has fallen into the fire, blood smothering the flames. He feels hooves trampling into the ashes, the rain and the blood are putting the fire out.

The sounds of battle are dimming. The ground no longer shakes with the stamp of horses' hooves. He pulls His horse to a stop and looks.

The camp is taken. His own men are standing their horses, panting and looking around, laughing. Ten or so are down – no, a couple more, maybe twelve or fifteen. Foot soldiers are coming up, making a final check to secure the field. He watches as one of them finds one of the wounded, looks about quickly to see who's looking, stabs him fast in the neck. 'Doctoring', as Tobias used to call it.

Osen and Yanis Stansel ride over to join Him. Osen's face is flushed with pleasure, his eyes glow. Yanis looks weary. Blood streams from a cut on his cheek. His left hand, too, is bloody. But it hardly seems fatal. Servants hurry over, unstrap Yanis and lift him down from the armoured frame that holds him on his horse, carry him to his wheeled chair. Yanis' horse snorts and shakes itself. Osen dismounts, kneels, holds out his sword. The bird bone hilt clotted with blood.

Chapter Twenty-Eight

'Marith! My Lord King!' Osen said proudly, 'we have your uncle — the king — Selerie — as you wanted.'

'Wounded?' Marith gestured for Osen to rise.

'Not mortally, no. His arm's cut up, his face is a bit of a mess . . .'

Marith frowned. 'But he's recognizable?'

'Oh, gods, yes. Basically. Just bruised.'

'Good.' Marith stretched, found his own body ached a bit. Strange how one never felt it, until afterwards. The usurper King of Sel fought naked and unarmed for three days without ceasing, mortally wounded in the belly and the chest, and, gods, he must have felt like shit when he finally stopped and the rush wore off. 'I'm going to my tent. Osen, you're in charge of things here. Get this mess cleaned up. I want the horses rounded up. See what's in the tents that's worth having. Burn Selerie's tent with everything in it.' He thought a moment. 'No, wait, give it with everything in it to the villagers. And they can have any of the horses too badly wounded to be fit for immediate use.'

Osen looked rather irritated that he'd be stuck out here directing corpse disposal duties. Think yourself lucky you're not digging the latrine pits, Osen, Marith thought.

'Clearing up the mess is harder than making it, you see?'

'And Selerie?'

'Keep him under close guard for now. That's for tomorrow.'

'And the queen?'

'The queen?' A shock went through him, cold bitter water, salt in the mouth. 'Why? What's wrong?'

Osen laughed. 'No, no. Not our queen. Calm down. Gods, to be in love like you are . . . There are other women living in this world, you know. Look there.' Osen pointed out into the bay. 'Her. Selerie's missus, poor bugger. The enemy.' Through the rain, the Ithish ship could be seen moving off northwards, its sails fat in the wind. Running.

Oh. Yes. Her. 'I meant her to go.'

'You meant them to go?'

'Well, yes. Of course.' Smiled at Osen. 'We've killed everyone here. Who's going to tell the soldiers of Malth Tyrenae what I've done, otherwise?'

He rode back to his own camp. Dreaming of a drink. Several drinks. A hot bath. Thalia. Thalia, Thalia, Thalia. She would be waiting at the grove of white trees, he ordered things prepared then without waiting rode down to find her himself, blood-covered and battered as he was. His heart sang as he went, the trees thick with birds and blossoms, long low evening sun breaking golden through the clouds, her horse whinnied sensing him. He came into the clearing where she waited, wrapped in her dark cloak before the white bark. The horse was tethered, grazing, her guards sat mounted a little way off from her. Her face lit as she saw him. Sun breaking through clouds. Gold and silver of joy. It's not all dust, he thought. Not all dying.

She said, 'Is it . . . Is it done, then?'

'Yes. It's done. Easily.' Marith smiled. 'You'll be Queen of Ith soon enough. Wait till you see Malth Tyrenae! We have nothing, even Malth Elelane, to compare with it. And Ith! The mountains. The forests. The great mines, where rivers of quicksilver run beneath the rock.'

As they rode back she looked askance at the men with loot

from the Ithish camp in their arms. But in the tent she helped him remove his armour. Her hands at the end were soaked with Ithish blood.

The next morning, he ordered Selerie brought to him.

Yanis Stansel brought him, chained so he walked with an odd waddle like he'd shat his breeches, green and yellow bruises all over his face, right arm heavily bound stinking of pus. Already? They rotted quick, these Ithish lords. All the quicksilver they drank, perhaps: they were already half dead and the sword stroke merely reminded their body of the fact. It looked kind of comic, the King of Ith bound and decayed with his legs spread apart, Lord Stansel of Belen with his withered legs in a wicker chair covered over by a rug, his big strong arms and his black beard, his left hand a club of bandages. Couldn't manage the chair himself now, the state his hand was in, an attendant who looked like he might be a young Stansel relation pushed him about like he was in a handcart. Marith saw at once that he hated it and so did the relation.

One of the soldiers with them kicked Selerie. He went down in a sprawl on the leather floor of the tent, a funny squishy sound as he landed on his injured arm. The smell got a lot worse.

'Hello, Uncle. I did say it was your decision to come. That I was perfectly happy sitting in my tent.'

Try to put some kind of strength into it. I am death and ruin and murderer incarnate, I am a man of power, I am a king: I can do this, I will do this, this is what power means, what kingship means, this is what I am, I am not afraid to do these things. I'm not, he thought. I'm not. I am an Altrersyr king, I am Amrath, I am born of the blood of demons. This is what I am. What is in me.

'I'm not going to kill you,' he said. Selerie's face registered nothing. Mad bastard, as Tobias once referred to him. 'Not yet. Later, maybe.' Frowned. 'Gods, you stink of death already. Perhaps I should kill you. You're disgusting.'

Familiar words. A shock, suddenly, a dim memory of Landra

staring down at him, dissolving into light and shadows, her voice screaming 'disgusting, disgusting' at him. Marith rubbed at his eyes, tried to steady himself.

'I'm not going to kill you,' Marith said again. 'Not yet.'

Selerie's face still registered nothing. Self-righteous old man.

'You told me to kill them. It's your fault.'

Selerie said then, 'I said nothing, King Marith.' His voice sounded horrible, thick and rot sodden, his tongue grown too big for his mouth.

Marith said, 'You told me to kill them.'

'I told you the truth about the whore and about your father,' Selerie said. 'I would have stood by you, King Marith *Ansikanderakesis Amrakane*. Fought beside you. So long ago, when you were a child, I had already decided that. I told you, I remember you as child, so full of radiance. I saw you and I was proud of you.'

'Thalia says you lied to me! That my father didn't kill her. That he loved me!' His own voice sounded like a child's voice, high-pitched, hurting. I remember that night in Sorlost, Marith thought, that night when I went through a house and killed everything that lived there, and I hated myself as I did it, but I did it, and I didn't want it to stop. What it feels like, to destroy everything. I remember that. So clearly.

'I would have fought beside you,' Selerie only said again.

'I don't need anyone to fight beside me. I can do it myself, all of it.'

Of course my father hated me, he thought. Of course my father wanted me dead. Filth that I am. Only a pity my mother wasn't killed off earlier, with me still in her womb. King Ruin. King of Death. I should have been destroyed before I was born.

Marith drew out his sword and cut his uncle to slow pieces. Hands, toes, nose, earlobes, lips. Smash in the face to take the teeth out, running off on the floor in little white lumps. Hamstrings. Kneecaps. The rotten right arm at the elbow, so that was a waste of the stroke he'd used to take off the right hand. But the arm was foul. There were already worms in it, even. Doctoring, as Tobias used to call it. Doing the man a kindness. Selerie stayed conscious through all of it, silent, his face set blank, only making little snorting noises to choke up blood, groaning a little when his bowel and bladder control finally failed. When it was done, the soldiers dragged Selerie out again.

Yanis had sat in his wicker chair through everything. He looked green and sick. The young Stansel relation looked mesmerized. The boy was only a few years younger than Marith. A kind of guilt, looking at him staring with big child's eyes, seeing the beauty of it for the first time, the way human flesh crumpled away so easily. Beautiful bleeding! Everyone enjoys it. Anyone who says they don't is a liar. The greatest thing in the world, destruction. Another thing to help one pretend. I'm not rot and dying! I am as a god! Behold my power! I am indeed alive, for I can maim and ruin and destroy!

Comforting, like.

Thalia came in while servants were still clearing up the mess. She wore green velvet, a posy of white anemones nestled in the bosom of her dress. Her hair was braided with gold. She stopped at the doorway. Her mouth opened. Tal and Garet were visible behind her, trying to see.

'What . . .? What have you done? Are you hurt? What's happened?' Then she understood. 'Selerie?' Her voice trembled with pain.

'I didn't kill him. It's less than he did to Ti. What did you think I'd do, let him go? He deserved it.' His voice echoed in his ears, running on and on.

'Did he?' she said, and then she looked at Marith very gravely and said, 'Perhaps he did.'

'It's what is done,' he said. 'No worse than he would have done to me. What Ti would have done to me. What he did to Ti.' Thalia sat down next to him, he curled himself down into her, she stroked her long fingers through his hair. His face felt hot and sore. The sweet, clean smell of her; musty damp seasalt traces on her dress from the ship. The smell of the flowers crushed against her, petals turning brown, pollen smeared on her skin. A tiny beetle crawled off the flowers onto her collar bones.

'Yes,' she said. 'It is what is done. So you said.'

They marched for Malth Tyrenae the next morning. Selerie rode at the front of the column, tied to his horse. Stank so badly they had to shoo the crows off him. Maggots were already breeding in his wounds. They dropped off him dying in a trail behind the horses. His body was poison. Quicksilver leeching from his veins. Still he was silent, though his breath came very loud. Marith tried not to think of him, up there in front. Tolling their passing like a leper bell. Osen rode up several times to look. The boy who'd watched with Yanis, Jeram Stansel, Yanis' nephew, rode up also. Fascinated. Try not to think of it. Try.

There were minor skirmishes on the roads, local men with pitchforks in fear for their farms and their children, a party of swordsmen under the command of a local noble, shouting 'death to the invaders' as they died. A barrel of banefire exploded when a cart jogged, killing ten men and a horse. Clouds gathered on the horizon around the towers of the Malth Tyrenae. All the men of Ith would be gathering to crush him. They must outnumber him ten, perhaps twenty times.

Scouts brought back word that Selerie's brother Leos was mustering on the plain of Geremela, south-west of Tyrenae. Rightly Leos must assume that Marith could not even think of besieging the city with the numbers at his command. Gods only knew what he must assume Marith was thinking. That Marith was mad. Or probably just that he was drunk.

'Is there . . . is there not some danger the Ithish will be preparing some kind of ambush? Fall on us from behind? It seems, um, strange, that we've met so little resistance this far. Can we really believe they are just sitting at Geremela waiting for us to arrive?' said Lord Erith of Third.

'They are afraid,' said Lord Jaeartes of Belen. 'They would not dare. They know we will cut them down if they try.'

Even Jaeartes himself couldn't believe that. The Ithish could fall on them and cut them to ribbons at any moment and they all knew it.

'They don't need to ambush us,' said Lord Nymen the former fishmonger. 'They don't need to pick us off in bits. The only thing we can do is engage them. We're here, invading their country. Proclaimed the *Ansikanderakesis Amrakane* their new king. We have to engage them. They just need to wait. Make us do the work.'

'And we just . . . "do the work", do we?' said Lord Erith. 'Walk straight up to them and engage them? Their tens of thousands or hundreds of thousands against our few?'

Shuffling. Faces looking away. Marith watched them, waiting.

'We —'

'We —'

Osen said, 'We just walk up to them and engage them. Their tens of thousands or hundreds of thousands against our few. Their horse and their foot and their great engines of war. Their choice of battlefield. Their choice of battle plan. Their advantage.' His lords, fussing and eying each other. And Osen Fiolt, who alone understood. Osen smiled with anticipation. 'Then we kill them.'

That night the camp was woken by screams in the darkness. Three men were reported lost the next morning. Two vanished. One cut open with his heart shredded up. The men murmured fearfully.

'Wolves,' Lord Stansel told the army. 'Wolves and deserters. Fuck them both. If you see either, kill them.' Marith knew what it was that had killed them. Thalia knew, had woken trembling. Osen knew, from the way his eyes laughed when Yanis Stansel spoke. Hungry things. Waiting things. But oh, not much longer to wait. The Mara Hills on the horizon, behind them the city of Tyrenae and the Geremela plain. Another few days' march. Scouts brought back the news that Leos had taken the title 'King'.

Three men lost the next morning, one vanished, two gutted and missing their heads. The men murmured fearfully.

'Wolves,' Marith told them. Tried not to see Osen laughing as he spoke. 'Wolves and deserters.' Thalia's eyes were red where she had not slept. They crossed the hills taking the river pass. Green woods and the smell of growing. Bright new leaves, sticky buds that caught on cloaks and the horses' coats. In the trees pigeons called. Blackthorn blossom like snowfall. Catkins. They forded the river at a village called Eseen Elevana: 'the place of the bright crossing' in Itheralik. Possibly. If you twisted the syllables enough. They made camp in the hills by the river, clearing out the village headman's house for the king. On the plain beneath, the lights of the Ithish campfires, like a hundred hundred stars. On the horizon, in the west, the towers of Malth Tyrenae showed, just visible as fine needles in the sky. The Fortress of Shadows. Flames flickered around the quicksilver pools at its height.

Silence in the darkness. Marith reviewed his orders, set down his final plans, slept.

Chapter Twenty-Nine

The army of the *Ansikanderakesis Amrakane* awoke before dawn. Mist was rising from the river. The strange hushed silence of the world. The beating of birds' wings making the branches of a tree rustle. In the village a cock crowed. A dog barking; the sound of water over rocks. A blackbird flew onto the eaves of the king's house and sang. White flowers beneath the hedgerows. The smell of wood smoke and fresh bread.

Quietly the men began to gather themselves. Feed and water the horses, prepare porridge and mulled beer for themselves, ensure ration packs of dried meat and bread are stowed on their belts, their water skins were filled. A final girding of armour, unsheathing and sheathing of swords. Libations before a godstone found at the riverbank: water, beer, coins, scratched smears of blood. The sky turning pink and silver. The blackbird sang clear. Crows and rooks in the woods cawing. A skylark. A thrush tapping on a stone. In the far west, over the city, the red star of the Dragon's Mouth was setting in a bank of pale cloud.

They lined up in the fields of the village, trampling the dark earth where the new corn was sown. Five hundred light horse. Three hundred heavy horse, armed with spear as well as sword, the horses armoured with red plumes on their heads. Three thousand sarrissmen in quilted and studded armour, wielding the jagged-tipped bronze spear. Six thousand swordsmen in bronze corselets. One hundred archers. Nine thousand nine hundred men. Slowly and carefully Marith led them down out of the village, an hour's slow march to the flat plain of Geremela. He himself had the light horse; Yanis Stansel the heavy horse; Lord Bemann the sarriss. With some discomfort, he had given Osen the bulk of them, the archers and the swords. At the front of Osen's lines a lone figure rode, his horse held by an armed man walking alongside. Selerie Calboride, maimed and rotting, his eyes kept whole so that he could see his soldiers die.

The Ithish were waiting. Their lines were longer, thicker, spear fighters ten, twenty deep, a mass of horses tossing plumed heads. The great Ithish warhorns, lower pitched than the trumpets of the White Isles, ringing with the music of bronze. Bells tinkling on the horses' harnesses.

On both sides, the beat of drums.

The armies halted, as far apart as a man might run without being winded or a little more. Marith trotted to the front. Out into the dead land between them, the killing ground where the grass would soon be watered with men's blood. The earth was already churned and pitted from the Ithish horses.

'Soldiers of Ith!' he shouted to the enemy. 'Yield! Your king is mine! Your kingdom is mine!'

Osen rode up beside him, leading Selerie. Hardly recognizable, his wounds black with flies. But the Ithish army moaned like storm waves, seeing him. Marith drew his sword. 'You see what I have done to him? So I shall do to you, and your children, and your cities, and your fields, unless you bow down to me and name me king and lord! Yield! Yield!'

A stir in the Ithish lines. The spears drew apart, opening like a door. A herald came forward with the blue and silver banner. His horse snorted, tossing its head, as it approached Marith. Its eyes were very wide. Blood flecked its bridle, where the bit had torn its mouth. It skittered and snorted and pawed the ground. Frightened. The herald wrestled with it in undignified panic to get it straight.

Another man rode up beside the herald. Leos Calboride. Selerie's brother. Ith's self-proclaimed new king.

'The soldiers of Ith will not speak with you, traitor and betrayer. Parricide, we name you, and false, and king of nothing but ruin and death! We outnumber you tenfold. We are the righteous, whose land you have invaded. The outraged. The betrayed. May the gods curse you.' Leos too drew his sword. 'Death, we name you! Ruin and death! Go back to your accursed kingdom and leave us! Or die!'

Tenfold! The liars! It couldn't be more than eight to one. And they were only ready and mustered at all because they'd been planning on helping him invade Illyr. The Illyians should be feeling pretty outraged themselves. The desire in Marith to ride out at them now, alone, cut them down. Death! Death and ruin! His hand itched on his sword hilt. The white horse reared. But he turned, rode back to his men.

A very long, aching silence, the banners snapping, the snorting of horses, the creak of leather, the tinkle of Ithish war bells. Metal moving on metal. Men coughing and shifting their feet. Neither side moving forward. The Ithish do not need to move. They can wait all day. Until the moon waxes and wanes and the seasons change and the seas rise to swallow the world. This pretty boy with a pretty sword who thinks he is the heir to a god. They outnumber him. Outflank him. They have more cavalry alone than he has men in his whole army. Heavy horsemen, thickly armoured, wielding long bronze spears.

The Ithish lines stretched almost a mile end to end. Horse in front, six or seven lines deep, a wall of infantry behind, sarriss points like the palisade of a town. And there, on a little knoll to the Ithish right, tucked back from the lines, scouts brought urgent word – some kind of defensive encampment, a screen of archers, heavy armoured swordsmen, a woman with a wooden staff. The whisper went down the White Isles' lines in horror. A mage.

Marith's lines were far shorter, interspersed blocks of infantry and cavalry, two corps of archers, one on either flank. A small line of sarriss dropped back behind his centre, in reserve. The Ithish flanks could easily encircle him, close on him like jaws. He therefore angled the flanks backward, his lines forming almost a square. The Ithish do not need to charge first. Marith cannot, for his men will be surrounded and overwhelmed. His whole battle plan must be defensive. And the Ithish have the mage. So they both wait. Drums and trumpets. The stamp of horses' hooves.

Hold.

Hold.

Hold.

The White Isles men begin edging forwards. Slowly, crawling, beetle slow. The Ithish too begin moving. Not even clear if it's in answer to an order: men lined up for battle must meet, and so they begin inexorably to move. All they have to do to live is refuse to go forward. Put down their spears. Nothing in the world and all the gods and demons and powers anyone could do to make them move and take up their arms and kill. But they move towards each other, slowly and inevitably, beyond any possibility of turning back. The secret hidden pleasure of every human heart, that it is waiting to die and to kill.

They are shifting sideways, also, as they move, drifting south-west, Marith's right flank coming slightly forward with his lines angled back, the Ithish lines shifting to keep in check. Again, unclear if this is in answer to an order or just something that is happening, like water flowing one way or another when the floods come. Marith's left are perhaps frightened of the mage, moving slightly more slowly. Or Marith himself holds the right and is too eager, his men moving slightly too fast. The Ithish right themselves move forward faster to keep their lines firm. Inexorable. Inevitable. Good sense. But because of this, the mage on the Ithish right flank is stranded further behind and away from the Ithish lines. Too far, and she will be useless: the Ithish need to keep in total control of the battlefield, keep her close enough to engage. And the Ithish are angry, confident of their numbers, sickened by this treacherous half-Ithish boy and what he has done to their king.

211

The Ithish lines break. The Ithish left charges Marith's right.

The ground trembles. Like an earthquake: in Tarboran they worship the earthquake in the form of a running horse. A crash like thunder and voices screaming. Metal ringing against metal. Dust. The line wavers, thrashing back and forth like a boy cracking a rope. Marith's right were going too fast, too eager: they have summoned the charge. But the Islanders hold. Don't go forward. Don't retreat. Just hold.

Hold.

Hold.

Hold.

The Ithish right, too, lighter cavalry, charge Marith's left. Osen's men. Swordsmen, banefire archers. Osen's voice roars at the troops to stand firm even as blue flames leap over the charging Ithish horses towards them, burning the front line, ripping at them like claws. Like water breaking on the seashore, pulling all that bends beneath it down. The strong, pungent smell of burned metal and burned flesh. Magecraft.

Hold.

Men from the reserve move into the back of the flanking positions, left and right. The centre, sarrissmen under Lord Bemann, move forwards, meet the Ithish centre lines. Long spears warding off the horses. Just dig in. Hold them. Keep them from breaking through. No heroics. No charges. Don't break them. Just hold.

Hold.

On both flanks, the Ithish pushing forwards, coming round to encircle. The last of the Islanders' reserve troops split left and right. Marith's lines now stretching backwards giving slowly backwards, closing in on themselves, the centre breaking apart, the Ithish shouting as they drive the Islanders back. Like a book being forced back against its spine. A crack appearing in the centre, like the spine breaking. The Ithish moving round to surround them. Close up. Cut them down. The crack in the centre of Marith's lines widening. The Ithish battle lines becoming two lines moving inwards towards each other like jaws. Biting. Closing shut. The Islanders holding, but giving ground.

Hold.

Mage fire searing into the left flank, taking Osen's men there apart. The left weakening. If they collapse it is over, the Ithish will cut through them and encircle the Islanders entirely, catching them as in a net, the mage burning them at will. A troop of archers crawling forwards on their bellies, edging round to try to shoot her down from behind. If the vials of banefire they carried on their belts should break . . . The Ithish don't seem to have seen them, too focused on the main body of the troops where the line is wavering, too many men burning, Osen frantically shouting 'Keep the lines! Keep the lines! Just hold them! Hold!'

Hold.

A gap in Marith's centre, his whole army slowly moving apart into two. Not retreating, not breaking, but being forced back and sideways, curved round and rolled up. The pressure on his lines growing. Crushing down and down. Keep pressing. Just keep pressing. Hold. Dead men are kept upright by the press around them. If a man or horse slips and falls, they're crushed. The ground churned to red liquid. Dust. Fire. Screams. Burning metal. Burning flesh.

A gap appearing too in the Ithish centre, the Ithish lines splitting apart to enfold the Islanders' army, moving forwards right and left, leaving the centre weakened. All their forces bent on shattering the two struggling wings. The archers on Marith's right crushed and annihilated. Osen's left falling apart. The archers on the left crawling towards the mage, half of them down and dead, shot in the back as they crawl or burned by their own flasks of green flames. The Islanders' centre, the sarriss under Lord Bemann, pushing hard but moving apart left and right, broken like a broken spine.

Hold.

Everything utter confusion, pressed so tight, everything shattering. Shredded. Choking. Drowning in each other. Crushing too tight to breathe. Eyes staring, swallowing each other's sweat. Everywhere swords and spears and horses and metal grinding remorseless against metal and skin and bone. Push. Push. Hold. The lines wavering. Thrashing like a boy cracking a rope. Osen's left burning. Osen's left falling apart.

Just hold.

Hold.

Hold.

Hold.

Dying. Burning. Shattering. The lines giving. So far outnumbered. Lost.

The lines giving. The cracks widening. Breaking like a broken spine.

The lines giving. The cracks widening. Opening like a door.

A gap in the lines. A doorway. An entrance. Inviting something in.

'Amrath! Amrath and the Altrersyr! Death! Death! Death!'

Marith charged with the last hundred of his horsemen.

The darkness followed him. The shadows.

Teeth and claws.

Chapter Thirty

The noise of the horses across the plain is a roar like men cheering. Hooves throwing up bloody dust. The riders behind Him shout His name over and over: '*Ansikanderakesis Amrakane*! King Marith! King Marith! Death and all demons! Death! Death! Death!' The shadows laugh beside them, dripping spittle, hungry. So hungry. The crash as they meet the Ithish lines like blindness. His coming is like night. His sword lashes out gloriously: Joy! Joy! Joy! Bright blood flies up at the stroke, spattering on His face, He licks His lips at the taste, blood and sweat and dust, the stink of the battlefield, sweet. He kills one man and then another. But you're all dying anyway. Don't you see? He kills another, and another, and another. The sword sings in his hand. Joy! Joy! Joy! His hands and face already filthy with blood.

The shadows come shrieking. Killing and tearing things.

A man is up in front of Him, heavy armour, sword thick and grotty with blood. No, not a man, green flashing eyes and fine cheek bones, a young woman. Blue and silver on her helmet plumes: royal kin. He kicks the horse forward at her, meets her head on, the two horses colliding, swinging out His sword with a shout. The Ithish princess hits back, the two swords colliding like the horses. Sparks. This beautiful moment, when everything is lost but the killing, hitting and striking each other, nothing else matters, nothing else just the two of them and the death in between. Killing. Killing. Kill and be killed. The shadows eat up the dying. They're all dying. All of them. Frightened wide eyes looking at Him a moment. Wounded. Blood on the pretty face that has traces of His own. For a moment it's Ti again, dying in pieces, cut up and slowly falling away into nothing, dissolving under slow long strokes of the sword. The wide eyes understood, looking at Him. No chance of winning. No chance of anything.

On the right flank the press of spears is breaking up, the enemy's soldiers beginning to run. Osen's swordsmen picking them off as they pull back from the spear heads. The horsemen swirling, birds in flight, eddies of water over rocks, swirling around the men on foot, cutting them, riding them down, Ithish cavalry engaging them but the shadows leap and tear and the horses screaming run mad.

The Ithish are dying. Oh, they're dying! Kill them! Kill them all! Death! Death! Death! The blade of His sword shines with light that is clear like morning sunshine. The ruby in the hilt shines red. The mage comes at Him. Blazing with fire. The heat of her power strikes Him like fists. He raises His sword, brings it down on her. Silver light flashing. The sword strikes her like striking stone. A crash that must break mountains. Open a crack in the world. The mage falls dead.

His shadows tear at the Ithish. Devour them. He cannot remember, after, quite what they looked they. Like great cats, sleek with hunting. Like a wolf pack. Like men with long clawed fingers and no face. They devour without mouths, ripping bodies, tearing the life away, gutting through armour, sinking talons into beating hearts. The ground is running with torn bodies. The depth and innermost soul of a man, spilled out there shimmering in the mud. Screams loud enough to tear the sky. A few of the Ithish are trying to fight them. Stabbing. Jabbing spears. The spears snap. The swords buckle. The metal corrodes into rust. The shadows laugh and the earth shakes.

The Ithish lines are retreating. Running. His men push on in pursuit across the plain. Filled with lust for blood. They have held and held and felt the Ithish vice close on them, holding on their spears perhaps five times their own weight. They have thought themselves dying. Now they know they are victorious. They will have no mercy. They will wipe the Ithish army from the face of the earth.

Chapter Thirty-One

At last, when it was over, Marith limped back to his camp. Exhausted. He could lie down and sleep for about a million years. His horse had taken a wound to the leg, he'd ended up dismounted, fighting on foot. On foot, soaked in blood like all of them, he was hardly recognizable. The men hardly gave him a second glance. A woman was handing out mugs of beer and bread crusts. And kisses. Marith sat down on a tuffet and drank thirstily. A troop of foot came in, laughing, singing the song about their beloved king and his big big sword and his cloak as red as widows' eyes. Marith beamed into his mug.

Oh, and there was his horse. Limping also, with blood on its right ear, but otherwise unharmed. A young cavalry captain had it, had obviously kindly thought to look after it. He was leading it looking delighted. Marith wandered over to him.

'I think you'll find that's my horse.'

The captain said, 'Your horse? I think you'll find it's my—' Eyes opened in terror. Went down on both knees with his face in the dirt. 'My Lord King. My Lord. My Lord King. Forgive me.'

Pause. Marith eyed him, thinking, warm and cheerful and holding a pint.

'Oh gods, man, get up. Of course, you were merely looking after it. "It's my Lord King's horse", I'm sure you were about to say. It's a lovely horse; I wouldn't want to lose it and you have my thanks. A purse of gold and a place in my personal guard a fitting reward?'

The man rose, gibbering, mud over the blood on his face. 'Thank you. Thank you. My Lord King. My Lord.'

'Take it to the horse lines, will you?' Marith smiled at him. The captain led the horse off, shaking with overawed delight.

So now, of course, everybody recognized him, he was surrounded by people kneeling, cheering, milling about shouting his name. Orders to be given, the camp to be secured; he sent Lord Bemann marching ahead to Tyrenae with a picked force of horse and half the sarriss. A squad of Ithish horse had got away south over the river, would need mopping up. A few hundred foot soldiers had broken through the baggage train and got up into the forest behind the camp: he sent Lord Parale after them with a troop of swordsmen and the surviving archers to secure a perimeter and set up watch posts in case they tried to creep back. A few Ithish nobles had surrendered: one or two he invited to join him, one or two he killed immediately with his own hand. Finally in his tent he sat down and began stripping off his armour. Osen himself knelt to help him with his sword belt and boots. Stiff and sticky, hardened with blood.

'You've done it.'

'I have, haven't I? The beginning, at least.'

'Well done.'

Thalia would be safe, back in the hills, watching the battle. It felt right, briefly, that it was an old companion of his youth who was here with him in his moment of triumph. Carin's ghost hung between them faint and fading. Osen, surely, had always been his friend. There is no bond closer than the bond of shared killing. Even with Carin there had never been that. Never would have been. The old battle hymns sang of the friendship forged in war, the trust of men knowing they held each other's lives like a gift, that what they did together was like nothing else in the world.

'I'll throw these away?' Osen asked of Marith's boots. They were astonishingly bloodstained.

'Please do. And the armour. It's a vile mess. Get that buckle cleaned up, though. It's a nice one.' His cloak hung from a peg in his sleeping area, burned and tattered at the hem, even more sodden with blood and gore. Almost like lacework. Marith stood up naked, stretched. Osen helped him into his bath.

'When shall I tell the other lords you'll see them?' Osen asked.

'Oh, gods . . . Yes, yes, I'll need to. And the Ithish one. Say two hours? Get wine and meat set out for them. And see if Leos' baggage has cups or anything we can use.' Gods, this had all been easier as a foot soldier with Skie and Tobias. Kill people, stop killing people when you'd run out of people to kill, get rat-arsed to celebrate/forget afterwards. Hot water sluiced deliciously over his head. He opened his eyes to Osen offering him a large cup of firewine.

'Gods, where did you spring that from? You're a mind reader. Thank you.'

'You sometimes have a very eminently readable mind, Marith. To the King of Ith, then.'

'The—?'

He almost looked round, looking for his uncle, then realized who Osen meant.

The lords filed in at the appointed time, some still bloody and armoured, having come straight from securing the field or preparing the next day's march. Beside the lords of the White Isles there were now two Ithish nobles, Lord Alleen Durith of Emralleen and Lady Kiana Sabryya. This last being a young woman with vivid dark eyes and wild brown curls who excited some attention among the men of the Whites. Everyone knew the Ithish and the Illyians had women warriors. They'd been fighting and killing Ithish women warriors a bare few hours ago. But gods, the way they stared at her you'd have thought they'd never seen a woman before. She looked at Osen with a smile: they'd fought hand to hand, apparently, she'd pushed him back before she had to break to help her comrades. Fought valiantly. For a while.

Then surrendered with all her surviving troops, turned on the nearest Ithish and routed them.

He should distrust her as a turncoat. But . . .

'Leos escaped uninjured,' she said shortly. 'Do you wish any pursuit?'

'Bit late for that, I'd have thought,' Yanis Stansel muttered.

'He'll be making for Tyrenae,' said Nasis Jaeartes. 'We hardly need pursue. Just walk in after him.'

'That may be something of an over-assumption,' said Yanis. 'With all respect to My Lord King, of course.'

'Their army is utterly crushed. Annihilated. They have no way of resisting.'

'They could try closing the city gates.'

Lord Durith of Emralleen stirred himself. A Calboride, some distant kin of Leos and Selerie and Marith. 'Lord Leos is not loved in Tyrenae. Especially not now . . .' He tailed off smoothly, looked at them.

'Not now what?' asked Osen.

'You have not heard? I had assumed you knew . . . Leos not only took the title of king. As soon as news came that Selerie was taken, he had the little prince and princess Selerie's children killed. He hardly made a show of it, of course, but enough people know or suspect. I very much doubt the people of Tyrenae will rejoice when he returns in shame.'

Osen said, 'Very thoughtful of him. That makes the king next heir to the Ithish throne.'

Lord Durith smiled at Marith. 'It does. Some might think it was a foolish move.'

'Some might think he had encouragement,' said Kiana. Her eyes narrowed. 'If the Ithish are wise, they will open their gates to you tomorrow without bloodshed and hand him over in chains.'

'If the Ithish were wise, we wouldn't be sitting here,' Yanis Stansel muttered. Gods, what was biting Yanis this evening? He'd led the heavy horse charge and laid waste to the Ithish spears. He couldn't still be pissed off because his left hand was buggered up a bit?

It was time for their king to bring them to order. Marith said crisply, 'We march on Tyrenae at dawn. We assume it will come to battle: gods know, they may still try to hold out. But they'd be fools. If they want a siege, I'll break their walls by dusk. Then let the men loose on them.'

One night's rest and then they marched. Long taut hours going, through sprouting fields slowly rising towards Tyrenae. The city stood on a long ridge overlooking the plain. At its heart the citadel of Malth Tyrenae on its rearing outcrop of stone. So high clouds sometimes shrouded its towers, hiding the flash of its copper roofs, the pools of quicksilver set there. Thus some said came the name the Fortress of Shadows. An ancient city and an ancient keep. Older than Amrath. Older than the Godkings. Older, some said, than men themselves. Before the world rose from the waters Malth Tyrenae stood, crowned in quicksilver, alone above the endless unbreaking waves of the first sea. Its stones were honeycombed by wind and weather, pitted a thousand thousand years. Its halls had seen men rise from the mud to crawl before its lords. Here Amrath had boiled alive Eltheia's parents. Here Eltheri her brother had watched and laughed. Here Marith Altrersyr the *Ansikanderakesis Amrakane* would truly be king.

The army crossed the river Ushen at midday, unopposed. A troop of horsemen rode out of the hills but drew back and scattered towards the city. Lord Bemann had sent word Tyrenae was preparing to surrender, so Marith let them go. No one else was visible, the peasantry huddling in their cottages or fled. The cherry orchards for which Geremela was famous were coming into blossom, pink flowers emerging in clots like thick heavy cream. Marith made a garland of them for Thalia, pink against her black hair. Osen in turn made one for Marith: he removed his helmet, rode crowned breathing in the faint scent. Several of the lords copied, laughing: Kiana Sabryya looked like a fresh young wood sprite and Osen made eyes at her. More a carnival than a battle march.

As the sun began sinking rich gold behind the city, they came to its walls and its eastern gate. The Tower of Shadows stood against the sky like a knife.

The gates were open. In the road before them, two wooden stakes had been set up. Leos Calboride's head topped one of them, staring out at the conquering army as they halted before it. On the other, Leos' body, impaled. A dark red banner flapped in the wind. Lord Bemann's troops lined the gateway. The powers and potentates of Ith knelt at their feet.

Lord Bemann nudged his horse forward. 'My Lord Marith Altrersyr, King of Ith and the White Isles and Illyr and Immier and the Wastes and the Bitter Sea. *Ansikanderakesis Amrakane.* The men of Tyrenae beg leave to speak with you. Will you hear them speak?'

Marith looked across at Selerie, looking back at his brother's dead face. Yes. That's how it feels, he thought. That's how it feels, Uncle, you callous, cruel, merciless, stubborn old man. Shall I tell you he killed your children? Shall I? What must he have felt for you, to do that? 'I will hear them speak. I might even think about listening to them.' He was still wearing the wreath of cherry blossom, he realized, as were most of the lords around him. Thalia beside him looked like a statue of a goddess, the afternoon sun glittering on her garland and her gown of silver thread.

One of the Ithish nobles stumbled to his feet. An old man, grey haired, his back bent. Blue and silver trim on his clothing: more royal kin. A great uncle, perhaps, the pretty princess's grandfather. Marith smiled encouragingly at him.

'My Lord King. My Lord King of Ith. Be welcome. Your city opens its gates to you. We rejoice that you have come.' He knelt very low before Marith's horse, his head so close to the gilded hooves. 'Tyrenae surrenders unconditionally, My Lord King. Malth Tyrenae itself also. We are yours to dispose of. We beg your mercy, My Lord King.'

Marith raised his eyes to the towers of the fortress. Things that might be clouds circling its heights. He raised his voice. 'I accept your surrender.' The man's breath came as a long juddering sigh.

A troop of boys came forward, scattering flowers. Two girls in crimson silk brought cups of wine for Marith and Thalia as king and queen. Two more girls in crimson presented them both with gifts, a first taste of the treasure stores of Malth Tyrenae that he had won. A jewelled sword, scabbard and sword belt for Marith, gold filigree and emerald, quicksilver encased in clear crystal on the hilt of the sword. A necklace of white diamonds for Thalia, tight like a collar around her throat. Ah, gods. He reached out and touched her hand. More flowers as they rode through the gateway, voices shouting a ragged attempt at joy. From windows and doorways the people of Ith stared out sullen and terrified. They had hung carpets and tapestries from the shutters, threw flowers, trembled with fear as he passed. 'The King of Ith!' a voice was shouting. 'The King of Ith!' Selerie beside him was slumped in the saddle, eaten up with flies.

'The King of Ith,' Selerie lisped through his maimed mouth.

Down the long processional roadway, through squares and marketplaces, the voices ringing on and on. 'The King of Ith! The King of Ith!' Blossom falling: they must have stripped the city's trees bare. It caught in Marith's hair, his horse's mane, his clothes. Thalia shimmered in it. In every square a troop of musicians sang the great songs of Amrath. At the windows of a brothel the women leaned out half naked, blowing kisses, shaking their long hair. A cloth merchant had spread his wares in the roadway, silks and fine linens, coloured wools, velvets sewn with copper thread. The horses pranced over them, trampling petals into their weave. From the alleyways, beggars shrieked and flapped their arms and cheered.

Up the slope to the gates of Malth Tyrenae. Here again the gates stood open, more young girls in crimson showering down petals from the walkway at its top, a fanfare of trumpets, a clash of bells. The king's steward came forward to receive them, kneeling with the crown of Ith on a platter in his hands. Servants prostrate, foreheads pressed to the ground. Another girl with the cup of welcome, robed in crimson and gold. Hippocras, this time. Someone had checked and remembered his taste. The tower's guards clashed their swords against their shields. Sang a hymn of praise.

At the doorway of the keep the queen herself knelt in surrender, bruised where she had fought off Leos' assassins, still in the bloody clothes she was wearing when Leos had locked her away. She did not look at Selerie, but clung to Marith's knees as a suppliant. Begged him to let her bury her children in peace. Marith nodded absently. She grasped his hands. Kissed them. Horror gripped him. Tears. I maimed your husband, he thought. With these hands. Her lips were dry and hot. Thalia looked sickened, he saw her touch her own scarred arm. 'Great Tanis. Great Tanis. Have mercy. Have pity.' Osen gestured something; two men in armour dragged the queen away, her voice still babbling out thanks.

Marith rubbed his eyes. Hatha. A strong drink. His hands felt dirty, like he'd touched dog shit and not been able to wash it off.

Lord Bemann came up to him. 'The gates are closed, My Lord King. All the men are inside. Everything is secured. The fortress. The Ithish troops. All is at your command.'

He turned and looked at the waiting faces. Could feel tears in his eyes. Petals. Trumpets. Cheering. Joy. 'King Marith! King Marith! Hail!' At the tower's height the shadows danced and writhed.

PART FOUR

WOUND SCARS

Chapter Thirty-Two

'He's adorable. Adorable. Sweety.' Lady Ameretha Ventuel tickled the baby's face and he made a snuffling sound at her. 'Oh Bil! His hands! And his ears! His tiny little ears! Oh sweet thing!'

'Do you want to hold him?' asked Bilale. She nodded to the nursemaid, who passed the baby over.

'He smells so lovely. Oh Bil.'

Bilale smiled at her friend. 'You should have one yourself, Retha.'

Nilesh the servant girl was amused to see Lady Ventuel make a shivery face.

The baby gurgled. It closed and opened its eyes, flailed around and spat its yellow milk spew onto Lady Ventuel's dress. Lady Ventuel didn't notice.

'Is he good?' said Lady Ventuel. She raised her eyebrows at Bilale. 'He looks so like his father. The same face.'

Nilesh looked carefully away from her mistress as Bilale said, 'He does, doesn't he?'

The baby mewed in Lady Ventuel's arms. It did the thing it did when it got angry, reared backwards in Lady Ventuel's arms like a caterpillar. The nurse hurried over, took it back. Whisked it off to be fed.

'He's a darling,' said Lady Ventuel. 'Oh Bil. And he looks so well and healthy.'

'He's strong for his age already,' Bil said proudly. 'Janush our doctor says he is holding his head very early.'

Lady Ventuel noticed the yellow milk spew on her dress then. Nilesh came up discreetly and dabbed at the dress with a silk cloth.

'Is he sleeping well?' Lady Ventuel asked. She swatted Nilesh away. 'Oh, never mind that. I'll get the dress replaced.'

'Janush says he is doing everything well,' said Bilale.

'Can I see his bedroom?'

'Of course.' Bilale, Nilesh knew, was desperate to show it off. The cot was mother-of-pearl and silver, the draperies very pale green silk lace. The walls and ceiling were painted with green and blue and purple flowers; between the flowers there were red jewelled birds with gold beaks. The room faced north and was deliciously cool.

Bilale cried, sometimes, when she was alone with Nilesh, because so few people had come to visit the baby, admire his room and his cot.

Rumours running everywhere: 'Lord Emmereth killed Lord Verneth! Lord Emmereth betrayed us to the demon! Opened the palace gates to him! Sold the High Priestess to the Altrersyr for a bag of gold!' No one knew where they came from; Lord Emmereth had saved the city, everyone knew that. And yet. And yet. 'Lord Emmereth betrayed us!' It had . . . a taste to it. The latest stories had the High Priestess Thalia presiding over the feast of Year's Renewal, sitting on a throne of diamonds, drinking firewine out of a human skull, wearing a dress so revealing she would have been more modestly dressed naked. No one believed them. But everyone believed them. 'She's certainly grasping life outside the Temple with both hands,' Lady Amdelle had said to Bilale. 'You've got to give her that.'

Lady Ventuel was their first visitor since Lady Amdelle. Bilale's dear friend, and it had taken her almost a month to gather herself to come. 'I've been so worried about you, darling,' Lady Ventuel had gushed when she arrived, 'it must be so dreadful for you, all this.'

The two ladies went up the stairs, Nilesh following. Lady Ventuel of course was enraptured by the baby's room, spent ages cooing over the silver rattles, the perfumed sleeping robes, the miniature bathtub of white glass.

'So how are you, Retha?' Bilale asked when they had examined everything in the room. They sat down on a couch together, Bilale sent a girl for wine and cakes. 'I haven't seen you for so long! You look well.'

'Oh, I'm well enough.' The wine was poured, sweet scented over the sweet baby smell of the room. 'Things are the same as always.' Neither Bilale nor Nilesh looked directly at Lady Ventuel as she sniffed at her cake carefully before taking a bite. 'Delicious.' Her eyes narrowed. Nilesh thought: ah. Lady Ventuel looked like a servant about to ask something, cajole something out of Bilale.

Lady Ventuel said, 'Actually, Bil, the real reason I came . . .'

The nurse came into the room with the baby, fast asleep and delicate as gossamer. It snuffled in its sleep.

'He's the most adorable thing I've ever seen,' said Lady Ventuel. 'You are so lucky, Bil.' Bilale lit up with joy, then, and all her scars seemed to fade.

'Aris is getting annoyed,' said Lady Ventuel. 'The ban on travellers from Chathe entering the city . . . My brother is not pleased. I thought I should tell you. You could talk to Orhan, couldn't you, Bil?' She cooed at the baby. 'Oh, he's such a darling, Bil. The guards at the gates are even stricter, now, and it's all Orhan's doing. You could talk to him.'

'There have been more outbreaks of deeping fever in Chathe,' said Bilale. She too looked at the baby. 'Orhan is entirely right to take precautions.'

Lady Ventuel's face went very sharp. 'The Nithque's refusal to let anyone from Chathe inside the city is costing Aris a fortune. And not just Aris. He's been talking about it to Cam Tardein. Cam is not happy either. Nor is Holt Amdelle. Orhan said it would be rescinded and instead it's stricter than before.'

'Whole villages die of deeping fever,' said Bilale, 'in Chathe and Allene. It's costing my own father. But Orhan is right.'

A mild fever, headaches, like being out too long in the sun. That was how Lord Emmereth had described it to Bilale, when she, too, had complained about the ban on travellers from Chathe entering the city, told him it was costing her father too much. The fever passed, the body felt healthy. Then fever again, worse than before. With the fever came vomiting. Bringing up blood. The body inside liquefying. The vital organs pouring out mixed with bile from the mouth. Raging fever. Screaming delirium. Agonizing pain. Final blessed death. It spread like a dust cloud, unstoppable. Then as suddenly it would stop. One in four might survive, if it were a mild outbreak. One in five. One in ten.

'A few people die in Chathe and it's impossible to get hatha anywhere, and rose oil costs twice what it did, and my brother is losing money.' Lady Ventuel said sweetly, 'I would have thought your husband had enough problems to deal with, without annoying people like this as well. My brother is thinking of petitioning the Emperor about it. As is Cam Tardein. People are not pleased. Really, Bil, do you want people to start feeling angry with Orhan about this, as well?'

They had been spat at, Lady Emmereth and Nilesh, coming back from the Great Temple to give thanks for the child, in the beautiful green silk litter that felt like travelling in a cool bower of leaves. Voices shouting 'Murderer! Traitor!', a rattle of grit and pebbles and then a horrible fat lump of phlegm running thickly down the silk, yellow and shiny, making Nilesh's stomach turn and Lady Emmereth retch.

'It cannot be proved,' Janush would say to Nilesh, over and over. 'Lord Emmereth did nothing. It cannot be proved.' It seemed sometimes to Nilesh that this was a strange thing for him to say. Bilale barely left the house now. The beautiful green litter with its silk like trees in morning rainfall had been hacked to pieces and burned.

'People are feeling the cost,' said Lady Ventuel. Her face was fixed with a smile, she took another bite of her cake. 'They might start to complain. Blame the Nithque. Ask why he's doing it. What it is he might be standing to gain.'

The two women stared at each other. Bilale's scars were very red on her white skin. Nilesh felt herself afraid.

'Your husband has made a lot of enemies recently,' said Lady Ventuel. 'I was so sad to hear about what happened to you in the street. You don't want people to have any further reasons to feel angry, do you? You just need to talk to Orhan . . .'

Bilale said very weakly, 'Retha . . .'

The baby made a little noise and Lady Ventuel said, 'Oh, he's so adorable. Listen to him!'

'I'll talk to Orhan,' Bilale said. The baby whimpered and Bilale took it in her arms, held it very tight. 'My beautiful beautiful baby boy.'

'Look at his little ears, he's a darling,' Lady Ventuel said. 'I knew you'd help me, darling.' She took another cake. 'Thank you.'

There was a knock at the door. Janush came in. He looked very strange. As though there was a weight on him. Crushing him. His face was rigid.

He bent, whispered something in Bilale's ear.

Bilale gave a cry. Her hand rose to her mouth. Her whole body flinched.

The baby stirred. Lady Ventuel said with concern, 'Bil?'

Bilale got to her feet and Nilesh got to her feet also. Stepped forward to her mistress, for it seemed as though Bilale might fall down in a faint on the floor. Bilale said very slowly, 'You need to leave, Retha. I . . . You will need to leave. Please.' She gave the baby back to its nurse, very stiffly, her hands shaking. The baby fretted, began to cry.

'What's wrong? Bil?' Lady Ventuel also looked afraid. And it was so strange and rare and terrible, to see these great ladies afraid. The look on Bilale's face reminded Nilesh of the time long ago when she had sat in Bilale's bedroom, heard a doctor tell Bilale the sickness she was suffering from was blackscab.

Lady Ventuel's face froze. She gasped. 'Oh. Oh Bil. Something has happened to Orhan.'

Bilale said, 'It's nothing,' in such a strange voice Nilesh almost began to weep.

When Lady Ventuel had left them, Bilale did begin to weep. Screamed. Howled. Shook.

'Please, My Lady,' Nilesh begged her. 'Please, please, be calm.'

'A messenger has come from Lord Vorley,' said Bilale finally. 'The Emperor has summoned Lord Emmereth to attend him. Sent guards to ensure that Lord Emmereth is protected on the way.' She raised her hands to her mouth, tracing out the whorls of scar tissue across her lip. 'Has he gone?' she asked Janush.

Janush bowed his head. 'Yes, My Lady. Lord Vorley wanted to accompany him, the messenger said, but My Lord refused. He took his guards, but was otherwise alone.'

'Of course he would go alone.' Bilale picked at the scar. 'Did he leave a message for me?'

Janush said, 'No, My Lady. He did not.'

His death, thought Nilesh. He has gone to his death. To all our deaths.

Bilale's white scarred hands closed over her stomach, her long gilded nails like worms against her dress. '*Your husband has made a lot of enemies recently.* But now it comes . . . Ah, Great Tanis. I should go to my father's. We had agreed that. Send someone to Lady Amdelle.' She looked over at the baby flailing red and angry in its nurse's arms. 'No one will believe it is not his child.'

He is your husband, thought Nilesh. It won't matter, whether they believe it's your child or not. The penalty for high treason: if one of the great families is found to have committed treason against the Empire or the Emperor, they and every member of their household must be burned alive. Janush had talked to Nilesh about it, over and over, on and on. There was no escape. No appeal. No mercy. Janush and Lady Emmereth had watched it done to Lord Rhyl's family. 'They burned the girl who sewed Lord

Rhyl's nightshirts,' Janush had said. 'A beggar Lady Rhyl ordered fed.'

'But it might not come to that, My Lady,' Nilesh said. 'It might be nothing.'

'Nothing?' Bilale's hands went back to the scars at her mouth.

'The Emperor . . . He may only want to talk with Lord Emmereth. Seek his counsel. That is what his post is, after all. Nithque. Counsellor and friend.'

Bilale shook her head. 'For weeks, now, we have feared this. Since March Verneth's death. I told you to send someone to Lady Amdelle!' Bilale shouted. Her voice was harsh: the baby's cries grew louder, more afraid. The nursemaid cooed at it, raised it to her breast. Bilale watched. Wept.

'Yes. Yes. At once.' Nilesh rang the bell. A young man came in, so quickly he must have been waiting outside the door. Every servant and bondsman would be waiting at doorways, whispering in the corners, sick with fear. Some were perhaps already preparing to run away. The man bowed low, pretty hair bobbing. Nilesh gave him his order. He nodded, wide-eyed, looking around the room. There was fire reflected in his eyes. Seeing all the beautiful draperies and gilded wood torn down and running with flame.

Bilale stared at the baby suckling, rubbed at the patterns of her scars.

'Everything will be all right, My Lady,' said Nilesh dully. 'Your beautiful boy . . . Of course it will be all right.'

'Better he had never been born. My beautiful beautiful baby boy.' She glanced at the window. The sky was beginning to grow dark. Thick, weary yellow light. In the gardens evening flowers were coming open; a gardener went around lighting the lamps. A bad time. Any moment they would hear the toll of the twilight bell. *Seserenthelae aus perhalish.* But now comes the time when the death things are here.

A knock on the door, they both started in terror. It cannot be fair, Nilesh thought, all I do is attend her, I know nothing about anything beyond the walls of this room. Why should I burn? Why should I die? What have I done? And the baby. So small . . . My beautiful beautiful beautiful baby boy . . . The door opened. Lady Amdelle came in. From the speed of her arrival and her face she knew what was happening, had set out before Bilale had sent for her.

'Bil!' Her voice frightened. Her face frightened. Nilesh had never seen her like this, this distant terrifying woman, perfect as gems, impossible to imagine how she lived or thought or went about her daily business, her world so far removed from Nilesh's life, so far even from Bilale's. Perfect. But here she was, frightened, looking older, tired, weak, afraid.

The two women embraced.

'You have had no word from him?' asked Lady Amdelle. 'But why now? Things seemed calmer. I had heard nothing. Nothing new has been said. Has it?'

Bilale shook her head. 'I don't think so. I don't know. That last absurdity about the false High Priestess . . . But that was nothing new. More nonsense.'

'Holt is going to see Darath and Elis,' Lady Amdelle said. Holt, thought Nilesh. Lady Amdelle's husband. Very powerful. Very rich. 'Perhaps if we can find some bargain with Cam . . . If we can offer him enough . . .'

'You should have got Symdle married off to Zoa before,' said Bilale. 'He'd have a stake in it, then.'

'That was Cam's choice. And it's obvious why, if he knew any of this. Or started the rumours himself. But it was too late anyway. As soon as March was poisoned, that was ended. We lost.'

'Can Elis not get Leada to try to win over Eloise?'

'How? Eloise told Ameretha she's going to take Leada back to the House of Silver tonight.'

Nonsense. Babble. A part of Nilesh thought: these are the great ladies of the Sekemleth Empire. The great high powers of the world. My mistress. My Lord Emmereth's own sister. How can they be powerless? How can they be afraid? A part of Nilesh thought: they sound like birds. Like little pethe birds, chattering away at each other, shiny bright and meaningless. Little pethe birds in cages, beating their little wings.

'Your father has influence with some of the merchant families. They seem to think Orhan has done well enough for the city. They won't want to see him fall.'

'He's afraid,' Bilale said hopelessly in response. 'Too afraid to act.'

'Then he'll see you and his grandchild die.'

'He says it will not come to that. He thinks—'

A part of Nilesh thought: how can my mistress's own father be afraid?

A part of Nilesh thought: stop talking! What do you think any of this will do? Do you think you can talk it away? Order it away? Buy it? Rattle off enough lordly names? If I was you, I would be running for the gates with a bag of gold hidden in my cloak, as some of the servants are doing already. They prattled on like birds in cages and she wanted to scream it at them. Run away! Run away!

There was a commotion in the corridor outside; Lord Emmereth came into the room. His face was haggard. He looked from his wife to his sister to the baby sleeping suckling, seated himself wearily on a couch. Slumped. One of his body servants fussed around him, fetched him a cup of water and a cup of wine. Finally he waved the boy away with a frown. Turned towards Bilale. His eyes fixed on Nilesh standing behind her chair.

'You, too, Nilesh. And the — and my son.' His voice was cracked as his sister's was. 'Doubtless my wife will tell you all, or the guards I took with me. But a man must have some dignity left in his own house. And a child should not hear these things.' He almost smiled at the nursemaid. The baby stirred, angry at being disturbed in its slumber, whimpering, flailing its arms.

Chapter Thirty-Three

Nilesh went to the library in search of Janush. He would know what was happening. Four of the new guards stood outside the door she had come from, one of Lord Emmereth's body servants prowled the corridor biting at his nails. Two girls were lighting candles in the hallways, looking nervously about them, expecting some great terror to come rushing through the walls. In the library Nilesh found Janush staring at a book without seeing it. He started as she put her hand on the desk in front of him. He, too, looked grey and older. He'd been Lord Emmereth's bondsman for a long time.

'You startled me, Nilesh. What is it? Does Lady Emmereth want to see me? Is the baby fretting again? Tell her I'm too sick to come and speak.'

'Janush. What is happening?'

Janush sighed. 'Why do you want to know, Nilesh? Lady Emmereth will tell you soon.' What he meant was, she wouldn't understand what was happening.

'Please tell me.'

'Did you not hear me? I'm too sick to speak. And I don't even know, for sure. Only spies' whispers. Though I'm told the Emperor shouted loud enough to be heard through a closed door. Lord Emmereth is dismissed as Nithque, Nilesh. Lord Tardein replaces him.'

She did not understand clearly what the title of Nithque meant. Power. More guards. Her mistress happier. Yet also more strained.

And Lord Tardein, she thought. The Lord of the Dry Sea. He had recently broken off his daughter's marriage to Lord Emmereth's nephew.

Bilale shouting at Lady Amdelle: *You should have got Symdle married off to Zoa before. He'd have a stake in it, then.* Lady Amdelle shouting back: *That was Cam's choice. And it's obvious why, if he knew any of this. Or started the rumours himself.*

Lady Ventuel saying sweetly to Bilale: *The Nithque's refusal to let anyone from Chathe inside the city is costing Aris a fortune. And not just Aris. He's been talking about it to Cam Tardein. Cam is not happy either. Your husband has made a lot of enemies recently.*

Our enemy, Nilesh thought. Our enemy. In power in my master's place.

Nilesh said, 'Why?'

Nilesh said, 'Will he burn us?'

'The rumours grow and grow, Nilesh. A man from a village in the eastern desert came to the Emperor seeking audience this morning. He had a long, tangled story about a young man who walked out of the desert, having come from the direction of Sorlost. A beautiful young man with black-red hair and a scarred hand, rich enough to buy half the man's village, he ordered the villagers to kneel to him, he had a sword that shone with mage light. He had a woman with him, rapturously beautiful, black hair, brown skin, blue eyes. Her left arm was covered with scars. As though she had been cut by a knife.

'The Altrersyr demon, they say, has a scarred left hand. From where he killed a dragon with his bare hands, they say.' Janush shook his head. 'The man was an ignorant farmer. The story was old, he was confused over the details. Could not explain why he had waited so long to tell. "I did not think it was important," he told the Emperor! But then, he was an ignorant old man from the desert. He wanted a reward, it seems. I would suspect that he is now dead.'

Nilesh said, 'If the Altrersyr demon truly was here, in Sorlost, then surely Lord Emmereth saved us all. He saved the Emperor's life. He warded the demon off. He cannot be blamed if the High Priestess betrayed us.' *They say he is the most beautiful man in the world,* Lady Amdelle had said to Bilale.

Janush sighed. 'Indeed. That would seem the rational conclusion. But the rumours go on. The Altrersyr demon is raising a war fleet, Nilesh. Recruiting troops. They say he has started to call himself the King of All Irlast. The King of Death.'

'But that is not Lord Emmereth's fault!' shouted Nilesh.

Janush laughed. 'No, Nilesh. It is not.'

'Lord Emmereth is a hero who saved the city. I don't understand. Any of this.'

Janush sighed. 'Neither do I, Nilesh.'

'What will happen to us, Janush?'

Janush shook his head. 'I do not know.'

Nilesh went back to Bilale's rooms. Servants bustled about, finding things to busy themselves with, looking round and staring hoping to see and hear. The baby's wails drifted through closed doorways. Banished, Nilesh thought. A child should not be present to hear of his family's ruin. Bad omens. Dangerous to the baby's mind and heart.

'Where have you been?' Dyani the perfume girl hissed at her. 'She's looking for you.' The boy who sang for Bilale slunk past, weeping. Dyani gestured: 'You see the mood she is in?'

Nilesh went into Bilale's bedroom. Her mistress sat on her bed, she had opened up her boxes of jewels and was looking at them. A boy scattered cedar wood and lavender oil on a brazier. Soothing. Calm. The coals flickered and hissed. Bilale also had been crying. Her eyes were very red. 'Where have you been?' she snapped at Nilesh.

Nilesh knelt at her feet. 'I . . . Walking around the house. I was frightened. Forgive me, My Lady.'

Bilale said, 'He's gone out. To see him. Lord Vorley. He can't be at home even now, didn't even look at the child, he has to go and see him, tell him he's fine. It's all his fault. Lord Vorley's fault. If he wasn't so blind with love for him . . .'

Did Lord Vorley then make it all happen? Nilesh thought. Betray us to the demons? Trick My Lord Emmereth into helping them? I don't understand.

'He cheats on him, you know? Celyse's spies have watched him at it. He weeps as he comes. And Darath knows about it. Maybe he's watched him too.'

Bilale picked up a heavy necklace of turquoises. A rope of green pearls, made two months' journey away in the impossible to imagine sea. Citrines in gold, carved into the shape of flowers, tiny as children's teeth. A ruby pendant the size of Nilesh's closed fist. 'I've never even worn some of these. My bridegifts, some of them.' She threw the pendant across the room. It struck the wall by the curved lattice of the shutters. A chip in the painted plaster. A clink as it hit the floor.

'Better I had died in childbed,' said Bilale. 'Better my son had died in my womb.' Her voice was savage. But she frowned, picked up the tangled useless lacework, took a long deep breath. 'What shall I do, Nilesh?'

'What did . . . did Lady Amdelle say, My Lady? And My Lord Emmereth?'

'Nothing.' Bilale placed her hands over the jewels again. Her nails clicked against them. 'Nothing! We will do nothing. The Emperor has accused him of nothing. They are all equally as weak and afraid.' Her hands went back to her scabs. 'He is dismissed. There is nothing we can do.'

The next morning, Bilale went to the Temple. Lord Emmereth had not come home; Nilesh guessed, from the looks on the guards' faces, the way the servants took an eternity preparing the litter, that he had forbidden anyone in the household to go out. Bilale was already forbidden to go out. Bilale shouted at them to be ready. She was wearing the ruby pendant, a dress of gold and silver silk. Her face was like a mask, with dry, white-edged lips. She kissed the baby tenderly before climbing into the litter. 'My baby baby baby boy,' she whispered. Her eyes ran with tears.

In the streets the litter went fearfully slowly. The curtains were tightly closed, yellow silk making the world beyond like honey or amber or Bilale's citrines. The soft warm pleasure of holding closed eyes up to the sun. It gave Bilale's whiteness a sickly look, though it shaded away her scars. The shadows of the guardsmen moved on the curtains and they could see nothing beyond them. The noise of the streets drifting in distantly, like sounds in dreams. Bilale twisted her hands in her lap. Touched at her scars.

We will all die, Nilesh thought. Not yet, but it will come. I am her servant. My whole life, nothing but her servant. And now when she dies, I will die.

'We only exist because they exist,' Janush had said to her once. 'We are like lice crawling on their bodies, for whom Bilale's beautiful red hair is the earth and the sky and the house of God. If they were to stop commanding us, do you think we would disappear, Nilesh? Cease to exist?' He'd been drunk on firewine. She'd had to call servants to put him to bed. His words had terrified her. Terrified her now.

The litter came to a stop. They had been recognized: voices shouted. 'Murderer! Traitor!' They had at least not been spat on. An attendant handed Nilesh and then Bilale down. Bilale moved so awkwardly, her body rigid with fear. She looked so pitiful, thought Nilesh. So vulnerable. So weak. Her hands shook, as she steadied herself on the attendant's arm. The guards drew close around them. Morning light on their swords. Bilale looked at them with indrawn breath, tears welling in her eyes again. More of them every day. They did not look at her or at Nilesh, looked stone faced at the muttering crowds in Grey Square.

They did not look, Nilesh, thought, as if they would disappear if Bilale or Lord Emmereth stopped commanding them. It came to her, with a dizzying stab of shock, that they could as easily decide to kill Lord Emmereth, or the baby, or Bilale. They had very sharp swords.

She followed Bilale up the steps to the Temple. The last time they had been there, their hearts had been so full of joy. It loomed over them, vast dark bulk as high as eternity, cold with sorrow, oh, Great Tanis, it was itself alive. Nilesh had heard stories of lands far away, Chathe and Ith and Tarboran, where the ground itself rose up hugely to meet the sky. But nothing, surely, nothing could be as high and as huge and as vast as the Great Temple of Great Tanis the Lord of Living and Dying, He Who Ruled All Things, the Sekemleth Empire's God. Bilale went forward through the Temple door that looked at them with wooden eyes. A high, narrow doorway, a narrow passageway, dark as night. Nilesh held her breath as they walked. Bilale's hair showed faintly in the darkness, her jewels, she turned her head towards Nilesh and her skin was visible like white shadows. The dark: is this what it will be like, Nilesh thought, when we die? Then out into the light of the Great Chamber, the bronze walls, a thousand scented candles burning, everywhere gold and bronze and gems. So bright and blinding. Nilesh gasped. Almost spoke her fear and joy aloud.

'From the fear of life, and the fear of death, release us,' Bilale whispered. She reached out, almost took Nilesh's hand.

A priestess was singing before an altar, a high soft song whose words Nilesh could not catch. Far, high up at the ceiling, pethe birds fluttered in a shaft of sunlight.

Before the High Altar, the little dark-robed figure of the new High Priestess was kneeling. She rocked back and forth. Silent. Her body was hunched, very thin, Nilesh looked at her and saw how thin she was, how tiny, her hair was matted and lank. Her body rocked. Twitched. They said she did not leave the altar now until she fell asleep and could be carried away. But that was surely only servants' gossip. The figure rocked, raised thin fingers to pull at her hair. Her fingers were bloody. The people in the Temple looked anywhere but at her. Bilale made a noise in her mouth. Bilale's hands went to her belly, where his body had lain.

243

'My Lady?' A priestess stood before them in her mask. Her eyes through it were sad, she too tried and tried not to look at the child. It was like trying not to look at a beggar with a rotting face.

Nothing can be proved against Lord Emmereth, Nilesh thought. She tried to lose the thought away.

'I wish to make an offering,' Bilale said. Her eyes went to the child and away and back and away, her hands moving to pick at the scars at her mouth.

The priestess tried to smile. 'Very well, Lady Emmereth.'

They went over to one of the many altars, a high one adorned with golden flowers, crowned with rose buds and hyacinth. Opposite to the High Altar, so that Bilale knelt with her face turned away from the child. Someone had placed as an offering a jewelled cage holding a scarlet bird. It trilled as Bilale knelt, showing a green mouth.

'Tamas bird,' said Bilale. 'Pretty.'

'*Nane elenaneikth,*' the bird chattered. '*Nane elenaneikth.*' It beat its wings. The undersides of its wings were black.

'What is it saying?' asked Bilale. She looked frightened.

The priestess said, 'Nothing. It makes sounds that sound like human speech. But it is not human speech. What is it that you wish to give, My Lady?' the priestess asked. Bilale had dedicated a life-sized gold statue of a baby when they came here to give thanks for its being born. Janush said Lord Emmereth had bought a thaler's worth of candles as an offering once.

Bilale reached behind her neck. She unclasped the great ruby pendant on its golden chain. She stretched her white neck as it came off. 'Here.' She held the jewel up to the candlelight then placed it on the altar. After the necklace, she stripped off her gold bracelets, her rings, placed these too on the altar. She said loudly, 'Great Lord Tanis, Great Lord of Living and Dying, Great Tanis who rules all things, protect me and my child, that by your gift of living was given life and birth, protect us and keep us safe and guard us from harm. Oh Great Lord Tanis, Lord of All Things, protect us and keep us from death today.' She bowed her head, her voice dropped. 'Great Lord Tanis, from the fear of life and the fear of death, release us.'

'Great Lord Tanis, from the fear of life and the fear of death, release us,' Nilesh whispered.

'*Ethald emn enik*,' the bird chattered.

Nilesh thought: we are like lice crawling on their bodies, for whom Bilale's beautiful red hair is the earth and the sky and the House of God. And what will we be, when the earth and the sky and the House of God are fallen to dust?

They travelled back to the House of the East. Shouts and murmurs, dust and stones rattling off the litter, sharp drawn swords visible through the yellow silk. Yet Bilale looked almost peaceful, comforted by her prayers. The God must listen, Nilesh thought, to Lady Emmereth. She is so great, so powerful. She must be close indeed to the God. Bilale went to her dressing room to change. Chattering eagerly about playing with her child, some new song she must sing him, how she must tell the nurse to eat more honey to make her milk sweet. 'Beautiful, beautiful, beautiful baby. Baby baby baby boy. Baby baby baby boy.' Tears running down her face. Nilesh sat in Bilale's bedroom on the floor by the window, closing her eyes, letting the breeze from the gardens play on her face. Honeysuckle, jasmine, roses; underneath a foetid odour where they must be cleaning out one of the fountains. A rhythmical clanging as they worked. Bilale came in in a loose dress of pale green like milky jade. The nursemaid came with the baby. Bilale fondled it, kissed its tiny fingers, crooned a song, exclaimed again in marvel at its tiny curled toes. 'What will Great Tanis name you, beautiful one? My baby boy, my baby boy, my baby baby baby boy.' A girl scattered spices on the brazier. Ammalene resin, calming to the mind. The baby made a beautiful babbling noise. 'He's smiling!' Bilale cried in delight, 'my baby!' Bilale sang, 'That's Mummy's hair, little one! Mummy's hair!' Nilesh began to doze.

Bilale screamed.

Nilesh opened her eyes.

There was a man in the room. He had a sword.

Nilesh stared at him.

'Death to traitors!' the man shouted. He waved the sword at the girl by the brazier. The girl fell down with blood coming out of her throat. Bilale screamed. The baby screamed. The man was on Bilale with the sword. Nilesh stared at him. Bilale threw up her left hand, it struck the sword blade and made the sword waver but he grabbed her hair, yanked her head back. Her face stared up at him. Her body was arched back, clutching at the screaming baby, she was making a horrible noise in her throat.

Nilesh threw herself at him, pounding with her hands. A terrible blazing pain in her body. She fell back screaming. Bilale was screaming. Everything was blind with pain. The sword came down on Bilale's arm. Bilale fell down on the floor. On top of the baby. The baby was screaming. Blood was pouring from Bilale's arm. Nilesh hit and hit and hit at the man's legs. Bilale's screaming went on and on. Another voice shouted. There was another man in the room. He had a sword. Nilesh stared at him. Nilesh's head felt very light, like it was floating, her vision fading to dark and movement, her body drifting, numbness in her arms and in her legs. She couldn't see things sensibly. There were lots of men in the room. She was watching patterns, water ripples, shadows, voices were shouting and screaming on and on. Her body was in pain. Something struck her, a voice shouted, she tried to roll away, they were fighting like the knife-fighters in the streets, something fell on her, there was more pain. Bilale's voice was still screaming and the baby was still screaming and a man's voice was shouting and her vision was fading away to white light.

She saw jewels. Candles. Bloody child's fingers, and the creased tiny face of the baby, and Bilale's red hair.

Her vision. Fading away to white light.

Chapter Thirty-Four

Orhan heard the noise from the entrance hall.

Screaming.

Bil, screaming.

The baby, screaming.

He began to run through the house, shouting to the guardsmen. People were running everywhere. Shouting everywhere. Up the stairs, almost falling. His hand went to the knife he wore. In the upper hall the screaming was louder. A smell of smoke. He stopped, shaking. Flesh burning. Bodies burning. The clash of swords. The Emperor's face white with terror, the walls burning and the boy raising his eyes to look at him, *'I'll kill you, then,'* men falling dying, Darath falling, blood and smoke and blood. All this. All this I wrought. The guards formed up around him, a defensive circle with swords out. Through them and over them he saw fire, bleeding, Bil dead, the baby dead, its grub's mouth screaming reproach.

'Get him away! Get him out of here!'

'My Lord—' A hand pulled on his shoulder. 'My Lord, this way, away from the danger.'

'No! No, this is my house!'

Bil, screaming.

The baby, screaming.

What have you done, Orhan?

Orhan pushed his way forward. The guards couldn't stop him, had to follow him. He ran down the corridor towards Bil's bedroom, where the screams were coming from, the burning smell, the crash of sword blades, the blood. The door to Bil's bedroom was open. A girl's body lay crumpled in the doorway. Cut up. Dead. He staggered over it.

The room was stinking chaos, a knot of bodies writhing together, crash and crash of metal, a woman's scream on and on on one note. Men fighting. Bil's guards, fighting each other. Why were they fighting each other? Bil on the floor, crawling. Blood all over her. A girl dead. The baby's nurse dead. The silver drapery on the walls on fire.

Murder, Orhan thought dimly. He stopped at the door. Impossible to go on, believe this, it's some kind of game, he thought, it must be, it will all stop in a moment and it won't be happening. A dream. He stepped forward into the room. Dizzy: the room seemed to lurch and move. Men fighting. Swords. His guards threw him aside, rushed past him, ten men with swords, trained to defend. Orhan held out his knife. His hand was shaking. Bil was trying to crawl towards him. Her hands were bleeding. She, too, was holding a knife. The baby, he thought hopelessly. The baby, the baby. My son.

Two of the guards were surrounded. The murderers. Helpless, against so many. 'Take them alive,' Orhan wanted to shout, 'question them,' but he couldn't bring himself to speak, he watched Bil crawling and the two men cut down. Then the guards were all around him, the murderers were dead, a man was lifting Bil and carrying her to her bed, a man was clutching the tiny lump of the baby that screamed with a contorted scarlet unhatched raw face, he sank down onto the bed next to Bil, watched a guardsman tear the silk hangings from the wall bare-handed and hurl them from the window, watched guardsmen fan out around the room, pull closed the shutters, kick the girl's body out of the way, slam the door.

It was dark for a moment, before a lamp flared. Its light threw the room into soft shadows.

One of Orhan's guards knelt before him. 'Are you hurt at all, My Lord?'

'No. No, I'm not hurt.' His mind wasn't working. Of course I'm not hurt. But Bil. Bil's hurt. The baby's hurt. He shouted out, 'Lady Emmereth — fetch Janush immediately. Why hasn't someone already gone for him?'

'We need to be sure there's no one else in the house, My Lord. It's best if you and she stay here, guarded.'

'But she'll die. The child will die.' Bilale was crumpled on the bed, her face and hands and arms a mass of blood. Her body looked so fragile, weak as eggshells. The baby screamed and screamed and screamed. Bil's bloody hands were cupped over her belly, trying to protect the baby that was no longer inside. 'Fetch Janush now. Or I'll kill you myself.'

The guard stared at him. Shocked. So Lord Emmereth the coward and the traitor does have some strength in him. Oh, I'm good at killing people I'm paying, Orhan thought bitterly. Hired men and servants and women, the old and the desperate and the very young. I only go to pieces when there's any danger to myself.

'Go! Now!'

He turned to Bil, placed his hands carefully on her forehead. She was very cold. Her scars were rough, standing out like faults in rock. This was, he realized then, the first time he had ever touched her.

'Bilale. Bilale. It's all right, Bilale. You're alive. You're safe. It's all right. It's all right.'

No response. Orhan wrapped the bed cover over her, tried to ease a pillow under her head. Her beautiful hair was full of blood. There was a savage cut on her face, snaking down her left cheek, it tore open her scars. Bruising around her nose and eyes. Her hands were cut down to the bones, her fingers shattered, more cuts to her arms, also very deep. Her eyes were open all the time, looking beyond Orhan into the gold of the lamplight.

She held the sword blade in her hands, Orhan thought. She warded the swords off with her hands.

The baby screamed and screamed and screamed.

There were other bodies in the room, slumped about, one at least was moving, making weak horrible noises in its throat. He should see to them, see if there was anything he could do to help them. But he couldn't leave Bil. Where was Janush? If he had gone out, gone down to the bathing rooms, if he was somewhere enjoying himself and Bil died . . .

Finally there was a bustling at the door, a knock and an exchange with the guards inside, Janush came in flanked by two guardsmen, his face rigid with shock. He stopped, stared dumbly at the bodies. A doctor, and he was terrified at the sight of so much blood.

'My Lord . . . Are you hurt?' His voice was shaking. He had crumbs of food around his mouth. 'Lady Emmereth. Oh Great Tanis.'

'Help her.'

Janush knelt beside Bil, inspecting her face and hands.

'Open the shutters. It's too dark to see anything. And bring another lamp close.'

One of the guardsmen said, 'It's not safe. There could be more of them, outside.'

'Open the shutters,' Orhan shouted at him.

'My Lord—' The man went and threw them open. Orhan blinked at the light. Bil's face was white and clammy, it looked like Tam's face had looked when he was dying. Maggot-white with pain. Blood soaked into the white bedsheets. Her eyes flickered slightly. The baby screamed and screamed and screamed. Her eyes blinked at Orhan.

'Wait. The baby first,' said Orhan. Bil's eyes blinked. *Thank you. Thank you.* Janush took it from the man holding it, bronze and red, rolling and thrashing in his arms. Put it down on the bed where it flailed madly like a fish out of water or a beetle on its back. Screamed and screamed and screamed. Blood on its tiny face, matting down its funny fluffy hair.

'He seems unharmed,' said Janush at last. 'From what I can see. But who can tell, the damage it may have suffered? In its mind and its heart.'

Bil's eyes flickered. The bloody stumps of her hands clawed at her belly. Orhan placed his hands on her hair. 'It's all right, Bil. It's all right. Be calm. Your son is safe.' He took the child in his own arms. Kissed its screaming face. Beneath the blood stink it smelled so sweet. My son, he thought again. This child is my son. It quieted a little, as he held it. Snuffled at him. Flexed its hands, screwed its face up, coughed, renewed its screams. Orhan handed it to a guardsman. 'Take the baby out. Find one of Lady Emmereth's women. Whatever she says the baby needs. Now. Go.'

The guardsman took the baby. The screaming trailed away through the house. God's knives. So tiny. What damage it may have suffered. So tiny, barely yet alive.

Orhan turned back to Bil. Janush was kneeling inspecting her. She flinched at his touch. But her eyes were fixed on the door where the baby had gone. Her lips moved. Praying. Great Tanis, be merciful. Be merciful. Please.

'Tear up the sheets, My Lord,' Janush said to Orhan. 'She needs bandaging. A dose of hatha, to make her sleep. Then I will have to try to stitch her wounds.' He looked down at Bil's body. 'But I do not hold out much hope for her hands.'

They started there. On the wreck of her hands. Orhan held a sheet to the wound on her head while Janush cleaned her hands with spirit alcohol, began carefully to sew. Two of the guards held Bil down. Orhan closed his eyes and clenched his teeth. My fault my fault my fault my fault. Even through the hatha her screams were like mage fire. He saw them through his closed eyes. Her hands. Her arms. It went on and on.

'I will not sew her face, or the lesser wounds to her arms,' said Janush at last. He sat back on his heels, sweat and blood dripping down him. 'They must be bandaged, bathed with herbs. I have charms I can place on her, spices to burn to help her heal. For the baby, also. But . . . Pray to Great Lord Tanis, My Lord, and beg

His kindness.' He pulled himself heavily to his feet. 'Pray to Great Lord Tanis, My Lord. I will go and fetch the charms and the herbs.'

Other people were wounded, Orhan remembered slowly. Servants. Guards. Or perhaps they had died while Janush was treating Bil. He ordered two guards to carry her into his own bedroom, had her placed in his own bed. Janush came back with a bone amulet to hang around her neck, a clay figurine in the shape of a bird to bind to her left hand. A brazier was lit and piled with cinnamon bark. The wide blind eyes finally slid closed.

'She will live,' said Janush. 'Great Tanis be kind. I have done the best I can, My Lord. But her hands . . . She was lucky, I suppose, in a way. The blackscab scars protected her, made her skin harder so the blades did not cut so deep. You or I might have lost a hand entirely. Made it more difficult to sew up, though. And may make it more difficult to heal. But I did what I could.' Bandaged thickly in white silk, perfect smooth white as the skin on them must have been before the disease took her. What was beneath looked like shredded leather. Like gristle that a man had chewed and spat out.

'You should see to the servants,' said Orhan. 'Send me word, how they are. If any of them are alive. Examine the child again, ensure it has whatever it needs. I will be here.'

His guards came to report the house clear of any further danger. Two of the new guardsmen, they said, had turned on Bil. 'Traitor!' they had shouted, when they started killing. Madmen, believing the lies. A disgrace to the household and their status as guardsmen, who must be loyal only and forever to their master and his kin. But they were newly hired, Lord Emmereth would need to make enquiries, where they had come from, why the man he had engaged to find them had chosen as he had. Orhan had thought the man he had engaged to find them trustworthy. In that too he had apparently been entirely wrong.

'Find him,' he ordered the guards. 'Punish him.'

'By why not just kill her when she was sleeping?' Darath asked Orhan. 'Or you, in fact?' He had come, of course, as soon as he had heard. So, a while later, had Celyse. Orhan almost ordered the servants not to admit them. He sat by Bil's sleeping body and did not want to be disturbed. The baby cried and gurgled by turns, seemed calmer, he held it for a while, breathed in the smell of its scalp and thanked the God over and over that it had survived. But . . . He clung to Darath, the warmth of his body, the grief in his eyes. And Celyse, also, capable and cold and broken-hearted, talking it through with him and helping him understand it was real.

'I was out of the house with most of the guards' — in your bed, Darath, joy of my heart, arguing with you then making it up to you, your cock in my mouth; let us not forget that, oh my beloved, another taint like ashes to the honeyed bliss of our love – 'I was out of the house, no one was around, they were stationed outside her very door. So easy. Such a show of power, in broad daylight, in my own home.'

'Power?'

'Oh come on, Darath,' said Celyse harshly. 'Think! They weren't deranged madmen. They were paid by Eloise Verneth.'

'My son,' said Orhan, 'for hers. In broad daylight, in my own house.' Darath's face darkened, still, even now, at the words 'my son'. 'It's clear it was planned. Another guard had overheard something, was watching them. That was what saved her, in fact. He rushed in, shouted, raised the alarm. Took a wound himself defending her. And Bil fought like a dragon. Shielded the baby with her body. Fought off the sword blade with her hands.'

The storm came exactly as he had known it would. 'Was watching them?' Celyse shouted. 'Was watching them and had suspicions, and said nothing to you? God's knives, Orhan!' Darath's eyes went to the man on guard in the doorway, searching him or maybe just willing him dead.

'He said he wasn't sure, didn't want to cause an uproar, thought they just wanted to steal some of Bil's jewels to sell. He was frightened, of them, and of me. Who would dare try to do such a thing, in the Lord of the Rising Sun's very house?' He looked at Darath. 'He never changed his story, even at the end. So it may have been the truth.'

Silence. From the next room a woman's voice spoke to the guardsman at the door, asking permission to enter to tend to Bil. The sound of the baby fretting. The cooing voice of a woman in response. How many people have I killed now, Orhan thought? Can I even count any more?

'So I suppose we have to kill Eloise now,' said Orhan wearily. Death breeds death breeds death.

'No,' said Celyse.

Silence.

'No?'

'Bil did give away one of my bride gifts to her as an offering at the Temple this morning,' Celyse said dryly. 'And her baby has just disinherited my son. But no, God's knives, brother! I'd rip Eloise apart with my bare hands if I could! But think. The city's in a state of turmoil. The Emperor's rather lost his burning adora-tion for you. It's pathetically obvious you poisoned poor March. You may still have some shred of lustre in a few eyes now it turns out you saved the Emperor from an Altrersyr demon, but to half the city you seem to be the man who sold the High Priestess's maidenhead to King Death. Your name stinks like carrion, Orhan. Don't make it any worse killing a grieving old woman. Sit back and be the victim who's above all this, and pray to the God things die down a bit now.'

'No—' Darath began.

Celyse cut him off. 'If you can prove it was Eloise, in fact . . . there may be some good in it all,' Celyse said.

Silence. Darath and Orhan stared at her. I think I will be sick, Orhan thought. Celyse said slowly, 'The Emperor wanted calm, given everything. Certainly no credence given to these absurd blasphemous lies. He'll be furious with Eloise. It swings the popular sympathy back rather towards you, Orhan, having assassins creeping around your house targeting your tragically disfigured wife and your baby son. The Verneths have tried to kill you twice now, with a big nasty terrifying mess left behind each time. You only did it to March once, and then very neatly so as it might not even be murder at all. Everyone knows March died of heat flux.'

'That's vile,' Orhan said. True, though. He found himself laughing. His mouth tasted of bile.

'Are you sure you didn't arrange it yourself, for the sympathy?' Celyse flushed. 'I'm sorry. That was horrible. Tasteless.'

But someone else will think it, Orhan thought.

'No,' said Darath. 'No! God's knives! March and Eloise both tried to kill him. March is dead. Eloise dies. Slowly. Worse than March.'

Celyse only rolled her eyes at Darath. A little, angry, blustering boy. The words made Orhan shiver: his lover, who used to think himself notorious because he occasionally chewed keleth seed and had once struck a hired boy in the face.

'Quit while you're ahead,' said Celyse.

So crude.

'You're still alive,' said Celyse. 'Both of you. So quit. Now. Before you're not.'

Darath almost bared his teeth at her. 'Eloise dies. I won't sleep until she does.'

'Then you're a fool,' said Celyse.

Orhan took Darath's hand. If Bil lives, Orhan thought. I owe her that. If she lives, Eloise lives and we go on and hope things can rebuild themselves and it was all worth the cost. Magnanimous in victory. A better and brighter world for my son.

If Bil dies, I deserve whatever will come for me. So Eloise dies. And never mind the consequences.

He looked at Darath. Squeezed Darath's hand.

And I'll do it myself, this time.

Chapter Thirty-Five

A man in a green jacket, bright in the afternoon sun. The sunlight flashed on his buttons. Flanked by men in gold armour. The sunlight flashed on their swords. The gates opened smoothly. Orhan watched them march towards the front doors.

The man in green stopped before the pearl doorway. Shouted clear and slow. 'A message for Orhan Emmereth, the Lord of the Rising Sun, Servant and Counsellor of the Emperor, Warden of Immish and the Bitter Sea, the Nithque of the Asekemlene Emperor of the Sekemleth Empire of the Golden City of Sorlost. Attend, My Lord!'

So the Emperor summoned him again. Of course. Orhan considered putting back on the blood-stained clothes he'd been wearing that morning. Cut a fine and pitiable figure, wife and son's body fluids bathing his favourite coat. Maybe tear it a bit in the hem and the sleeve lining, make it look battered, muss up his hair and get Darath to knock him about in the face.

'My Lord?' The door keep, with a pale frightened face. 'My Lord, a message—'

'From the palace. Yes.' Darath stirred in his chair opposite, where he was sitting trying to read. 'I'll come.' Eyes met Darath's. 'No. As I said before. Alone.'

'Orhan—'

'Send a message, if Bil wakes, or . . .'

Darath stood up. 'Don't order me around, My Lord Emmereth. I'm richer than you are. Even got a faint stream of semi-divine blood, which is more than you can say. And you're not even the Emperor's Nithque any more. Are we walking, or taking the litter? I'd suggest the latter. Marginally safer that way. I don't want too much spit on my coat.'

Thank you. Thank you, Darath. Oh Great Lord Tanis, thought Orhan, oh Great Tanis I am indeed grateful, for You are indeed sometimes kind.

He went to see Bil and the baby. Bil still lay sleeping. The baby was sleeping, he bent and kissed its face. Darath was waiting by the door for him. Looked at him with an unreadable face.

'I do love you for more than the beauty of your cock, remember, Orhan,' Darath said.

They went out accompanied by Orhan's guards, and Darath's, and those the Emperor had sent. So many men with drawn swords. The servants — the surviving servants — no, most had survived, he could not think like that — seemed to hang around the corridors as they passed. Orhan found himself shaking. His head was hurting him, his body rang with tiredness. After-effect of shock and terror, like the dregs of wine. I am the victim here, he kept thinking. As Celyse says. Or it was nothing at all. March died of heat flux. Two of my guards just suddenly ran mad.

The people in the streets stared at the litter. He felt their eyes through the silk. 'Traitor! Murderer! Blasphemer!' Everyone would know something had happened this morning. Everyone would know where he was going, with guards in gold armour at his heels and head. Whispers. Jeering. A few attempts even at a cheer. A great hero! An arch traitor! A master of intrigue! A gullible fool! He himself had lied so many times about that night he no longer had any idea what had occurred. They were Immish sellswords. They were dead bodies. I hired them. I killed them. I remember. Except that he kept seeing those beautiful terrible gaping eyes.

I saw him, Orhan thought. I saw Amrath. I stood and looked at him face to face.

Great Tanis lives in His house of waters. The Emperor lives in a palace of dreaming. The demon is loose in his tower of joy and despair. From the fear of life and the fear of death, release us. Great Tanis, Lord of All Things, hear me: I don't want any more of us to die.

'Stop it,' said Darath, nudging him in the ribs.

'Stop what? What?'

They were almost at the palace. Its dome gleaming in the light. Gold and silver and white porcelain. The bare blind windows, through which a boy who was Amrath the World Conqueror had fallen in shards of brilliantly coloured glass.

'Your face, that looks like you're about to open your throat in the street. You're shaking like a leaf, Orhan. Stop. Try to pull yourself together a bit. Please.' Darath took Orhan's hands. 'Please, Orhan. Try to look like you think we might survive.'

And in through the gates of the palace, where once he and Darath had marched with a troop of men behind them to save the Empire from decay. Up flights of marble stairs, through wide corridors painted with flowers, past open doorways giving on to empty dusty rooms. Past the hallway off to Orhan's suite as Nithque.

Yesterday. He was last here yesterday. It felt like a thousand years.

The doors to the throne room were closed as they always were. Beautiful new carved cedar wood, still with the slight smell of metal and glue from when they were made. Men and women danced beneath a golden sunrise, trees spread forth cooling branches, birds sang in a hymn to the dawn. Eyes and faces peered from the borders. Dead bodies piled invisible just off scene. Great Tanis. Great Tanis. Ah, God, Great Lord, be merciful. Help me, please. Be kind.

'Stop.' Darath squeezed his hand. 'Breathe. You're trembling.'

The doors opened. Smooth and slow. There beyond the blaze

of lamplight. So bright there were no shadows. Walls of gemstones dazzling to the eye. Confusing, like stepping into pure colour. Patterns that made no sense, that moved and shifted until they had no ending, things moving in them, never quite visible, too many angles, too few, walls and floor and ceiling all the same, no depth, no space in the world. Walking forward felt like falling. Or climbing. Walking upside down. The room was huge as the space between the heavens. Flat and tiny like the page of a book.

Orhan had seen it built. Agreed its design principles. Argued with the craftsmen over the price. He'd watched a boy of six stick tiny tiles down into wet mortar, his face screwed up, already half blind. Like the doors, it still smelled faintly of glue and hot metal and men's hands. His skin crawled. Cold sweat running down his clothes. Utter terror as he stepped forward. This room, this room is the power of life and death and the God. The centre of the world.

At the end of the room, floating in the jewels, the great golden throne. Hard to look at, like it had no shape. But the eyes were pulled to it, even as the patterns moved. Painful. It hurt to look. It hurt to look away. The greatest power in this dying dreaming mummified dust city. The centre of the centre of the world.

'You are dismissed as Nithque,' the Emperor had said to him in this room yesterday. 'I do not believe these stories. Of course I do not. But I cannot have you as my Nithque, now, even so. Pray to the God that there is nothing more.' And all his hopes in ashes, there, in those words, everything that he had tried to do, all his crimes for naught.

Darath and Orhan knelt. Darath bent his body forward, awkwardly angled, back curved. Orhan knelt upright, back perfectly straight but head deeply bent. Like a man offering up his neck to the blade. One of only two men who had the right to kneel upright before the Asekemlene Emperor, the Eternal, the Ever Living, the radiant dawn light of the Sekemleth Empire of the Golden City of Sorlost.

The other man was March Verneth's heir.

Everything seemed designed so neatly to remind them all of everything.

Orhan held the formal pose of his status a moment longer, then prostrated himself fully, face flat on the floor. Stronger smell of glue and workmen's bodies. The sharp cold stones pressed on his forehead and nose.

Silence. Dark before his eyes, sparks of colour from the gems as the lamps burned. He could feel Darath beside him. Uncomfortable, unpleasant pose. Still as statues, and his heart pounding and his head hurting and the fear and shock thrumming through him like the beat of a deep drum. Yesterday, he'd last been here. Yesterday. It's just a room, he thought. He's just a man. I almost succeeded in killing him. I saw this room in blood and flame. The gems were cutting into his knee caps. Darath shifted, trying to hold still. I'll have the marks of diamond tiles on my forehead, Orhan thought suddenly, when if ever I'm bid to rise. God's knives, whatever possessed me? Why didn't I choose carpet, or Chathean seamarble, or a layer of smooth cool beaten gold? To be condemned to the fire with the marks of floor tiles embossed on my face . . .

The Emperor said, 'Raise your heads,' in his thin voice.

'March started it!' Orhan wanted to scream. 'He tried to kill me first! I didn't know about the boy! I didn't know!' He pushed himself up carefully back to kneeling. Heard Darath's knees creak. The Emperor sat on his throne looking down at them. A youngish man with a puffy face and a puffy stomach, dressed in black that drained the colour from his skin. Orhan kept his eyes fixed carefully on the bones of his eternal neck. Never look at his face. Never. Apart from that one mad night. 'I didn't know they were led by a demon!' he wanted to scream. 'Tam strung me along! I didn't know! I didn't know! I did it to save the city! I thought it was for the best!'

'The Lord of the Rising Sun. The Lord of All That Flowers and Decays.' The thin voice paused a moment. 'I did not summon Lord Vorley, I think.'

Darath said, 'My Lord Emperor, light of all the world, glory of

260

the Empire, radiance of the dawn that sweeps away the dark of night. You did not. But Lord Emmereth's business . . . is my own.'

'Is it?' Orhan could feel the Imperial eyes tracing between them.

'Yes, My Lord. It is.' The Emperor was eternally alone, without wife or child or parent or lover. And so in all his thousand thousand years of living, he would never understand love, or companionship, or loyalty to one's heart.

Pitiable, then, Orhan thought. So raw and lonely. I have Darath. My sister. Bil. My son. Even Amrath seems to have found his Eltheia, unfortunate though that may be for Darath and myself.

'Very well, then. You may even be right.' The Emperor made a gesture. A pause, then the sound of footsteps approaching across the jewelled floor. Walking slowly. The click of heels on the gems. The Imperial guards behind the throne shifted very slightly. Tensed. A figure came down to kneeling on the other side of him, slowly and uncomfortably, with a creak of knees. Orhan could not move his head to look at the new-comer, visible only as a flickering of gold and scarlet in the corner of his eye. But it was obvious who it must be.

'Raise your head.'

Eloise Verneth did so, awkwardly poised in a deep bow. Darath's knees creaked again.

'My Lord Emperor, eternal glory of our eternal city, joy of the Empire, the dawn sun before whom the world turns its face in joy.' Eloise's voice was afraid.

'Lady Verneth. Lord Emmereth assured me only yesterday of his shock and grief at your son's untimely death. Lord Emmereth sadly agreed that he could no longer continue in his role of Nithque. The city is in turmoil, filled with vile lies. You asked me to dismiss him. I dismissed him. I had ordered you both to behave yourselves. I had believed this business at least was at an end. You told me it would be at an end.'

One should not tremble at a thin petulant voice saying such things.

Eloise shuddered. Her hands twisted against her dress. 'My

Lord Emperor . . . I . . .' She sounded genuinely, deeply afraid. 'Concerning . . . what happened today, my heart grieves for Lord Emmereth, rejoices that Lady Emmereth and her child live. I give thanks to Great Tanis for His mercy.' And she did, indeed, Orhan thought, she did sound grieved. The note of fear dropped for a moment. 'Given that I know, better than any, deeply and painfully and raw in my heart, what it is to mourn a child's death.'

At least your child had forty years of life behind him, Orhan almost thought. The room fell silent. Darath's knees creaked. Everybody weighing up everything, the Emperor trying to think where to go.

Eloise was weeping. Orhan saw that from the far corner of his eye, the tears wet on her face. The Emperor saw it, he thought. The Emperor was frightened by her tears. By the love and grief in this room.

The Emperor said carefully, 'Lord Emmereth and Lord Vorley rescued the Empire from great peril. Far greater, it now seems, than even they knew. We all owe them thanks and praise. Your son, Lady Verneth, began this, I believe. I was displeased by his actions then. I am equally displeased by what has happened now.'

Eloise seemed to flinch. 'My Lord Emperor . . .'

'Lady Verneth. Your son's death was unfortunate. It was deeply' — the head turning towards Orhan — 'deeply to be regretted. I mourn for your loss, and your grandchildren's. I fervently hope such a thing will not occur again. As I told Lord Emmereth only yesterday. Lord Emmereth's household has now also been the victim of a cowardly outrage. This too I fervently hope will not occur again. Am I clear?'

You hope? 'Thank you, My Lord,' Orhan said loudly. Trying to keep the tremor from his voice. 'I fervently hope the same, and am certain Great Tanis will hear us and so grant us our hopes.'

'Thank you, My Lord Emperor,' said Darath. 'I am assured Lord Tanis will hear us and feel moved to grant us peace. We mourn Lady Verneth's loss, and Lord Emmereth's, and rejoice that you pray such a thing shall not befall us again. You grant us the gift of peace, for the God will grant your prayers.'

'Thank you, My Lord Emperor,' said Eloise. 'I am certain that you are right in all that you pray for.' She seemed almost confused. 'Peace in which to raise my grandchildren. One of them so newly wedded. That is all I ask. Peace and safety for my grandchildren and their children after them.'

'A blessing, that he lived long enough to see them begun,' said Darath. 'An honour, to share the wedding rites with him as bride and groom's kin. A tragedy, that he did not live long enough to see these hopes realized.'

These absurd rituals. Twisting, writhing games. They talk like a man farting in his sleep, the great families. As Orhan had once overhead Janush say.

The Emperor made another gesture, nodded his head almost imperceptibly at Eloise. She bowed down, rose, vanished backwards out of Orhan's vision. He heard her footsteps slow and awkward as she walked backwards to the door. A long silence while they all waited. A big room, bigger even than you'd think until you had to wait through someone formally walking out. Finally the doors must have closed. The Emperor moved again, Orhan saw him swallow, the knob at the base of the Imperial throat jumping. Site of a man's soul, the Chatheans believed.

His knees were aching so badly. Gemstones so hard on his shins. Poor Darath's back must be near breaking. Trying to keep looking at the Emperor's neckbones and not at his podgy stomach or between his Imperial legs. The Emperor made some other gesture. To Orhan's surprise and alarm the guards trooped slowly out.

The Emperor said, 'Rise.'

Orhan and Darath got up painfully. The blood rushing back into Orhan's legs hurt. Hot sand dance from toes to knee caps, skipping across his skin. Darath's bones cracked loud. They both kept their heads respectfully downwards, still staring with fixed attention at the Imperial neck. The Emperor swallowed and the site of his soul jumped.

'Lord Emmereth. Lord Vorley.'

'My Lord Emperor.'

'My Lord Emperor.'

Another jerk of the throat. 'A letter arrived this morning. From a source of reliable information, I am told. A man in Ith who was a member of Leos Calboride's deputation to me here. A man who was also a part of Selerie Calboride's deputation to this new King of the White Isles. A man who swears on his life that the new Queen of the White Isles is the High Priestess of Great Tanis Who Rules All Things whose body you showed me in a silver box. He saw her close up, here and there. Says that her face would be hard to forget. And then . . . Lord Tardein my Nithque showed me another letter, Lord Emmereth. One now quite a few days old. From the same source. One of the Secretaries showed it to him. After he had asked for it several times.'

The blood draining from Orhan's face. Darath shifted beside him.

Darath, of course, didn't know about the letter Gallus had shown to Orhan.

And Orhan had ordered Gallus to burn it.

'The King of the White Isles! Here! Drew his sword on me! Claims I cowered and wept at his feet! The sacred title of the Chosen of Great Tanis, on the filthy lips of an Altrersyr demon slumped insensible in his chair! And you knew! All this time, you knew!'

Trying to find anything inside him he could speak. A rock on his tongue. A worm in his belly, gnawing at his heart. Beside him, Darath seemed to burn.

Orhan said, 'My Lord Emperor, I . . . I did read the letter, My Lord Emperor. The . . . the Secretary Gallus showed it to me. He was concerned. We agreed . . . it was lies. Absurdities. I still . . . I still cannot believe. My Lord Emperor—'

The Emperor's throat jerked again. 'I could have you executed for High Treason, Lord Emmereth.'

A knife blade.

And why did he think first of the child?

'I am persuaded by Lord Tardein, however, that I should in my mercy spare you,' the Emperor said. 'Lord Magreth, also, believes that it would be rash to punish you. My people need stability, as I told Lady Verneth. These claims are absurd. Lies. And even if they are not – I defied Amrath when he came for my city, did I not? Drove him off. Sent him away. I protected my people against Amrath's army once. The doings of some petty barbarian who claims descent from him are of no concern to me or to Sorlost. Are they not? If the Altrersyr king came to my palace, he did not harm me. I defeated him. I am the Sekemleth Emperor of Sorlost and thus he failed to lay so much as a finger on me.'

Orhan bowed his head. 'You defeated him indeed, My Lord Emperor.'

'You are spared, then, Lord Emmereth. In my mercy, I will spare you.' That weak, foolish, terrifying voice. 'But. But. Lord Tardein and Lord Magreth, they will be watching you. I shall be watching you. Both of you.' The Emperor shifted on his throne. A new idea in his voice. His own idea, a sudden flash of Imperial brilliance, Orhan thought. 'Lady Verneth will be watching you.'

Darath moved his head. The Emperor said, 'Well?'

'You are glorious in your mercy, My Lord Emperor,' Orhan said.

'You are kind beyond all kindness, My Lord Emperor,' Darath said.

Orhan thought: Cam Tardein and Samn Magreth are merciful and kind beyond all things.

The Emperor said, 'You will remember everything I have said to you. And you will be thankful I am a merciful man.'

They prostrated themselves again, faces pressed into the jewelled floor. Darath's knees creaked. Orhan's neck felt like someone was strangling him. His head was pounding, his legs shook, the sick feeling in his stomach like his entrails were full of molten lead. Silent rage radiated off Darath. Hot dry wind from which there was no possibility of relief. They remained prostrate on their faces for forever, until the Emperor bade dismissively for them to leave.

'Remember I have been kind,' the Emperor said. 'The Emperor cannot be deceived, Lord Emmereth, Lord Vorley.'

Rose with another crack from Darath's knee bones and from Orhan's back. Walked backwards carefully, heads bent to look down at their feet. Hot sand dance down Orhan's legs.

When they got outside the palace, Darath said, very, very slowly, 'I think perhaps we need to talk, Orhan. Don't you think?'

What could he say to that? Orhan said, very, very slowly, 'Yes.' He looked away. 'I'm sorry, Darath. There's nothing else to say.'

Chapter Thirty-Six

Dark room. No one else even breathing. Beams of light picked out the shutters. Raised her head. Beams of light picking out a small door. The light hurt her. Very very bright in the dark. Closed her eyes again. Rough sheets. Thick soft pillows. Her skin hurt. And too hot. She pushed a leg out of the bed. Painful. Her leg hurt. Heard herself groan. It sounded odd. Far away. She coughed. Like a dog barking. Her mouth was dry. Tried to move a hand to look for a cup of water. Her hand flailed. Couldn't move. Hurting. A dry painful sound in her throat. Too dark.

Blind, she thought. I'm blind. Her body was clammy, like she'd been running. Sticky. Been in bed a long time. Blind. Paralysed. Bed-ridden. Bandages on her head and arms. Thirsty. Blind.

The door opened. Very bright light. A figure behind it. Wavered. Too bright. Closed her eyes, whimpering. Light burned into her eyes. The figure like a ghost. Still see it. Too bright. Blind.

She thought: Bilale? My Lady? Bilale?

'Nilesh?' Janush's voice. Worried. Relieved.

'Janush?' Her voice was so dry. Struggling to make her mouth work. Hurting. Odd.

'Nilesh. It's all right. Lie still.'

'Water.' Opened her eyes again. Too bright. Too dark. No vision.

Just shadow. Janush, flickering. Black shadow. White light. Hurting. Wrong.

'Here.' Hands on her head, lifting her. Drank water. Sweet. Cool. Bitter. Something in it.

'Janush—'

Sleep.

Dark room. Someone by the bed. Breathing quietly. Still. Light at the shutters. Easier to see. Dry mouth.

Hurt.

'Who's there?' Her voice sounded funny. Not like her voice. Coming from the corners of the room. 'Who's there?' Whispery. Hurt to speak.

'Nilesh. It's all right. Can you see?'

'Dark . . .'

Light. A lamp, flickering. Hands, bringing the lamp.

'Janush?'

Face. Blinked in the lamplight. She blinked. Face shimmered. Drew together. Mosaic tiles. Making a face.

'Nilesh. Are you in pain? Can you see?'

'Janush.' Coughed. 'I . . . can see.'

'Great Tanis be praised.' Raised her head, held a cup to her. 'Drink this.'

Drank. Hurting. Sweet. Cool. Bitter. Dry lips.

She spat. 'No. Don't want . . . to sleep.'

'It will stop the pain.'

'No!' Dry, cracked mouth. Voice sounded all funny. Coming from somewhere else. Hurting. 'No. Don't want to sleep.'

Cup at her lips. Sweet. Cool. Bitter. Janush holding her head. Thirsty. Dry mouth.

Sleep.

Light room. Shutters open. Sunlight. Breeze. Birdsong. Dusty gold sky.

'Janush?'

The figure by her bed turned his head. Been staring out of the window. Watching birds.

'Good morning, Nilesh.'

'Janush—' Sickness. She bent forward and vomited. Crying. Hurt.

'It's all right, Nilesh.' Held a bowl under her. Vomited again. Silver. Blurred through her tears. Thin yellow spatter of bile.

'Sick . . .' Her eyes were hurting her, sore and hot. Rubbed her eyes, spat into the bowl. 'Janush!'

'Try to keep calm.' He poured her a cup of water. Drank gratefully. Sweet. Lemon and flowers. Washing the taste out of her mouth.

Janush said, 'We had to give you hatha. To help you rest. You're suffering . . . after-effects.'

'To help me?' Memory coming back to her. Fighting. Bil screaming. Pain. 'The baby! The baby, Janush! Bilale's baby!'

'The baby is fine, Nilesh. Alive. Babbling. Smiling at our mistress's face.'

'And Bilale?'

Frowned. His face sad. 'Alive.'

'And?'

'You should rest, Nilesh.'

Sick again. Water and bile in the silver bowl. So violent her shoulders ached. Itching eyes. After-effects of hatha. She had seen them, the hatha eaters, vomiting and crying in the streets. Their faces running sores.

'Janush. Please. How is Bilale? Please?'

Winced. 'Her hands . . . Her hands are . . . She has lost both of her hands, Nilesh.'

Oh Bilale. Bilale. She asked slowly, 'How long have I been sleeping, Janush?'

Janush sighed. 'You were wounded in the head, Nilesh. I thought you were dead. Then I thought you were going to die. Then I thought you might stay . . . as you were. Sleeping, and waking, and screaming. All day and all night. In pain. Blind. Our mistress could not bear it. The sound you made. I gave you hatha, to keep you asleep.'

Eyes itching. Heaviness in her. Tired. Hatha. Janush gave me hatha. Screaming all day and all night in pain. 'How long, Janush?'

He said slowly, 'A month, Nilesh. You have been sleeping and drugged for almost a month.'

She wept. A month! And other things came back to her. 'Lord Emmereth. The Emperor. We went to the Temple.' Her head felt so heavy, confused. 'We have not been burned, then. We are . . . we are safe?'

Almost laughed. 'The girl Dyani died in the attack, and two of the guards. The assassins also. Lord Emmereth sent their bodies back to the House of Silver with bags of gold talents and garlands of copperstem around their necks. Lord Emmereth sits in his study, writing long lists of plans. Then he burns them. He has borrowed money from Lord Vorley, to pay the guardsmen's fee. Lord Vorley came yesterday to demand some of his money back The cetalaso-phrase was reported to have blossomed early. We celebrated the Festival of Sleeping Eyes. Lord Tardein's daughter Zoa married Lord Magreth in a gown sewn with a thousand yellow diamonds. The dead High Priestess was crowned Queen of Ith in a gown sewn with human skin. The Lord of Empty Mirrors held a party last night, they say he served wine spiked with hatha while his lamps burned rose oil.' He tried to smile. 'But yes, Nilesh. We would seem to be safe.'

'That's good, then.' So much of everything she did not under-stand. Why should she understand?

'It's good.' Janush got up, roughly, choking on his words. 'Now that you are awake, I'll see that some food is sent up to you. You may vomit it up, at first. But you must eat. The sickness will ease, as the hatha leaves you.'

Nilesh thought: but the itching. The feeling in my head. That won't leave, will it? Everyone knows that, about hatha eaters. Her hand jerked, as she thought it, to her eyes.

'Try not to scratch, Nilesh,' said Janush. 'I will see if I can find anything, to soothe the skin. Keep the scratches from becoming inflamed.'

She dozed. Empty. A pounding needing clouded feeling in her head. Craving hatha. And exhausted. The vile sticky feeling of her limbs, that had lain so long in the bed. Jumpy, wanting to run around. She pissed and shat in a bowl in the corner. The effect of getting up made her vomit again. Her head hurt. Her arms hurt. Felt strange to walk.

They brought her some food: bread and creamy cheese and soft red fruit. She ate and felt a little better. Then vomited again. Hatha cravings. Her body jittery, like a fly buzzing round and round a room. Two body servants came to help her wash herself. Change her clothes. She felt better. Ate again. Kept it down. Slept a little, afterwards. Didn't remember her dreams. Woke in the night, sat up listening to the silence. Been used her whole remembered life to hearing Bilale breathing in her sleep.

Janush didn't come the next morning. He no longer felt guilty, perhaps, now she was awake. Ate and kept it down, drank water, her lips and skin feeling less dry. Another wash. More clean clothes. Itching madly around her eyes. Already scratched and bleeding. Janush had forgotten the lotion he had promised to send.

It was strange, not having Bilale to tend to. Just lying down. She kept starting up in panic, thinking there must be something she should do. Janush had said something about that . . . About servants, and masters . . . But she couldn't remember. Some things were hazy. It was hard to think, anyway, with the itching pain in her eyes. And her body ached, where the wounds were. Her legs shook from the effort of walking across the room to the pot.

She was lying on the bed staring at the ceiling. The door opened. Janush came in.

'Nilesh. Nilesh. Get up, Nilesh.'

She sat up. Too fast: her head swam and she felt her eyes burn. Sick feeling coming up in her. Fought it down. Janush hanging around the doorway. Disappeared. She went to lie back down again and suddenly the door opened again and Lord Emmereth was there.

He sat down by her bedside on the chair Janush had sat in. Looked at her but didn't speak. His face was tired. More grey in his hair. Heaviness around his eyes, a thinness to his cheeks. It shocked her. He looked like a tired servant. Not like Lord Emmereth at all.

Still he was silent. He shifted and stirred in his chair, seemed about to speak but said nothing.

'My Lord?' she said at last. A servant of a household should never speak to her Lord without first being spoken to. Never. She should be whipped for it.

He shifted in the chair. 'Nilesh. I . . .' Looked away at the window, ran his hands through his hair. 'I am sorry. I owe you great thanks. You and Lady Emmereth, and the child — and our child. I ordered candles lit at the Temple, prayers said for you. Any good a healer or a magic worker could do you. But your head was injured. You may not . . . You may not entirely recover, Nilesh. Janush and I . . . we both fear that.'

Lord Emmereth was the master of her world. If he spoke a thing, it was true.

Lord Emmereth had studied medicine and the mysteries of the body. He would know.

'And Lady Emmereth . . . Your mistress. She . . . As you perhaps can understand, she does not wish to see you again.'

No.

Bilale had burned the litter. The green one. After they had been spat on. Nilesh saw the green before her eyes, cool and lovely, like being in the garden after rain.

Burned.

'It reminds me of what happened,' Bilale had told Lord Emmereth. 'I cannot look at it. I will not have it in the house.'

Lord Emmereth said, 'And so I do not know what to do with you, Nilesh. The proper course for an unwanted servant would be to have you thrown out on the street. But that . . . as you were

272

harmed in Lady Emmereth's service . . . I do not think . . . I can find you a room somewhere, give you some money. A pension. I did that, after all, for others who were injured on my account.'

A room? Some money? Nilesh said, 'Thank you, My Lord.'

'You almost sound as if you are thankful, Nilesh. Curse me, if you want.'

Her eyes were hurting. She rubbed her eyes. Lord Emmereth winced as she did so. Frightening, to see him look so sad and weak. Like Janush did when he'd been drinking. Like he wasn't the great strong centre of the world.

She jerked her hand down.

A tap on the door. The door keep. Familiar. She should know his name. She couldn't remember his name.

'My Lord? Forgive me, but you wanted to be told at once, you said. Lord Vorley is here.'

'Darath?' Lord Emmereth got up. His face was changed. More and even less himself. Eager and frightened, both together, light flashing in his eyes. He left without speaking. The door was still open. She heard the clatter of men's footsteps. His guards.

Chapter Thirty-Seven

They moved her into a room in a lodging house over to the south of the city, a long way from the House of the East, in an area she had never seen before. She went in a hired litter, small and cramped, a bag of her clothing in her arms. The curtains were tightly closed, so she couldn't see where they went. To stop people seeing her, she wondered, or to stop her seeing the way back? As she left the house she had heard the baby crying. Bilale singing it a song. Janush sat beside her, trying not to press his legs against hers. Awkward and hot, his face dripping sweat. Airless. He fanned himself with his hand.

They stopped with a jolt. Nilesh jerked forward, knocked against Janush. Janush tried uncomfortably to pat her hand.

Janush said, 'It's all right, Nilesh. Don't be frightened. Look. It looks nice. Homely.'

A tall house, walls painted green-yellow like preserved egg yolks, stucco crumbling in the sun. Shutters bleached pale. Pale yellow flowers curling around the door. A fig tree grew in a pot by the doorway; a cat slept in the dust in a pool of light.

'The Five Corners,' said Janush.

Got her baggage and scrambled down from the litter. Warm dusty flagstones under her feet. The flowers smelled heavy. The cat woke up and rolled over, stretching out all its legs. Nilesh walked slowly to the door. Strange. So strange. Her legs were still weak. Her eyes itched. So strange. This was where she was going to live.

Janush did not get out of the litter, stayed back behind the curtains, pulled them quickly back closed. Nilesh raised her hand to wave.

'Goodbye, Janush.' Never see him again.

The room was much smaller than Bilale's room. A bed, a cupboard, a table with a jug and a cup. Nilesh looked around for the alcove in which she would sleep. Then realized this was her room. Her bed.

Put her clothes away in the cupboard. Drank a cup of water from the jug. Glazed painted clay, not bronze or silver or gold. Tasted different. Wrong against her mouth. The water was warm from being in the room. Not freshly drawn.

Walked to the window. Walked back to the door. Smoothed the clothes in the cupboard. Walked to the window. Walked to the door.

Sat down on the bed and wept.

She did not sleep well. Different noises. Street noises, coming in through the window, dogs and cats and people and handcarts. Two women arguing in the middle of the night. Gilla fowl arguing at the dawn. She was used to hushed creeping servants' footsteps, ferfews calling, wind in the tree branches, Bilale's breath. The clay jug was empty: she wondered when it would get washed and refilled. The pot under the bed was brimming: she looked at it and wondered what to do, how to empty it. After a little while she went over to the window. From the window there was a view of the street and the houses opposite: people bustled about, two children playing with a ball, a man begging, a woman closing her door behind her, carefully balancing a tray of cakes. A dog came out of an alleyway and almost upset the tray. The children ran off. The woman gave the beggar man a cake.

Nilesh got dressed. She was hungry and thirsty. The pot under the bed stank. She went out of the room. Down the creaking stairs. The creaks made her jump again. On the stairs down there was a mirror, old greening polished bronze, showing her reflection blurred and strange coloured, wide eyes looking back.

She wasn't used to seeing herself alone. Other faces should be there in the background. Bilale, or servant girls, or a boy who came to sing.

At the bottom of the stairs she met Alyet, one of the three sisters who owned the house. Alyet looked her in the face and smiled. Friendly. Nilesh didn't know how to speak to her. Her hands were rough like servants' hands and her hair smelled of work, but she looked at Nilesh in the face and this was her house.

'Good morning,' said Alyet. 'Come into the courtyard. I'll get you some breakfast.'

Nilesh sat down at a table under a fig tree in a pot. Alyet brought her herb-stuffed bread, sour milk, and walnuts. She ate in silence, looking at the tree. There were three other people sitting eating at another table, two men and a woman, talking in a language Nilesh didn't understand. They wore dark embroidered clothing, very different to her own clothes, or lords' clothes, or the clothes servants wore. The woman wore a gold chain in her hair. She laughed, stretched out hands that were worn and rough but decorated with rings and gold paint. One of the men saw Nilesh staring and smiled at her. Nilesh lowered her eyes quickly, went back to looking at the tree.

For five days, Nilesh sat in her room, ate in the courtyard looking at the fig tree, ventured occasionally out into the city to try to walk. Her eyes itched her. Her legs shook. Walking alone, without Bilale and guards and servants, she stumbled through the streets utterly lost. Stared at the streets hoping to see Bilale. The baby. The beautiful beautiful baby baby baby boy. Stared at the people wandering about buying selling arguing laughing. Doing things.

'We are like lice crawling on their bodies, for whom Bilale's beautiful red hair is the earth and the sky and the house of God.'

That was what Janush had said, that she hadn't been able to remember.

On the fifth night, she went to bed early, worn out from walking about. Her head ached. It often ached. Her eyes itched painful as cuts. Janush had said it might stop, eventually. She did not think it would stop. Once in bed she lay awake a long time, listening to the noises of the building that were not the noises she was used to. It came to her that she was tense, waiting for Bilale to call. She was always tense. Always waiting. It came to her that she didn't need to wait. The realization went through her with a shock. Like drinking ice-cold water. She sat up, clutching her body in fear.

Then she heard the screams.

It was so very like the screaming before, in Bilale's room. A woman's screams. Terror. Grief. Nilesh whimpered and screamed herself. Saw the things she couldn't remember, blood and men with swords and Bilale without her hands.

The screaming stopped. Started again, more like crying. Someone shouted something she couldn't understand. Voices in the corridor outside, whispering, urgent. A door opening, slamming again. Footsteps, moving fast. Nilesh opened the door a crack and peered out. The ghosts of men with swords fighting, Bilale crawling in blood. Closed her eyes, opened them. The corridor of the lodging house, the creaky stairs, the old bronze mirror, cobwebs in the furthest corners of the walls. Nothing. Then the door of the room opposite flew open. Lamplight, flickering, making shadows; in the light, the foreign woman with the gold rings. Her dress was stained. It looked black in the lamplight. She was crying. Screaming. She was terrified. A vile smell filled the corridor. Sweet and bloody and fishy and rank. Nilesh choked, nauseous. The woman ran down the stairs into the dark. Nilesh saw what was behind her in the room. A bed, with a man's body in it. A man by the bed, looking down, appalled. Dark stains on the bedclothes and the floor.

The woman ran up the corridor again, still screaming. Alyet's sister Navala came up after her, holding a knife. Navala shouted, waved the knife, gestured at the room. The woman's screams grew louder. Moved forwards towards Navala. Navala leapt backwards, raising the knife.

Navala shouted, 'Get away from me! Get away!' Jabbed the knife at the woman. The woman screamed, trembling between the doorway and the knife blade.

'Get away! Get away!'

A creak from the stairs. Alyet came down from the top floor, holding a lamp. Tamale, the third sister, behind her.

'No!' Navala screamed. 'Go back upstairs! Go! Now!'

Tamale pushed past Alyet, came down the stairs. Saw the woman and the open door. Screamed. Navala was still screaming 'Get away! Get away!' The lamp in Alyet's hands and the lamp in the bedroom flickered, made the shadows dance. The smell in the air was choking. Latrines and filthy bodies, menstrual clouts, the muck at the bottom of the fountain when a bird had got caught there and drowned. Nilesh thought she would be sick at the smell. The man in the room came out to the doorway, grabbed at the woman. The woman struck at him. Navala brandished her knife, shouted, 'Stay back! Stay back!' The woman bent forward like she was bowing. Vomited stinking steaming bloody filth at Tamale's feet. Tamale shrieked. The woman swayed on her feet, making a gurgling choking noise, black filth dripping down her face; the man caught her, pulled her back into the room, slammed the door. Tamale stood with black vomit on her dress, shaking. Her sisters stared at her. The lamps they held shook and shook in their hands. From behind the door the woman's voice screamed out.

For the next two nights and days, Nilesh kept in her room. The house rang with noises, sobs and shouting, footsteps up and down the corridor, a woman's mad despairing laugh, the tramp of soldiers' boots on the stairs. The woman with the gold rings died in the morning. Or stopped screaming, at least. More screams later, wailing crying howls of pain. From upstairs, this time: Alyet, Nilesh guessed, or Navala, or Tamale. She heard them stumbling up and down the stairs, fetching water, trying to find herbs and charm spells that might bring relief. They brought a wonderworker, the first morning, shortly after the foreign women died. Then a doctor. Nilesh listened to his shouts of terror as he fled the house. Cursing them. It was after that that the soldiers came. Nilesh heard Alyet pleading with the soldiers downstairs in the entranceway, begging them not to come in, telling them all was well. 'Just a flux from bad meat,' she kept sobbing. 'Bad meat. A butcher sold us bad meat.' Footsteps on the stairs. The sound of a door opening. Nilesh crouched by her door. A crack she could peep through, just about, a little view of floorboards and the opposite wall. The soldiers trooped into the foreign woman's bedroom. Cries of horror. The smell when they opened the door. The soldiers ran out again, shouting. One stopped in the corridor outside Nilesh's door and was sick. Nilesh crouched trying not to gag at the man vomiting. Trying not to move as he leaned moaning against her door. Her heart pounded so loudly. Trying not to breathe. The soldier stumbled off down the stairs, muttering. 'God's knives, God's knives.' The smell of filth came so strong under the door. She heard voices shouting in the entranceway. A crash of metal. Silence. The door to the house slammed.

A while later came the sound of hammering.

Confusion. And then she understood.

They were nailing the front door shut.

'What then is the cure?' Nilesh had asked Janush. 'For deeping fever. If it is as terrible as our master says.'

'Burning lavender and sysius berries can help ward it off,' Janush had told her. 'Mint, for a general cleaning of the air. The Chatheans sacrifice cats to the disease as god-brought, drink a medicine of wine lees and rose hips and cats' blood. One can repeat the chant of Semethest. Bind to your chest the ashes of peacock feathers dipped in honey. Sing the hymn of the new sun.

'But all these remedies only work if the disease is caught early, before the sufferer realizes that they are sick.'

'What if the sufferer does not realize, then?' Nilesh had asked. 'Until after they have become sick?'

'Ah. Then, then, Nilesh, there is only one remedy. Pray to the Lord Tanis. And open the veins in your wrists.'

The morning of the third day, the house was silent. The stink coming in under the door was heavier. Even worse than before. Nilesh sat on the bed staring at the wall and the light coming in through the shutters. The water jug was empty. Had been empty for a night and a day. The pisspot was overflowing. Her stomach ached with needing to eat. The sounds of the city drifted up. But more distant. Quieter. Some kind of hard edge. She kept thinking she heard screaming. But that was maybe in her mind, a ringing echo, like when Lord Emmereth had had some work done in the courtyard and the workmen had dropped a bronze slab.

She had to get up. Get out. She was sticky and sweaty and thirsty and hungry and the room stank from the pisspot that buzzed with flies. The whole house stank. The whole house was full of flies. Everyone in the house, she supposed, was dead.

Nilesh opened the door. Clouds of flies in the corridor, fat and heavy, buzzing joyful at the threshold to the woman's room. Black beetles. Don't look, she thought. Don't look. Don't look.

She made herself walk to the stairs. Black beetles on the floor and walls. The air was thick with flies. The smell. Oh god's knives, the smell. Her legs were weak with hunger, her mouth dry; her lips felt puffy and sticky, not a part of herself. The house was very hot. She paused at the stairs, listening. No human sound from above, where the three sisters slept. She went down the stairs into the entranceway. Alyet lay on the floor on the bottom step. Her stomach was cut open. Dead. Blood and filth and beetles and maggots and flies. Nilesh would have to step over her to get past. Thought for a moment of going back, upstairs, hiding back in her room.

You have to go past, she thought. You have to get out. Thirsty. So thirsty. You have to get water. You'll die of thirst. She gathered her skirt high round her thighs. Could feel the filth sticking to her as she stepped. The flies rose in a cloud around her. The noise the beetles made. She froze with her foot raised, couldn't get over, a dead thing before her with beetles scrabbling in its stomach, the flies getting between her legs, getting caught in her clothes and her hair, landing on her, putting the filth from the thing on her skin.

You have to go past. You have to go past. She put her foot down, the blood was spread and seeping and running so that she had to step in it, blood and liquid on her sandal, slippery, she clutched at the wall, got over, ran down the entranceway to the nailed up door.

I have to get out, she thought. If she knocked on the door, screamed, shouted, pleaded for help? Or the walls, the next house, she could beat on the walls, open the shutters, shout.

This is a plague house, she thought. Sealed up. So if they found her alive, they'd kill her, as a bearer of the plague.

She looked out through the viewing holes in the thick wood of the door. The street was empty. A dog wandered across the street, panting. Two sweetsingers bathed in the dust. People should be about, doing things. Instead, silence. She could hear, distant, still, an echo in her head of screams.

The dog trotted towards the sweetsingers, barking. It drew Nilesh's eyes. The door of the cake maker's house was boarded shut.

The door of the house opposite opened. A woman came out. She stood on the threshold. Raised her face. Screamed. The scream hung in the air like the echoes Nilesh had thought were in her mind.

The dog barked and ran. The sweetsingers flew up in a beating of wings and a flap of dry dust. The woman screamed. Her dress was stained dark down the front, like the foreign woman's dress had been.

Nilesh realized what was so obvious and inconceivable.

Deeping fever was loose in Sorlost.

PART FIVE

THE WONDER

Chapter Thirty-Eight

Thalia Altrersyr. Queen of Ith and the White Isles.

Did I not say, once, that I would live, and live, and live?

The strange thing is how much I think of my former life in the Great Temple. As though it were both so long ago and only yesterday. Things here make me think of it, and I wonder about it. The news we hear from Sorlost, of what is happening there . . . I think about them. The little child Demmy. Demerele. It had not occurred to me that she would be made High Priestess so young. I think about myself as a child before I was made High Priestess, knowing what I would have to do. I do not know, truly, which would have been better or worse, at that age: to do it, or to know that I would have to do it when I was older. I lived for ten years, knowing I would have to do it. I pitied Demerele, when she drew the red lot, because I knew she would spend the next ten years waiting knowing she would have to kill me.

No. In truth, I have no idea whether I pitied her. So much has happened since then. But I like to tell myself I did. One would, surely? You would, wouldn't you?

Like Marith talking about his childhood, I seem to think a great deal of my life in the Temple. Sitting on my bed talking to Helase of gossip and poetry and girl's fantasies of the world beyond us.

285

It astonishes me, how wrong we were. Or we would go down into the gardens to play with the little ones: Demmy; the baby Sissly with her fat brown legs; the tall girl whose name . . . what was her name? She had yellow hair but I cannot remember her name. And yet it was so little time ago.

Our times of innocence. The past, that shines golden. We both think so much about these things.

'I dared Ti to climb the highest tree in the orchard at home, once,' Marith tells me. We are walking in the gardens of Malth Tyrenae, his gaze lights on a fruit tree. 'Right to the top, to bring back an apple from up there, I pointed out the apple I wanted to him. We were only little, he was maybe five years old, I don't remember. He climbed it, got stuck, I went up to join him, got stuck as well. We were there for what felt like forever. We were helped down and beaten. Our nurse Glytha was whipped, for letting us get away from her like that.'

'And?' I say to him.

'We learnt to climb down.'

Innocence, indeed.

'I feel sorry for your nurse,' I say.

Marith laughs. 'Looking back, so do I.'

He says then, 'If we should . . . should have children . . .' And then he is silent. And I am silent.

We should not talk of the past, perhaps.

But if there is guilt for both of us, it was worth it. Ith is a very beautiful kingdom. Tyrenae is a very beautiful place. Its buildings are of dark stone, tall, wild. Spires and towers that leap into the heavens. Sharp, like spines. Their roofs are made of copper, green with verdigris. The copper roofs are beautiful like cold green water. The city is beautiful like bare winter trees.

Marith does not seem to like it as much as I do. He is already talking of us moving on. It reminds him of Sorlost, Marith says. Its beauty. The sense of the city, of its grandeur that is fading, of a place that is old. Tired of itself. Decaying. Do I not think?

'I don't think I understand,' I say to Marith. 'Is that like Sorlost?' Sorlost, my city, the greatest city that ever was or ever will be, decaying, tired of itself?

'It's what Sorlost is famous for,' he says. Puzzled. 'Isn't it? The decaying heart of a decayed empire. A city of such wealth and such squalor. A rotting corpse.'

'I . . .' I feel my face hot with something that might be shame. 'I didn't know . . .'

I have seen old pictures of emissaries from half the world kneeling in the Great Temple, spellbound and trembling before the might of Great Tanis Who Rules All Things. Now I officiate to peasants and petty merchants, while foreign kings laugh at us for our beliefs behind fat fingers. Pointless, it seems sometimes. All the candles, all the gold and silver and bronze. Pointless, in the way most lives are pointless. A ritual motion we must go through, for want of anything else to do or believe.

I said that once. Told you that. But I did not understand . . . I thought that I had some kind of power, when I was the High Priestess of Great Tanis, the holiest woman in all Irlast. I killed men and women and children, to keep my city as it is.

'It's so strange, isn't it?' Marith says then. 'That I know Sorlost better than you?' He blinks with astonishment, thinking about it. 'All your life, in one building. Locked in. I would have gone mad, not being able to get about. It's impossible to imagine it.'

It is strange. That he knows Sorlost better than I do. That he knew of its decay, while I did not.

'I was the Chosen of God,' I say. My voice sounds stiff and foolish.

'I'm sorry,' he says. 'I shouldn't have said that.'

'It doesn't matter. Truly. I don't think of Sorlost.' Try to laugh. To brush it away. 'If I lived in a cage, at least the women who cared for me never had to be whipped.'

'And you would never have lamed your first horse riding it into a peat bog, or lost your best boots to an incoming tide, or been yelled at for tearing your clothes climbing a tree. I was beaten for that last. I was supposed to be being presented to someone at court. Not covered in mud falling out of a tree.'

'No,' I say.

Ah, Great Tanis. We should not talk of the past. Either of us.

Yet I begin to see what Marith means, about Tyrenae. I have seen it, I realize, I have seen it and known it for longer, now, than I have seen and known Sorlost. Strange, yes. And I look at it with new understanding. It does, somehow, feel something like my Temple. Beautiful. But tired. Dried out. The great lords and ladies here drink quicksilver every night and every morning. They claim it keeps them in good health. But they and their city are so worn down. Weighed down. The air here is heavy. This, after all, is all that is left of Caltath that was home to the Godkings, who lived and lived and could not die and were so very afraid of death.

And there is squalor here. Decay. Poverty. I begin to see that. I saw it, I think, in Sorlost, briefly in the streets, and in the faces of the people who came sometimes to the Temple. The people who came offering themselves for sacrifice, especially, I saw it in them. I begin to understand that, here. What it was. Some of the people who came to the Temple dripped with jewels. Others had the thin pinched faces of those who have nothing. No food, no shelter, no hope. I saw that without understanding, in Sorlost. I did not wonder at the blank broken faces that came to me, laid themselves before my knife. I see it now in Tyrenae, and I begin to understand it. Blind children and madmen go begging in the streets here. The wealthy look at them and turn away and do not care. 'The quicksilver mining kills them,' Kiana Sabryya says. 'That is all.' One day, riding through the city, I pass a private garden, very beautiful, very lush. At the gates a woman is standing. A servant. She throws fruit through the bars of the gates. Rotting apples: I can smell the heavy scent of them. A group of beggars gathers. They begin to fight over the fruit. 'Come away, My Lady Queen,' Tal says.

'But . . .'

'All great cities are full of hunger, My Lady Queen,' Tal says.

'I didn't see it like this,' says Marith, 'when I came here before. I just thought it was exciting, being here. Standing in the footsteps of the Godkings. Of Eltheri. I don't think it can have changed much, even, since Eltheri's day.'

The first thing we did when we came here, of course, was go to the room in Malth Tyrenae where Amrath boiled Eltheia's parents alive while Eltheri watched him. The second thing we did was to order the door to that room locked and barred, and to throw away the key.

'It's lucky, don't you think, that you married a woman with no parents,' I heard Osen say to Marith one night. We had all been drinking, I don't think Osen had any idea I could hear what he said. As I say, we had the door locked and barred. The next morning, I threw away the key.

Terrible things were done here, in Tyrenae. Over and over. Torture and pain and hunger and neglect. The city and the fortress . . . they are well named indeed.

But it is still a beautiful city, Tyrenae. In its tired old beauty. Despite what it is. Ith is a beautiful kingdom. Malth Tyrenae, for all its past, is a very beautiful place. Its towers rise so high that the clouds gather around them: we climb the stairs of the tallest tower one day, round and round, up and up, we are exhausted when we reach even halfway, gasping and laughing. When we reach the top, there is a room that opens out onto a balcony. We are above the clouds. They lie below us, a thin grey mist. We can see the city, ghostly, through the clouds, the copper roofs glowing green. Then the clouds grow thicker, higher, we are surrounded by cloud, everything is damp and silent. Before us, just out of reach, is a pool of quicksilver, a lake of quicksilver, perfectly still. It seems to glow in the cloud-damp. Marith throws a coin into it. The surface moves in slow ripples, heavy like the clouds, then is still.

'What is its purpose?' I ask Marith. 'Why are they there?'

'No one knows,' he says. 'Perhaps only to be beautiful. The sky up here burns sometimes,' he says. 'Burns with cold fire. I should like to see that, up close. I saw a woman's head bathed in mage fire once and wondered, what must it feel like?'

Another day we go up there when the sky is clear blue, see the city spread before us, the dark forests and the meadows, the Bitter Sea. The mountains, north of Tyrenae, beyond which lie the Wastes and Illyr. It grows dark and all the lights of the city flicker beneath us. Like stars. Beautiful like stars. I am glad I have seen this place. Seen this.

'What is that?' In the mountains, too, I think I see lights flickering.

Marith looks where I am looking. Smiles. 'You know, don't you? Surely? What that is?'

I look at him. 'No. What is it?'

'Think. Guess.' He smiles. 'Wonderful things.'

Oh! I think . . . I think I do. Oh. Oh! Fear and delight, both at once. 'Truly?'

'We'll see,' he says. 'Soon. You'll see.'

Yes. It is time to move on. To find new kingdoms. Make our own world. Our future, not our pasts. Places neither of us have ever seen. Who knows, I think, looking at the mountains, who can say what is out there, to take away our memories of pain? To give us new things. New life. The *Emnelenethkyr*, they are called. Which means, in Itheralik, the Empty Peaks. For we who are burdened by our pasts, surely a good name?

Chapter Thirty-Nine

More plans. More logistics. More work. More feeling his head ache.

A bigger army, now. Half of Ith seemed to have signed up for the adventure. Kiana Sabryya had brought him a small army just by herself, a lot of them women, which was proving . . . interesting for the White Isles troops. 'They've got breasts and they're wearing swords and armour,' Osen had honestly genuinely actually ended up having to shout at Lord Parale. 'Amazing. Just bloody well get over it.' Some people could be very odd. Alleen Durith had a lovely troop of cavalry on beautiful creamy white horses, fast and strong with proud, clever eyes. The best four he gave to Marith, adorned with gold and copper trappings, cheekpieces set with rubies, red feather plumes on their heads. Marith, Osen and Alleen had a glorious day riding them very fast along the coast south of Tyrenae, stopping at every inn they found on the way back. But a larger cavalry contingent was something of a mixed blessing, rather like the inn visits had been. More horses meant more fodder to lug across a mountain range. And these particular horses looked like they'd be a nightmare to keep comfortable en route, being proud and fast and strong and clever and very, very, very highly strung.

So they had something like forty thousand men — men and women — people — argh — forty thousand *soldiers* and horses and tents and food supplies to get over the mountains. Again, the roar of the forge, the rattle of grain carts. Again, the long hours poring over maps and plans, talking with Osen and Yanis Stansel and his lords. Again, the ringing sound of soldiers training, readying themselves. The women of Tyrenae sat and wove cloth for ten times a hundred tents.

Thalia's wagon palace on wheels was coming on well, at least. Marith was very pleased with it. All green and gold and silver. The horses that pulled it had pearls plaited into their manes. A bed, a bath tub, a tiny desk, lamps. He and Thalia had a lovely morning choosing a selection of books.

Illyr. It called to him. To rule in Ethalden! To raise again Amrath's walls, Amrath's throne! See the silver towers rebuilt, the walls raised in splendour, the glory of Illyr restored. Bury Amrath with honour. Avenge His death. The whole army was alive with it, staring away north with longing, it was the first and last word on every soldier's lips.

Just a lot of work first . . .

Marith was reading over a list of troop units one evening when Osen entered his study, with Thalia's guardsman Brychan behind.

'What is it? I gave orders I was to be left undisturbed.'

Osen looked at him and Marith saw that Osen was afraid.

Osen said very slowly, 'My Lord King — Marith — The queen . . . This man here . . . he has things he needs to tell you. About the queen.'

I need not fear. What have I to fear in the world? Cold gripped his heart. I'd know. If anything happened to her, he thought. I'd know. She had gone out riding early that morning, to see the Ithish woods all in their richest spring green. Two guards had accompanied her, Tal and Garet. She, too, had nothing to fear.

'What is it?'

'She—' Osen's eyes fixed on the floor at his feet. Brychan staring around the tent, anywhere but at his king in front of him drawing up his war plans. Brychan's eyes wide and rolling, young horse's eyes when a man comes to break it.

'What about the queen?' The air harsh as boiled metal. Trying to keep his voice level. Trying to keep from screaming so loud the men before him were shattered bones on the floor. His hands went to the hilt of his sword on the table. Trying to keep his hands from tearing them apart. 'Tell me. What about the queen?'

Osen pushed Brychan forward. 'Tell him. As you told me.'

Brychan said faintly, 'The queen . . . My Lord King . . . You ordered me to guard her. To accompany her. To obey her, do as she ordered me.' The man's voice shook, but defensive as well inside it. *'I did my duty'. 'I followed orders'. 'You told me to'. 'It's not my fault'.*

'Yes,' Marith said. 'She is your queen, is she not? You obey her.'

'She is my queen . . .'

Brychan lapsed into silence. Stared at the floor.

'And?' I don't understand. The burning pain back at Marith's eyes.

'Tell him,' Osen said. His voice was cold and strained and taut, like ice cracking underfoot.

Brychan shuffled. 'This morning, she wanted to go riding. She loves the woods around here . . .'

'Yes?'

'My Lord King — I — I swear this is the truth, true as I'm standing here. We were riding, she was ahead of us, she ordered us to go behind her, she was riding, she stopped her horse, like she was waiting. And a . . . a white deer came out of the woods. To meet her. White as snow. And its antlers, they were huge, they reached out like a tree, like branches. And, My Lord King, I swear, I swear this is true, it had a human face, My Lord. The face of a man.' His hands made a gesture. 'It was a . . . a gestmet, My Lord King. A god.'

Brychan lapsed into silence.

A sick heavy dark.

Marith said, 'And what did Thalia — did the queen — what did the queen do?'

Brychan's voice shrank to a whisper. 'She was not afraid. She looked at it. It looked at her. I thought she was going to go towards it. Then she stopped, and made a gesture with her hand to shoo it away. And it went.' The head went up a little, defensive and on surer ground. 'And she rode on. And we followed her. She went on, and then rode back.'

Silence.

'Thank you.' Still he kept his voice level. 'That will be all. Thank you, Brychan.'

Brychan turned to go. He'd pissed himself. A pool of piss dribbling down to the floor. Marith watched him, trembling. After Brychan had gone he sank down with his head resting in his hands.

'Why did he tell you?' His voice was dry as though he hadn't spoken since the world was born.

Osen said, 'He was afraid. And he is in love with her, of course.' And Osen too looked older when he said it, stone man, remorseless, driving in the pain.

'Why did you tell me?'

Osen the stone man said, 'I thought you needed to know.'

'So now I know.' Marith gestured to the doorway. 'Leave.'

Osen took three steps, stopped, turned again. 'And something else. I have to tell you something else. About her. Something else the man Brychan told me, that solved something that was puzzling me.' His eyes met Marith's and they were as cruel. His friend. 'It is not only . . . whatever it was he saw, that she has been meeting with. She is betraying you, Marith.'

On the red leather surface of the table, on top of the lists of soldiers, Osen placed a gold necklace set with amber, that had once belonged to Queen Elayne, that Marith had given to Thalia.

'I got this from a girl in Morr Town. She got it from a market seller. He got it from a young woman with a grand lady's voice and a burned face.'

Drive the knife in. Harder. Harder.

Death! Death! Death!

* * *

Confront her.

Betrayer. Like all the rest. Mother, father, brother, friend, wife.

Kill her. Her and Carin both. Killing him, and he had to kill them first.

Gods, yesterday they'd been standing on the tallest tower of Malth Tyrenae, looking at the darkness of their kingdom, and he'd told her he loved her, and she'd told him she loved him. Which she never had before. 'To our future,' she'd said.

Put his hand over the necklace. The amber was almost warm under his hand, softer and warmer than metal. The sap of ancient trees. Once, once it had been alive. A living thing.

She had worn it at a feast one night at Malth Elelane. Danced, with the candlelight on her, dressed in white. The gold had glowed against her skin.

Thalia. Thalia my love. The beautiful shining weight of her hair and her hands pushing through it like through dark water. Her slender fingers like branches, her hair rippling like water, a soft scent of roses and honey, cool dark river against his skin. Her hands on his skin, her slender fingers like branches brushing against him, like leaves, like water, like light. Her eyes. Her lips. *Saleiot.*

He put the necklace into his pocket. Felt it burning there, malign, mocking at him. I killed Carin, he thought. I loved him. He loved me. Yet he betrayed me. Destroyed me. Yet I killed him.

Marith sat alone, with the necklace in his pocket, the lists of troops spread before him on the table. Thinking. Making plans. The shadows crawled on the walls. The red star of the Dragon's Mouth rose. The Twin Children. The Worm. The Dog.

A good star, the Dog.

Marith went up to his bedchamber. Thalia was sitting by the fire, reading.

His bedchamber? It had been Selerie's bedchamber. The bed, the chairs, the hangings, the coverlet of blue and silver and seed pearls. Suddenly, surely, the room smelled of rotting flesh.

Thalia started. 'I didn't hear you come in.' She looked nervous, he thought. Afraid of him. Awkward. 'You've been so busy today,' she said.

'Yes.'

The room smelled of rot. Couldn't she smell it? The necklace burned in his pocket. The amber looked like the dried crust of pus on Selerie's wounds. The amber looked like the honey in which they had preserved his father's corpse. She had sat in Selerie's tent on Seneth in his ruins, eating apples and cream and honey, licking honey off her perfect lips.

'Come here. What is it? You look terrible.' She held out her arms to him.

She lost the necklace, the catch broke and it fell from her neck, my mother lost a necklace like that once, out riding, not my mother, Elayne, the whore, she lost a necklace like that when the catch broke. A maidservant stole it – so I'll have every maidservant in Malth Elelane whipped. She gave it to a beggar girl who was burned as a child, because she is such a kind and good and caring woman and her heart was moved with grief.

The man Brychan is mad. I should have him killed. Have his eyes put out. He is lying. If she met with a god in the forest, it was . . . it was . . .

Look at her! Even god powers must worship her! The sea and the sky and the rocks and the sea. That's all. She is radiant and pure and bright with life.

I can't ask her, he thought. I can't speak the words.

King Ruin. King of Death. What did I expect?

'What are you reading?' he asked her, trying to find something to say to her. His voice shook on the words.

She flushed. Hesitated. 'Marith—'

Held up the book.

The story of Hilanis the Young. He had to bite his tongue, to keep himself from crying out.

'I didn't hear you come in,' she said again. 'Osen said he was going to get you to go out somewhere with him tonight.

'I wanted to understand the history of the White Isles,' she said.

296

'And of Illyr. Places we've been. Will go.' She put the book down. 'I'm sorry,' she said. 'But I wanted to know.'

Gods, all we do is say sorry to each other. Tiptoeing round all the stories. I tell her her birthplace is a corpse's death rattle. She reads stories of just how vile my bloodline is. We apologize for knowing what everybody knows.

'There's nothing to understand! It's a vile story about my vile accursed family. My vile accursed poisonous blood.' His father's sad cold face, listening, nodding a little, his eyes flicking between his two sons, the queen beside him watching, sighing, sometimes taking her husband's hand. 'Sitting after dinner in the hall, some sycophant who calls himself a poet reciting the great deeds of our ancestors, Ti and me sitting looking at each other. Sitting listening. Me. My blood.' King Ruin. King of Death. Divine demonic cursed filthy blood. 'My past. My blood. That's what you need to know! To understand! My blood! Hilanis who skinned his older brother Tareneth alive to claim his crown, Hilanis who dressed Tareneth's widow in the skin on their wedding day! What we do to each other. What we are and do. My blood. What I am and can't escape.'

'Your past?' She stared at him blankly. 'Your blood? You – Marith, it's an old story. About someone who lived and died hundreds of years ago.'

'About my family. About me.'

'Marith.' She stood up, came over to him, she was dressed in green, she looked like forest pools, she looked like light and shadows on a green tree. 'Marith, the Asekemlene Emperor of Sorlost is reborn anew each lifetime, the son of a wineseller or a farmer or a crippled beggar or a, Great Tanis, I don't know, a street whore. It doesn't matter whose child he is, a great lord's, a murderer's, a mad idiot. He is the Emperor, and he is what he is. I don't know who my parents were. No one can know.'

'Stop it,' Marith said.

Thalia picked up the book. Opened it. Flicked through it.

'I remember,' she said, 'the day I chose my lot. I put my hand into a box and picked up a wooden token. I let it go. Picked up another. Drew it out. If I had not put the first lot back again, I would, I don't know, I would be a lowly Temple priestess like Ausa or Helase. Or, more likely, I would be fifteen years dead. Another girl drew her lot ten days after I did. She is fifteen years dead.'

She tore a handful of pages out of the book. 'In a story I once read, a kitchen girl swaps her own fatherless baby with the king's son, her child grows up to be king. If you found out tomorrow that your father was not your father, that you had no . . . no Altrersyr demon blood . . .'

She dropped the pages into the fire. 'It would change nothing that has happened. Would it? Nothing about you. About any of this. There. It's gone.'

The flames leapt up. Licked the parchment. It crumbled away. The fire was bright but the room was darker. Marith cowered away from the flames.

'Come here,' she said. 'Please.' Held out her arms to him. *Saleiot.* So bright with life.

They went over to the bed. The sheets smelled of rotting wounds.

She is betraying you.

I thought you needed to know.

Marith thought: I shouldn't have come here. I hate this place.

Chapter Forty

'Why did you tell me?' the boy asks his uncle.

His uncle looks . . . sad, the boy thinks. Weary. Ashamed. Filled with guilt.

His uncle toys with the books before him on the study table. Picks at a scratch in the red leather that covers the table top. His uncle says at last, 'Because I thought you needed to know.'

Chapter Forty-One

'Amrath! We stand before You clad in bronze and iron. We stand before You with swords drawn. Our swords are ready. Our swords are sharp. We will make the music of bronze and iron, the music that lifts joy in Your heart. Blood we will bring You. Death we will bring You. War we will bring You. You who delight always in blood and death and war.'

Behold the Army of Amrath, preparing to march on Illyr.

Gods, there are a lot of the sweaty buggers.

Tobias, Raeta and Landra going to join them.

It takes a long time, planning to kill someone. Tobias has thought and thought round and round. Infiltrate Malth Elelane. Bribe the guards. Co-opt someone close to him. Get Raeta a job as a scullery maid, poison his wine. But it wouldn't work. It wouldn't godsdamned work. And the Army of Amrath — yes, they were referring to it as the Army of Amrath in capitals and portentous voices now, with entirely straight faces, seriously – and the Army of Amrath sailed to Ith and he still hadn't thought of a plan as he watched them go in their black ships, and he still hadn't thought of a plan when the news came that they had taken Tyrenae.

'Fucking hell. I mean . . . fucking hell.'

Landra had laughed hysterically. Raeta had bitten her lips white.

Tobias had looked at Raeta bleakly. 'To be fair to myself, it's harder than you'd think, killing someone.'

A vast crowd of chancers, gamesters, shysters, hucksters, cut-throats, con men and whores were pouring over to Ith in the Army of Amrath's wake, mad keen to follow it to Illyr. Morr Town was even more crowded than it had been for Sunreturn. Every inn was heaving with people, ships sailed every day across the Bitter Sea to Tyrenae with another load of soldiers, salesmen and interesting if undefined types looking to make a quick bit of cash. Amazing, the skillsets the people of Morr Town turned out to possess.

'They can perfectly well get fleeced by the Ithish, you know,' Tobias told one sweet and lovely young lady who was boarding in his inn. She was sailing to Tyrenae the next morning. Planning to sign up with the heavy cavalry, obviously. What else? 'There are sexually transmitted diseases, loaded dice and ruinous loan rates in Ith already. You don't need to export them.'

'Why,' Sweet Face said sweetly, 'should foreigners get all the fun? He was our king first.'

Gods, he should pray for another storm to drown the whole bloody lot of them. Wipe the earth clean.

'Thirty years ago,' said Tobias when Sweet Face had left them, 'thirty years ago, Marith's own grandpa led an invasion of Illyr. There's a very famous song about it. The refrain goes something like this: *Glorious they sailed, a mighty host in golden ships. I alone came back.* Most of this lot probably still have empty places at the dinner table where their dad or uncle used to sit.'

'Never underestimate people's desire to hopefully possibly get rich while hopefully possibly being part of killing things,' Raeta said.

Making a killing in every sense. Yeah. I know. And the good people of Tyrenae were reported as being remarkably accommodating to their new king's followers. Very little a White Isles accent couldn't get you. The drink flowed like water. 'Hurrah for King Marith' shouted everywhere. Various very grand Ithish ladies alleged to have developed quite a talent for striptease.

Tyrenae could have held out against him for bloody years, behind its walls. Cowardly sods.

'You fought with him,' said Landra. 'You shouldn't be surprised.'

'What can I say?' said Tobias wearily. 'Maybe I'm just too much of an optimist.'

And then it had struck him. The answer struck him.

All these plans he'd made, rejected, *break into Malth Elelane, bribe the guards, co-opt an insider, poison his drink*: they all had one stupid stupid stupid flaw.

It's easy as piss, to kill someone, if you're quite happy to die doing it.

Endless, endless soldiers in bronze armour, armed to the teeth, their helmets covering their eyes. Men and women and children. The injured. The half-dead. Parading before Good King Marith, swords and spears and knives sparkling in the sunshine. Men and women, voices and faces from all over, chaos and confusion of half the world flooding into Tyenae to fight for the new king. *We stand before You with swords drawn. Our swords are ready. Our swords are sharp.*

Sail to Ith. Join them. March into Malth Tyrenae. March up to the boy. Stab him in the gut. Die.

He dies. We die.

Hard? It's easy as piss. His death and my death, Tobias thought. A kind of dim pleasure, in thinking that.

By a truly staggering coincidence, the next boat sailing for Tyrenae turned out to belong to Raeta's brother. His new ship, bigger and flashier than the last one, the one Tobias had arrived on the White Isles on. The figurehead was a woman, her hair dark, holding a silver disc like a shield. The sails were new and black.

Lan stared at the ship for a long time before they embarked. She looked very white.

'What's wrong?'

'Nothing. I . . .' She stared at the figurehead. 'I . . . I thought I recognized this ship.'

'Seen it in Toreth Harbour, maybe.' Winced, as he mentioned the place name. Lan jerked like he'd stabbed her. He said hurriedly, 'You're holding everyone up, come on.'

'*Another's Luck.* No, I'd remember the name.'

'Bloody stupid name.' Oddly enough, it did look vaguely familiar. Something about the figurehead of the woman, the way her face looked. Familiar in a not-good way. Made him nervous. 'Raeta said her brother only got it recently. The paint's all new, you can see it's been repainted, done up. So you probably wouldn't recognize—'

Oh.

Another's Luck.

Oh.

'It looks like a lot of ships do,' said Tobias. Gods gods gods, if she realizes, if Landra realizes what ship this is. Another's bloody luck, gods yes. 'Let's just get on board, yeah, before it whatever the term is. Casts off. We're holding the queue up. Come on.' Before she realizes what ship this is. Was. The *Brightwatch,* it had been called when she last saw it. The figurehead had had yellow hair, had been holding a sunburst. Had had as its cargo a dead man.

First chance he could, Tobias cornered Raeta.

'You know, don't you? What ship this is?'

Raeta shrugged. 'My brother got it very cheap.'

'I'll bet he did. What happened to the last owner, then? Your brother tell you that?'

'I would rather imagine,' said Raeta, 'that he's dead. Wouldn't you?'

'Gods, Raeta! And if Landra — if Lan finds out?'

'She will not find out,' said Raeta.

'She's wracking her brains right now trying to work it out. She'll remember. It's hardly the kind of thing you don't remember. This being the ship she brought Marith back to Malth Salene in and all.'

303

Raeta looked at him. Her blue eyes opened very wide. She looked . . . ah, gods, she looked like something . . . something . . . A sound in Tobias's ears. Rustling leaves. Like . . . like . . .

'Raeta?'

'She will not find out,' said Raeta. 'It's not . . . ideal, no. I'm sorry. But unless you want to wait . . . My brother did get it very cheap. And the name fits.'

Painless journey. Sea smooth as silk. Smooth as a well-paved road. The winds were very favourable, the sails bellied fat and shining, the sky was cloudless blue. A school of dolphins raced the ship one afternoon; they even saw a whale blow. The fishermen off the coast of Sel Isle waved and cheered their passing. 'Good luck! Good luck to you! Joy to the king!' Tobias and Raeta and Landra sat on deck and watched the sun rise, watched the sky change, watched the sun set. Tried to relax.

'Pretty.'

'Pretty enough. Not much different to yesterday. Bit more cloud.'

'One of nature's wonders, the sunset. Never the same twice.'

'Yeah? Could say the same thing about a bleeding wound.'

A few of days of life left. Wondered if Raeta and Landra had worked that out yet.

Hard to relax.

They'd reach Tyrenae in record time, Raeta's brother said. Benefits of Good King Marith having a weather hand in his service. Sweet west wind and calm sea and the ship fair danced on the wind. How kind of Good King Marith. Another's luck indeed. Poetic, like. Or something.

And Tyrenae! Soldiers everywhere, not so much a city as an army camp. If Morr Town had been crowded with eager young faces longing for battle, Tyrenae was filled to overflowing, bursting at the seams, the air heavy with bronze and leather and horses and men's sweat. The perfume of ten times a thousand pairs of muscular thighs. The smoke of forge fires and cook fires. The endless, endless clang of the smith's hammer. The sheer amount of piss and shit and body fluids an army in peace time can produce. Almost nostalgic, the smell, like the way Tobias's tent had smelled on damp mornings, in the Company. All those strong, excited, pent up young men . . .

A grain ship was mooring up at the quay beside *Another's Luck*. Wagons waited to take its load. Marith must be stripping the White Isles bare to feed his soldiers. Sailors on their own ship shouted as they got everything secured; the human cargo surged for the gangplank, the crew strained to unload bales of wool cloth for soldiers' cloaks.

'I remember him when he first arrived in my squad,' said Tobias. 'He was dressed in tatters, his hands shook, he hadn't had a bath for gods know how long, his hair had lumps of dried puke in it. He looked about twelve. He looked like someone had just nicked his favourite toy. He looked like he'd wet himself if someone spoke to him.'

The buildings around the quayside were so tall they blocked out the light. They were built of black stone. Looked like teeth. Lodging houses, whole families living five, ten people to a room. So inhabited by a lot of people. So a lot more young men looking for a way to prove themselves while making some cash.

'Mind your backs!' a voice shouted. A wagon of tin ore went crashing past them. Ith was famous for its tin. Made very good bronze, did Ithish tin. Bronze that kept an edge very well. A troop of soldiers marched past in the other direction.

'We could still . . . not do this,' Tobias said pointlessly. 'We could just go home again. Boat's not sailing until tomorrow night.'

Raeta said, 'We could.'

'Someone has to be king,' Tobias said pointlessly.

'Someone has to use all that Ithish tin,' said Raeta. 'All those strong healthy bodies, all that wheat. Couldn't just leave them alone to sit around doing nothing, could we?'

Another wagon went past, carrying a load of sarriss. The sarriss certainly weren't pointless.

The boiling mass of people and goods pushed them up the streets further into the city. Dancing on it, like the ship at sea. Whirled round and along. Eager eager crowds: like a festival, the atmosphere in Tyrenae. The air fairly buzzed.

'We'll find an inn today.' Tobias almost had to shout over the chaos. 'Get the stuff we need tomorrow. Scout out.' The paving stones were bobbing up and down after days at sea. He felt tired and worn down. His leg was killing him. The crowds shoved past him, looking for the same thing. 'Watch your backs,' a voice shouted as a wagon rolled past, almost knocking into him.

They got settled in an inn called The Weeping Woman, beside the west gates, where they could have a cupboard beside the scullery-cum-latrine for double what a room had cost in Morr Town. The west gates, it quickly turned out, being the major point of ingress for the city's meat supplies and egress for the city's effluent.

'Bloody hell,' said Raeta.

'That, Raeta, woman, is the true smell of war. Bronze, hot metal, sweaty men's bodies and all that, yeah, maybe, but twenty thousand tons of human shit and horse shit and cow shit . . . that's the authentic odour of glory.' Tobias's head was hurting something desperate. In the common room, two women were talking loudly in the harsh rough accents of Immish. Tobias slumped over a beer listening to them. Immish women. His own countrywomen. The older woman had a voice and a turn of phrase that reminded him of his mum.

Back and forth, like a loom working, discussing the beautiful young soldiers, the fine ships in the harbour, the bountiful nature of the new king.

'A statue spoke aloud, today, in the Great Square,' said the older woman. 'A statue of Turnain the Godking. Milk and honey ran from its eyes and its mouth. It spoke in praise of the king.'

'What did it say?' the younger woman asked. Her eyes went dreamy, thinking about it. A moment of splendour in her foetid life. She was only perhaps as old as Landra Relast.

'Milk and honey flowed down from its eyes and its mouth,' the older woman replied. 'People caught it in their hands, said it was sweet to drink. *Nane elenaneikth,* that's what they say it was saying. *Joy to Him.*'

'It was a trick,' a man at the next table shouted to them. 'I saw it.'

The two women raised their cups to him. 'It probably was at that,' the older woman said. 'But it spoke. I heard it.' A pause. 'Course, I was off my tits on firewine. It might have been saying anything.'

'We'll need to get ourselves armour,' said Raeta. She didn't look entirely comfortable saying it.

Tobias touched the purse at his neck. 'I've got plenty of blood money, haven't I?'

They had something resembling a wash and a meal, went out again into the city. Even in the evening twilight, the place was running with people, all the shops and stalls were open. Everyone caught up in the preparations, buying and selling their lives before the war. And it's remarkably easy, buying arms and armour, when everyone and his wife and his kids and his dog is buying it too. Churning the stuff out night and day. Selling it alarmingly cheap. 'If you're fighting for Him,' the armourer shouted, 'you can have it at cost. Amrath! Amrath!' The state of the bloke suggested he hadn't stopped to eat, or wash, or sleep, for the last week. He looked basically insane. Six children in the back of the shop were hammering bronze as if their lives depended on it, and one stopped for a breath and another screamed 'Don't fucking stop!' and hit him. In the dark, the whole thing was lit by the forge fire. The children's faces looked scalded red. Fucking hell, thought Tobias, and I thought people were looking to make money out of this.

'If you're joining the Army of Amrath, joy to you!' a woman shouted, seeing them gathered at the shop door.

'It'll be ready in three days,' said the armourer. 'Can't do quicker than that, I'm afraid. Rushed off my feet.'

Part of Tobias thought: too slow. Too slow, damnit.

Part of Tobias thought: three more days!

'So I'll have a scout around tomorrow morning,' said Tobias. 'Get things sorted.'

Raeta nodded. Landra nodded. The children's hammers came down and it was too fucking symbolic. Like all this shit.

They went back to the inn in silence. Condemned bloody men. Three days of life. The common room was filled with singing and laughter, the two women hawking themselves unsteadily, toasts and shouts of 'Illyr! Illyr!' Tobias ran into Sweet Face. She was wearing a very nice dress and jewels, drinking beer with two soldiers of the Army of Amrath.

'Tobe!' she shouted, waving at him. 'Fancy seeing you here! Isn't this fun? Aren't you so glad you came? Get him a beer, Acol,' Sweet Face ordered one of her friends.

Depressingly, she looked plumper and in better health than she had back in Morr Town. War is always good for some people.

'Oh, yeah. Definitely.'

Friend came back with a cup of beer. You could almost smell the beer over the stink in the air.

'To Illyr,' Friend said. He, Sweet Face and Lover clunked cups. Tobias reluctantly joined in.

'My grandpas died in Illyr,' said Lover. 'Both of them. Never even got their bodies back to bury. One of the survivors said he thought the Illyians ate them.' A long pull of beer. 'Can't fucking wait to get stuck into them back.'

'I need to see my brother,' Raeta said the next morning. She looked like Tobias felt. Lying awake all night, all three of them, thinking 'I should be doing something, I've got three days left of life, I shouldn't be trying to sleep.'

Left Landra in the inn. 'I'll bring you back a meat pie,' Tobias told her. She winced.

Again, the city was bustling, bursting with people, have they slept at all? Tobias thought. Detritus of last night mixed with the filth of the morning. All bathed over with fresh light rain. The sun through the rain was silver. It felt good on Tobias's eyes. Soft; soothed them. He was noticing these things more, it occurred to him.

He walked fast, up towards the fortress of Malth Tyrenae. Listing in his head all the things he needed to find out. Gates that were open. Gates that weren't. Soldiers' marching patterns. Ideal plan: march in with a whole load of soldier boys, swords drawn, faces eager, yada yada yada, march up to Marith, kill him. Easy. Only three more days of staying in an inn that stinks of shit.

A shadow fell on him. All the plans gone from his head. Easy? Easy? Just give up and die now. Kill yourself.

So cold.

He was standing in the shadow of Malth Tyrenae. Towers thrusting themselves up shredding the sky. A scream, a curse against happiness; someone, something, had taken stone and wood and iron and built all of life's pain. It was almost pitiful thinking of someone trying to live there. I am not going in there, Tobias thought. Gods, no way in hell am I going in there. Several thousand years of people torturing each other, in there. Eltheri Calboride watched his parents murdered, in there. Undyl Silver Eyes killed his own children, in there. Until Ysleta his sister killed him. In there.

A troop of soldiers marched up to the gateway. Huge black gates open to admit them. Fools! he wanted to shout. Go back! Go back! Go and live in bloody boring peace, like I once did. They marched in with their heads high, armour gleaming, the tramp of their feet was musical. The open gates yawned after them. The shadow of the towers seemed to devour them.

How much do I really value Lady Landra Relast's life? Tobias thought. Like, really? She's so keen on killing him. Get her in, armed and smiling. Leave her there and leg it halfway across Irlast.

That's, like, my job.

Thirty men had marched into the Imperial Palace of the Asekemlene Emperor. Four men had marched out.

A wagon laden with grain sacks went in through the open gate, the driver singing cheerfully to the oxen pulling it. Two men on horseback rode out of the gate.

Tobias drew back in horror as Thalia rode out after them. She was all dressed in white, a white cloak trimmed in thick gold fur. She looked more beautiful than he had ever seen her.

He was wrapped up against the rain and she didn't see him. She rode off down into the city. 'Out into the forest,' he heard her say to the men guarding her.

Stood by the walls and watched after her for a long time. The rain stopped.

Another troop of soldiers marched up, so young some of them looked, their armour badly put on because they didn't have a clue what they were doing. Their armour smelled new. New leather, new forged metal, gods, some of them you'd think their swords and helmets were still hot from the forge they looked so new and bright. Disappeared into the gate.

Thought of the nice eager young men he'd led to their deaths, in the Free Company of the Sword, because Skie had paid him.

The open gate was like a hole in the world. His head felt full of screaming. It sounded like Marith's voice screaming. Echoing round and round, screaming for death. Shook his head and stared, wondered that the whole damn city couldn't hear it.

No, he thought. I kill Marith myself, and I die, and that's the best fucking thing for both of us.

Three more days of life left.

So a strange few days. As you'd expect. Sitting in the inn, waiting for death. Landra sat in their tiny room, not speaking, refusing to go out. Waiting. Counting it down. 'We should have paid more,' she said, 'to try and get the stuff sent more quickly. Couldn't we go back? Offer the man more money?' She polished her knife and sharpened her knife. She had begun to scare Tobias like Marith did. He and Raeta spent a lot of time in the inn common room or sight-seeing trying not to look at any of the sights of Tyrenae. Avoided being in the same room as Landra with her eyes watching the sun move across the sky only waiting, waiting for her death and Marith's death.

Two more days of life left.

They went to visit the statue of Turnain the Godking in the Great Square. Some kind of sticky, milky smelling something was indeed dripping down its marble face. Which was a shame, as Tobias had always kind of wondered what the Godking of Caltath could possibly look like, and now he'd never know. People were collecting the stuff in cups, rubbing their hands in it. Flies buzzing all over it.

One more day of life left.

Been close to death so many times. But never quite knowing, like this. Always assumed in the back of his mind, no matter how bad, even when he'd been fighting the dragon — always assumed he'd survive. Your own death's an impossible thing to think about.

If all goes well, tomorrow, this time tomorrow, I'll be dead and Marith'll be dead. How can you really think about that?

Stood and watched the sun set over the walls of Tyrenae. Last fucking sunset. Three helmets, three mail shirts, a small sword for Landra were delivered to the inn as the evening light was fading. Cheap, ugly, rough work. The boys carrying it all ran off exhausted, more orders to deliver. Everyone in the city armed and waiting.

'Dinner and drinks are on me!' the landlord shouted, when he saw the equipment. 'Conquer Illyr for us, Tobe!' Seated them at the best table, served them stale bread, stale butter, meat stew that was nothing on the stew at the inn in Morr Town. It smelled greasy and not entirely appetizing over the smell of human shit and animal shit. Predictable: this is our last night alive, so the food's inedible and the drink's worse. Tobias took a long swig of beer that tasted of piss over the smell of shit.

Sweet Face at another table was eating stew with her mouth open, had slopped some down her dress. Tobias's leg was aching like a bastard. He let out a belch and tasted rancid stew again. He thought: fuck, but I liked being alive. Looked at all the people crowded into the inn gulping down beer and stew and talking and laughing, a bloke had his arm round Sweet Face's waist. You all like being alive, thought Tobias. And tomorrow I'll be dead, and if I fail, a few days after tomorrow you'll all be dead.

Fuck, Tobias thought slowly, why do we all do this?

Sweet Face came over, maybe seeing him looking like death and murder. Tried to chat. Hard to chat. She had stew round her mouth. Terrible fear he'd tell her. That it'd burst out of him. 'Guess what I'm going to do tomorrow, Sweet Face? Want to give me a last kiss?'

'I like your necklace,' Tobias said at last, desperately.

Sweet Face giggled. 'Have a look. Isn't it lovely?'

Now he was actually looking at it, it was. Gold and amber, fine thin links like it had been spun. Very fancy. Meant leaning in close to her chest, too.

'Acol found it just this morning,' Sweet Face said. 'In a latrine dump. Isn't that a joke? Wiped the shit off and it was beautiful.'

One night of life left. Tobias watched Landra sharpen and polish her knife. Sharpened and polished his own knife.

'What if we can't find him?' said Landra. 'What if he's closeted away in a throne room somewhere, guarded by forty men?'

'Then we wait until he comes out,' said Tobias.

Raeta said, 'We'll find him.'

Yeah. They would. A huge bloody fortress, but they'd find him.

'He's the king,' said Tobias. 'I think it'll be pretty obvious where he is.'

They went to bed early. Two options, the night before you're going to die. As Raeta and Landra were with him, Tobias chose the sensible one.

Tobias thought: I could betray them and run I could I could.

Raeta and Landra were asleep beside him, like they weren't worried or scared. Slow gentle sound of Landra's breathing. Smell of her breath. Smell of her hair.

One night of life left.

Comforting, like.

Chapter Forty-Two

Marith, sleeping.

Tobias, sleeping.

Swords and knifes sharpened.

A few hours of life left.

Chapter Forty-Three

Awoke and the sun was shining. Clouds and sunshine chasing each other across the sky. Slept in, slept late. So . . . peaceful. There's a story about Fylinn Dragonlord sleeping late the morning of a battle, because he was so at peace with himself. The utter calm stillness of knowing that today he's going to die. And so nothing else in the world matters anymore.

Landra doesn't know, Tobias thought, watching her eating breakfast. She was watching the city around them, the beggar children fighting in the street opposite, the crossing sweeper shovelling filth. She ate and watched with a look on her face that said she still felt alive.

Raeta's eyes met his own. Raeta knew.

They got themselves equipped. Mail, swords, knives, helmets. Their vision closed down by the helmets. Everything less real. Can't see so well. Can't hear so well. Like being drunk, or fevered. Looking through a window at the world straight ahead. It's easier to kill people, Tobias had sometimes speculated, wearing a helmet, because it doesn't feel quite as much like it's you inside it killing a real person.

Tobias rarely wore a helmet.

Remembered Marith shuddering saying he hated wearing helmets.

Raeta looked kind of foxy in hers. Shameful to admit it, but she did. More than kind of. Landra looked . . . Landra had realized, finally, Tobias thought, that killing Marith meant killing him.

Raeta might look foxy but she obviously hated the armour. Itched and wriggled her shoulders, twisted her head around.

'You look like a bloody hatha addict,' said Tobias. 'Or like you've got fleas in there. Stop it.'

'How can you wear this stuff?'

'With practice.'

Landra carefully packed up all her things, left them in a bundle on the bed. Landra got her things together. A horse-bone spindle. A scrap of yellow cloth. A broken twig. A gold ring stamped with a bird flying, her father's crest.

'Eltheia,' Landra whispered. 'Please. Please.' Raeta shot her a glare like ice.

They walked through the city, towards Malth Tyrenae. Thick grey clouds coming over, the sky growing dark. About to pour with rain.

Tobias looked straight ahead of him. Trying not to walk too fast or too slow. No different to walking up to the gates of the Imperial Palace. No different to any other job he'd done. Just walk.

A few hours left to live.

Nobody noticed them, and like always that was strange, that no one could see and knew.

Malth Tyrenae was there ahead of them. They came within the shadow of its towers. So high, its towers, that they blocked out the light of the sun. The gates were open. A long path up and they would be in.

Tobias could feel him. Marith. A light in his mind up there ahead of them. A pressure. Waiting for them, up there.

A few heartbeats left to live.

They stopped and looked up at the fortress. Its towers were lost in the clouds. Every window was brilliant with light.

'I'm afraid,' said Landra.

My death and his death, Tobias thought.

'You can still leave,' he said to Landra. 'Go back to the inn.'

Saw her eyes blink beneath her helmet. She shifted her hand on the hilt of her sword. 'No.'

She said she wasn't looking for vengeance, Tobias thought.

A trumpet sounded, high and clear. Again. Again.

A voice shouted. Too far away to make out the words.

More voices began to shout.

The trumpet sounded. Trumpets and drums. A horseman came racing out through the gates towards them, past them, a man in armour, a red banner raised, shouting 'We march! We march!' More horsemen. 'We march in an hour! King's orders. Go! Go!' The fortress before them boiling over with shouts, crash of metal, blare of trumpets, horses galloping out. The city shouting and stirring, soldiers and camp followers pulling themselves together, running in panic, preparing themselves.

'King's orders! King's orders!'

'The king says we march!'

The skies opened. Rain pouring down.

Behold the Army of Amrath, preparing to march for Illyr.

You really thought they'd even get close?

Really?

Chapter Forty-Four

The Army of Amrath filed out of Malth Tyrenae. Rank upon rank of bronze helmets, red plumes nodding, a sea of bronze and red. It was raining heavily; the rain ran down their armour, looked like the metal was weeping. The sarriss they carried were tall as tree trunks. A sea. A flood. A forest. Not men. Landra watched them from the shelter of an alleyway and thought: these soldiers are no longer men.

Marith rode at the very head of the first column. White fire flashing on his sword. Landra saw him a moment, so clearly she could have reached out and touched him. He was wearing a new cloak in deep twilight blue. Supposedly the colour of the Godkings. Then he was gone past into the city and the rain hid him.

Tobias cursed and cursed and cursed.

'What do we do?' said Landra. Her mind felt numb. Everything numb. The impossibility of it all made her laugh and weep.

Vengeance! she thought. I should have stayed with Ru learning to weave stinking gold cloth.

'We can still catch him,' said Tobias. His body slumped. Spittle round his lips. 'We can catch him in the street, run up to him, stab him. This is chaos. This isn't an army marching, it's a bloody stampede. We can do it. Come on. Come on!'

'Don't be stupid,' said Raeta. 'We're too late.'

'We can't be too late!' Tobias screamed.

They went back to the inn. Nothing else they could do. What else could they do? In the common room the woman Tobias had befriended stood with a pack at her feet. She was blinking, still half-asleep, smelled of drink and dirt and sweat. She was crying.

'What's wrong?' Landra asked her.

'Nothing. I'm scared,' Sweet Face said, 'for the soldiers. Now it comes to it.' She ran her hands over her amber necklace. 'He was a nice man,' she said. 'Acol. I liked him.' She said, 'We got woken up so sudden, he ran off and didn't even say goodbye.'

Up in their room Raeta started to pack up her things. Landra looked pitifully at her already packed bundle and thought: fool. Gods, I was a fool.

'We go with them,' said Raeta. 'Out in the forest, up in the mountains . . . the Empty Peaks, the Wastes . . .' She looked a little brighter, she had taken off her helmet and her body looked less tense. 'Out in the mountains,' she said, 'he will be vulnerable.'

'He'll be surrounded by a fucking army,' Tobias shouted. 'We won't be able to get near him. He'll fight a fucking war, and maybe he'll die in battle, even, but I won't have killed him. We go now, we catch him in the street, stab him. Now.'

Trumpets. Horses. Tramp of feet. The army pouring out of the city. It was like a storm.

Tobias sagged against the wall. 'I dragged him out of the way of a fucking dragon once.'

Raeta put her hands on his shoulders. Landra thought of a mother comforting a child.

'I was ready to die today,' said Tobias.

'I know,' said Raeta. 'So was I.'

The two of them got Tobias's things in a bundle, while he stared out of the window at the tides of men, cursing.

The innkeep gave them all a cup of beer. 'Victory to the king!' he shouted. 'Joy to the king! Conqueror Illyr for me!' They all

drank. Landra thought Tobias was going to be sick when he drank.
The streets were thick with people, utter chaos, children wailing,
women cursing, people running back and forth. The rain seemed
to be washing them all out of the city. Landra thought: just follow
and follow him. I've followed him from Sorlost to the White Isles
to Ith, I can follow him onwards now to Illyr. Through the west
gates, past the fields and gardens around Tyrenae, marching into
the vast forests of Ith. Three people in a mass of travellers, swept
up in the hunger for gold and blood. The Army of Amrath, sarriss
points raised to the sky, red banner fluttering in the wind.

Tobias muttered, 'Days and days left to live.'

'King Marith!' the soldiers shouted. 'King of the White Isles and
Ith and Illyr!'

'Death!' the soldiers shouted. 'Amrath and the Altrersyr! Death!'

Silver trumpets rang joyously. Drums pounded like heartbeats.

Tens of thousands, hundreds of thousands of people, soldiers,
servants, camp followers, baggage wagons, horses, spread out in
confusion over the fields and forests, the army still wrestling itself
into any kind of order after the sudden command to march. They
lost any trace of Sweet Face. Perhaps, Landra thought, the woman
might find her man Acol, be able to share his tent at night.

A great cloud of crows and gulls flew above them. The crows
and the gulls knew what following an army meant.

Before them, rising jagged, the high mountains. The
Emnelenethkyr. The Empty Peaks. The border of the world of
men. Beyond them, the Wastes. The dead place. No man had ever
lived there, not since the raising of the world. A place indeed
where men should not go. The highest of the mountains were
capped with snow, even in full spring. Yet the forest was full of
life, Landra saw as they marched. Pale pink windstars bloomed
beneath the trees, catkins danced on the branches. Oak and ash
put out golden green leaves. Even the dark pines looked young.
The kind of place, Landra though painfully, where one should feel
filled with hope and happiness. The earth smelled very strongly
of growing: rich heavy soil, rotten wood. Bees humming drowsily.

The first butterflies. Big black beetles with red flashes to their wings. If she turned her face away from the mountains, she saw sweet running water, flowers, green leaves.

They marched until nightfall, stopped and made camp by the side of a stream. Soldiers and camp followers all mixed up together. Fires lit, food prepared, chatter, laughter; again Landra hoped that Sweet Face had found her friend. Marith's camp was off somewhere ahead of them, only a few miles, someone whispered in an awed voice. Absurd that it was the same day as the morning they had tried to kill him.

Landra's body ached. Her mind ached. The shock slowly wearing off, perhaps. Replaced with guilt and pain. She was so tired but she could not sleep. Everything going round and round in her head. Everything changed yet again.

She stared up into the night sky. The flow of the stream made a clear bright sound. A murmur of noise from the next fire, someone still awake. The jangle of metal, the distant sounds of horses, an owl hooted, all the strange human sounds of the night.

She had known him since they were children. Absurd beyond absurd, thinking that he might have been dead, and that she would have killed him.

I hate him, she thought. Yes. But impossible to think of these things.

She tried to think of Ru. Of Ben and Hana and Saem.

Of less shameful things.

There was a splash from the water. Landra sat up.

The night was very dark and very still; the stream was a movement like a shadow, almost visible. She thought: do I see it, or do I only imagine I see it, because I know it is there? Far off in the north she thought that she could see lights moving, in the high mountains on the horizon. Or were they stars moving in the sky?

Tobias was sleeping.

Raeta was gone.

'Tobias.' She shook him. 'Tobias. Where's Raeta?'

'What? Having a piss, I expect. Bugger off. I'm sleeping.'

'Her cloak's gone.'

'Having a piss. Go to sleep.'

He got up stiffly. Landra heard his knees creak. Scratched himself. 'Damn it, Lan, now I need a piss.'

An owl hooted. In the trees ahead, something white moved.

A white shadow. White light.

A sound. An animal smell. Sweet.

There is some kindness in the world. There is. The world is a good place.

Landra stepped forward.

The creature moved towards them.

A deer. White in the light of the stars. Vast antlers reached up into the sky. Vast as trees. Spread and splayed and twisted, a forest of bone branches in which a bird sat and a squirrel ran. Eyes seemed to gaze from the patterns. The deer's own eyes were human eyes. Its face a human face. Neither male nor female. Not a child's face, nor an adult's, nor the face of someone old. But a human face.

It came towards them. Almost looked at them. Its nostrils flared, sniffing. For one moment there was the terrible possibility it might speak. The stars blazed above it. The bird in its antlers fluttered its wings. The deer's hooves pawed the ground. The human face looked at Landra. Landra almost knew its face. Almost spoke to it. Almost called it by its name. Then it lowered its head, snorted a deer's snort from its red human mouth, moved away off into the forest.

Gone. Silence. The stars. The stillness of the air.

A gestmet. A god.

Sat beside the stream for the rest of the night, watching the stars, two dark shapes against the illusionary movement of the water. Landra thought of Ru, sitting by her fire, spinning wool, weaving golden cloth. Swimming in the sea as a seal. Free. Uncaring. Alone. Mindless.

'A god,' she whispered. 'A god.' Wood god. Wood demon. Wild, life power.

'It wasn't a god,' said Tobias. 'It was a . . . a freak thing. A monster. I've seen dragons,' said Tobias. 'A dead whale. Lost cities in the forests of Neir. Cetalasophrase blossom luminous under the moon. I once saw a woman spurt beer from her nipples. I once saw Thalia smile at me. I did not just see a god.'

'It was a gestmet. You saw it. You know.' Its image shaped in gold on old shields; wooden carvings painted in bright colours now chipped and faded, displayed sometimes by the harvest fields; dolls of plaited straw that were burned at Sun's Height. The old unhuman powers of the land, the forests, the wild creatures who lived and died there. Not things to be worshipped. Things to be feared and venerated and left undisturbed, like the wild places and the wild beasts. Unhuman things.

'What did it mean, do you think?'

Tobias was silent for a long time. 'A life god. A life power. What the bloody hell do you think it meant, Landra?'

There, again, far off in the mountains, a tiny flicker of light.

Suddenly Raeta was shaking her awake. 'He's gone,' Raeta hissed in her ear.

I . . . I was sleeping, Landra thought. Dreamed it. I didn't think I could fall asleep, after seeing it. Her body felt grubby and damp. I didn't dream it, she thought. The stream rang very clear and loud, swollen with rain. Mist was rising from it. The sky was pale with dawn light.

'He's gone,' said Raeta.

'Who's gone?' asked Tobias. He got up slowly, stiffly, from where he was lying huddled beside her. Landra could see and feel every part of him hurting. 'Where in all hells have you been?' he asked Raeta.

'The king,' said Raeta. 'He's not with the army any more. He left in the night. I've just come from his camp. The place is an anthill, soldiers massing for something, arming. But Marith has gone.'

'He's left the army?'

Raeta rolled her eyes at Landra. 'That's what I just said, Tobias.'

Tobias looked around as though Marith might appear behind him, sword drawn. 'Where is he then?'

'Marith, Thalia – they've both left,' said Raeta. 'Rumours a small group of horsemen slipped off in the night.'

'Gone back to Tyrenae?'

'I . . .' Raeta looked up at the mountains before them. Their peaks lost in grey rain clouds. 'The horsemen went north,' Raeta said. 'They could be doubling back, I suppose . . .'

Lights in the mountains. Lights in the wild dark night. Gods walking near to the world of men.

'But I think not,' said Raeta. There was fear in her voice.

'One day and we've lost the target? That's a record even for the Free Company at our height.'

'The army's still here,' said Landra. 'It's just Marith who has left.'

'The army's not really the bloody concern, is it?'

'No, Tobias.' Gods, the man really was being hopeless. 'The army,' said Landra, 'the army is not a concern. Not if he's not with them.'

Long pause.

'Yeah,' said Tobias. Half asleep and confused. Who can keep track of what's going on? 'I see what you mean.'

'So we—'

Broke off. A sound coming towards them. Horses' hooves.

Loud as heartbeats. Drumming drumming on the earth. Filled Landra's head. Filled her vision.

Marith, she thought. Marith. Coming to kill me. I saw a god last night, it looked at me, I would have spoken to it. Now Marith is coming to kill me.

Raeta reached over. Took her hand. Squeezed it tight.

Horses' hooves, thundering towards her. A mass of horsemen came past them, armed and in full armour, the horses armoured and masked. Osen Fiolt was at their head. They rode past like a river flooding. So many of them. And then infantry, marching fast behind. Their faces were hard and set. Eager. Hungry.

A very long time it took, for the columns of the Army of Amrath to march back past. They were going back towards Tyrenae at double speed. The camp followers milled around, wondering, some beginning themselves the march back.

'He's going back?'

'He's retreating?'

'He's giving up?'

'There must be some plan . . .'

'The White Isles are under attack?'

'Ith has been invaded?'

'Lord Fiolt has betrayed him?'

'What does it mean?'

'What does it mean?'

The baggage, all the food stores, the army servants, were reported to have been left where they were camped, with guards around. A woman who had spent the night with one of the officers swore the order to march had been given by the king himself.

'Should we follow them?' Landra asked. Such a terrible fear in her, that Raeta would say yes.

'We're looking for Marith,' said Raeta. She looked suddenly very tired. 'Not . . . whatever this is.'

I know what this is, Landra thought then. I know what they're going to do. Oh gods.

Raeta looked strained, sick. Raeta knew, also. Her face was grey, her body bent and hunched with pain. She looked like a tree battered down in storm. Looking at her, Landra heard the creak of breaking wood. The sound of stones shattering against the earth.

'We must go on,' said Raeta. 'Into the mountains. Find him. Kill him. There is nothing we can do here.' Her face was like an animal's face, wounded, suffering. Her mouth moved awkwardly. 'I said that he would be vulnerable in the mountains.'

Destroy him like a rabid dog.

Landra nodded.

Tobias sighed. Spat in the dust. 'I can't let you go to Ith, boy,' he said quietly, half to himself. 'You know that. Can't let you have power and command. I know what you are. What you'd do.' He pulled his pack onto his shoulders. 'Gods. How much more guilt can any one man bear? If we'd done as you wanted, Landra. Paid the weaponsmith more.'

They went on along the road through the forest. Slowly, as though bowed down by a great weight. The forest was green and rich with life. I saw a god, thought Landra. A god of life.

The next morning, great palls of black smoke could be seen on the horizon, coming from the direction of Tyrenae.

Chapter Forty-Five

'Go back to the city,' He tells His army. 'Destroy it. Every stone. Every life.'

'Tyrenae surrendered.' One of His lieutenants. A sensible, clever man. 'Tyrenae is Your city, My Lord King. You are King of Ith.'

'Destroy it,' He says. 'Every stone. Every life. Everything.'

'As My Lord King wills,' the man says.

In Tyrenae, Undyl Silver Eyes tamed the dragon Aesthel by feeding it on the flesh of his own children. In Tyrenae, Ysleta White Hands slew both man and dragon with the sword Goldlight. Sons betrayed their fathers. Fathers betrayed their sons. Children starved while their parents killed each other. Blind children and madmen go begging in the streets there. The wealthy look at them and turn away and do not care. The rich feed on the suffering of paupers. The poor fight each other for food scraps. Terrible things were done there. Torture and pain and hunger and neglect. Tyrenae is not a good place. Three people plotted to destroy King Marith here, and perhaps if they had acted sooner they might have managed to do it, and perhaps things would not be as they are.

Every stone, the Army of Amrath destroys. Every life, they take with their pitiless sharp bronze. They pile the bodies in the rubble.

Pile them into towers of dying. The ground is churned to mud with the river of bloodshed. The ground is slippery with human fat. The city of Tyrenae is wiped from the face of the earth. Everything is dead.

Chapter Forty-Six

'Why?' said Landra.

'Because he could,' said Tobias.

'Half the army . . . half the army were from Ith. From Tyrenae. He forced them to do it,' said Landra. 'He made them. He'd have killed them if they didn't, maybe . . .'

Malth Salene falling in ruins. Marith shrieking, 'Destroy it!' Following him, cheering him, breaking it down with their swords and their bare hands.

I followed him, Tobias thought. Cheered him. This shouldn't be a surprise either, not to anyone. 'Every soldier's wet dream,' said Tobias, 'a rich city, open gates, undefended. Your commander yelling at you to attaaaaccckkkk!!!!! Don't suppose they cared, most of them, whose city it was. Easier, in fact, for the Ithish guys. Knew their way around. Knew where that girl who'd always spurned them was living. Knew where the people in their families keep the secret money stash.'

For three nights, the sky over Tyrenae was lit by red fire. For three days, the sky over Tyrenae was black with smoke. On the fourth night, the sky was dark.

'They'll be heading back this way soon,' said Tobias. 'Back towards Illyr. Suggest we possibly think about getting out of their way.' He turned away from them. Not going to let them see him cry.

They met a woodsman on the road. He knew nothing about what had happened to Tyrenae. Knew nothing about fighting, or a new King of Ith. But he had seen a party of riders, some days past, riding fast into the mountains, hooded and cloaked, richly dressed like great men.

'What in all hells is Marith doing? Where's he going? He can't be planning to conquer Illyr on his own?' Not expecting an answer.

Landra looked blank and puzzled. Raeta shrugged. 'Making himself vulnerable.'

'Very considerate of him . . .' He just didn't want to face it, maybe. Face seeing Tyrenae sacked and slaughtered. *'It was nothing to do with me, I was miles away, I was drunk, I didn't want it to happen, someone must have misunderstood.'*

The forest grew darker. Thicker, less alive. Cutting out the light. The road went sharply upwards, into the mountains, there was no human life visible but they passed sometimes old marks where mine workings had been. The earth was dark and heavy, slimy underfoot. All poisoned, Raeta said, by the mine workings. Quicksilver was once mined here. And then the mountains themselves, their slopes forested with black pine trees, the track leading through high passes where the air was thin and cold. In dark sheltered places there were still patches of snow.

They came to the river Elenanen, that cut through the mountains. It had once flowed all the way across Caltath, the greatest river in Irlast. Flowed past the palaces of the Godkings There was a bridge over the river, the road running along its northern bank. The stones of the bridge were pale yellow, dry and crumbling. They did not look like the stones of the mountain. They did not quite feel like stone under Tobias's hand.

Still no sign of Marith. No trace of a group of horsemen. They were walking through a landscape bigger than the whole of the bloody White Isles. He could have turned off the road. He could be anywhere. Doing anything.

Raeta, Tobias realized, was beginning to look afraid. Staring around her at the trees. She flinched and trembled, as they crossed the bridge.

'*Elenanen*,' Landra said, 'means—'

'Quiet!' Tobias held up his hand. 'Stop. Get down.'

Voices. Coming towards them.

'. . . not my fault . . .'

'. . . bloody stupid . . . tell him . . . tried . . . not . . .'

'. . . kill us . . .'

Not happy bunnies.

Three men came out of the trees. Armed. Dark cloaks. Dark red badges on their armour. Shapeless formless pool of colour, like a scab over where their hearts would be.

'He's near,' Raeta whispered in Tobias's ear.

Tobias nodded. 'What do you think?'

Raeta sighed. 'Yes. Do it.'

The three men came up to them. Hostile and curious. But swords not yet fully out. A man and two women lost in the mountains, what harm could they be?

About to find out, guys. Sorry. Bad luck. Nothing personal.

Music of iron and bronze! Hadn't drawn his sword for a long time. Hack and smash. Smash and hack. Kill two. Take one alive. Easy. Yeah? Gods, this was tiring, his leg ached, his sides ached. Swung his sword aiming for one of the men's chest, and felt his ribs scream. Sword in his face, stabbing, hacking, warded it off, drove his opponent back a few steps, the sword back in his face again. Driven back himself. Ward it off. Just ward it off. Hit and smashed and hit and missed and his ribs were killing him, and so was his arm, and gods he really didn't want to mean that literally.

I used to be a good swordsman, me.

Hack and smash. Artless. Bloody hard. Just ward it off. Kill the bloke before he kills me. Taste of blood in his mouth.

This was a mistake. Should just have chatted to them nice. Asked leading questions. Never mind taking one alive. Just try to stay alive myself. My ribs fucking fucking fucking hurt.

Tobias only got his one down because the bloke stumbled on a rock. Landra was bloody useless, stood there staring with her sword in her hands like she was waiting for someone to be good and helpful and fall on it. Looked terrified. Raeta finally killed her one with a swing of her sword that took his head off. Rolled away, got up some momentum, went over the riverbank. Plop. The body lay there bleeding. Sword still in his hand. Looked really surprised by it, even despite not having a head.

Strong woman, Raeta. Possibly hadn't realized quite how strong.

The last bloke looked at his friends' bodies and howled and dropped his sword and got down on his knees gasping 'please'.

Thank the gods. Tobias held his sword over him. 'You surrendering?'

'Yes. Gods, yes.'

Landra said faintly, 'You're with Marith?' Let's hope, eh? Tobias thought painfully. Bit pointless, all this, otherwise. Might be a bit late to apologize and wish them well on their way.

The prisoner stiffened. 'I serve the king.' The way his voice said the word 'king', sweet in his mouth, sucking on it as if it was honey. Made Tobias want to puke.

'What are you doing here?' said Raeta.

Silence.

Tobias held up his sword. 'What are you doing here?'

'One of the guides deserted, ran off over the mountains. We were sent to track her down.' The weak face looked helplessly at Tobias. 'Are you going to kill me? Though I'm dead whatever, now.'

'Oh gods, man, don't be so bloody melodramatic. And she meant, what's he doing here? Your king?'

The poor bloke stared all round him. Stared at Tobias's sword. At his mate missing his head. 'I don't know. We've been camped here for days now. But I don't know what he's doing here. I swear. Nobody knows.'

'What's your name?' Landra asked the bloke.

'Graventh,' the bloke replied. 'Grav. From Sel Isle. You're from the Whites?'

'From Third Isle.' Landra turned away. Pretty sure she was crying. She made a choking sound. 'Third Isle.'

'He'll kill you,' said Grav.

'Yeah, yeah. What did I say about the melodrama? But before he kills us, you're going to have to take us to him.'

Landra's voice came up suddenly in a scream. 'I've trained to use a blade! I killed a man, when the bandits had attacked outside Skerneheh. Stabbed him in the hand, knocked him down, I rode my horse over him. I didn't even manage to hold my sword properly.'

Raeta said, 'It was a good thing, Landra. He's alive, he can lead us to Marith. You did a good thing, not killing him. Tobias and I . . . we failed, killing the other men.'

Raeta looked at Tobias. Shook her head at him. Failed. Yeah. That was it, definitely. He nodded back. 'Raeta's right, Landra. We needed one alive. Well done.' Just don't tell that to my bloody ribs and leg.

The prisoner led them up along the bank of the river Elenanen. Whose name, Tobias had realized, must mean something like 'Sorrow'. Or 'Joy'. It rushed down in a torrent of snowmelt, ice cold, sharp and fierce. Well named, yeah, the way it rushed down. Kites and crows circled above. Watching them. They had come down in a cloud for the dead men. Raeta looked exhausted. Frightened. Landra was white faced, still mumbling about her knife. After a while, they turned off the road, scrambled up a narrow track like an animal track. The trees gave way to scrub grass and thorns and bare grey rock. Hard, bitter ground. Every step hurt the body, hard pain down into the bone.

Gods curse this bloody godsdamned bloody place. I'm a sellsword, I'm not a fucking mountaineer. The rock beneath Tobias's feet slipped suddenly, twisting his ankle round. He stumbled, landed hard on jagged stone, scraped his hands on thorns. 'Gods! This godsdamned place! What in all gods is he bloody doing up here? He's supposed to be bloody well invading bloody Illyr. Not fucking around camped up a bloody mountain.'

'Treating the wife to a walking holiday? Taken up landscape painting? Heard about a particularly good hatha den hereabouts?' Raeta's voice was harsh and drawn. She sounded so bloody afraid. 'Think about it, Tobias. Think.'

Landra said quietly, 'He's looking for something.'

'Looking for what? Particularly viciously bloody rocks?'

Grav smiled like daggers. 'I lied. I do know why he's here. Clever girl, Landra. He is looking for something. But not rocks.'

An empty landscape. The Empty Peaks. The border between the world of cities and the wasteland where nothing lived. Why does nothing live here? Do you think?

Raeta moaned. Landra wept. With fear or with pity or with laughter. Tobias pissed himself.

From over the mountain came the sound of beating wings.

Chapter Forty-Seven

Night, and almost dawn. Thalia was sleeping, breathing softly, her hair hanging over her face, one hand raised near her mouth. Barely visible in the dark, the faint glow from the brazier catching on her skin. Marith sat and watched her for a while. His breathing in time with hers. Never ceased to wonder, watching her. Luminous bronze, like flowers opening, like water and light. The first time he saw her face, shining like that . . . Perfect beauty. Hope.

Misplaced. Like everything. The pitiful illusion that life was worth something. Life is death, Marith. Love is death. There is no hope. He had not told her about Tyrenae. She would understand, perhaps. But it would burn like ice, to see her face if she knew. She would have to know in the end.

I wish I hadn't done it, he thought. Osen had asked him if he was certain. He had paused a long time, before he had said yes. And there, now, another guilt. I shouldn't have asked it of him, he thought.

Betray me, he thought, looking at Thalia. Destroy me. Please. If you love. Carin loved me enough to help me. You . . . do not, I think. The Chosen of the God of Living and Dying, radiant with light. You do not understand. You cannot.

Osen understands, he thought then. It sickened him, then, to think that. Osen had always understood.

He got up, wrapped the thick fur blanket carefully around her. Caring. Taking care of her. Even despite everything. She moved and frowned and sighed. Didn't wake. He dressed quickly, feeling his clothes in the dark. His sword caught with a clatter on one leg of the brazier: he froze, guilty, waiting for her to wake. She stirred and sighed again, her eyes blinked open blindly, then rolled back into sleep. Marith counted to two hundred in his head. When she was certainly asleep he buckled his sword belt, fastened his bloodstained blood stinking cloak. The movement of the fabric raised a stench of rot in the tent. Flakes of blood moving in the draft blowing in through the tent's seams. He trailed blood where he walked now, like a man who had been walking in the muck. Slug trails. Sometimes Thalia had to brush it out of her hair.

He pushed aside the curtain separating the sleeping room from the main chamber of the tent, went through. A candle burned there on a low table set with fine worked silver jugs and cups. He lit a second candle, poured himself a drink, splashed water on his face. The wine was as cold as the water. He drank the wine off, refilled his cup, drank again. The cold sharp sweetness of it sang in his head. He drew a long breath. Stepped outside.

It was perfect dark, no moon, no stars. The cloud had thickened overnight. The torches had all burned down to embers, the campfire was dead. Utter silence in the camp. Tal sat hunched in the tent doorway, sleeping, his sword drawn across his knees. Should have the man cut to pieces, for falling asleep on watch. Cut him and maim him and feed his eyes and his tongue to the dogs.

He walked carefully over the curled bodies of the guards who should be watching. It was too dark to see, but he walked as if he could see. His eyes open. Staring into the dark. He walked further up the slopes of the mountain, his feet crunching on the stones. The air itself smelled of stone. In the sky in the east the very first faint whiteness of morning. He could see, without seeing, the tents damp with dew, the men sleeping, the dead fires, Thalia sleeping with her hands against her face. The slopes of the mountain were dead and silent. Everything still. Waiting. Afraid.

A memory came to him: walking on a riverbank, in the dawn, watching the mist rise, the world pale and strange, his own vision pale and strange. The bog smell of the water. Silence, and then the harsh sad cry of a bird. A terrible, fearful knowledge of impending joy and horror, of something coming in the dawn. A keening grief struck through him as of something lost. A pain.

I should kill her, he thought. Destroy her. Like I killed Carin.

He stopped walking. He'd come far enough. The camp was below out of sight in the rocks. The sun was rising. It was time. So.

Marith sat down on a rock, took a drink from the wineflask at his belt, rubbed at his eyes. His hands were shaking. Stupid. No need to be afraid, he thought. I have no need to be afraid. Not now. He took another drink of wine. Looked at the ragged face of the mountain before him. Stood up and raised his arms.

'*Athelarakt! Mememonsti tei essenek! Ansikanderakesis teme tei kekilienet! Athela!*'

Come out! Show yourself! Your king summons you. Come!

His voice echoed on the rock. Nothing moved. Pink breaking dawn. Thick black clouds at the peaks. A dead land.

'*Athelarakt! Ansikanderakesis teme tei kekilienet! Ansikanderakesis teme! Athela!*'

Nothing.

'*Athela!*'

A crow called, off to his left. Marith almost laughed: was that it, all he would find, his voice's echo and a crow?

The crow called again. Stones rattled behind him. Ah, gods . . . He swung round.

'Marith.' Thalia was there, wrapped in her furs, Ithish diamonds at her throat. 'Marith.'

He said in confusion, 'What are you doing here? It's not . . . not safe.'

'Not safe?' She smiled. 'I chose to come. I think I will be safe.'

'I thought you were sleeping.'

'I was. You woke me up. Crashing around with your sword

trying to be quiet.' Her smile faded. 'You shouldn't drink in the mornings.'

'I needed it, this morning.'

Opened her mouth to speak, then sighed. Laughed. Bitter laugher. Sad. 'I'll have a drink too, then.'

'You don't need it.' Drops of wine red on her lips. It made him flinch, to see her drink. She gave the wineflask back to him.

'Come on then,' said Thalia. Marith shook himself, followed her further up the slopes of the mountain, the path winding up and back on itself, a hard scramble over rocks that cut at their hands. Thalia's cloak caught, he had to detach it, ripping the lining; her hair came loose and blew in the wind. She was panting a little. Enjoying herself. He'd taken her climbing at Malth Elelane, on the cliffs of the headland that ran down to deep rock pools and caves and the sea. She'd laughed as she climbed.

They came to a narrow gap in the rocks, a thin passage through like an open door. The path ran through it, water running down in a stream making the ground shine. So narrow they had to go through sideways. It opened out into a wide gorge, sheltered and green, its walls great tumbled masses of stone. A peaceful place. Calm out of the wind. The cloud was coming down over the mountains, making it misty, as though seen through a hatha haze. Marith rubbed at his eyes again.

'Here,' Thalia said. She took his hand. '*Ynthelaranemyn mae.*'

He almost snatched his hand away from her. Then grasped hers more tightly. Warm. '*Ynthelaranen,* beloved. It will come. Singular. I hope.'

They stood together looking at the rocks and the grass and the gathering cloud. Slowly the world fading, grey mist covering everything, closing off their vision. Grey mist and grey rock. The side of the mountain merged away. Morning light dimmed. Silence, different to the silence before the cloud came down, heavier and waiting. Like the memory again, the river mist, the dawn, knowing something was near.

No, Marith thought. That, that was a memory of this place.

Ah, gods. Flee. Run away from here. Take her away. She is betraying me? Then beg her to kill me here, now, before it's too late. She is betraying me? Then she is as wise as she is beautiful, and all the world should thank her.

The cloud stirred. Sounds in the rocks: scrabbling, stones shifting, stones dragging against stone. Stones shattering under great weight. A rasping breathing that sounded like a man breathing as he died in pain.

Athelenaranen.

It comes.

Smoke smell. Hot metal. Charred meat. Colour, coming towards them through the cloud. A glow of burning. Something too huge to be properly seen.

Marith drew a breath. His eyes itching. Fire. Smoke. Burning. Scalded metal. Fear. Joy. He clawed at his eyes. Thalia was trembling, her hand cold with sweat, fingers clutched into his palm. Marith squeezed it tightly. It's all right. It's all right, beloved. I've done this before, remember? That didn't end . . . quite as badly as it might have done.

It came closer. A vast shape, vast as buildings, blocking out the weak little light of the sun. Its own light, red as coal fires, flickering from eyes and mouth and scales. The scrape of stones breaking beneath it. A hissing of steam and the rasping raw breath.

The dragon bent out of the mist. Lowered itself before Marith. Bowed its head.

Like a horse, waiting to be mounted. Like a dog, beaten and begging for treats.

Like a lover, kneeling in desire and surrender at his feet.

Chapter Forty-Eight

The camp was finally stirring as they made their way back down. Tal sat up and stretched, blinked heavy eyes. Marith smiled at him.

'Pleasant sleep?'

'My Lord King . . . Gods . . . My Lord King . . .' Groggy look on his face, that horrible feeling one got from sleeping in armour, sticky clammy like the skin was half rust. 'My Lord King . . . My Queen . . .'

'You're forgiven. Everyone seems to be asleep this morning. Get people awake and a bath drawn. Some breakfast.' Marith went into the tent, began pouring himself a drink. Thalia's hand came to rest on his arm.

'You promised.'

Kill her. Destroy her. If she will not destroy you. 'It's not every day one commands a dragon, beloved.'

She considered this. Smiled. A wide, delighted smile. She picked up the flask and the cups and led him through into the sleeping area. 'That's true. Marith the dragonlord. Marith to whom dragons kneel in homage. That, we should celebrate.'

A very nice day. Wine and love, and he could almost forget what she had done. Get deliciously drunk and fuck for hours. In bright sunlight, and in the evening shadows, and in the dark by candle-light. In the mountains, the empty places, it all seemed so far away. I'm wrong, he thought again. Osen was wrong. Thalia gave Landra a necklace. So what? I destroyed Landra's home and all her family. Left her less than I ever was. Why should I grudge Landra a necklace? She sold it to buy bread. Bread! Thalia is so beautiful and so alive even the gods come to worship her, and yet she stays here with me. In the cold emptiness, in the tent, it reminded him of being in the desert, facing down another dragon, triumphant, glorious, beneath the endless sky. They whispered to each other of the dragon. Wondered in it, together. How can I think she will betray me, Marith thought, when we together have seen and done such things? Whatever comes after, she has stood by my side and seen such things. 'Marith the dragonlord. Marith to whom the dragons kneel in homage.' Ah, gods, yes! Wine, and love, and memories of the desert, when he first met her, and that night they stood together drunk and laughing and watched dragon fire burn in mountain heights through soft spring rainfall, and stumbled together back into bed.

Chapter Forty-Nine

Watched the dragon circle high into the morning sunlight, beating its vast wings, breathing out fire, shrieking out a song. At last, long after it had vanished into the horizon, they crept onwards. Tobias saw it and felt it every moment, watching him. They went on bent over, crawling through ragged undergrowth, painfully vulnerable. The sound of wing beats, dragon song in the air. Hot faces, as though they already burned with dragon fire.

'There,' Grav said after a long time crawling. 'There. Over that ridge. His camp.'

Tobias closed his eyes.

'I'll go and scout it out,' said Raeta.

Tobias let out a sigh of relief.

There was a tumble of rocks nearby, the remains of an old rockfall from the heights. Or from where dragon claws had torn and rent the earth. They found a sort of cave there. Landra found faded marks on the cave walls, letters carved in Itheralik. 'Amrath's soldiers,' Raeta said, 'perhaps. When He crossed into Ith. Or deserters from His army, running back to Illyr.' She took off her pack, her cloak, left everything but her knife with them in the cave. 'If I'm not back in an hour,' she said, 'then . . .' She smiled at them. 'You'll have to kill him anyway.'

She came back in much less than an hour. Yes. His camp. 'Four tents,' she said. 'Perhaps twenty people. Most of them armed soldiers. Nothing much seemed to be going on. I didn't see him.'

'No dragon?' Imagined it curled up like a watchdog, outside Marith's tent.

She snorted. 'No.'

'He'll kill you,' said Grav.

'I told you to stop being so bloody melodramatic.'

Tobias considered Grav for a while. Sat on the other side of the cave looking at him. Went up close to him. He's shown us to Marith's tent. So his job's done.

He stuck his sword into Grav's chest.

Grav gasped like a fish and was dead.

Landra cried out. Raeta cried out. Soft. We're on an assassination mission here, you two, Tobias thought. He felt sick.

'Extra couple of hours, he had, thanks to you,' he said to Landra. Could hear the tremor in his voice.

She looked down at her hands. 'Yes.'

Neither of them helped him drag Grav's body to the back of the cave. He wiped and swiped his hands on the scrub outside the cave.

Landra came over after a while, gave him a torn bit of her skirt to clean himself up with.

'I had to do it,' Tobias said. She didn't say anything. She was squeezing her vile bit of yellow cloth.

'We'll do it tonight, then,' said Raeta. Her voice sounded strange. Heavy. There was a roughness to it. Like sawing wood. Her eyes flashed. 'Tonight.'

Here we are again, then. One more day to live.

The day passed forever and much too quickly. They sat in the cave, stared at the walls, tried not to gag at the smell of Grav's blood. I really shouldn't have stabbed him, Tobias thought. I'm sorry, man. Nothing personal. Honest. Look, you'd have done the same thing to me. Probably with more relish.

The sun set. Through the mouth of the cave the sky was liquid gold.

'Pretty,' said Raeta. 'Not much different to yesterday. Bit more cloud.'

Tobias stared at the sky waiting for the light to fade. Fucking hell. Fucking hell.

'Come on, then,' said Raeta. She drew out her knife and Landra drew out her knife.

'Leave the swords and the armour,' Tobias said. They both nodded. Too heavy. Too noisy. Don't need armour, fighting stuff. Defensive stuff. Landra's face was flushed and eager. It seemed to take forever, just to walk out of the cave.

Did this for a living, once.

Fucking hell.

'This way,' said Raeta. They crept towards the camp. Crawled on their bellies the last bit, like worms. Like maggots, Tobias thought. Lay on their bellies in the dark watching soldiers and servants moving around, murmured voices, an evening meal being prepared. Marith and Thalia came out of their tent briefly, spoke to someone, went back inside. Tobias's body tensed and his heart screamed in his chest. A servant went into the tent a little later, carrying a bottle. The camp began slowly to settle for the night. Clouds over the moon. Tobias's body was aching and his leg hurt like shit.

The camp silent. Most of the torches were extinguished.

A few heartbeats left to live. Landra's eyes shone in the dark.

'Now,' Raeta whispered.

Crawling fear all up Tobias's back, stomach in knots, his bowels churned up to mush. Through the camp, bent low like animals, knifed two guards round the campsite perimeter, knifed two guards dozing outside Marith's tent. Stopped with a hiss. Raeta reached out. Pulled open the door curtain. Slipped inside. A servant sleeping in the main chamber. Raeta slit the poor bastard's throat in his sleep. Dim lamplight on fine worked metal tableware, a stand with armour, a table with a pile of papers and maps. A scatter of wine bottles and a smell of alcohol. The air stung like knife blades. Shadows moved in the corners like birds. Raeta hissed through her teeth. It did not somehow sound like a human sound.

Go back! Go back! every part of Tobias's body was screaming. Too fucking easy. We'll all die here. Put out his hand to pull Landra back, run away out of here this place is dying this place is death.

Raeta smiling, knife glinting in the lamplight, pulling back the curtain to the inner chamber. Something in her hands, in her body, as she moved that rippled like blood.

And there he is, Marith Altrersyr King Ruin King of Darkness, lying sleeping naked as a baby with his chest showing silver-white. Like a fucking target. White skin shouting 'stab here'. Easy. Too easy. Oh gods. Oh gods and fuck. Beautiful Thalia asleep beside him, hair like a waterfall, perfect arched curve of her arm. Strained to see her perfect arched curved bubs. But still the terror in Tobias: go back! Go back!

Raeta smiled and her smile was reflected in her knife blade. Her eyes and her teeth were huge and sharp and she wasn't quite a human thing.

Landra raised her knife.

One heartbeat left to live.

Chapter Fifty

A hissing sound. Marith sat up, jerked, rolled sideways, a blade came down hard burying itself in the bed. Thalia sat up screaming. Silver light flooded the tent. Dark to light was blinding: Marith blinked as a shape threw itself at him, spitting through its lips. Flailed for the knife under his pillow. Thalia! Gods, Thalia, my love! Pain in his shoulder. Bright as the light. His hand closed on the knife handle. A voice shouted. Pain again. Bright in his heart. Thalia! He struck out with the knife, felt it meet something hard and yielding. Sunk in deep. Blood smell. Blood spattering his face. Voices cursing whispering in panic. The light exploded brighter. A kind of howl. Lonely. Heartbroken. Afraid. The weight on the knife jerked away from him. Killed it? Shrieking hissing sound. Smell of hot musky earth. Sweet.

The light faded. Dim cool shadows, the lamp by the bed flickering into life. Thin traces of dawn coming in through the tent seams. A gentle music of rain on the leather and the smell of fresh damp. Thalia was sitting up in the bed. Naked. Shining. All the light in her face. Landra and Tobias and a woman with yellow hair were kneeling on the ground before him. Blood on Landra's fingers. Blood on Tobias's arm.

That would be what had stabbed him, then. And that would be what he'd stabbed.

Landra was holding a knife. The blade ended half way in a jagged line of rust. She was staring at it mesmerized, like a woman looking at a snake. Tobias was looking at Thalia. The yellow-haired woman was looking at Tobias. There was blood running down the yellow-haired woman's cheek bones. Running out of her eyes.

Thalia pulled the bedding up around her. Flushed and trembled at Tobias staring. Weeping. Afraid. Ashamed. Her eyes closed, opened weaker and pale. The light flared and dimmed again. The spell broken. Tobias looked away from her. Groaned.

Hot musky earth smell. Sweet. Like an animal scent. The yellow-haired woman turned away from Tobias. Got up onto her feet. Raised long clawed arms. Like birds' wings.

'No!'

The light bursting out again. Marith threw himself at the woman, hitting out with the knife. He was on top of her, his weight knocking her over, they rolled on the floor of the tent. Her breath stank in his face hot musk and stone. Eyes like furnaces, weeping blood. Cold and hard as iron ingots, writhing dissolving under his hands, he stabbed down at nothing, cold and hard as iron, dissolving like wrestling storm clouds, the stinking breath in his face. All he could see was yellow. Sulphur fires and yellow dust. He hit again and again with the knife blade. Sparks flying. The ring of metal on stone. Keening weeping howls. Yellow, and behind his eyes black star-lit dark. A thing like a hoof struck his shoulder. Earth stink. Life stink. The smell of flowers. The smell of bread baking. The warm smell of sweat and skin. Rolled and got some kind of purchase on it, lashed out with the knife blade, got something soft. His hand sank into it. Growling sound. Pig grunts. Filth like grass blades thrust in his mouth. Taste of flowers. Scalded metal. He spat and bit down. Shrieking. He'd hurt it. His shoulder was bleeding. It had hurt him. But you can't hurt me, he thought. You can't! From a long way off he could hear Thalia screaming. Soft floppy things like dead fingers rubbing themselves over his body. His eyes stung worse than hatha. Soft floppy dead finger things peeling at his eyes and mouth. Taste of flowers. Scalded metal. Shrieking. Pain in his chest. Hurting. Hurting me. Taste of blood in his mouth. Hit and hit and hit with the knife blade. Blunted metal. Rang like hammers on an anvil. Bright flashes. Musk. Hit and hit and hit with the knife blade. Shrieking. A soft, warm weight.

You can't hurt me, he thought. You can't. He burned up in white fire. Stabbed out with the knife. Eyes staring at him, huge as mill stones. Bleeding. A vast white explosion of light.

Thalia's voice, screaming. Shouting. 'No! No!'

Hit it. Hit it. Hit.

The lamplight flickering, dawn light coming in picking out the seams of the tent.

Thalia standing with the light pouring out of her. Tobias crouched in the corner. Landra crouched beside Tobias. The yellow-haired woman lying huddled, blood on her face.

The door curtain pulled open. Brychan and Lord Durith and Lord Parale and a whole lot of people, all armed, falling over each other to get inside. The thing that was pretending to be a woman spat at them, stretched out her claws. Lord Parale rushed at it. His sword went up like pitch burning. Fingernails long as sarriss tore off his arm.

'Get back! Get back!' Brychan. Shouting.

Thalia was still shouting 'No! No!'.

The thing reared up in front of them, huge and silver, shapeless like the branches of a tree. Marith reached his sword where it hung in the corner, so very close, so very far from the bed. Drew it in a shower of white light.

He screamed, 'Death!' and rushed at it, hacking down with his whole strength. The bedchamber filled with shadows. Rainbows dancing on the leather. Rainbows dancing on Thalia's face. The shadows rose like a maelstrom. The bedchamber stank of rot.

The sword bit home.

All there is, in the end, he thought. The dark. The dust. This creature, this god, this thing is weaker than I am. Is life. Is lies. Death is the one true thing.

He struck again with the sword, felt flesh and blood yielding. Soft heavy drag of the blade through skin.

Killing it.

Landra's voice, screaming. Shouting. Pleading. 'Marith. Please. Marith.'

The tent exploded in silver shadows. Marith fell backwards. The sword rang in his hand. Thalia's voice crying out rejoicing. A thing like a great black bird shot upwards into the roof of the tent, a deafening beating of feathers, a smell of burned bones. The leather of the tent ripped open. Dawn light flooding in on them, damp soft morning rain. A mass of leaves swirled up out of the hole. Dead leaves blown on the wind. Black before his eyes a moment, and when he could see again Landra and Tobias and the woman were gone.

Marith stood naked and uninjured, shining white in the morning, rain picking out the fine bones of his shoulders, the muscles of his arms and chest. Blood and leaves and feathers caught in his beautiful blood-clot coloured hair.

Chapter Fifty-One

'Fucking fucking fucking what the fuck?' Tobias kicked the ground. Stamping and swearing trying to keep the fear out of him. His arm hurt like murder. Like it was alive with insects. Like every crow in Ith was pecking him alive. But nothing compared to the fear and anger. Betrayal. Shock. Failure.

Humiliation.

Again.

I had a shit in front of you once, Raeta, he thought. And you turn out to be a . . . a . . .

They were hidden in the cave. It was dark in the cave. Dark and damp. Landra sat in the corner. She had her scrap of yellow cloth in her hands, kept looking at it, turning it over.

'Fuck fucking fuck fuck fuck.'

Stone crunched under Tobias's boot heel. He kicked the wall of the cave and his leg hurt. A shower of dust from the ceiling. Landra glanced briefly up.

'He wasn't injured,' said Landra. 'I stabbed him. I did.'

'Yeah.' Who knew what had happened?

'My knife . . . It just . . . It rusted away. The blade. Stabbed him and it just . . . rusted away. Didn't harm him.'

'Yeah.' Like you stabbed Grav, he tried to think. Like that.

'Look at it!'

She held out the hilt of something. All kind of ashy at the base, where it should join to a blade. Looked old as mountains. She prodded it. A bit of it fell off.

Amrath returned. Dragon kin. Demon born. All that crap.

Oh, gods. Oh fuck.

She just missed him, he thought desperately. Missed and her knife sort of . . . sort of . . . broke . . .

'He's just a man,' said Landra. 'I stabbed him.' Twisting and twisting the scrap of yellow cloth. 'My brother bedded him. I used to sit opposite him at dinner. I was going to marry him.'

'It's a bloody good thing we didn't make it into Malth Tyrenae,' said Tobias. 'Would have looked pretty dumb, wouldn't we, rushing him shouting "Death to King Ruin!" and our swords just bouncing off?'

The thing that was pretending to be Raeta came in through the mouth of the cave. Her breath was wheezing out of her. She was bent over like sticks and looked a thousand years old and a thousand leagues tall. She sat down slow as an old man. Rotting smell. Sweet. Dead animals. Old dead wood. All her different faces. She looked like an owl and a skull and a dead horse and a fallen tree. Bones and splinters poking out all wrong. Lots of different bits of her crawling and moving, like she was covered in insects. Bark and leaves and fur and hide and feathers. Old, old god thing. Old power of earth and life. Whole forest of life growing over and around her. If you listened carefully, you could hear birds singing and beetles' wings. Gestmet. Wood god. Life god.

'He's gone,' she said. 'They broke camp. We're safe for now.' Turned to Landra. 'You named him King Ruin, Landra,' it said.

Landra kept turning the yellow cloth over. Staring at it, not looking anywhere else.

The thing that was pretending to be Raeta got some bread out of her pack, chewed it. Crack of bones shifting as she ate. She ate very slowly, like it hurt her to move her mouth. Stopped, spat a tooth into her hand.

Tobias took a drink from his water bottle. Meltwater from the river Sorrow, cold as stars. Got out some bread and chewed it himself.

Landra kept turning the yellow cloth over. Staring at it, not looking anywhere else.

The thing that was pretending to be Raeta finished the bread, drank water from her own bottle. Winced. Cold pain on the wounds in her mouth. Her breath reminded him of a loom clacking.

He could still almost see her woman face. One eye was sealed up puffy. Oozing. Green-blue-purple-red-black. Her real eye stared through beneath it, furnace hot, huge as the world. Kind of like being a weaver, he kept trying to think. Seeing the pretty cloth with its pretty dancing patterns, flowers and swirls and that, masterpiece of the weaver's art, that is, got to envy the talent what made that, while also seeing the mess there'd be on the other side too, just a whole lot of jumbled colours, the bloodstains from a child's fingers for the fine bits, the tears of frustration up at midnight bent frantic over the loom, the slowly going blind eyes. Seeing both things, at once.

Kind of like that. Kind of.

Blood was beginning to seep out again from the bandage round her left shoulder. Black bones shoved out through coarse skin. He'd had to sew it up. Crack the bones back into place. Looked one way and it was nice white lady skin and pinky lady bits. Then blinked, and . . . Couldn't see it. Or could, but couldn't fix it in his mind.

His own arm wasn't much better. Wouldn't stop bleeding, no matter how tightly Landra tied it.

'Who's the bloke in the boat you say is your brother?' he asked. 'You really got a dead ma back on the Whites?'

The thing that was pretending to be Raeta spat blood, laughed then caught her hands to her chest. 'You've got a god sitting beside you and that's what you want to know? Who's the bloke in the boat? You really got a dead ma?'

'Gods and demons, Raeta!'

The thing that was pretending to be Raeta laughed again,

wheezed her breath. 'The bloke on the boat had a sister called Raeta. They had a ma back on Fealene.'

'Had?'

'I told you: she's dead. I am that Raeta, Tobias. I'm just . . . this, as well.'

'A gestmet. A wood demon. A failure. A not actually all that powerful god thing.'

'His destruction.' Wheezing breath like a loom clattering. 'Basically, yes.'

Best part of two months, he'd had Marith poxy gods' cursed Altrersyr King Ruin King of Shadows the second coming of Amrath marching around making him tea and digging the fucking latrines.

Best part of six months, he'd had Raeta whatever the fuck she was god thing nagging at him and being whined at back. He'd shat himself in front of her. Very nearly once asked her if she'd be interested in having a feel of his cock.

Still saw it. Every time his eyes closed. Every time he stopped concentrating on not seeing it. Fire blast. Blinding. The two of them fighting.

Death and Life. White light and shadows. Wingbeats. Knife blades. Seeing things it wasn't possible for a man to see.

Seeing Raeta fail. Seeing Raeta dying. Seeing what Marith really was.

Running in the dark. Lost. Running. Back to the cave, with Grav dead behind a pile of rocks.

Failure.

Again.

Oh, gods.

'So,' said Landra. 'What now, then?'

'We die,' said Tobias shortly. 'Or I do and you do.'

The thing that was pretending to be called Raeta's breath came even worse, clacking like loom weights. 'I'm not far off dying, Tobias,' she said. 'A lot closer to dying than you are. But yes, we go on after him.' She said. 'What else is there we can do? Our

death and his death.' Bent her head. 'I had not realized he was so
. . . so strong,' she said.

Landra looked at the hilt of her knife and laughed.

'We should get out of here,' said Tobias. 'There'll be men out
looking, I should think.'

'You're both wounded,' said Landra.

'Rather wounded than dead.'

Grav's body fucking stank already. The clouds had come down
very low, thick like fog, hiding everything.

Tobias drew his sword. 'Come on, then. His death and our
death.' Or just our death, more like.

The thought of what would have happened if they'd been a day
earlier in Tyrenae again. Really clear image of it: him running at
Marith screaming, the sword hitting, the sword bouncing off in
little bits of rusty metal, Marith grinning at him. Invulnerable!
Gods, yet another reason to hate the poisonous little shit. I risked
my fucking neck, he thought, in Sorlost, warding a sword stroke
off him.

'Did you magic me?' he said to the thing that was pretending
to be Raeta. 'Did you maze me, make me follow you to help you
kill him? Like he magicked me to fight for him on the White Isles?
Is that why I'm here, not safe in a warm bed somewhere? Did you
magic me?'

'Did he magic you to fight for him on the White Isles?' said
Raeta.

Thought about this. Malth Salene, Marith's voice screaming
'Destroy it', killing everything.

Landra looked at him. He looked back at her. Met her stare.
Held it.

'Go back to Immish, then,' said Raeta. 'Find a warm bed.'

'Fuck him. Fuck him.'

Got up, shouldered his pack, began to walk on. Bent over,
limping and gasping with pain.

Chapter Fifty-Two

Marith thought: I've always known.

And it did not surprise him. But it felt almost . . . almost shameful.

He had been injured before. Of course he had. Many times. Had his hand half burned off by a dragon. Torn all the skin off his knees slipping in a rock pool. Put a broken branch through his arm falling out of a tree. That last had almost killed him, the tree had been rotten, the wound had mortified, wept pus. He remembered, dimly, his mother kneeling by his bedside holding his hand, crying, begging Eltheia for aid. Heal him. Heal him. An older woman's voice in the background, chanting over and over the old rune words. *Hel benth, tha:* health, safety from disease, hope. The weight of stone charms and wood charms pressing on his arm.

(Not my mother, he thought. She killed my mother. She hoped I would die that day, I expect. Was begging Eltheia for that. Wasn't she? Closed the thought away.)

But this . . .

Hard to kill, the Altrersyr. Famous for it. I always knew, he thought. Always.

'I saw you wounded,' Thalia said. 'I saw your blood.' She pointed to ruined bedding heaped on the floor of the ruined tent. 'There. There is your blood.'

Thalia sat running her hand over and over his shoulder. Where the wound should be. In the morning light flooding in through the rent in the tent's roof, with bright lamps burning, his skin was perfect as a child's skin. Creamy white like new milk. Smooth lines of muscle and bone and sinew. His skin tingled deliciously under the touch of her hand.

'Yes. That's my blood.'

'Amrath conquered the world,' Marith said after a while. Her hand on his shoulder was distracting. He lifted it off. 'He fought a lot of battles. Survived them all.' He drank wine. Looked at her. Rain was still coming in through the rent in the tent's roof, glistening in her hair. But neither of them could bear to leave the tent, step out into the world beyond, now they knew what they had both already known about him.

There were leaves and flowers on the floor of the tent at their feet. Spatter of blood. Flakes of rust.

'You knew that Landra was alive,' he said.

Thalia pulled her hand away from him. 'How do you know that?'

'Someone recognized the necklace you gave her.'

'Someone?'

'A servant in the palace.' It came out of his mouth so smoothly. Didn't know if she could tell he was lying. Didn't think she could tell he was lying. 'I should have your guards flogged,' he said, 'for letting you talk to her.'

'They didn't know who she was,' said Thalia. 'I told them she was a beggar. They are my guards. Not yours. She was cold and hungry,' said Thalia. Oh gods, she looked so beautiful. So earnest. 'She was alone and broken, and I pitied her.'

Pitied her? 'She wanted to kill us!' Marith said. It came out as a shrill shout.

Landra kneeling in his tent, burned . . . she had looked so much like Carin did in his dreams, with his sword sticking into him. 'She wanted to destroy me. She hates me. She hates you.'

Thalia said nothing.

'And Tobias. And that . . . that thing. You were talking to that thing. You were conspiring with that thing. I know that.'

'The gestmet,' Thalia said. 'That is what your people call it, I believe. Did my guards tell you that, too?'

'I needed to know. Don't you think I needed to know?'

Silence. Her face was unreadable. 'I speak with whoever I choose,' said Thalia.

'You were conspiring against me! That thing just tried to kill me. Landra Relast just tried to kill me.'

'I drove the gestmet away,' said Thalia. 'I did not speak with it. I did not let it speak to me.' But there was something in her face. Some guilt. 'I speak with whoever I choose,' she said again.

Marith thought: that's it? That's all you can say?

'I did not know that Tobias was alive,' she said. 'I . . . If I had . . .'

Marith thought: oh, didn't you know? Something in her face. Days, he thought, Thalia and Tobias had travelled together, with him Tobias's prisoner. Days and days and nights.

We called a dragon together, he thought. We saw all the wonder of the world in its eyes and in the beat of its wings. A dragon, dancing! And now this.

Remembered how Tobias had once looked at him, in the lodging house called the Five Corners in Sorlost, after he had stolen the company's money to buy firewine. Tobias had trusted him, for a little while. Had then realized with disgust what a mistake that had been.

He had feared that he would die, he remembered, in Sorlost. Stared at the walls and been so, so afraid of death. He looked at the ruined bedding on the floor. Laughed.

Thalia's face was cold, watching him. Angry.

Wedded bliss! He thought: if I had known what you would do . . .

Felt the blood rush to his face. Sickness and shame. Horror. My father killed my mother, he thought. My father killed his wife. I killed Carin.

'I love you,' he said to Thalia. 'I do. I do.' Got down on his knees on the bloody bedsheets. 'I love you.'

'Even though you think I am conspiring against you?' It was difficult to hold in his mind, sometimes, what it was that she had been, before he met her. The High Priestess of the death god of the Sekemleth Empire, killer of men and women and children for the glory of her god. And he felt now as her victims must have felt, bound and naked beneath her knife.

'We need to leave,' he said. Change the subject. Everything felt so soiled. The wonder of it, the joy, the melancholy. Get away, block this thing out. Remembered the inn in Reneneth, trying to find anything to say to her, knowing she had seen him drugged out of his mind on hatha, soaked in his own filth.

Days and days and nights, she had spent, travelling with Tobias, while he lay drugged out of his mind in his own filth.

Why do you stay, Thalia? he thought.

He walked out of the tent. The campsite was all chaos: they were supposed to be leaving today anyway and no one seemed to know what to do, whether to pack up. The tents were fuzzy with the rain. The mountain turf was beautiful, in the rain. Heavy raindrops like jewels. A gorse bush, hung with raindrops. A white flowering thorn tree. There was a spider's web between two of the tents, beaded with rain. The sky was soft pale grey. The clouds had come down, hiding the higher slopes of the mountain.

Different, strange, looking at it now. All this living beauty. A living world. And he was what he was.

'Amrath was a living man,' Carin had once said. 'A lucky man with good armour and a chronicler who lied about certain things.' Carin had rolled his eyes. 'I seem to remember, it might just be the drink confusing me, but I do seem to remember that Amrath died.'

Thalia came out and stood beside him. Did not touch him. She, too, looked around her at the grass and the gorse and the thorn tree. The spider's web. The low cloud. She, too, he saw, was thinking of life and death and other things.

'Marith—' she said. He turned away. He felt her walk away.

Alleen Durith came up to him. Knelt. Very formal. Everyone in the camp should be flogged, Marith thought, for letting danger get so close to him.

'Five men dead,' said Alleen. 'And Lord Parale. We've buried them. There's a trail, very faint, the scouts say, goes off south over the ridge.' He pointed into the cloud. 'Did you want us to pursue?'

'Shouldn't you already be pursuing them?' Marith asked lightly.

Alleen Durith shifted from foot to foot. 'In the . . . the cloud . . . The . . . My Lord King, the men . . .'

Are terrified and confused and terrified and perfectly well aware of what's out there. Marith stared at the raindrops on the spider's web. Tried to think.

Poor Lord Parale. He'd been so excited when Marith let him come along.

'We leave them,' he said. 'Pack up, as was arranged. I have done what I came here to do. We will rejoin the army, as was arranged. March for Illyr.' It felt good in his mouth, saying it. Solid. Bronze and iron, he thought. Swords and spears. Solid things. And rejoin Osen Fiolt. The air grew colder. He wondered if the dragon was flying, up above the clouds. *Athela!* he thought. *Athela, Tiameneket!* That would cap everything. Calling the dragon down and riding away on its back.

He drank wine and looked at the raindrops on the spider's web, until the servants had to dismantle the tent. Thalia kept away from him. They rode down the mountain, to rejoin the Army of Amrath marching through the Wastes.

Chapter Fifty-Three

Marching through the Wastes. Marching to the edge of the world. Trying to find a way to kill a man who cannot die. Landra and Raeta and Tobias went very slowly. Tobias and the Raeta-thing slow as old women, accompanied by grunts and groans and crunches and yelps. Difficult bits, the Raeta-thing had to hold on to Landra's elbow on account of how she couldn't see properly out of one eye. So they were going to walk across the Wastes to Illyr? Take them, what, several years? Marith Altrersyr King Ruin King of Shadows Invulnerable would be dead of old age before they got to him.

The landscape got bleaker as they travelled. Bare high grassland, broken every few miles by outcroppings of grey rock. Like a sea with whales breaching, said the thing that had once been Raeta. The rocks tumbled into shapes that tricked the eyes into seeing patterns: pillars, doorways, faces, thrones. A perfectly round lake reflected the sky pale and empty. Nothing moved on it. Smelled funny as they got closer. The water was smooth, solid looking, glistening dark. Fine silk velvet, picked out with gold thread. The water bottles were almost empty, so Landra suggested they get water there. Maybe even wash.

'Water's poison,' said Tobias.

'Poison?'

He picked up a handful of soil, threw it into the lake. The water hissed, closed over the soil without a ripple. Perfectly smooth surface, like muscles and skin and good cloth.

'Poison.'

Landra blanched.

They tried to camp every night in the shelter of the rock formations. Woke each morning at dawn to the cawing of crows. High off screams of kites and kestrels. The crows sat on the rocks hoping they'd die soon. Flies buzzed round Tobias, drawn by the smell of his smaller, just about scabbing wound. Left Raeta alone.

The Army of Amrath were ahead of them. Spurred on by its exploits in Tyrenae. Eager for more. Three days down from the mountains they had seen the dust clouds behind them, the sound and smell of ten times a thousand horses and men. Kept their distance, cowered in the cover of some rocks when a scouting part rode by.

'Let them get well ahead of us,' Tobias said. 'Safer that way. Try and fall in with the idiots following them. If any of them survive this.'

That Marith knew they were all three alive and following him in order to kill him was a stumbling block they didn't mention. Like the broken sarriss they came across: entirely pointless. That Marith might be unkillable was a stumbling block they didn't mention either. Like the next broken sarriss they came across: even more pointless.

'What are you?' Tobias asked Raeta. 'What is he? Explain!'

She only shook her head, slowly and painfully, and Tobias saw leaves dancing and birds flying and heard the sound of the wind in bare dead trees. 'Death,' she said.

They stopped in a place where a troop of soldiers had camped before them. A discarded water bottle, an empty pork barrel, bits of pig bone alive with flies and beetles. They were running out of bread. So the thing that had been Raeta suggested they eat the beetles. Landra looked sickened. Tobias felt his stomach heave.

They crunched almost nicely, you shut your eyes and your mind to what it was. Landra blushed scarlet when she traced out graffiti on a rock reading, 'Sarene is the most beautiful of women. Sarene likes it up the arse'.

Gods, reading it was wonderful, out here in the filth. Someone out here thinking about sex and love and women, feeling alive enough to scratch it laboriously into solid rock.

Once they found the body of a soldier, stretched out with a clawing hand reaching off to follow his comrade's tracks. Sword wound deep in the belly. A very slow way to die. The next day they came across a cart and cart horse, abandoned in one of the smooth dead pools. The horse was so covered in insects it was thrashing around like it was still living. So was the man who'd fallen in trying to rescue it. Made a funny sort of high-pitched squeaky clicking sound. Another two dead men a few hours later, floating face down. Another cart sunk and broken. Another dead horse. No more graffiti or salt pork bones. Occasionally they came across groups of stragglers, camp followers staggering dying of thirst and hunger and exhaustion, unable to keep up to follow the army, unable to go back. 'Gold,' one woman repeated over and over as she died in the dirt. 'Gold. Gold.' 'The Illyians killed my father,' a man shouted, stumbling away from them into the dusk. 'Revenge!' Tobias felt a nagging horror they would come across Sweet Face.

Landra pointed. 'Look there.'

Raeta followed her hand, squinting. Her face all screwed up. 'Interesting,' Raeta said.

After days and days walking through the dead landscape, actual living breathing moving not dying life. Or some of it wasn't dying, anyway. They had caught up with a squad of soldiers. A baggage wagon, floundering hopeless in a patch of shimmering poisoned marsh. A thousand yellow irises, a thousand blue and silver dragonflies, the smell of mint. And a dying horse in the water, five men gathered around cursing. Frantic attempts to unload a cargo of grain sacks.

'Fucking gods don't let the sacks sli—'

Splash. The horse jerked. Poisoned water sprayed up. Sparkling. Dancing. Raised a cloud of dragonflies iridescent in the evening sun.

'Oh gods. Oh hells.'

'Get the rest of the damned sacks.'

Watched sympathetically as the soldiers wrestled most of the remaining cargo onto dry land. The wagon and the horse slowly sank.

'Let me give you a hand there.' Tobias helped a young man lug a sack clear of the marsh water. His leg and arm and ribs shrieked like the horse.

'Bastards fucked off and left us. Thank you.'

Tobias blinked. 'Acol? Sweet Face's friend?'

'Tobe, man! What in all gods happened to you?'

So there was nothing for it but for Acol's squad of soldiers to adopt them for the duration, promise solemnly to help them get all the way to Illyr. The bulk of the army was well ahead. Days. Maybe weeks. The going was, uh, maybe a bit harder than anyone had anticipated. King Marith had split his forces in two, sent them up along the north and south coasts. The baggage wagons were getting further and further behind. Getting lost. The army was starving, must be. But rushing on. Leaving them behind. Curse it, Friend said, the war will be over, by the time we get the bloody baggage to Illyr.

'You should have joined the army, Tobe,' said Friend. 'Still could, you know. You're still about young enough. You should have seen what we did to Tyrenae! Oh, gods, you missed out there.'

Death, Tobias thought. The sum total of my life now. Raeta wheezed out a breath that sounded like waves crashing on the shore.

I followed him. I was part of his army. I'm no different to these guys. Why me? Why do I have to see it? See him? A little house in Alborn, and a girl to clean it, and a beer or three in the evening, and a fat soft flatulent gut . . . But we go on, because there's nothing else. Me, and Landra with her face burned and her heart broken, and a dying wounded cursed damn god.

At night, the soldiers sat round and told stories about Amrath. Every. Single. Night. The *Treachery of Illyr*. The *Wooing of Eltheia*. The *Fall of Tereen*. The *Burning of Elarne*. The *Burning of Balkash*. Even the *Song of The Magelord Symeon and the Gabeleth*. Name a city. Name a way of blowing it to buggery. Yell 'Victory!' Repeat.

Gods, that last one brought back happy memories. If he'd known. If he'd only bloody well known.

'Tyrenae was like that. Like something from the songs. Like the Fall of Tereen. We went through it like we were slaughtering cattle.' Acol's eyes were rapt. 'They put up no defence: gods, the look on their faces, when we marched back in through the gates, they thought maybe we were retreating, had given up on the idea of invading Illyr, you could hear people sniggering at us. And then we went for it! Their faces were a picture.' Acol held up a gold necklace. 'Look at this! Even nicer than the one I found in Morr Town. And a lot more fun to get.'

Tobias tried to introduce a bit of variety, tell a story from Immish. They told him as one to shut the fuck up.

Landra writhed in discomfort, listening. Every night.

Raeta's wound was getting worse. It stank. She looked old and grey faced and terrible. Cold grey like the cold grey stones. She sat and listened every night to the stories, her eyes closed, her face turned to the west. Searching for him, Tobias thought. The nights were very dark, out here. The stars were very bright. Hateful, staring down on them. The red star of the Dragon's Mouth looked huge, out here. Tobias found himself staring back at it.

Acol said, 'We'll be at the Nimenest soon. Three days, tops, if the wagons can keep from getting stuck.' And then bloody what? None of this is real, thought Tobias. I'm dying, somewhere in Sorlost, in the Emperor's palace, that mage is torching me, I'm bloody dying delirious, I'll wake to see myself die and that, gods, I'll feel so relieved about. Oh gods. Please.

'Anyway,' said Acol. 'I'm turning in. Need to keep rested for the fun ahead.'

'Good idea, mate. Keep your strength up.'

'Gods,' Tobias said when the soldiers were all bedded down in their possibly familiar looking wool blankets, 'any chance I can kill him?'

'I . . . I have an idea,' said Landra.

'What?'

'To kill him.'

'Him?'

Landra's face was pale. Her voice had a shake in it. Oh. Him. Tobias thought: this is not going to be good. I really think this is not going to be good.

Landra gestured to them to move a little further away from the soldiers' campfire. 'I . . .' She looked at them, edgy, frightened, eager. 'I . . . There is something,' she said, 'the stories . . . made me think of it. There is something in . . . in Illyr. In Ethalden. That might . . . that could . . . Bronze and iron cannot kill him. Men cannot kill him. But there might be something in Ethalden, a thing powerful enough to destroy him. Might be.'

Ethalden. The Tower of Life and Death. Shit yourself in terror saying it even as you marvelled at just how naff the old bastard's taste in names had been. No. Please. No. I've been there once. I'm not going there again, with Marith there. Said kind of trying for casually witty: 'The Illyian army, perchance?'

'Shut up, Tobias,' said Raeta. 'Well?'

'What's the one thing Amrath was ever afraid of?' said Landra.

'His mum,' said Tobias. 'The pitiful size of his willy. His total sexual inadequacy. Someone finding out who his dad really was.' *Something Amrath was afraid of.* A story I think I might have heard recently, and once before in a caravan inn. Oh gods. Oh gods.

'The gabeleth,' said Landra. 'The one thing that defeated Amrath and Serelethe's power. The magelord Symeon had to destroy it for Him. And Amrath was afraid of Symeon, that he could do it where

He had failed. Had him killed in turn. The gabeleth could destroy Marith. Perhaps. Don't you think?'

Two nights ago, their dear friends the soldiers of the light infantry, the mighty guardians of the baggage cart, had told the story, singing it loud out into the night.

A great fortress, Amrath raised in Illyr. Its walls were made of gold and mage glass, and its banqueting halls were carved of onyx and red jade. A mustering ground for armies. A prison for his enemies. A warning to all men. Its towers were so high they blocked out the very sunlight. Its chambers rang with shadows and screams. Blood was its mortar. Tears were its mortar. Ashes were its mortar. It was built on the bodies of the dead.

But Amrath could find no pleasure in his fortress. For each month at the dark of the moon, a soldier or a serving maid or a noble was found dead in their bed, and not a mark on them but the burning marks of a great fire running all up the length of their right arm. But no smoke was smelled, and no cries were heard, and what was killing them and how they died no man knew. And the guards and the maids and the nobles began to lose faith in Amrath, if he could not keep his own people safe within his own walls.

So Amrath and his mother Serelethe were in despair, for try as they might, they could not find an answer to the mystery, and their people were dying and muttering against them. And Amrath had angry words with Serelethe, who had promised him mastery of an empire but could not defend his own men for him. And so things went badly in Ethalden.

Now, this had been going on for a year, and no man was any closer to finding the truth of it, when there came to Ethalden a young mage, a wandering sorcerer from Tarboran where the fires burn. And he stood before the throne of Amrath, and dared look even Amrath full in the face. And he promised Amrath that he knew the secret that was plaguing his fortress, and could destroy it. And all he wanted in return was a chance to stand beside

Amrath, and be his lieutenant, and lead his armies with fire and blood.

So Amrath roared a great roar of laughter, and promised the mage gold and silver and precious jewels, and a lordship, and the command of his armies, if he should only defeat the evil that was plaguing him. For he saw in the mage a brother, and a comrade, and a tool to be used. He gave the mage a great chamber for lodgings, and put all of his wealth and his power at his disposal.

The mage walked the corridors of the fortress, sniffing the air and looking at the stone. And at length he stopped in a certain place, a small room in the outer keep looking down over the city, and he gave a great cry and said, 'This is the place. And now we shall see what we shall see.' And he ordered the men with him to dig.

The men dug and the men dug, and they broke open the great stones of the walls, and they found there buried the body of a young girl, with her right arm burned through to the bone from her wrist to her shoulder, and the marks of a knife on her throat.

Well, Amrath, he ordered the body buried with full honour, as though the girl was his own sister. Ten horses, they burned over her grave. But still the dying did not stop, for at the next month at the dark of the moon one of the mage's very servants was found dead and cold with no mark on him but the burning marks of a great fire running all up the length of his right arm. And the mage knew then that he was dealing with no ghost but a gabeleth, a demon summoned up from the twilight places by the shedding of the girl's blood. And he was greatly afeared, for such a thing is very powerful.

But the mage had promised Amrath he would destroy that which was harming his people. And he feared Amrath near as much as he did the gabeleth. So he locked himself away in his chamber with his books and his magics, and for three days he did not eat or sleep but only worked at his spells. And at the end of three days he went back to the room where he had found the girl's body, bringing with him his staff, and his sword, and a silver ring. And there he fought the demon.

Three days and three nights they fought, and fire raged through the skies above Ethalden, and Serelethe herself cried out for fear. So terrible was the battle that every child birthed on those three days in all Ethalden and for thirty leagues beyond was born dead. So terrible was the battle that the sick died and healthy men went mad and ran screaming into the sea, or set themselves afire and were burned to death where they stood.

And at the end of three days, the mage overcame the demon, and peace returned to Ethalden, the Tower of Life and Death. And Amrath's heart was pleased.

For Amrath had feared the gabeleth.

'The gabeleth.' Landra was very pale. Her hands opening and closing on her stupid little scrap of yellow cloth. 'The demon was so powerful, even Amrath and Serelethe feared it. If Marith cannot be killed with bronze or iron or a gestmet's magic, then perhaps . . . a demon . . . a thing even Amrath feared . . . perhaps he could be killed with that.'

'The demon, uh, was destroyed . . .' Oh no, Tobias thought. Oh hells. Oh gods. Oh fuck. Oh no. I could have been in his bloody army, Tobias thought. Victorious and glorious and all that. I could have been home in Alborn. A little house and a girl and a pint of Immish gold or three of a night. I could have been warm and safe and cosy and dead.

'Symeon overcame it. But he didn't destroy it. It was not alive, and so it could not die. He imprisoned it. He imprisoned it in the silver ring. In my family,' said Landra, 'we have a story that Amrath wore the ring all His life, out of fear of it. No one says what happened to it after Amrath's death. I always assumed that He . . . that He died wearing the ring.'

Amrath lies unburied, somewhere in the ruins of Ethalden. Wearing a silver ring?

'There's nothing in Ethalden,' said Tobias. 'Nothing. Just rubble and dead earth. I've been there. I've seen it. Just dead earth.'

So many things, he thought, that I've seen. A dragon. A dead whale. A god walking the forests, my friend and my companion. Beautiful Thalia smiling at me. And what else is there we can do, indeed? See Marith destroyed. What else is there left for me? I've been dead since Tyrenae, he thought.

Landra shivered violently as a night bird screeched out in the marshes. Far off, staring into the dark, Tobias thought he could see the lights of ten times a thousand campfires. The army of the *Ansikanderakesis Amrakane.* Somewhere out there in the dark. Like trying to think that there were whales out swimming beneath the cold grey sea, dragons dancing on the west wind.

Not campfires, he thought. Marsh lights. Glow flies. Tricks of his eyes.

'If bronze and iron cannot kill him, if he is Amrath returned, if he is Death,' said Landra.

Marching through the Wastes. Marching to the edge of the world.

Marching to find a ring with a demon in it, on the finger of a dead god, unburied in the ashes of a ruined tower. To kill a man who cannot die.

Gods and demons and fuck.

Chapter Fifty-Four

Marching through the Wastes. Marching to the edge of the world.

Marching to rebuild a great city. To find the betrayed body of Amrath the World Conqueror.

Marching triumphantly to war.

The soldiers walked in near silence, neither hungry nor tired. The nearer they got to Illyr the more they hardened, silent and uncomplaining, tramping on and on. They barely seemed to need to eat or drink. To think. Their faces stared fixed on the horizon, towards Illyr; at night their faces turned towards the king's tent and the king.

Thalia kept in her wagon. Marith had arranged, while it travelled to catch them, for it to be even more sumptuously decked out, gold silk lining the walls and ceiling, three layers of green dyed kid skin for the floor cover, jewelled flowers set into the struts of the roof. A glade of light and blossoms for her, fragrant with sweetwood: he had had in his mind, perhaps, the Great Chamber of her Temple, glowing golden bronze in the morning sun.

The wagon jogging along slowly with the wheels catching and slipping and sticking in ruts. Four times they had broken a wheel on hidden rocks. One day it stuck for hours, under a burning sun and a cold wind. A man's hand got caught, trying to mend the back axle; when they got him free his skin was black from fingers to elbow. Thalia asked Tal to find out what happened to him. For days he refused to tell her anything; finally he admitted that the man had had his arm cut off, but had still died. In the marshes the pace was almost painful, the horse straining, the wheels fouled so they could barely move. The weight of two kingdoms' treasures, pressing down in the mud. Often they had to stop while men scrambled behind pushing. Lay out the canvas coverings of the supply wagons in the mire to help the wheels turn. The water got in on the green leather flooring, made it rank with mould. The sweetwood rotted. Huge flies caught inside the window slats, whined and rattled till they died. Tal swatted them, burst them in clots of red on the silk walls. Two men led the horses at a crawl pace, cursing at them to keep on.

'Amrath campaigned rough with his men?' Thalia asked Marith. 'The old ways of war?'

'You deserve better.' He'd been drinking with Osen the night before, hard rough spirits distilled by the men. Sat in silence now in her wagon watching Tal swat the flies.

'We should have got a ship there,' she said bitterly. 'I can't go on, in this.'

'No one sails to Illyr.' He shuddered. He, who loved the sea.

'It cannot be as bad as this. You didn't tell me it was like this.'

'I didn't—' He rubbed hard at his eyes. Hatha itch. He and Alleen Durith took hatha together. In Tyrenae, and on the march. Despite her pleading. Despite her threats to Alleen. 'Stop talking about it.'

'We should have got a ship there,' she said.

'My grandfather Nevethlyn sailed to Illyr. His fleet was driven all the way round Illyr, into the Sea of Grief, wrecked on the south coast. His army was destroyed. One of his ships made it back to the Whites. Hilanis the Young sailed to Illyr. Every one of his ships was destroyed. No one knows if he even reached the Illyian coast.' He looked away from her. Frowned. Almost bared his teeth. 'Is that what you want for me, then?'

'What?'

'Me, all my army, dead?' His voice was poisoned, like the water of the marshes.

'What?' Sickness filled her. 'Marith?'

Rubbed harder at his eyes. 'Are you still meeting with Landra?' he said. 'Giving her more of my mother's jewels?' He stumbled to his feet, pulled open one of her chests of clothing. 'She's following us, isn't she? She and that thing. Which of these shall we give her, then?'

Tal was staring at them. Terrified. Flies buzzing around his head, around the dead flies on the walls, on his lap where he had been scraping them off.

'That's enough,' Thalia said. High Priestess of Great Tanis. Chosen of God. Queen of the White Isles and Ith and Immier and Illyr and wherever else he claimed to rule. 'Enough.'

'Are you meeting with Tobias? Did you give him gifts of jewels too?' His eyes. His mad eyes.

The light blazed up in her. Golden. Tal cried out in fear. The horses leading the wagon snorted, also in fear. The wagon juddered, almost stopped.

Marith cowered back into the corner of the wagon. A dark clot of shadow by the wagon's door. Raised his hands over his eyes. Clawed at his face.

The light died. Thalia knelt down beside him. 'I thought of killing you once.'

'I can't die,' he whispered.

Walk out. Leave him. Curse him.

She had begun to hear rumours, about Tyrenae. Whispers. He had said something himself, then closed his mouth on it, looked away in shame, tried to speak of other things.

Vile.

Disease, he is.

'*Come away now with me. We can get away,*' Landra Relast had said.

'I gave Landra a necklace, yes. Out of pity. As I said before. To

371

buy food. She was freezing. Starving. As I was, when you found me. I was starving and cold and alone, and you cared for me, gave me your cloak. You were kind to me. I was kind to her.'

He whimpered. He sounded like the horses drawing the wagon, snorting and afraid, stupid dumb fearful things. My husband the dragonlord. My husband who defeated a god.

'Get out,' she said.

The Army of Amrath marched faster, singing the paean. Their mouths bitter with thirst. Thalia's wagon rattled over dusty stones. The horses were thin and sore in their harnesses. They held up their heads and trotted eagerly onwards. Their nostrils pricked. Smelling coming blood. Tal brought word to Thalia that Illyians were massing to repel them. Rumour amongst the men said that the Illyians ate their enemies' still beating hearts. The men jogged on waiting. A heavy impatience hung over them all. Thalia sat listless in her wagon. Tal reported to Thalia that Marith rode with Osen Fiolt or Alleen Durith. Thalia was sleeping in her wagon. She and Marith had not spoken since they argued.

They reached the Nimenest five days later. The river that marked the border between the Wastes and Illyr. Marith came to tell Thalia. Ask her to come and stand on the bank of the river and see it by his side.

'And Illyr, too, you will raze to ashes? Butcher everything that lives?'

'This is war, Thalia! That is what war is. What did you think I would do to Tyrenae? Tyrenae deserved it.' He rubbed his eyes. 'If you don't like people dying, you can—'

'I can?'

'What did you think would happen in war?' he shouted. He walked out.

They made camp in the hills a few hours' march from the river. From the hilltops the river showed as a thin band of silver, bordered by scrubby trees. Tiny figures swirled on the plain beyond it. Their swords glinted in the sun. It felt very strange, to Thalia, setting up tents with the enemy out there so near. Marith had the troops draw up in full battle order, paraded the horses, then ordered them all to get some rest. The baggage wagons were a long way behind them still. Marith had sent Yanis Stansel back after them, with a large contingent of foot soldiers. The river was wide, fast flowing. The land beyond huge. They had little spare food. They seemed suddenly very small.

Marith rode out the next morning to inspect the river, look over the grassy plain beyond, where the battle was to be fought. Thalia watched from the crown of the hill. Distant figures wheeled on the Illyian bank. Shouting things, waving spears and swords. Been watching them since they arrived. Several brief exchanges of arrows. At night they could see the Illyian campfires, spread on the plain like stars.

There are a lot of them, she thought.

'But they could come over and attack us,' she said to Tal. Marith looked so small and vulnerable, with just Osen and Kiana and a handful of soldiers. More and more Illyians were riding up to stare at him. Their first proper sight of him.

Tal snorted. 'They could. They won't.'

'How can you be sure?'

Tal pointed at the silver river. 'Because they'd have to be suicidal to cross that when there's an army waiting for them on the other side.'

Thalia considered this. 'And we cross . . .?'

'Day after tomorrow, at first light. Not that I'm supposed to know that, mind.'

Thalia went to her wagon. It smelled very strongly of marsh damp. The air outside rang with the preparation for battle. The wind shifted direction: she caught the scent of hot iron, the clang of the smith's hammer, ensuring at the last that the horses were all well shod. A low rasping noise hung over everything. Thalia realized after a while it was the sound of an army's worth of swords being sharpened. The air must be full of tiny fragments of metal dust.

Hours passed. She had nothing to do. She decided to go for a walk around the camp. The king's tent was closed off, Brychan and one of Lord Erith's sons and another man standing guard at the door. Voices buzzed inside, too quiet for her to catch them. Then a cheer and a laugh. Kiana Sabryya came up in full armour, flanked by two attendants. Said something as she entered, stopped in the doorway and smiled at Thalia, then the leather closed behind her. Men's voices cheered.

Thalia thought, for a moment, of going in there. Confronting them all.

She walked the circuit of the camp. Tal followed her, very close behind. The whole place was churning with activity. Bright glow of excitement. Like the day before a great festival, or the morning of her wedding. She laughed bitterly to herself at that. Like the day she was dedicated. The day of a sacrifice. Everyone waiting with such impatience, trying to find something to do. Soldiers' faces smiled up at her. The great omen of their king's prowess, the holy beauty of the Yellow Empire he had mastered and made his wife. Pain filled her. She smiled back at them smiling at her with love. The soldiers had set up a shrine place at the bank of a stream, she knelt carefully in the damp and placed a necklace in offering. Piles of green branches, piles of wet round pebbles, pieces of bark and stone and metal scratched with the names 'Amrath', 'Eltheia', 'Marith', 'the king'. Locks of hair, human and horses'. Feathers. Crumbs of bread. Bird bones. Bird entrails. Smears of blood.

There was nothing more she could do. Indeed, she rather suspected from Tal's expression that she was getting rather in the way. Soldiers hurried about doing . . . things. Some horses got loose, overexcited, charged off through an encampment and almost brought down a tent. From the king's tent came the sound of singing. She could tell from the voices that most of them were drunk.

'The old ways of war, My Lady Queen,' Tal said. Mistaking her face. 'It'll be all right. The king's not expecting it to be anything difficult, tomorrow. Just some fun and a bit of spilled Illyian blood.'

She was awoken that night by a great mass of noise ringing around the camp. In the dark, torchlight flickering in through the closed windows, she had no idea what was happening, panicked that they were under attack. Outside was a mass of activity, soldiers moving, horses being led up. The sky was black as pitch. No stars. Raining heavily. The torches hissed and sputtered in the rain. Firelight shone on bronze armour. Helmeted figures gripping swords, spears. They reminded Thalia of the priestesses, masked for Great Tanis. God things. Holy things. Priests of ruin and death.

The camp was emptying. In silence, in the dark. Brychan and Tal stood guard by her wagon, watching them go with hungry eyes.

Thalia dressed herself. A rich silver gown, jewels for her hair and throat. Wrapped her furs around her. Her horse would already be saddled. Waiting if necessary for her to flee back across the Wastes to safety somewhere.

'We go with them,' she said to Brychan.

'My Lord King ordered that we were to stay here,' he said. His eyes would not meet her face.

'Your queen orders you to escort her to the field of battle. Or I will go on my own.'

Tal said, 'I said that My Lord King ordered that we were to stay here.'

'I said that your queen orders you to follow her.' Thalia pushed past them towards her horse. 'Or she will go alone. Your Lord King will make you answer for that, I think.'

Tal and Brychan sighed and cursed and followed her. They rode down the hill out of the camp.

Marith had spoken of a good ford upriver. To Thalia's confusion, however, the bulk of the soldiers were moving back the way they had come a few days before, away from the river, into the Wastes.

It was too dark to see clearly; the heavy rain confused everything. But she was certain they were heading away from where they should be going. She looked at Tal in alarm.

'Do you want to turn back, My Queen?' he asked shortly.

'No. We follow.' It was very dark. Dawn, Marith had said. It couldn't be anything near dawn. She felt as though she had had only a very few hours' sleep.

They were following a squad of foot soldiers, sarrissmen, walking silently carrying weapons twice as tall as a man. Their raised points made a forest. A palisade to block out the sky. No one spoke or sang the paean. Faces turned to look at Thalia, puzzled, then turned back to staring ahead of them into the dark.

After what seemed forever marching away from the river they swung sharply to the right. Thalia tried to guess the direction, but there was nothing to judge direction by. No stars. No moon. No light. Nowhere near dawn. The ground under the horses' hooves was soft. Sandy. Churned up and soaked with rain. It muffled the sound of their footsteps. Sucked at their feet. They were turning again, swinging again right. The ground of the hill had been sandy. So they were near the camp again? But she could see nothing. No lights. They marched on and on. Changing direction again sharply. So dark. She, she who had walked so often in darkness, she felt the dark like a blindfold and could see nothing and was blind. They went on looking straight ahead in silence. No light. No moon. No stars.

Claustrophobic. This horrible black silent march. It would go on forever, she thought suddenly. They had gone out of the world, beyond the light and the life things. They were marching forever and forever in the endless dark.

There was nothing but darkness. He had taken them beyond living. They were lost in the dark.

She wanted to cry out. To make light. To raise up fire. There is nothing out there, she thought. This wall of darkness is everything there is. So weak, the barriers between the darkness and the illusion of living. They had followed him and followed him and marched through out of the world.

She couldn't speak. Couldn't move. It had been raining, but now she wasn't certain whether she was soaking wet or scoured dry. Silent. No footsteps. Not even the sound of men's breathing. The men were dead. The horse was dead. The horse walked on fixedly into the dark. The faces of the soldiers staring ahead of them. Seeing nothing. No longer human, in their helmets and armour. Death things walking in the dark.

And then suddenly she saw light, very faint, pale and barely visible, ghost light in the furthest reaches of the sky.

Dawn coming, in the east. The traces of trees emerging. The waiting ranks of horses and men. She could see, in the half-light, the outlines of the land.

They had marched round in a great half circle back to banks of the Nimenest. But not upriver. Down.

The troop stopped. Drank from water bottles, chewed on crusts of stone bread.

The light got stronger. The sky in the east soft blue, then blue-silver, then rosy pink. Bronze armour gleamed. The light flashed on the points of the sarriss. A horse whinnied. Hushed. The strange waiting silence. Thalia remembered it from her Temple. The roar of it loud as the wind.

No birdsong. She remembered that, later. A smell of smoke in the air. The men stirred, looked together all at once to the east. She could hear, suddenly, now that she was aware of it, the sound of metal clashing. Shouts. A crash like thunder and an answering scream.

Finally she could speak. 'What's happening?' she whispered to Tal.

He grinned. 'We're crossing the river. That's what. My Queen.'

'But the fighting . . .'

'Upstream of us, My Queen. My Lord King mentioned the ford?'

'But that's where we were crossing . . .'

He was close enough she could see him laugh at her. 'Bit obvious, wouldn't that be, My Queen?'

The sky was flaming pink and orange. Glorious dawn. Thalia raised her head to it. Raised her eyes to the light. It shone on the armour, the horses dressed and ribboned, the points of the sarriss. The dark red banners, silk and leather and men's flayed skin. The sandy ground and the scrubby trees and the tall dry grasses gleamed pink in the sunrise. Sparkling with rain. The light catching on the water. The river mist rising like steam.

The sounds of distant battle redoubled. Shouts and cheers and screams. A mile away? Two?

The heavy waiting silence. The soldiers stood perfectly still. The light was fading. Thalia blinked her eyes. A bank of cloud rushing up in the east. Thick and vast. It covered the sun. The world suddenly dark as night again.

The soldiers dimly visible around her. The horse shifted. Frightened, she thought, as she was.

Not frightened, she realized. Eager.

'We should go back, now, My Queen,' said Tal. 'Back to the camp.'

The press of men began to move forward. Marching forward in slow steady lines. A drum began to beat.

Gulls and crows. The shrill cry of a hawk.

The men went on again in the dark.

They were at the river. The water shimmered black. Slowly and steadily the soldiers began to cross. It was raining again, heavily, a curtain of water. The rain drummed on the soldiers' armour, a wild thundering roar like horses' hooves at the gallop, or the rapid hammering of an ironsmith beating out a sword.

'We have to turn back!' shouted Tal in Thalia's ear. 'We can't cross with them! We have to go back to the camp! My Lord King ordered you to stay in the camp!'

The horses pushed on, ignoring him. The soldiers around them seething over the bank into the river. Thalia's horse slithered down the bank in the river following them.

The water came up to the horse's belly. Her body was soaked and cold. The men around her must be almost swimming. How did they manage, she thought, with their sarriss? The weight of the armour alone must threaten to drown them. The current was strong, the horse had to push. It was so dark she could hardly see her hands holding the reins. The sound of the rain on the water and the rush of the current was so very loud. The rain on the soldiers' armour. So heavy it stung her skin. Waves broke over her body, water stirred up by the press of men. It tasted like metal in her mouth.

The horse scrambled up the opposite bank. In Illyr, Thalia thought. They were in Illyr. Amrath's kingdom, where they ate their enemies' hearts. The bank was very steep and stony. Men and horses slipped and slithered in the mud. Voices shouted, panicked. Something happening behind her. She tried to turn, caught a glimpse of men falling. Sliding back into the water. Trampled by those behind them. Drowned. She cried out to the men to stop. Help their comrades. But the columns of soldiers pressed on. Moved on away from the river into Illyr, taking her horse with them. It staggered through the churned mud. Voices shouted orders. The press of men began to shift eastwards. Downriver. Towards the distant battle. Again Thalia tried to pull back her horse. Tal, close to her, reached for her horse's bridle. He shouted something indistinct, the columns moved and he was lost in the dark.

There was a clap of thunder. Deafening, roaring on and on. A sound over it. Men's faces raised in glory.

The beating of wings.

The dragon lit up the sky like the sun.

Crouching at Marith's feet, it had been huge as buildings. Flying with spread wings it was vast as a world. Crimson red like new bleeding. Like the inside of a mouth. Its wings and tail were tinged with gold. It breathed out fire and the clouds burned around it. The armour of the soldiers marching beneath it glowed fiery red.

The sky was on fire. Dust in the air burning. The rain boiled up in a cloud of steam. The dragon came down lower over the army. Vast crushing shape. The flames faded, utter darkness, the dark body darker than the clouds. Lines of fire glowing around its jaws. It spurted fire again, joyful. Dropped lower and lower until its claws were hanging above the soldiers' heads. Threw back its head and spouted flame upwards. A shimmering fountain. A tree burning. Columns and palaces of flame.

The men screamed in frenzy. 'Amrath! Amrath! *Ansikanderakesis Amrakane!* Victory! Victory!' And the deeper, bloodier cheering, the clash of swords and spears. 'King Ruin!' 'Death and all demons!' 'Death! Death! Death!'

Tal was shrieking and shouting somewhere over to the left: 'The king! The king! Victory!'

Intoxicating. Throbbing in her head like wine. She had forgotten, almost, the glorious feeling when one waited to kill. Thalia laughed, shouted, 'Victory! Victory! The king!'

Again the dragon spouted fire. A great rushing wall of light. Like storm waves. A thousand banners of red and yellow rippling silk. The wind of the dragon's wingbeats stirred burning eddies in the sky. Currents of fire. Spirals. Sparks falling and the grass was ablaze.

Voices shouting: 'Victory! Victory! King Ruin! Death! Death! Death!' A blare of trumpets. The thud of drums. Thalia pulled up her horse and the soldiers surged past her. Like water around a rock or the prow of a ship. They saw and recognized her. Cheered her. Their queen. Their beloved's beloved. The chosen of their new god. She raised her arms, shouted them onwards.

'Victory! King Marith! Amrath returned! The king! The king!'

In the light of the dragon fire the army of Illyr could be seen rushing towards them. A charge by a troop of horsemen, tall heavy men on massive horses, encased in plates of bronze. The ground thundered with the weight of them coming. Their armour was already slick with blood. They flew red pennants, red like the Altrersyr. They too had once been the men of Amrath. They carried trident lances that ended in poisoned barbed bronze tips.

The army of the *Ansikanderakesis Amrakane* drew up in formation. The sarrissmen came forwards, a solid wall of bronze and iron, the terrible points of their weapons gleaming hot red. They stood like statues before the oncoming charge. Trident lances rushing up towards them. Filthy with their comrades' blood. The darkness fell again. Metal flashed in the darkness. The thunder of hooves and the snorting gasps of breath.

Coming. Coming.

Here.

The dragon spurted fire. The crash of it like a breaking wave. So Thalia had imagined, terrified, the surge of liquid metal from a smelting cauldron overturned. Boiling eating the world. The heat and the light left her blinded. Glowing shapes of men and horses danced behind her eyes. The earth thundered. Molten bronze trickling down the grass. The line of Illyian horsemen struck the line of Marith's sarriss. Explosion of flesh and wood and metal. Then darkness. A ruck of dying bodies, churning like worms.

Voices screaming: 'Victory! King Ruin! King Ruin! Death!'

'Why we march and why we die,
And what life means . . . it's all a lie.
Death! Death! Death!'

Another gout of flame. The battlefield was lit up in splendour, the Illyian horsemen reeling back terrified across the plain. A cheer. The sarrissmen began to press slowly forward, a single unwavering line of bloodied points. Beyond them to their left a block of horse lancers in crimson armour, crimson crests on their horses' heads. The dragon soaring on huge above them. Drums and trumpets blared to urge them onwards. On, on into Illyr!

Thalia spurred her horse to follow. Raised her arm to shout again to her men. Tal caught her reins, checked her.

Tal shouted, 'We have to get back across the river, My Queen! It's not safe here.'

'But we're winning! We're destroying them!'

'At the moment.' Tal pointed before them. Black darkness, and then a brilliant flash of glittering white light. The dragon shot flame in answer. Shrieked in pain in the sky. 'They have mages.

Powerful things of their own.' He smiled coldly. 'They are the men who betrayed and rejected Amrath. They have destroyed any number of Altrersyr armies. This is not like it was in Ith, My Queen. We must go back.'

'But—'

A great howling in the dark ahead of them. An explosion of light showed up clawed shadows, flying in panic, a thing like a golden bird tearing at them. The dragon spat fire. The shadows wheeled, turned on the bird thing, ripped at it with their claws. Light and shadow wrestling. Chunks of shadow flesh and golden feathers crashing down killing the men beneath. Another charge of Illyian heavy horsemen thundered towards the Islander's horse. The two lines met with a juddering smash. Darkness fell again, thick and absolute. Lit again by the sky burning, and the Islander's lines were broken and pushed back. Dead horses. A man running past with his face ripped off.

Thalia stared. Terrified. Appalled.

This is war. This is what they do for me. This is what they endure, to make me queen.

This is what Marith endures.

Her horse began to pull forward again. Caught up in the press of soldiers moving forward into the battle lines. Its hooves slithered in the mud.

'Marith!' She stared terrified at the rushing lines of soldiers, the flashes of burning maiming light. 'Marith! Where is he?' We quarrelled and parted in anger, and I was right to be angry with him, and now he is here, in this, doing this, suffering this. If he is harmed, she thought. If he is harmed . . .

'You said we weren't expecting it to be difficult,' she cried to Tal.

'I said he said it wouldn't be difficult.' Tal said, 'My Lord King led the first attack at the ford. He's pushing round to meet us now. He must be, he's got the Illyians turning to face us here, moving back.' He pulled desperately at her horse's bridle. 'My Queen, we must go back. If My Lord King was in any danger . . .' He looked at her face. Kind. Soothing. 'If anything were to happen to him, do you think we would not all of us know?'

Another brief moment of sweet blind dark. She could not see, so it must not be happening. She wheeled her horse, pulling hard at the reins. It snorted angrily. Trying to press on. She fought with it. Tal was pulling and fighting his own horse.

He cannot be harmed, she thought. I am being a fool. Swords and spears, bronze and iron, they cannot harm him.

'We go back then.'

The two horses turned, flicking their heads sorrowfully at the battle lines then trotting towards the river. Their hooves sucked in the mud. A handful of wounded were already limping back around them.

The river had risen. A fast rushing current. Churning up foam as the soldiers' feet churned up mud. The banks on both sides seemed far steeper. Collapsed stone and earth. In the firelight the water looked red. Thalia regarded it in dismay. Her horse snorted, tried to go back.

A man rushed past her down into the water. On fire. His bronze armour burned. The water hissed up in steam. He stood submerged to his neck. A moment's relief. Then the current took him, whirled him away.

'Come on!' Tal shouted. He spurred his horse. 'Swim the horse! Come on!'

A voice shouted off behind them: 'The king! The king's coming!' Thousand-coloured explosions ripped across the sky.

Thalia hesitated. The horse trying to pull back to the field of battle. A burst of dragon fire showed up Tal's horse in the river, Tal struggling on its back. Red light on the black water. Beyond the river only empty dark.

'Swim the horses! Come!'

The current rose up higher and faster. Rain beating on the surface of the water turning it alive.

'My Queen!'

Something was screaming behind her. All the pain in all the

world. The earth shook with an explosion. Drums beating harder and a thousand voices shouting 'Death! Death! Death!' A thunder of hooves, a crash. Thalia wrenched at the horse and forced it forward into the water. Cold water struck her like the explosions of light. She gasped and struggled, water smashed into her open mouth. Choking. She swallowed, spat. The water tasted of blood.

They were downstream of the battle at the ford, Thalia remembered. The water was not just red with reflected light.

The horse pushed forward, half walking half swimming. Its hooves sinking in mud. Something crashed up against Thalia, tearing at her hair. She shoved it away and it was a severed arm. Screamed again and her mouth filled with water tainted with blood.

The water was rising. Pushing round the horse's neck. The current stronger. The horse staggered. Tal's horse was almost across. In a flash of fire she saw Tal reaching out for the trees on the bank.

Her horse's head jerked and turned sharply. It shrieked in fear, bucked so that Thalia was almost thrown. She turned in a panic of fear.

A vast wave reared up out of the water. Reaching like claws. In the crest of the wave Thalia saw eyes and roaring mouths.

The bank collapsed where Tal was trying to scramble up it. The wave towered higher. Sucking up all the water, so that the dry riverbed was exposed. In the black mud were ancient bones.

'Go! Go!' She tried to spur the horse to the bank where Tal was floundering trying to get the horse up.

The wave hit. Broke over Thalia. Claws tore her from her horse.

Blind in the water, thrashing, fingers squeezing her throat, trying to force open her mouth. Pulling her into pieces. Ripping at her heart. The water was lit up in a flash of silver. Her head downwards, seeing fresh dying bodies, old broken Altrersyr bones.

Anger rose up in her. The holiest woman in the Sekemleth Empire of the Golden City of Sorlost. The Queen of the White Isles and Ith and Illyr and Immier and the Wastes and the Bitter Sea. The Beloved of God. She would not die like this.

The water burst. The river retreating. Falling away.

Gold light. Warmth. Perfume. Flowers, birds singing, soft summer rainfall, the drowsing hum of bees. Cool swirl of water lapping around her ankles. No sign of her horse. Or of Tal. Dead things poking up through the water. The water looking up at her with sad defeated broken eyes.

Thalia splashed across to the bank and scrambled up. Mud and roots pulled at her clothing; she brushed them away scornfully. A crow came low overhead shrieking. She raised her head and it wheeled away with a cry of pain. Sat down panting on the bank in the sunshine, watching the shallow river dance. *Saleiot*, she thought. To shine, to sparkle, to dance like the sunlight on fast flowing water. She thought suddenly of Marith sitting by her side on the banks of a stream in the desert, throwing stones into the water and telling her who he was.

On the far bank a great cloud of dust had been thrown up by the fighting. Smoke, also, in thick heavy plumes. The sky was pale grey. A light rain falling, bright in the morning sun. Tiny figures hacking and pushing. A wall of sarriss raised at the back like a wall, then they dipped all together, smooth as an arm lowering, she saw them move forward, heard a shout and a crash as they met something. Another flash of silver on the horizon, dazzling, reaching up into the sky. A scream. Shadows falling. An answering burst of red-gold dragon fire. More screams.

Two men came slithering down the bank opposite, splashed across and pulled themselves up. Very near her. Both wounded, ripped open, pink raw burns. Their armour was mangled, like something had smashed at it. They wore red and yellow badges and Thalia realized they were Illyian. They moved oddly, awkwardly, groping about them as if they could not see. They had not noticed her, stumbled off past her up the riverbank. She thought they had been blinded. Then she understood. The battle was being fought as she saw it, in summer rain and fresh morning light. But the battle had brought a darkness over all their eyes.

The men disappeared behind a clump of trees. She should have killed them, she thought. Her enemies. She sighed. Got to her feet to walk back to the camp.

A noise. On the Illyian side of the river the gestmet stood. Watching her. Its antlers were broken and fire blackened. Its face burned down to the bone. A gash ran down its right shoulder. Red and raw and filthy with rot. It looked at her very sadly. Dumb animal eyes.

Chapter Fifty-Five

We are alone. Utterly alone.

'I told Landra Relast to leave me in peace,' I say to it. 'Can you not accept that?'

A bird sits on the burned antlers. A red bird with red and black wings. It flaps its wings. The gestmet does not speak.

'Leave me alone,' I say to it. Three times, now, it has come to me. Each time, I have sent it away before it speaks to me.

On the lich roads, when first we came to the White Isles, we walked there and I was afraid. The things that walk the lich roads: I was so afraid of them.

'I wish that Marith had killed you.'

The human mouth opens. The burned face cracks with blood. 'He will, I should think.'

'Then perhaps you should leave him be. Leave me be.'

Dumb animal eyes. 'I cannot. I will pursue him to his or to my death. You should understand that, Thalia Altrersyr.'

And now I feel anger. I make the light come, all around me, lighting up the gestmet's wounds. Still, still, you think me his prisoner!

'I do not need to justify myself. Not to anyone.'

The bird cocks its head at me. Flaps its wings. '*Ethald emn enik*,' it trills.

The gestmet says, 'Bronze and iron cannot kill him. But you could still kill him, Thalia Altrersyr.'

'I know that I could kill him.'

A sound in my ears of birdsong. Bees and insects. The sound of the rain. The earth shifts and softens beneath my feet. Flowers growing up around my feet. The gestmet steps towards me, its head lowered, its antlers out towards me. Dead blind eyes on the burned antlers open and close. Its antlers are sharp. Like weapons. It lowers its head to gore me.

'*Ethald emn enik*,' the bird trills.

It steps towards me. Light flickers on its antlers, on the wings of the red bird.

'If you touch me, I will kill you,' I say.

'Please, Thalia,' it says.

'Tell Landra Relast and Tobias also.'

It turns away and raises its head and is gone. I watch it run into the green of the hills.

Chapter Fifty-Six

All morning, Tobias and Landra had sat on a hill watching the battle flow around before them. Kind of like watching a dye vat boiling up cloth. Lines moving hither and thither. Pushed forward. Pushed back. Breaking, being swallowed up the other side, going down trampled and dead. A charge of horses against light armed footmen and the ground would go red and pulpy. Stained. Spearmen raising and lowering in formation, long shafts like the movement of a loom. Two lines of the spearmen meeting was like watching hands clasping. Found himself, in fact, interweaving his own fingers and clasping his hands.

That hadn't happened for a while now. Most of the spears had long since been lost or dropped. Lines had pushed and shoved and held and broken, and the surviving spearmen were down to hacking crudely at each other with fat little swords. Long time, they could hold on, just shoving at each other, shoulder to shoulder, like drunks supporting each other, kind of funny intimacy to it he'd never have suspected, never having been a one-in-the-ranks spearman himself. Front row must be half buried in each other. Pressed up in each others' thighs. Until one side broke and fell apart and the other lot ran through them shouting. Or a mage or a dragon turned up and deep-fried them all. But finally mostly given it up now. A few reserve lines still trooping in, one neatly holding off a charge of heavy-armoured horse. But mostly dead or hacking inexpertly at each other and getting expertly hacked down by the sword guys, who'd been worse than useless spinning around en masse in clever circles holding metal tipped tree trunks but had a demonstrably better grasp of how to cut someone's arm off with a short fat blade.

A cavalry-on-cavalry charge early on in the proceedings had been simply spectacular. Slower than they looked when they were coming towards you personally, heavy-armoured horses, he'd noted with interest. Then the smash, and bloody bits actually bloody flying up in the air. Crashing past each other, crashing into anyone severely unlucky enough to be thinking a line of massive armour plated horses made a good defensive barrier between you and the enemy, pulling round excitedly to see if anyone else had survived it, then doing it all again from the other end.

Actually, it looked kind of funny, from a distance, that bit, the aftermath of a big cavalry charge. Great lords on great horses slightly surprised to find themselves still alive popping out the back end of the battle with nothing left to fight but a couple of crapping themselves runaways who'd adopted a strategic defensive position very deep field. Always looked a bit sheepish, you imagined. Had to have a quick row with the horse about turning round.

It was fascinating, seeing it all spread out like this. An education. Didn't often get a chance just to sit and watch and judge a battle on artistic merit in his line of work. Only needed a pint and a pie to make a proper good day out.

Raeta had woken them before first light, hissing there was something up in Marith's camp. Not surprising: classic time to attack, dawn, over the river, mist rising, hopefully catch the enemy half asleep. Suited the boy's taste for drama, also. The Illyians had been lined up on the other side waiting for battle. Good hard looking lot of them, horses, long spears, heavy iron armour, red flags. The three of them had been settled in a good sheltered spot on the ridge of hills shielding Marith's camp. Bit near Marith's camp, for Tobias's liking, but it wasn't like many people would be looking their way. Scrambled up a bit higher on the hillside, bedded down in a thorn bush out of the rain to watch.

'I have to . . . to do something,' said Raeta. 'Stay here.'

'Do something?'

'Be careful,' said Landra.

Raeta nodded. Shadow of antlers and branches and leaves nodding, branches blowing in the wind.

'Be careful,' Tobias said.

The sky began to lighten. On both sides of the river, the darkness seemed to stir. Crowds building into armies. Lines eyeballing each other, grim faced.

The sky turned palest pink silver. Flickered on iron and bronze.

With a yell, Marith stormed straight over the river at the Illyians. Straightforward half-suicidal cavalry punch charge.

The Illyians just stood there, long rows of spearmen, long rows of cavalrymen also with spears. Arrows shooting over their heads ripping up the water, cutting a big swathe in Marith's horses before they even got off their side of the bank. A couple of mages chucking fire at Marith, making the water burn. Lot more Illyians than there were Islanders. Lot more. Lined up five, ten deep.

He's going to do something clever like pull back and do something clever, thought Tobias. Marith's archers started shooting banefire. The Illyians began to burn. But that in itself was a bit surprising as a tactic, seeing as Marith and his friends were charging straight at the things they'd just started setting on fire. Also because the miss-shots had an inevitable tendency to fall on Marith's own men.

Marith didn't pull back. The horses came over the river, a good third of them falling behind him dead or dying, went straight into the Illyian spears. A crash Tobias could feel up there watching. Landra, despite herself, he heard gasp and scream. Beautiful shining Marith disappeared in a mass of spears and horses. The Islanders kept shooting banefire. So now they were basically under orders to barbecue their own king. A file of Islander infantry started across the river, spears in perfect formation, marching slowly through the water towards the seething morass that had just swallowed up their horse. The Illyians kept chucking mage fire and arrows at them. The Islanders kept up the banefire back. The footmen kept marching through it all up the riverbank and straight into the Illyians. Stoic fuckers there.

He's going to do something clever, thought Tobias.

Bugger me if I know what.

Die?

That would be both clever and extremely helpful.

Another line of infantry, light armed swordsmen this time. Having to queue to get across the river, the lot in front of them were having such a job of it fighting their way up the bank. Marith had got impressively far back in the Illyian lines, from the churning boiling patterns of the fighting, but he couldn't possibly think he could get enough men all the way through this to turn and flank . . .

Shadows came down at the Illyians. Came out of the dawn sky like a plague. Spat down on the seething battle lines. Impossible, from that far away, to pick out individual figures, but Tobias saw, he was sure he saw, Marith raise his sword arm in welcome.

The press in the river redoubled. Men almost fighting each other to get across and fight the Illyian troops. Pushing forward. Rain of arrows. Maelstrom like a red dyeing vat.

Mage fire ripped upwards. The shadows were burning. The shadows were unpicked like loose thread. Rose up in a cloud, shrieking murder. Scream after scream after scream. Wild light exploding. The air smelled of burning flowers. Sizzling hot meat. Mage fire shot upwards again, again the shadows were burning. Tumbling tossing upwards. Little dark holes in the world. A column of fire erupted in the midst of the battleline. Again, Tobias thought he could see, somehow, from half a mile away on a hillside, Marith Altrersyr fighting a mage with his eyes singing joy. The fighting boiled in turmoil. A horse charge hit a wall of mage fire. Went up as steam. Landra covered her ears at the screaming. Raging torrents. The river running red.

Though he's not actually doing as well as I'd have thought he should be, Tobias thought then. Seeing as he's Amrath returned King Ruin King of Death and whatnot. Only bloke in Irlast worthy of getting between beautiful Thalia's beautiful thighs. Not quite being creamed, but actually not as far off it as you'd think. All those people crossing and they weren't actually getting very far. And the famous shadows they'd heard so much about in Ith were a bit of a wash-out, if one was being brutally honest. Never want to fight one himself, obviously, but the Illyian magecraft was shredding them. Some big shiny huge bird thing falling on Marith's cavalry from behind, cutting them up bad like so many meat pies. Gold and silver feathers, light incarnate, plumed head like horns or branches, eagle talons long as men are tall. Singing, up in the sky as it killed them. Sweet lark song. Chorus to the summer dawn.

Cavalry dispatched to pie crumbs, the bird god thing turned on the shadows. The shadows did the sensible thing and bricked it. The bird thing gave chase. Mage fire blazed through the ranks fighting. Lines moving and eddying, pushing, Marith's troops wavering and then gathering themselves to push on. Going forward a bit. The remains of Marith's cavalry grouping for another charge.

Where's the dragon? Tobias thought suddenly. They'd seen it fly over the mountains every morning for days now, spurting flame and generally showing off. Marith had called it. Marith had a dragon. So where . . .?

A commotion at the back of the Illyian lines. Men beginning to split off. Legging it? But they're kind of winning. He saw horses coming up from beyond a bend in the river. Moving fast. So why . . .?

Oh where. Oh why. Oh hell. Bastard had a whole other army crossing somewhere. Plus a dragon. Could be as careless as a baby with the men here, because there was a whole other lot plus a dragon crossing somewhere else, heading round towards the back of the enemy in the classic old hammer and anvil technique.

Maybe the boy had learnt something from following him and Skie around.

Mage fire broke again over the horses charging. Marith himself was lit up a moment in the rush of light. Could tell it was him, 'cause he was the only person who came out the other side.

Funny, how small he looked. Thought he'd have grown bigger by now. Like a giant. Towering over the wreck of the world. Should be bigger. Big as dying. Since every single fucker dying here was only fucking dying 'cause of him.

Marith cut down Illyian soldiers. Light shining. Light and joy. Kill and kill and kill and kill. Death! Death! Death!

He's cutting it mighty fine, though, thought Tobias, even so. His losses to the mage fire alone must be enormous. Hammer and anvil strategy and all, but at the moment he's more just getting hammered. Almost as hammered as he was last night.

Moment of intense smugness with himself for thinking this up. Need to repeat it to Raeta later, get her to really appreciate it. *'Almost as hammered as he was last night'*—

Moment broken. Great big solid dark shadow falling over the hillside from behind them. Hot metal smell and a roar.

Oh look! There's the dragon! It's flying over Tobias's head!

The dragon plunged red and gold. Swept out over the brow of the hill. Plants withering. Air boiling. Warm sun beat of its wings. So close Tobias could almost touch it. Silver staring eyes.

The boy's eyes. The same staring grief shame pleasure hate joy.

It hung suspended up over the battlefield, watching down, its body humming still. One great beat of its wings. Its neck twisted. A shudder ran down the muscles of its flanks.

Its tail flicked. Sucked in breath like a bellows.

Dived. Spewed out flame.

The whole world disappeared in a blast of fire. A hot wind blew back over Tobias's face. Hot metal smell. Roast meat stink, rolling in his mouth. Better than steak. Chorus of a thousand desperate voices screaming. A tiny shining figure, head raised in triumph, silhouetted against the flames.

The dragon soared up into the wet sunshine. Rainfall sparkled on its wings. Mist rising around it. Warm clouds of metal and blood. Danced in triumph. Dived. Breathed out fire again.

Watching felt like slow eternity. The most beautiful thing a man could ever see. Scoured the mind clean of anything other. Couldn't remember there was anything other before this moment. Just a dragon dancing on the wind.

A blast of white light shot upwards. Great towering twisting wondrous pillar of light. Smashed into the dragon. Dragon shrieked like the whole world hurt. Hung in the sky crackling all over silver. Madly beating its huge wings. Roared fire. Vomited up fury. The pillar of light collapsed.

Some magic broken. Tobias could almost draw his eyes away from the dragon back to the battle beneath. Figures frantically running, regrouping. The one he knew without seeing was Marith Altrersyr surged forward, horse rearing, slashing out with his sword, horse's hooves treading blood. White light burst out around him. Like the dragon he shrieked, shook it off. A ragged line of horsemen formed up behind him. Charged the Illyian ranks.

Slaughter.

Trampling men like rotten waste.

The Illyian lines were retreating. Pushed back towards where the other army of the *Ansikanderakesis Amrakane* was marching up. The hammer and the anvil. The dragon swept the skies, herding them on. In his mind and his heart, Tobias heard the paean echo. 'Death! Death! Death!'

And then gold shadows. Birdsong. Cool of the dawn dew over the searing dragon heat. The bird thing, wing beats soft as cobwebs. Singing its song to the pain and joy of being alive. The sudden, terrible memory in Tobias of childhood, lying in his bed watching the dawn break in the quiet beautiful hopeful wholeness of the world.

The dragon screamed. Hovering. Reluctant. Looked almost like it might be going to fly away. Some have worshipped dragons, Tobias thought. But they can be tamed. They aren't gods. They can be harmed. Killed.

The god thing waited, circling. Calling. The dragon hissed and snorted flame.

They closed.

Like all the powers of life and darkness dancing. The sky lit up in splendour. A thousand suns rising, and a thousand shining silver moons. The very air filled with the clash of swords meeting. The ring of metal rising higher than the circles of the stars. All men long to see dragons. Dream of wonders. Hope deep down in the depths of their souls to see wonders blaze and burn and die. We worship the sky and the trees and the earth and the sea and the rocks we walk on. We dream of light and shadows and the glory of something far greater, the old wild powers of the world. Gods and demons parading. The secret things we cannot see that fly somewhere far beyond our human eyes. And there, there in bright magnificence, wrestling together, blinding beauty, dazzling to the mind. Dragons and gods and demons. Singing and crying and weeping as they fought. Bleeding light and darkness. Tearing great holes in the fabric of the human world.

The triumph of life. There! Glory! Tobias almost, almost believed himself a good man, just for seeing that. Seeing it winning. Kill the death things! The enemy! Life will triumph over darkness! Life! Life!

The dragon flew away screaming. Wounded. Took its pain out on the men around it. The earth of the plains. The clouds of the sky.

The last of the shadows rushed at the god thing. Were torn to pieces. Scattered. Burned up in flames like silk cloth.

Life!

Marith came up on his stallion. Cloak oozing blood behind him. Eyes like knife wounds. Bright white light shimmering off the blade of his sword.

The god thing blazing in the sky in glory. This tiny man on his tiny horse with his tiny sword. White light and golden rainbows. Life! Life!

Come on and die, thought Tobias. Vile little shit Marith Altrersyr. Just die. Men can't kill you, maybe. Raeta couldn't kill you. But that . . .

The god thing dived. Blazing golden. Pure pure perfect perfect life and hope.

Marith killed it down with one blow.

Chapter Fifty-Seven

Even from half a mile away on the hillside, Tobias felt the look in the boy's eyes as the god thing fell. His voice rang across the battlefield calling his men to fight for him. The battle cry raised by a thousand eager voices. 'Death! Death! Death!'

Battle redoubled. The dragon swept back, fire blazing from its mouth. More shadows dragged themselves in its wake through the rents it made in the sky. The Illyians died by the thousands. Turned even on each other. The world a blazing mass of white light.

'*Why we march and why we die,*
And what life means . . . it's all a lie.
Death! Death! Death!'

So loud it blocked out Tobias's breathing. Put his hands to his eyes and screamed. White light and golden rainbows. Trumpets sounding victory. The currents of slaughter calmed. The dragon lumbered forward, came down resting at Marith's feet. Men's voices cheered to the heavens. The sun burst through the rain wet sky.

Never go up against a drink- and drug-addled death-obsessed invulnerable demon with a pet dragon. Old secret sellsword's wisdom, that.

Chapter Fifty-Eight

He comes back in triumph. His eyes dance with bright joy. He kneels at my feet in his filthy armour, holds out his filthy sword. 'Thalia Altrersyr, Queen of Illyr. Eltheia come again. I swear it. I'll build you a temple on the foundations of Ethalden, with walls of pure gold.' I kiss him and his mouth tastes bloody. He holds me and his hands are dripping with blood.

'I'm sorry,' he says. 'I should not have been angry with you. I should not have doubted you. I'm sorry. Forgive me.'

I cannot speak. Such horror, kneeling here before me.

But he is safe and unharmed. I am safe and unharmed. Another battle has been fought and we have won.

He has the few surviving Illyians paraded before us. Orders them to get down on their faces prostrate at our feet. We move the camp to the other side of the river. A fine, flat plain with rich soil: Marith says he might think of founding a town here in memory of this day. The bones and bodies of the Illyians are piled up to make a tower, a marker of our victory. We bury our army's fallen. Heroes, Marith calls them. The conquerors of Illyr. The hallowed dead.

A party of Illyians comes in to do him homage. Not soldiers: they have old men and children with them, gifts of livestock, fruit, wheat, wine, gems. They throw themselves on his mercy, beg him to forgive them. 'Spare them,' I beg him. 'Please.'

'I should make an example,' he says sadly. 'I would spare them. But I can't.'

'More of them will surrender, don't you think? If they see you can be kind.'

'I don't want them to surrender, beloved,' he says. 'We need to destroy them all, if we are to take Illyr.'

That night I lie awake and look at him sleeping. So beautiful. Beautiful as the stars and the sky and the moon. 'Carin,' he whispers. 'Thalia . . . Carin . . . Father . . . Ti . . . Please. Help me.' The moonlight shines white on his white body. Like he is made of white silver. Mage glass. He shines in the dark like the blade of a knife. The shadows crawl outside the walls of my wagon. I hear overhead the beat of the dragon's wings.

We have come so far. Done so much, he and I.

This is war. What did I think that he would do?

I am as guilty in this as he is.

PART SIX

THE TEMPLE

Chapter Fifty-Nine

Concerning the outbreak of deeping fever in Sorlost, a thousand explanations were given. The God's anger at the turmoil in the city. The God's anger at the elopement of the High Priestess Thalia with the Altrersyr Demon King of the White Isles. The God's anger at the idiot blasphemers who believed such a patiently absurd lie.

As far as Orhan could see, however, the explanation was glaringly obvious. Cam Tardein's first act as Nithque had been to rescind every restriction on travellers from Chathe. The hatha addicts and the rose oil merchants and the High Lords had all been delighted. March Verneth's death, it would seem, had not been entirely in vain.

Orhan occasionally wondered: all I did, all my crimes, and they brought about my dismissal as Nithque over a travel ban?

From the Street of the South and Yellow Birds Square, the disease spread like flood water. The Gold Quarter. The Bloody Echoes. The Dead Harbour. Starlight By The Gateways. The Street of Bones and Longing. The Court of Evening Sorrows. The Court of the Broken Knife. The air rang with screaming. Bodies piled up in alleys and doors. People running mad to escape watching their children dying. Fighting to drink at the fountains to cool their fevered heat. Death stench began to permeate even the seclusion of private gardens. The rich locked themselves away and burned mint and lavender and sysius berries. The poor staggered about with rags clutched over their mouths.

For the first few days, bizarrely, predictably, the city had seemed entirely unconcerned. People were reported dying. But not real people. Not like real people were really dying of something real. They themselves wouldn't get sick and die. All lies, anyway. Another attempt by someone to cause alarm. Someone would start saying next it was caused by the ex-Nithque, or the dead High Priestess, or the dead Altrersyr king.

Then panic. Cam Tardein ordered the Emperor's soldiers out onto the streets to board up plague houses. A man fell down in a pool of his filth in the Court of the Fountain, cursing Great Tanis and the Emperor as he died. A woman killed her three children in the Grey Square on the steps of the Great Temple, screaming she would rather cut their throats than see them take sick.

People crowded into the Temple. Trampled the children's blood-stains under foot. Lit candles scented with herbs and spices. Gave offerings of jewellery. Said endless begging prayers.

The price of lavender and sysius berries and mint leaves doubled. Good candles cost a silver dhol each. People began to hoard bread.

The numbers dying started subsiding. The God had answered their prayers! The Sekemleth Empire would stand against any dangers. The Lord of Living and Dying protected them. The Asekemlene Emperor loved his subjects. What was mere illness, beside the power and wealth of the Golden Empire of the Eternal City of Sorlost?

The gates were barred to Chathean travellers. The price of lavender and sysius berries and mint leaves halved.

The disease flared up again. More savagely than before. Rumour had it that half the population of Fair Flowers were dead or dying. Children wandered the streets crying for their parents. The bakers' shops and food stalls began to close.

Lord Caltren took sick. So did Samneon Magreth. The Emperor ordered all the doors of his palace locked.

Everyone knew the villages of western Chathe had been the centre of the last outbreak. So anyone from Chathe was sought out and hunted down and killed.

Everyone knew the villages of western Chathe were the chief producers of hatha. So hatha eaters were sought out and hunted down and killed.

As the days went on, this came to mean anyone with a funny accent or funny clothing, or anyone who was seen publicly rubbing their eyes.

The price of lavender and sysius berries and mint leaves trebled. Good candles cost five dhol. Even the wealthy began to run short of bread.

A fire started in a boarded-up house on the Street of the Butchered Horse. The whole street was burned to ashes before it could be put out. Rumour had it that the dying had fought back the bucket chains to hurl themselves into the flames.

Ameretha Ventuel took sick. Samneon Magreth died.

Lavender and sysius berries and mint leaves were traded for family heirlooms, sexual favours, food. Good candles cost a talent each. People fought in the street for bread.

Bil shut herself in her bedroom with the baby. Ordered servants wearing gloves and silk masks to leave food in covered dishes outside the door. She would eat only milk curds, fresh mint leaves and raw gilla fowl eggs. Burned lavender oil day and night. The cost would be crippling Orhan, were he not certain it would all end very soon when they both died. Through the door he heard the muffled sound of her crying. He wept himself, when he thought of the baby kicking its pathetic legs in its clout cloths, that would die before it had really been alive. The smell of it. The odd inhuman sounds it made, that tore his heart to pieces with love. It seemed so . . . unfair.

Such an absurd word to use. Like every other word in his vocabulary. Language was pointless in the face of such endless disasters. 'Dead'. 'Unfair'. 'Sad'. 'Hurt.'

Ah, Orhan, you grow too bitter. Don't you know that bitterness is bad for the blood? You need to keep happy and smiling. That will help you keep your health. Burn lavender flowers and sysius berries. Repeat the chant of Semethest. Bind to your chest the ashes of peacock chest feathers dipped in honey. Smile. Keep your pecker up. Live in hope any of this rubbish actually works.

It would be nice if Darath could survive somehow, he thought to himself occasionally, when he and Darath weren't arguing again. And Bil. His sister. The useless lump of his sister's son.

Tam Rhyl's family would probably survive, it occurred to him, since they were safely tucked up in isolated starving poverty in rural Immish forbidden to leave their house. The irony was biting. Tam's death ultimately not in vain. Tam might, Orhan thought in his most generous moments, have been happy to see it end this way for them. His death saving his children's lives.

Or not.

'Let's run away to Immish,' Darath said that evening. They sat in Darath's splendid bathing chamber, trying not to breathe on each other even as they kissed.

'We'd never make it.' Streams of people crowded the gates each day, running away to Immish. The desert dwellers killed them, or just the desert; if they made it through to Immish, the Great Council had placed armed guards on the roads and in the border towns. Sensible safe precautions, when he'd insisted on the same thing for anyone coming into Sorlost from Chathe.

'We could bribe the Immish soldiers. For a sack of diamonds a man, they might close their eyes.'

'I suppose we could . . .' The idea astonished him. Run away.

'Just the two of us. Buy a house somewhere in Alborn. We could.'

'We can't. What would it look like, to the city? The two of us leaving? What about Bil, and Bil's child, and Elis, and everyone?' Bondsmen. Servants. Hundreds of lives tied to their own. 'It would panic people beyond anything, the two of us leaving, the Lord of the Rising Sun and the Lord of All That Flowers and Fades. There'd be utter panic. Where would we go, anyway? We couldn't just go and live somewhere else.' Orhan thought: I'm the Lord of the Rising Sun, Servant and Counsellor of the Emperor, Warden of Immish and the Bitter Sea, the custodian of the House of the East, the former Nithque of the Sekemleth Empire of the Eternal Golden City of Sorlost. I can't just leave and go and live somewhere else.

'Change your name,' said Darath. 'Stop being all that. Darath and Orhan, two men living together with nothing but a lot of money to their lack of a name.'

'But . . .'

'Fuck the city,' said Darath suddenly. Irritably. Orhan looked at him in astonishment. 'Fuck Elis and Bil and her baby and everyone and everything, who'll probably all die in agony anyway pretty soon. The Emperor publicly humiliated you, Orhan. You saved his eternal life and he showed you no gratitude at all. Eloise Verneth wants to kill you. The city either laughs at you or wants her to succeed. You almost destroyed the both of us thinking it was for the good of the Empire. The Empire ignored you. So fuck it. Leave them to it. Come away with me. Leave.'

We could. We really could. Orhan's head spun at it. Be two people living in a house together not having to think about the wider world. Darath and Orhan. Read and write poetry and talk and go food shopping together and just . . . not care.

The baby, he thought then. My son. I . . .

I'm sorry, he thought, to the baby. If you'd had a chance to live, I would have loved you so much.

'We'd have to go soon,' he said slowly. 'Today, even. Cam's finally said to be considering closing the gates.'

Darath's turn to look astonished. Sat bolt upright, splashing water. 'What?'

'You're surprised?' God's knives, the look on Darath's face was almost comical.

Breakdown of words again.

'Closing the gates?'

'Yes. Closing the gates. Obviously.'

'Obviously? Obviously?'

'He should have done it days ago. I'd have done it the day the plague first broke.'

Darath stared at him. Trying to see he was joking, perhaps. 'But . . . We'd be sealed in. To die. The whole city. Would die.'

'Yes. As you said yourself. We'll all die in agony pretty soon.'

'But . . . The whole city? The whole city? You . . . you callous bastard, Orhan.'

Darath really hadn't thought it. How could he still be so naive? That's what power is, Darath, thought Orhan. What I almost destroyed us both for. Choosing who lives and who dies and why and when and how. Buying and selling people's lives. Hoping it's worth it. Knowing it's probably not. 'Yes. The whole city. But not the whole world. Tam Rhyl, for the good of the city. The city, for the good of the Empire. The Empire, for the good of Irlast.'

Darath's face still look horrified. Shocked. Could feel them coming on to arguing again. Anything they said to each other now always ended up going wrong.

'An apple, for five cimma fruit! A cake, for a cup of wine! God's knives, Orhan! Where does it end? All of Irlast for . . .?'

For you, Darath. For Bil's child. For myself. Like we all would. All Irlast, for a few more brief moments of my life.

'Stop it, Darath. Please.'

'Your whore died,' said Darath.

'What?'

'Your beautiful beautiful filthy whore. He died.'

Like a knife blade. His hands twisting the wound in Tam's belly, squeezing out every drop of pain. 'I know.'

'Heartbroken, are you?'

'I . . .'

'I paid a man a talent to bury him. With a wreath of copperstem round his beautiful beautiful filthy neck. A talent, for a dead whore.'

Orhan got up. 'I think I should go now, Darath.'

'Run away, then,' said Darath. 'You callous, cheating, cowardly bastard.' Got up too. The two of the facing each other, dripping wet, stark naked, warm sweet scented oiled twilight dark with birds cooing and fluttering in their cages in the walls. Absurd.

Had to get dressed before he could go. Further absurdity. Orhan stood in the dressing room damp and sticky, holding out his arms while a body servant wrapped his clothes around him. Sticking to his skin. Just go back, he kept thinking, just go back into the bath chamber and tell him you're sorry again, like you always do. In the corridor he heard splashing from the shade pool. Darath trying to show him how well he could be happy alone.

The onyx gates of the House of Flowers opened smoothly and silently before him. Carved huge petals of precious stone. The last heat of the sun clung to their surface, butterflies and flies resting enjoying the warmth. Green lizards with red legs eating the flies. Every time he left, now, he imagined it was for the last time.

The gates swung closed again. Sealing themselves. Crowd of flies rising buzzing, then settled back to bask on the hot stone. There were a lot of flies, now, in Sorlost. Big and fat. The city of Tyrenae was reported a fly-blown wasteland. Flies buzzing in clouds over the White Isles and Ith. Flies flies flies eating the ruin of the world.

I just wanted to make things better, Orhan thought.

The streets were largely empty, even the Street of Flowers. The low distant background noise of screaming hung in the air like the dust. Like the dust, one hardly now noticed it. One day soon, thought Orhan, it will stop and the silence will drive the last few survivors mad. A dead man lay sprawled on the flagstones, hands thrown out, his shirt torn, blood running from the cracks in his head. A hatha addict, or a Chathean merchant, or one of the Sorlostian merchants banished from Immish, also somehow being blamed. Or a man selling candles, or lavender flowers, or sysius berries, or bread. Desperate people will kill for desperate things. Fever and despair are already driving us mad. Orhan walked slowly with his entourage of guardsmen around him. Costing him a fortune, and the chances were one of them would go down with it and bring the plague raging into his house. No need for them, given the number of different ways he was dying. But not even a dying man wants to die.

He found himself stopping in the Court of the Fountain, watching the water plashing, silver pale on the marble. Pretty. A warm gust of wind blew water droplets into Orhan's face. Cool and sweet. A soldier with a sword stood beside the fountain, watching the few people milling around still trying to buy and sell and walk about like the world wasn't coming to an end. Four people had drowned throwing themselves into the water to soothe their fever. Bad omens. Must be stopped.

In your embrace I dream of water! Orhan skirted round it, trying to avoid looking at the fountain or the man's blade.

The Grey Square, alone in the city, was crowded. People came to the Temple day and night to pray and beg. A new rumour had it that the disease could be avoided by lighting a candle while repeating the Chant of the Sun. It was noticed, also, that the priestesses were not dying, so this must surely mean something. Orhan wished like the rest to believe that it was the God's kindness. Knew really, like the rest, that it was some kind of pious lie. The priestesses wore masks, apart from the High Priestess. So no one could really say how many of them there were.

A rational man, Orhan Emmereth. Darath would even say a cynic. But trying to cling to some broken fragment of hope.

'Candied lemons. Candied roses. Candied salted cimma leaves.' A street seller, her tray piled high with sweets. All the pretty colours, the yellow-green of the lemons, pink rose petals, plump green leaves. Flies, fat and excited, buzzed around her, sated with dead flesh. Some things cost so much now no one could afford them. Other things no one wanted, and their sellers starved. 'Candied lemons,' she called hopelessly, 'candied lemons, a dhol a bag.' Orhan bought three bags, handed two over to his guardsmen. Dry and too chewy. Not sharp enough. The sugar crunched in his mouth.

'Thank you, My Lord, thank you,' she said. Her voice was

pathetic. 'Here. Have a bag of roses with my gratitude, My Lord.' Orhan took the bag carefully, passed that too to his guards. Beautiful big petals, a deep glowing pink like the morning sky. All the flowers were blooming in rich profusion. Like a plant with silver-rot, the city seemed to be decking itself in beauty before it died.

The square fell silent. From deep within the Temple, the twilight bell tolled. Scent of incense on the wind.

A sacrifice night. A little girl with old, old eyes and bloody hands.

The bell tolled again. In the Small Chamber, a man had just died.

'Every night!' a voice shouted from the square. 'We should be making a sacrifice every night! As we once did.'

'We were a great power, then!' another voice shouted. 'Never had the plague! Great Tanis is angry! We neglect the God, and this is our reward.'

'Every night!' More voices shouting. 'Every night!'

And you'd volunteer, would you? Orhan thought.

The first voice shouted, 'I have a daughter. Great Tanis would be happy, to see her sacrificed. Strong, she is, to help the God. Every night! Every night!'

'Every night!' More and more voices.

'The Lord of Living and Dying! The living remain living, and the dead may die! Every night!'

'This blasphemy, the High Priestess abandoning the Temple! Great Tanis is angry! Every night!'

'Every night! Every night!'

God's knives, Orhan thought. Is this now what we've come to?

If it makes them feel better, he thought then.

He walked on. Empty streets. A knife-fighter wounded and panting, sweat clinging to his brow. Two more fighting together in a courtyard, a handful of spectators gathered round shouting, chanting one of the men's name. As Orhan watched, the taller figure slipped, stumbling; the other was on him, cutting down hard

411

with his knife; the loser fell back in a mass of blood. His eyes stared round imploring his audience to help him. Dying. Dying. Don't want to die. The victor raised his arms. Bloody sweat on his forehead. His face fever bright. Two child whores drifted past the spectators with bells tinkling. Like the knife man, their faces oozed sweat beneath their paint. A man in a green coat pulled one of them roughly towards him. Child's lisp: 'One dhol. One dhol.' She's dying, Orhan almost shouted. She's dying, can't you see? Man and child went off together down the street into the shadows. The air around them seemed to moan and laugh.

Is this now what we've come to?

He drifted aimlessly with his guards around him. Floating in the golden dust. A group of women kicked a man to the ground on a street corner, shouting that he was a Chathean plague carrier. Two children ran past, dressed in rags. Two houses boarded up and screaming. A shop boarded up. The planks had been smashed open to loot the shop. A cloth merchant's, from the look of it. Orhan bent down, picked up a length of vivid pink and gold embroidered silk. Flowers, stems intertwining, the spaces between one picture the outline of the next. The same colour as the candied petals. The gold thread unravelling in his hands. A beetle was clinging to the embroidery. Fat and black. Bloodstained. He made a choking sound and dropped it back to the ground.

Chapter Sixty

The next day, Celyse came to visit. Orhan was surprised she was still leaving the house. But they were all taking risks now, abandoning caution, giving themselves up to the certainty of the plague. And life must go on, or something similar. The plague will not defeat us! We will survive! We are the richest empire the world had ever known! Keep our spirits up! and all that.

'Hello, Orhan.' Her face looked thinner, her hair greyer. Her eyes were red with tears.

'Celyse.'

'Ameretha Ventuel died.'

'I'm sorry.'

Celyse sat down. 'I should tell Bil.'

'Bil won't see anyone. Even me.'

'No?' A harsh little laugh. 'Wise woman.'

'You're hoping her son dies, I suppose?'

Celyse's face went rigid. 'God's knives, Orhan! That's vile.' She stood up, started back towards the door. 'I can see why Darath threw you out.'

'Celyse . . . Wait. I'm sorry. I'm sorry.' Orhan grabbed her hand. 'I'm sorry. I don't know what's wrong with me.'

'You are becoming hateful, Orhan. That's what's happening to you. The things you say . . . You're becoming what you did. Or

413

are you just bitter you failed at everything? You even failed at punishing March, since he hasn't had to live to see today.'

'Shut up,' he said suddenly. 'Stop it.'

Celyse pulled her hand away. 'I was worried about you. God's knives, why do I bother? I thought you might want to talk about it. Need to talk. I was obviously wrong.'

Need to talk?

'Celyse? What?'

She was through the door when she turned back at looked at him. 'Orhan . . . I'm sorry, though. Truly. I'm sorry. If you need me . . . need to talk . . . Once you've stopped being so vile.'

Need to talk? Sick panic. Terror. 'What? Wait! What's happened? What's wrong? Wait!'

Sick panic. Knew, in his belly. Almost screamed it. 'Tell me!'

Her eyes narrowed. Shadow on her face. 'You don't know.'

'Know what? What don't I know?'

No, he thought. No no no no no no no no no.

Celyse sucked in a breath. 'I wish your spies weren't quite so hopeless, Orhan. Leada is sick. She fell sick this morning.'

Reeled like someone had stabbed him. Like mage fire going off in his ears and eyes. Knife blades in his stomach. His hands twisting Tam's wound.

'At the House of Flowers, yes.'

Why didn't Darath send to tell him? Why didn't—

Celyse said perfectly calmly, clearly, tonelessly, 'Darath has ordered the gates of the house sealed.'

'But . . . But I . . . '

She sighed. 'Would have been sealed in too, if Darath hadn't thrown you out.'

Dead.

Dead. Dead. Dead. Dead.

Screams welling up upside him. But . . . It can't . . . But . . .

Celyse walked over to him. Awkwardly put her arms around him. Fell into her arms and screamed in grief louder than Bil's child.

* * *

414

A boy brought date cakes, salted melon, iced lemon wine. Poured with a pretty curve of his arm. Warm wind blew in from the gardens, perfumed with honeysuckle and jasmine, ruffling the bells of Celyse's headdress, the silver draperies hung on the wall. The sunlight had a heavy, yellow quality to it: Orhan had hoped and wondered that it might rain. God lives in His house of waters . . . Cool rainfall to quench the city's fevers, wash them a bit cleaner, freer from disease. Drown the cursed flies.

He drank. Sharp in his dry empty mouth. His hand shook on the cup. We always know we are all dying. But . . . But . . . Those we love . . . they can't die. They won't ever die.

'He may recover,' said Celyse.

'He may.'

But . . . But . . .

'Nistryle Caltren's youngest son recovered.' She laughed in pain. 'An orphan. Five years old. But he recovered. Do you know what I saw yesterday in the Court of the Fountain, Orhan? A woman was standing holding a basket. In the basket was a cat. She shouted that Great Tanis has abandoned the city. That Great Tanis the Lord of Living and Dying is an empty lie. "There is no such thing as living!" she shouted. "Hail King Death!" Then she killed the cat.'

'The Chatheans sacrifice cats to ward off deeping fever. They drink the blood as a cure.'

Silence.

'What happened to her?' Orhan asked.

'Who?'

'The blasphemer. The woman who killed the cat.'

'What do you think happened to her? She was mobbed. Everyone in the square turned on her. The guards at the fountain had to intervene.'

'She survived?'

'The guards dragged her off somewhere. Still shouting that life is a lie.' She laughed in pain again. 'I don't know what happened to the dead cat.'

'People drank its blood, I expect.'

'I was trying to make a joke there, Orhan.'

'People are selling cats for ten dhol a body. Fifteen, if it's still alive.'

Bit her lip. 'That's disgusting. And blasphemous.'

'It doesn't work, anyway.' Pain. Such pain in his heart. I'd kill a hundred cats for Darath, otherwise, if I thought it even possible it might. 'But that's probably why they mobbed her. Not because she was blaspheming. To get hold of the cat.'

Celyse left. Cakes and melon uneaten, wine undrunk. Loss of appetite an early sign of fever . . . But we mustn't all become paranoid about our health.

Orhan went to the Great Temple.

Not quite true. He went first to the House of Flowers. The gates loomed over him, sealed shut. He went right up close, pressed his hands on the carved onyx. Even in the midday heat, the stone felt unnaturally cold.

The last time. The last time he had gone through the gates.

'Darath,' he whispered, running his hands over the stone. 'Darath. Let me in. Please.'

No response.

We could have been somewhere in the desert together. Heading to Alborn to lead new lives. There is nothing left for me.

No, he thought suddenly. That's not quite true.

If my son dies, he thought, I will kill myself.

So he went on to the Great Temple. Through the Court of the Fountain, where a man stood and shouted 'We're dying! We're dying! God has abandoned us and we'll all die!' Through the Court of Petals, where a woman danced in silence for the dead. Through the Court of the Broken Knife, where the faceless statue with its knife and its burden stood and looked over at the horizon, and it seemed to Orhan that the statue had almost a visible face. A diseased, rotten, time-eaten figure, eyes fixed on nothing. The city embodied. The very image of Orhan Lord Emmereth Lord of the Rising Sun, ex-lover of Lord Vorley, ex-Nithque of the Eternal Golden City of Sorlost. A man sat beneath the statue, weeping. There was always someone weeping, in the Court of the Broken Knife.

Yet, as he approached the Temple, Orhan felt somehow a warmth and a peace. In the Grey Square the wind was blowing stronger; a few children, untroubled by fear of sickness, flew their little coloured silk kites. His heart lifted, watching the colours float. Little jewels against the golden blue evening sky. Little bright fragments of hope. He's not yet dying. He may recover. Some do. He'll recover and we'll stand here together in gratitude and watch the kites. In the Temple itself the throng was crushing. Flushed, feverish faces, desperate red eyed supplicants, the priestesses slipping between them with shadowed eyes beneath their masks. It was noted that none of them had died. The lapis and silver masks looked the more beautiful, against the hot frowning faces kneeling around them. But despite the crush and the heat of the candles the Great Chamber was calming to the mind. People stared and murmured at Lord Emmereth. Hissed. Made signs with their hands. The city's saviour, some of them still thought him. If Amrath really had visited the palace, some still believed Orhan had been the one who had fought him off. At least, he thought wearily, he could not be blamed for the plague.

They knew, he saw, that the House of Flowers was closed up with sickness. They pitied him, even those who thought him a murderer who had sold the city to a demon for a bag of gold. All and everything is washed away, all sin, all evil, in the face of such death.

So many candles were lit the chamber shone without shadows. Light brighter and clearer than the light of the sun. The air so scented with spices it was almost solid before him. Tasted sensual in his mouth. He knelt, felt the eyes staring at him. Whispers. Hisses. Pity. Prayers and songs. It felt like someone running cool long fingers across his face and down his skin.

'Great Tanis. Lord of Living and Dying. He Who Rules All

Things. Oh Great Lord Tanis, I come before You, to ask Your blessing of my life. Grant that I will live and die, as all things must live and die. Grant that I will know sorrow, and pain, and happiness, and love. Grant that I will endure Your blessing and Your curse. Grant that I will be grateful for the gifts You give me, that I yet live and one day will die. Let Darath live. Great Tanis, Great Lord, let Darath live.' Closed his eyes, saw the golden light of the candles through them, the holy shining presence of the God. 'Dear Lord, Great Tanis who rules all things, from the fear of life and the fear of death, release us. We live. We die. For these things, we are grateful.' Warm and soft. Soothing on his heart. He felt, almost, some kind of joy.

The child High Priestess knelt before the altar, pulling at her hair with chewed hands. Thin white wrists. Orhan thought of the child whore he'd seen yesterday. Noted that none of the priestesses had died, and it would be a kindness if this child did.

A figure came to kneel beside him. Orhan ignored it, staring into the candle flames, thinking of Darath and Bil's baby and the God. We could have been running away, in the desert together. Or dying together in each other's arms.

I could run away with Bil and my son, he thought. Take them out into the desert. Try to let the baby survive. Fuck the city, as Darath so musically put it. The city, for a single child. Go incognito, a bag of diamonds and no name. Live in Alborn. Be spared all this. Darath was right. We can just leave.

A surge of terror suddenly running through him. The candles seemed to dim. Dark, cold wind in the Temple, making the light flicker, writhing sudden shadows, and there in the flames a young man's face, beautiful, blood covered, eyes like knife blades. Red blood waves rising. Red blood boiling, crested with dark smoke. The eyes staring into him, filthy, oozing. Running pus like rotted wounds. Falling flashing shining shower of coloured glass.

Orhan thought in sudden panic: I saw him. I saw Amrath. He's riding across the world bringing ruin and blood. Nowhere will be safe from him. Every village and every man and woman and child will die under his sword. The world's burning. There's no escape. Nowhere to run to. We'll all die in pain.

Darath's dead. He's dead he's dead he's dead.

Orhan shook himself. Closed his eyes. Candle flames, voices praying, bronze walls gleaming, priestesses in lapis and silver masks. Soothing. Soft on his skin.

Night comes. We survive. A little while longer to live is still a little while longer to live.

The light in the Temple blazed golden. Light. There's always light. The child priestess rocked and stared at the High Altar. At least, thought Orhan, she's alive. He moved to get up, go back to the House of the East, tell Bil to get some things together, run away out of the Maskers' Gate into the barren desert tracts of sand. My son, he thought. I can still save my son.

The figure kneeling next to him moved also. Gestured to catch Orhan's eye.

Secretary Gallus. Grey in his gold hair.

'My Lord Emmereth,' Gallus said softly. 'Would you believe me if I said I was surprised to meet you here? I need to speak with you.' He gestured towards the entranceway. 'Please.'

The dark of the passage rose up suffocating Orhan. He almost choked as he followed Gallus out. Death and horror. Amrath's pale filthy staring eyes. This is death, this darkness, crushing, the weight of dying, the blind empty gnawing hunger of the void. This is what Darath will suffer. What he will become.

Darath's dead, he thought. He's dead he's dead he's dead.

The sunlight of the Grey Square poured over him as he stumbled out through the great doors in Gallus's shadow. I was going to leave, he thought. Save the child. The light was sickly yellow, clouds building in piles like walls in the far west through the gaps in the city's domes. The ghosts of the foreign plague dead, who still believed that they had souls. It's going to rain, thought Orhan, looking at the clouds. Wash the city a bit cleaner. Drown the flies. The smell of the city's stones, after heavy rainfall . . . Water, running warm and heavy on the face . . . A few final moments of something good.

Voices shouted in the square: 'Every day! Every day!' 'I have a son for the God's hunger! He longs for it!' 'Every day! Every day!' People milling around, looking up at the Temple. Waiting for some miracle to appear.

No sign of the kite fliers. Gone and flown. Sickened, perhaps, in the brief while he had been inside.

'What is it, Gallus?' he asked wearily.

Gallus glanced at the people shouting. 'Not here.'

'Half of the city just watched us walk out of the Temple together.' Memory: walking with Darath, talking about treason and murder, Darath claiming they were less likely to be overheard. Darath's dead he's dead he's dead he's dead. 'I'm told it's safer, walking and talking. Less easy to be eavesdropped on. We'll all be dead soon anyway. What does it matter, at the end of everything, who's seen talking to whom about what? Who's left to care?'

Still, Gallus hesitated.

'What it is, Gallus? What do you want?' You sold me out to Cam Tardein, Orhan thought. The man I have become should kill you.

Gallus coughed nervously. 'My Lord Emmereth . . . My Lord . . . It has been several months now, since you were dismissed as Nithque. In that time . . . In that time, things have not gone so well.'

'Possibly.' Dancing the dance again. Farting at each other. Round and round.

Darath's dead he's dead he's dead he's dead.

'The city is dying, My Lord,' said Gallus in a rush. Orhan thought: really? Is it? I never knew. Who knew? Gallus's voice dropped. 'The Emperor took sick this morning. Only a mild illness, he says it is nothing more than a cold. Shortly before I left, he was reported to be feeling a little better. That . . . that was when I knew I must speak to you, My Lord.'

The Emperor, dying.

He could die as easily as any man. Had died in many strange and spectacular and pointless ways. Not a great reign, this one. Better luck next time, perhaps. Should have been dead months past, dead and buried with a mewling baby on the throne. But . . .

The Emperor. Dying. Further chaos. Nothing left to centre them.

'My Lord, the new Nithque . . . You will have heard, My Lord, that he ordered the gates sealed?'

Orhan looked at the people milling uselessly in the square behind them. Shouts of 'Every night! Every night!' A distant voice weeping. The background hum of screams. 'No. No, I hadn't heard. When was this?'

'Last night, My Lord. He ordered that they not be reopened this morning.'

'But the gates are open.' The uproar if they had remained closed would have been audible throughout the city, blocking out even the screams. Someone surely would have had the courage to tell him that.

'The guards refused to obey the order, My Lord.'

'Then have them removed from their station, and have the gates closed.'

'Who would remove them?' said Gallus. 'Half the city guard are dead or dying or have already abandoned their post. Perhaps not half, I may exaggerate. A third, perhaps.'

'What did Cam — did the Nithque do, then?'

Gallus tried to look anywhere but at Orhan. 'What can he do, My Lord? His daughter is dying. His son took sick three days ago. Do you think now he even cares?'

Orhan sighed. 'He is Nithque. That should be above all.' His family, for the city. The city, for the world.

Darath's dead he's dead he's dead he's dead.

'He—'

'The gates need to be sealed, Gallus. You know that.'

Gallus nodded wearily. 'Perhaps, My Lord. If we have the men left.'

'The gates must be closed before the Emperor dies. Half the city will flee, otherwise.'

Gallus nodded wearily. 'Yes, My Lord.'

Orhan looked at him. 'You know all this. What is it you really want from me, Gallus?'

A long silence. They went through the square onto the Street of Flowers. Two women fought over the headless body of a cat. Orhan turned sharply away from the walk down to Darath's house, making instead for the Street of the Butchered Horse.

Gallus said quietly, 'Lord Tardein is in contact with the Immish, My Lord.'

'Lord Tardein—?'

Ah, God's knives.

Here it comes.

Gallus had worked well for him, when he was Nithque. Only betrayed his trust when it was clear he was already down. So here now was the price.

'He dictates letters to members of the Immish Great Council for me to write. I write them. Give them to him to seal. A reply comes. I am forbidden to open it. He tells me it must be opened only by the Nithque's own hands. Later he shows me the letter. It is a bland reply to the letter I sent. I write a lot of pointless letters. I read a lot of pointless replies. But there are other letters, folded up beneath.'

'You . . . You know this? You can prove this?'

Gallus reached into his coat. A small packet of silver paper, stamped and sealed in white. Orhan caught only a glimpse before it was tucked back away.

'A letter came yesterday morning. The palace is in chaos. The Emperor is sick. Two Secretaries are sick. Servants are dying every day. My Lord the Nithque is waiting to hear if his children are dead.' Sighed. 'As you say, no one will be left soon to care. I do not know what if anything it contains. Do you want to open it, My Lord?'

No. No. God's knives, no. I was going to abandon all this. I tried to change things. I failed. I was going to run away with Bil and my son and try to make some attempt at giving them a life.

Orhan held out his hand slowly. Like it almost wasn't his own hand. 'Give it to me, then.'

The seal of the Immish Great Council, a circle of interlocking circles around a broken tower. Fine sundried clay painted white, smudging off on his fingers, a small thing the size of a piece of candied fruit. Orhan flexed the letter. Broke the seal. Like stabbing someone, he thought. Something else from which there is no going back.

Unfolded the letter. A single sheet of fine silver leaf paper, inked in large letters in the awkward Pernish script in shiny black. Another, smaller letter nestled inside it. Like a present in a box. Plain rough coarse greyish paper. Plain porcelain seal with no stamp.

Gallus said with a kind of satisfaction, 'You see, My Lord?'

'It could still be nothing.' Orhan's hands trembled as he broke the seal.

A single word: 'Yes'.

A single bronze dhol fell to the dust at his feet. He bent and retrieved it. The image of the city embossed on it had been scored through.

Running feet on the flagstones behind him. Voices shouting. Orhan and Gallus swung round. A group of men, running, carrying torches. Carrying drawn swords.

'The Emperor is dying!'

'The God has abandoned us!'

'The blasphemers in the Temple! The High Priestess betraying us to the demon!'

'Every night! Every night!'

Shouts coming from several directions. A woman ran past clutching a baby. A group of children holding sticks and stones.

'The Emperor is dead!'

'The God has abandoned us!'

'We are impious! We deserve the God's anger!'

'Every night! Every night!'

A man staggering sick with fever. Vomiting his innards up in the street and staggering on. Another group of men with torches and swords.

'Every night! Every night!'

Orhan and Gallus began to run with them, Orhan's guards jogging behind. Horror mounting in Orhan. The letter crumpled half forgotten in his hand. Back down the Street of Flowers. More people running. And more, and more. Into the Grey Square. A single child had returned to fly her kite. Staring in confusion, open mouthed, at the crowds building suddenly around her. Men and women and children, the sick, the dying, armed men, men with torches, children holding stones. A few soldiers in gold armour in a group, uncertain, mouths open in confusion like the child's. A group of street girls swaying on bound legs, bells tinkling, also uncertain, making lewd comments to the crowd.

'The Emperor's dead!'

'The God has abandoned us! Great Tanis is angry!'

'The High Priestess betrayed us to the demon! The plague is our punishment for her crime!'

'Every night! Every night!'

'I have a child for the God's hunger! Every night! Every night!'

The woman raised her baby. It shrieked its odd heart-breaking grating shrieking noise. 'Every night! Every night!'

The crowd rushed towards the Temple. Up the steps, flowing like flood water, pushing and shoving each other, swarming crowding around the entranceway, fighting their way in in a rush. Still clutching torches and swords. The woman led them, the screaming baby still raised in her arms.

Orhan stared in sick wonder. There was light flickering out of the dark entranceway where light had never been. People fighting and trampling each other to get inside. Stared in sick wonder as a woman fell and was stamped on. People still running into the square, drawn by the shouting, the soldiers drew their swords hesitantly, looking at each other, the whores muttered to each other, shouted to the soldiers and the crowds.

Shouting from inside the Temple. The long rays of the evening sun through the gathering clouds on the black stone. And then suddenly Orhan understood. He bent forward and almost vomited. Gallus muttered something, fled back towards the palace. The soldiers moved slowly towards the despoiled entranceway. Those around the Temple began to shout at them. The whores jeered them. Someone threw a stone.

The sun sinking. The twilight bell tolled. From deep inside the Temple came a wild ecstatic hundred-voiced shriek.

Voices in the square screaming again: 'The God is angry with us!' 'The Emperor is dying!' 'The Emperor is dead!' 'The God has abandoned us!' 'Every night! Every night!' One of the whores untangled her bindings, went to join the crowds ebbing around the Temple steps. Men whistled at her, made catcalls. The soldiers looked at each other dizzily. 'Every night! Every night!' The woman who had been holding the baby came out of the Temple. Stood on the top of the steps. Her hands were bloody. She raised her hands. The crowd around the Temple cheered. 'Every night! Every night! Every night!' A stone flew from the crowd, hit one of the soldiers on the arm. The crowd cheered. Another stone fell short at the soldiers' feet. Another stone struck a gold helmet. Another stone. The whores began jeering. His guardsmen pulled tight around Orhan in a thicket. 'The Emperor's dead! The God has abandoned us!' 'Every night! Every night!' The woman waved her bloody hands: 'We must reclaim the Temple! Win back the love of the God!' 'The God has abandoned us!' 'The Emperor is dying!' 'Every night! Every night!' More stones, rattling on gold armour. The guards staring at each other, waving their swords. The woman screaming: 'The God must be placated!' The soldiers charged the crowd. Orhan saw blood spurting. Voices howling in fear and outrage. More people running into the square shouting. Stones flying. Then swords.

'The God has abandoned us!'

425

'Every night! Every night!'

Orhan stood in the dust trying to keep himself from vomiting. Tears running down his face.

Is this now what we've come to? Flies flies flies eating the ruin of the world.

The clouds opened, heavy warm rain, washing the dust up in swirling patterns.

'Every night! Every night!'

'The God has abandoned us!'

'Every night!'

Bodies falling. The soldiers cutting their own people down.

Orhan bent and wept in the wet dust.

Chapter Sixty-One

Twenty injured. Three dead. They piled the injured and the dead together against the west wall of the Great Temple. Thus the injured could see their future awaiting them as they died. The soldiers retreated to the mouth of the Street of Flowers, water dripping off their helmets. The rain fell like a wall between them and the crowds. After a long while paused talking, they disappeared into the rain.

Nilesh crouched at the edge of the square. She had seen Lord Emmereth from a distance, talking to his guardsmen, pointing at the Temple, waving his hands. Then someone had recognized him. Pointed. Shouted. A momentary flicker in the crowd. Shouts of 'traitor', 'murderer', 'hero'. His guardsmen drawing around him. The people had almost turned on him. Then he fled with his guards. Nilesh had been pressed behind a pillar, hiding from Lord Emmereth's gaze. This had kept her safe from the soldiers' swords.

Once the dead and injured had been carried to the shelter of the Great Temple, some of the crowd began to dance in the dark in the rain. A woman came round giving out wine from a heavy clay jug.

Another man Nilesh thought she recognized appeared in the square, grandly dressed, shining with gemstones, flanked by more guards. Soaking wet. He tried to talk to the assembled people. Got shouted down. His voice was weak and frightened, 'Your Emperor' he shouted hoarsely, the crowd roared so loud his words were lost, 'your Emperor . . . concern for the city . . . Great Tanis our Lord . . . High Priestess . . . I know . . . prayer . . . I know . . .' Voices jeered at him. The hard-faced street women shouted things Nilesh didn't understand. 'Every night!' voices shouted. 'Every night!'

'. . . Your Emperor . . . Great Tanis . . . I . . . good . . . city . . . Emperor . . . I . . .'

'The Emperor's dead!' a voice shouted. 'Stop lying to us!'

'Every night! Every night!'

'. . . not the way!' the man shouted hoarsely. His words were high-pitched and shrill like a child's.

'The God is angry!' a voice shouted.

'Every night! Every night!'

A stone came flying. Hit the man on the side of his head. Another, harder, drawing blood. The man swayed, staring, panicked. His guards surrounded him in a wall of golden armour. For a moment it looked like the violence would begin again. Then, like Lord Emmereth, he was hurried away. Stones and catcalls showered after him. People began to move hesitantly after where he had gone.

'Coward!'

'Betrayer! Liar!'

'The God is angry!'

'Every night! Every night!'

A cry from the steps of the Temple. Faces whipped around. A woman's voice screaming in fury.

'They're bolting the door!'

The great door of the Great Temple. Three times the height of a man. It was never locked. Not in all the history of the city. 'They're bolting the door!' The crowd streamed up the steps, rushed at the entrance. The door held against them, then gave. The crowd streamed into the Temple. Voices shouting. Howls. A while later a man's body was carried out, held triumphantly aloft.

'They have betrayed us!'

'The God has abandoned us!'

'The Emperor is dead!'

'Every night! Every night!'

Nilesh shrank back in the shadows. Many people like her, gathered on the edges, watching, unsure. This, this, surely, was going too far?

'Tolneurn,' the man nearest Nilesh said. She jumped, stared at him.

'Tolneurn. The Imperial Presence in the Temple. He must have ordered them to bar the door.'

The speaker was well dressed, silvery shirt, green embroidered coat. Nilesh bowed her head to him. 'Yes, My Lord.'

'Few will mourn him.'

Nilesh kept her eyes down. 'No, My Lord.'

'You were not tempted to take part?'

What could she say? 'No, My Lord.'

'You do not think, then, that the God has abandoned you?'

Eyes down at her own dirty feet. 'I don't know, My Lord.'

He snorted, strolled into the square to join the crowd swirling around the Temple. His fine green coat stood out vividly until it was soaked dark like the rest by the rain. Nilesh watched him moving between groups of people. It put her in mind of a leaf caught in the eddies of a flood.

The rain stopped shortly after. The water that ran ankle high across the flagstones began to recede. Wet rubbish and mud. Nilesh almost shivered, cold in the night air. The clouds parted to show a brilliant glittering band of stars. The Maiden, the Tree, beside it the great single red star the Dragon's Mouth. The stars looked huge. Because there was no dust in the sky after rain, Janush had said. She had never been able to see the Tree as a tree with branches, saw instead Bilale's hair dressed for a party with a net of diamonds and a single red pearl.

The drier air brought out more people. A flower stall was torn up and turned into a bonfire; it took a long time to light, the wood being soaked from the rain. When it lit it went up in a rush of blue fire and a smell of lamp fuel. Voices cheered. Sang the hymn to the rising sun. The Temple door, Nilesh saw in the light of the bonfire, had been pulled outwards and wedged open. The passageway behind showed black against the black marble wall. The crowd edged round it, not wanting to stand too close.

The violence seemed to be over. The bodies of those injured or killed by the soldiers lay undisturbed in the shadows of the west wall. A woman made her way through the square selling candied roses and cinnamon sweets. A kind of calm over everything. Nilesh went cautiously into the thick of the square into the press of people. The crowd milled aimlessly, gathering around the bonfire, sitting on the steps of the Great Temple, singing hymns, drifting past each other in blurred confusion, moving towards and then shying away from the dead body of Tolneurn the Imperial Presence in the Temple, moving towards and then shying away from the woman who had sacrificed her baby, who stood by the open door of the Temple, face raised to the stars. All directionless, confusion: like a lord's house must be, Nilesh thought, if the Lord and Lady were to stop giving orders and no one knew any more what to do. Voices shouted occasionally 'Every night! Every night!' 'The God is angry!' 'The God must be appeased!' In the firelight and the light of torches some of them looked flushed and haggard. Feverish. Sick. Yet a voice would start up singing a hymn of praise to the God Great Tanis the Lord of Living and Dying and the healthy and the sick would sing together, dance, even embrace. Nilesh moved in their rhythms, confused and in confusion like the rest. The whole night must be passing. In the east behind the domed rooftops the first light in the sky perhaps showed. Her legs felt weak and weary: she found herself near the sweet-seller on the steps of the Great Temple, bought a bag of sweets. The sweet-seller smiled at her with teeth as black as the shadowy passageway of the Great Temple. Her white face was flushed and damp with sweat. She shuddered as she handed Nilesh the bag, winced, bit her lip with a pained grimace. Nilesh dropped the bag onto the wet flagstones. It burst open, spilling out pink crystal petals that winked in the fire's light. Nilesh stared down at them. Rising rushing fear of the plague.

A man's shoe trod neatly on the fallen petals. Crushed them into the wet dust. Into little shredded limp pink grey pieces of rag. Firelight winked on jewelled shoe buttons. Nilesh looked up into the face of the man in the green coat.

'That was wisdom,' he said shortly. He ground the petals further into a smear on the flagstones with the toe of his shoe.

'She is sick with the fever,' Nilesh said suddenly. 'The sweet-seller. She's sick.'

The man in green nodded. 'Many are sick.' He pointed. 'Look.'

A man in the white silks of a knife-fighter was kneeling on the flagstones vomiting. The crowds swirled and moved around him, trying to avoid him, curling round him to include him in their endless movements around and around. Even as Nilesh watched he fell forward slowly on his face, lay still.

'He's dead?'

'They have made a sacrifice to the God,' the man in the green coat said. '"Every night! Every night!" So should the God not now be appeased and stop them dying? Cure all who witnessed it of the plague?'

He spoke like Lord Emmereth sometimes did, in such a way Nilesh could not quite understand what he was saying.

'Look,' the man in the green coat said. Two women lifted the knife-fighter back to his knees. His head rolled upwards, Nilesh saw that he was not quite dead. The women lifted him between them while a third put a cup of something to his lips. Then they let him drop again. He fell heavily, caught himself with his hands, knelt in a crouch. Spewed up whatever they had given him, began to crawl across the square towards the Temple steps.

'But he's dying?'

'I would think so, wouldn't you? Unless the God miraculously cures him in the next little while.'

'You're joking,' said Nilesh awkwardly.

After a while, she said, 'There was a man in the Court of Evening

431

Sorrows yesterday who claimed he could cure the plague with the touch of his hands.'

The man in the green coat looked at her. 'He's dead.'

Another bonfire flickered into light in the square. A circle of figures danced around it, dark against the flames, writhing and twisting and jumping hand in hand.

'It's almost dawn,' said the man in the green coat.

Nilesh turned her face around the square, gazing up at the sky. Her eyes imagined they could see pale faint light. Yes. Dawn.

'You served Lady Emmereth, didn't you?' said the man in the green coat. 'Until you were thrown out?'

'My Lord Emmereth was merciful and generous,' she said stiffly. How good it felt, to hear someone want to speak to her the Emmereth name!

'You are wondering, perhaps, how I know who you are?'

Nilesh looked at him in puzzlement. 'All in the city know My Lord of the Rising Sun and his household, My Lord.'

He paused. Nilesh thought that he seemed at a loss. He seemed about to speak, then stopped himself.

After a moment he said, 'Your name is Nilesh, I think? Mine is Cauvanh.'

Nilesh bowed her head even lower. 'My Lord Cauvanh.'

Laugh. 'Just Cauvanh.'

A shout went up in the square. Dawn! Dawn! Voices calling the Great Hymn to the rising sun, the most beautiful of all the songs of the God. Nilesh felt her heart rise in joy. The flames of the bonfires leapt higher, trying to match the light of the sky. The dome of the Summer Palace came alive in a blaze of gold. Even the black marble walls of the Great Temple were softly tinged in dreaming pink.

'Great Tanis! Great Tanis! Lord of Living and Dying! Great Lord Who Rules All Things!' The people in the square began to dance again, embracing and kissing one another, spinning like glorious joyful birds. Nilesh was caught up with them, one of the women who had tended the knife-fighter grasped her hands, pulled her into a circle of women dancing, street girls in sheer beaded dresses, merchants' wives in billowing satin, a little girl in a foam of yellow lace. 'The sun rises! The sun! The sun! The sun!' As if they had all believed, deep in their hearts, that the sun would never rise on them again.

Men in armour appeared again in the square at the mouth of the Street of Flowers. Glittering like the dome of the Summer Palace. Young men, silent, looking fixed straight ahead. Young men with tall barb-headed spears.

The dancers whirled to stopping. The voices singing the hymn died away.

A few ragged shouts and catcalls: 'The God is angry!' 'Every night! Every night!'

The lines of soldiers opened to let through a man in a fine blue coat. Nilesh recognized him with a start as the man Lord Emmereth had been speaking to the night before. He had come to the House of the East a few times to see Lord Emmereth. Gallan, his name might be. Gallise? Gallus?

'People of Sorlost,' Gallus said loudly. The crowd fell silent.

He knows My Lord Emmereth, Nilesh thought. So surely they must respect him for that, what he said would be worth hearing and give them cheer.

'People of Sorlost. I come to you from the side of the Emperor himself. The Emperor understands your fears. Fears and mourns with you. Like you, he has watched all that has befallen us with grief. Like you, he fears that the God is angry with us, that such strife and fear has befallen our great city. Like you, he feels anger. Like you, he seeks a way to heal our city and placate the God.'

'The Emperor's dead!' a voice shouted. 'He's dead!'

And a new shout, in a voice rich and tremulous: 'We'll all die!'

'The Emperor is not dead.' Oh Great Tanis! Lord Emmereth himself stepped out from the line of guards to stand beside Gallus. Nilesh flinched, seeing him so close. He must see her, surely, standing only a little way across from him in the light of the morning. Cauvanh, near her, stiffened. She felt him look briefly at her.

433

Shouts of 'traitor', 'hero', 'murderer'. Cheers. Murmuring. Curses.

'The Emperor is not dead,' Lord Emmereth said loudly over the noise. His face was grey, his body was clenched tight. He was shaking. Like a man in the wind. 'I have come from his chambers, where he has sat all night awake in prayer. He desires only to come to the Temple to give offering to Great Tanis. But he cannot come, for there has been violence done here. He is not dead, but he is afraid. The priestesses cannot hold the service of the dawn sun rising. So the Emperor implores you to leave and return to your homes and let the Emperor and the priestesses pray for the city, as is their task and their duty.' His face turned to the body of Tolneurn the Imperial Presence in the Temple, then to the dead and injured mixed together against the Temple's wall. 'Enough violence has been done here! The God has surely heard you! The Emperor hears you! He begs you, people of Sorlost the Golden, people of the Sekemleth Empire, the Empire of the Golden Dawn Light, of the Lord of Living and Dying, the richest empire the world has ever known, your Emperor begs you, his children, to return to your homes in peace and let him pray to the God for us all!'

Silence. Murmuring, like birds waking. A few uncertain movements. Catcalls, but quieter now. People's faces looking almost half ashamed.

Then Cauvanh shifted. Shouted.

'The Emperor is dead! He is lying!'

Threw a stone.

The soldiers moved into life around Lord Emmereth.

The crowd began to run.

People running up the steps into the Temple. Voices shrieking from inside. A child's scream. The door to the Temple slammed.

The spears came down.

Chapter Sixty-Two

'The Temple's clear.'

Orhan nodded wearily.

Gallus said, 'I had the men put the bodies in a pile in the Temple gardens. You're right, we don't want people to see them being carried out.'

'Burn them,' said Orhan.

Fever and contagion. Putrefying diseased bodies. Sickness of madness and of plague. 'They need to be destroyed now.'

Things you learnt. The destruction of the body by fire. The stacking of the pyre, the pouring on of the oil, the kindling of the flame. The way the fat sizzled. The smell of burning hair.

We're all dying.

Flies flies flies eating the whole world.

Gallus nodded. Equally wearily. He ran his hands through his hair. 'And the . . . the High Priestess, My Lord? Should we . . . should we bury her?'

Even you, thought Orhan, even you doubt, now, that the High Priestess Thalia is dead, that that poor child was rightfully High Priestess.

He thought: the child was an abomination before the God, indeed. A curse on me. Filth on my skin. Just not in the way you and all the rest seem to think.

'Display her body on the steps of the Temple. Don't try to pretty her, or disguise it. And if you can, wreath her in copperstem.'

'I could put up a notice,' said Gallus. '"So die all who blaspheme against Great Tanis the Lord of Living and Dying".'

Orhan in turn ran his hands through his hair. 'You could.'

'Have you got any rest, My Lord?'

Almost laughed. 'Rest? I'll rest soon enough when they come to kill me. Or when I kill myself. But I don't think I can ever rest again.'

Gallus looked at him and their eyes met bleakly. Sharing something deeper even than he'd ever shared with Darath. Pain and self-loathing like no one should ever feel.

'It was necessary, My Lord,' said Gallus.

'Yes. It was.' 'Kill them,' he'd ordered the soldiers, after the mob killed the High Priestess in the Great Chamber of the Temple itself. 'Kill them all.' An apple, for five cimma fruit. Half the city, for something and no one could say any more what. Plague and fire and madness tore at them. But something, something must be saved. Nobody else was doing anything. Lord Tardein the Nithque of the Asekemlene Emperor of the Sekemleth Empire of the city of Sorlost was hiding in the House of Breaking Waves stuffing a scarf into his mouth to smother his screams, a table against his bedroom door. Someone had to try to bring some kind of order. Keep them all from killing themselves.

Orhan Emmereth and his wife and his son and all his household, for the last few sane people in Sorlost.

'How soon will someone come for us, then?' said Gallus.

Orhan sighed. 'Soon, I should think. Cam will have to try to take some control back of something sometime, if he wants to stay alive himself.'

'His son died,' said Gallus.

'When? You should have told me.'

'Only very recently, late last night or this morning. The boy crawled from his sick room trying join the people in the street. Died as they tried to get him back to bed.'

'Go and burn the bodies,' Orhan said. 'That needs doing. It has to be done. And get the girl's body displayed.'

'Yes, My Lord.' It was raining again. Orhan watched Gallus splashing across the Grey Square. He did not look at the men accompanying him.

I hoped it would rain, Orhan thought.

One of the pyres in the square flickered. The rain, trying its best to put it out. The smell was indescribable. Far, far worse than the smell of Tam Rhyl's house when it burned. The square was so full of smoke it made Orhan's eyes water. The faces of the soldiers tending the pyres were blank and hard and empty. Poisoned. Ruined. Sick unto death themselves.

Shame, Orhan thought, looking at Gallus walking stiffly up the Temple steps, disappearing into the gaping dark. What it means to be a God is to live in constant grief and shame.

Just let me die of deeping fever, oh God, Great Lord Tanis, Great Lord of Living and Dying. Be merciful. Let me die of deeping fever here now.

Instead, one of the soldiers tending the nearest pyre approached him. Alyen, his name might be, one of the commanding officers in charge of these wretched men.

'The fires aren't burning properly, My Lord,' said Alyen. There was soot and blood on his white face. 'They won't burn in the rain, My Lord.' He shifted uncomfortably. His eyes staring respectfully hatefully at the ground. 'The men . . . The men say the rain's an omen. Unnatural. That Great Tanis is angry. They are afraid, My Lord.'

'Pour more fuel on the bodies,' Orhan said. His voice sounded distant in his ears. Alyen looked deeply unhappy. Glanced over at the fires with pain in his eyes. Orhan sighed. 'Tell the men the rain is Great Tanis weeping, that His city has come to this. The God mourns for the dead.'

'Yes, My Lord.' Alyen went back to his fire, trying to march like a soldier man. Brisk false officer's voice called to the man nearest him: 'Fetch another couple of barrels of oil, Jal.'

He was risking all the soldiers' lives, ordering them to clear the bodies. Their bodies were sticky with blood. Filthy, stinking, alive with flies. Contagious: the raised heat of the diseased blood warmed the blood of the healthy, made them sick in turn. 'The God will keep you healthy,' he kept repeating to them. 'The God will reward you, for what you do. The God will keep you healthy. The Emperor is grateful. He is praying to Great Tanis for you even now.'

'The Emperor's dead,' someone muttered occasionally. 'The God's abandoned us.'

Another squad of soldiers was coming back into the square from the Street of Flowers. The rain washing their spears clean. Their commander presented himself to Orhan. 'My Lord. We've cleared the streets east of the square right up past the Gold Quarter. No one's about now. And I'm to report that the Gate of the Evening is closed and guarded by ten men.'

'Yes. Thank you.'

'If I may ask . . . how fares the Emperor, My Lord?'

Orhan ran his hands through his hair. 'The Emperor is pleased. He is grateful for all that you have done.'

The Emperor must be a screaming mewling newborn baby, somewhere. Six, seven, eight hours old? Oh yes, he must be grateful. A newborn baby wouldn't stand much chance if the city collapsed entirely in bloodshed and disease. It's not lies, Orhan thought again. It's not lies. None of this. It's the truth, in that it's the only way that we can go on.

Gallus returned from the Great Temple. He looked even worse than he had when he went in.

'It's done,' said Gallus. 'Or doing, anyway. I set five men to tend the fire. Another four are working with the priestesses trying to set things at least partly to rights in the Great Chamber. Another two cursed me and ran away.'

'You should get something to eat,' said Orhan. 'A rest.'

'As you said, I don't think I'll ever rest again. Or be able to eat. I couldn't find any copperstem in the Temple storerooms. Not the kind of thing they'd have thought they'd be likely to need.'

'Never mind, then. We need to get her body set up on the steps outside. With a sign, if you wish. As soon as the Temple's halfway in order, we should get it open. Get some of the great families in there saying prayers. I'll send a note to Lady Amdelle. Remind me.'

'My Lord . . . The Emperor's supposed to be going to the Temple to pray for the city, My Lord.'

Ah, God's knives. He was. Desperately eager to do so at the earliest possible moment, his corpse had told Orhan so several times. Orhan rubbed his eyes, tried to think. 'Find a kitchen servant in the palace, stick them in a big black coat and bring them here. We'll have to announce the truth at some point. But not until after he's come here and made a dedication and said his prayers. Offered his life to the God for the lives of his people.' His voice was coming out from somewhere else, somewhere he'd never been, not even that night at the beginning of all this when the demon came into the city at his command. Heard it droning on and on, saying things he couldn't bear it to say. It was necessary. I did it because it was necessary. I did it to save us. I wanted to make things better. I wanted to help the world. 'Kill the man once he's back in the litter. Make sure no one can recognize his face.'

Gallus looked up at Orhan, their eyes meeting. Wet with tears. It's just the rain. Just the rain. 'Yes, My Lord.'

Gallus paused, looked around the square at the bonfires. 'Why did this happen, My Lord?'

Orhan said slowly, 'Because people are desperate, I imagine. The same reasons people usually have for desperate things.'

'But . . . A woman killed her child, My Lord. And the crowd killed that . . . that young girl.'

'She thought she was saving the city.' Orhan almost wanted to take Gallus's hand. 'Perhaps, Gallus, she loved her own life, or another's, more than that of the child.' What would you kill, Gallus, he thought, if it kept you a little while longer alive? Answer me honestly. Really, truly, honestly, deep down.

Gallus said, 'You were about to give me back that letter. Tell me to put it back. Walk off.'

The day wore on. The rain stopped again. The mud baked back to yellow dust and dog shit. The fig tree in the corner of the Grey Square shone verdant green. Pethe birds drank from a last shadowed puddle. Dogs slunk spittle-eyed looking for scraps. Orhan sat in the shade of the loggia giving orders, sending men out, watching the pyres slowly, slowly blaze up and burn down. Days, they would take. Days, hanging over the city in a fog of rancid smoke.

The things you learnt.

Chapter Sixty-Three

In the blazing afternoon sunshine the Emperor's litter arrived at the Temple. It floated in the heavy light, a great black box reminding Orhan of the black entranceway of the Great Chamber so obscenely exposed. Carved of bone that was said to be dragon bone, dug out of the sands of the eastern desert barely a day's walk beyond the city walls. Hard and dry and silvery, knotted ends like tumours, cold to the hand like thick cracked ice. Blue flames licked the curtains of the litter. Raced over the cold cold metallic bones. Basins of ammalene resin, dried lavender, dried mint, copperstem flowers preserved like sugared roses, a servant in gold and silver net like fish scales scattering them before the litter, the lumps of incense smouldering on the stones. Let the feet of those who carry the Emperor never touch the city's ground.

'All kneel! All kneel for the Ever Living Emperor! The Emperor comes!'

The litter bearers wore hoods and masks so that one never saw their faces. Embroidered all over with pure white pearls. They walked with a slow, heavy, rolling, tripping gait. The God alone knew if they were even human. Demons summoned up from the bones of the litter, yoked to it by the power of the God. Immortal and ageless and mindless and formless, inhuman things of light

441

and shadow, curling teeth and curling horns. Or servants in padded costumes. Sworn to silence for cheap effect.

From out of the litter a man emerged. A thick black cloak covering his face. So great his grief for his city that he could not bear to let the light touch his skin. He was carried up the steps of the Great Temple in a golden chair canopied with simiseren feathers, in which, it was noted, he sat awkwardly twitching and hunched. So great his grief for his city that he boiled with pain in his chair. In black-gloved hands he carried a single white candle, as offering for the God. His life, Orhan told the soldiers closest to him in an awed whisper. His life he would pledge, to die when the candle died, to purchase the lives of all in the city, to suffer in exchange for his people's salvation all the agonies of death and rebirth.

What exactly transpired in the Great Temple no one but the God and the man in the black cloak would ever know. Except that it didn't last very long. After what seemed to Orhan no time at all the golden chair was carried out again and the black-cloaked man placed back in his litter. 'All kneel! All kneel for the Ever Living Emperor! The Emperor comes!' The soldiers shouted a cheer as the litter departed swaying and rolling.

Lady Amdelle, robed in cloth of silver with a headdress of red glass, came to the Temple a little later in the first lengthening evening shadows, bringing her son and half of her household in her train. They lit a hundred beeswax candles. Lady Amdelle dedicated a moonstone the size of a serving plate and a rope of green pearls as long as a man's body and a statuette of a magnolia tree in flower cut from a white striped ruby, only as tall as a child's finger but so perfectly carved that every flower had petals and stamen and pollen grains. Lord Aviced followed her, weighed down in a coat encrusted with jewels, half his household following in torn clothing with bowed heads. He lit a hundred candles, dedicated a golden bowl of hens' teeth and an emerald the size of his clasped fists. Both, it was noted, threw gifts of gemstones and coins to the soldiers tending the fires. Lady Amdelle, it was noted, bent her head before one of the pyres and wept. To Orhan's astonishment, Eloise Verneth followed, all in white and yellow, mirrors on her gown reflecting his puzzled eyes. She stopped her litter and looked at Orhan. A long look he could not understand. She brought the petals of a cetalasophrase preserved in rose oil, a wreath of clear ice that was enchanted against melting, a vine of amethyst grapes with gold and emerald leaves. Her servants gave out bread and cold roast meat to the soldiers. Another couple of lesser nobles, one of them some distant cousin of Darath's, his face near enough to Darath's face that the line in the set of his mouth stabbed at Orhan's heart. A handful of the richest of the merchant families, just about a measurable proportion of those still left alive.

A kind of calm descended on the city. The desire for violence choked out, smothered like the flames. Sanity returning, people waking to stare at each other, curse themselves and look away, grieving shame for themselves and their city, unaccountable, frightened, sick at heart but also purged and calmed in themselves. It was announced shortly after dawn that the Emperor had died peacefully, His last words a prayer for His people and a thanks to the God for granting His only wish. In the eastern desert, it was rumoured, dragons danced red and green and silver on the wind. The air grew hot and stifling. The city was plagued by clouds of great fat black flies. The House of Flowers stood sealed and silent. Orhan sat outside Bilale's bedroom, listening to her croon to his son behind layers of locked doors.

Chapter Sixty-Four

It delighted Nilesh's heart, that Lord Emmereth was reinstated as Nithque.

The proclamation was made at midday on the steps of the Summer Palace. Thick crowds swirled around it, had done so since the Emperor's death was announced. The Emperor had named the Lord of the Rising Sun as Nithque again in place of Lord Tardein, who was too broken with grief at his family's deaths to go on. The gates of the city were to remain sealed. But the early signs were that the outbreak of plague was coming to an end. The prayers of the Emperor, the great sacrifices made by his people, the purging of the false High Priestess by those who had acted out of love of the God: all of these things had saved them. Great Tanis was merciful indeed.

'He will help us,' Nilesh assured the woman standing next to her in the Street of Closed Eyes. 'He will put things to rights, now.' A regency council was appointed, headed of course by Lord Emmereth, including also Lord Tardein, Lord Amdelle, Remys the new Imperial Presence in the Temple, Lord Lochaiel the new Lord of the Moon's Light the new Dweller in the House of Silver the late lamented Lord Verneth's cousin and heir.

'You see? It will all be well now.'

The woman next to Nilesh grunted. Grudgingly hopeful, Nilesh thought.

The city was to remain under curfew. The Great Temple was to remain under guard.

Mutterings in the crowd at that. Angry, frightened voices. Nilesh sighed at them. Why could they not see?

The crowd shifted. Soldiers outside the palace. The crowd began reluctantly to disperse. Nilesh began to move with them. She was beginning to think about things like what to do with herself. Clean up the Five Corners and live there, perhaps. Or beg Lord Emmereth for help.

The man in the green coat, Cauvanh, was suddenly near her. Nilesh felt great surprise that he had not been killed in the Grey Square. He noticed her. Smiled.

'Hello, Nilesh.'

'Hello.' She remembered him shouting to the crowd to attack Lord Emmereth on the Temple steps. Drew back from him, afraid. Angry.

'Nilesh?' He seemed sad that she was afraid and angry. 'I just want to talk to you.' He had a bruise on his face. He was no longer wearing the green coat, but his shoes were the same and they had dark splashes on them, one was missing a button, its leather torn.

'Go away,' she hissed at him.

'You should be pleased,' Cauvanh said. 'Your Lord Emmereth is Nithque again. He would not have been restored to his power had the rioting not broken out.'

'Go away.'

He looked saddened. 'Keep safe, Nilesh. Go inside. Stay there.'

'Why?'

He shook his head. Went off into the crowd. She heard, she thought, his voice raised talking to a woman in a red dress. '. . . And why should the Temple remain under guard?'

Nilesh stood in the street. Confused. Everything was good

again. Peaceful. Lord Emmereth Nithque. The city restored. She remembered Bilale talking with real excitement of some plans Lord Emmereth had to clean and improve the housing in Fair Flowers.

If only Lord Vorley would recover, she thought. Lord Vorley was in some way an enemy to Bilale. Yet to think of Lord Emmereth having to live without him grieved Nilesh's heart.

She went back to the Five Corners. She had got the door mostly open, one of the women living further down the street had got her son to help. The rotting bodies still sat in the hallway, by the fountain, slumped on their beds. But she had found a storeroom that was clean. Soon, she thought, she would ask the soldiers patrolling the streets to help her. She had seen them stripping clean the baker's house opposite, where all the inhabitants seemed to have died.

Noise woke her in the darkness. Shouts and cries. The rioting, she thought in horror. Lord Emmereth! Bilale! She pulled on her clothes and ran out into the street. Torchlight flickered on the walls. People stirring, stretching their heads from the windows, peering out. What is it? What is it?

A man came running towards her. He came from the direction of the palace. He was shouting, so fast and panicked Nilesh could barely understand.

'The Immish! The Immish! God's knives!'

'What? What's happening?' A woman in the street grabbed his hand. 'Sit down! Tell me!'

'The Immish! Ah, God! I need to get back to my home! Bar your doors! Pray!'

He pushed the woman away, ran on.

Nilesh stood staring after him. People in the street were staring after him, talking, repeating 'the Immish' in confused tones. What is it? What? More shouting, coming from the direction of the palace, the direction the man had come from.

The bell of the Great Temple began to sound. The twilight bell.

446

Ringing out loud in the dark. It sounded like the strangest thing in all the world.

On and on.

'The Immish'. 'The Immish.'

Nilesh began to run in the direction of the shouts.

The Temple bell fell silent. As terrifying as when it had begun to ring. More and more people were running, milling, standing staring caught in the flood. Everywhere the cries 'what is it?' and the confused words 'the Immish have come'. Nilesh ran on. Legs shaking. Bilale! she kept thinking. Bilale! Bilale! She came to the Court of the Broken Knife. An overturned candle beneath the faceless statue, a man sitting beside it panting, a crowd around him buzzing like flies. He was talking, telling them something, the crowd shouted angrily, swirled in the square, the same angry words. 'The Immish!'

'What is he saying?' Nilesh asked a woman on the edge of the crowd.

'The Immish have come,' the woman said. She was weeping. 'Returned. Not just the palace. Soldiers. So many soldiers. We are overrun.'

They had come in at dusk. The Maskers' Gate had been opened, though at dusk it should have been sealed and sealed. A company of soldiers, an army, thousands, heavily armed, a magelord at their head. The city was surrounded, besieged, occupied. The Immish were rounding up the great families. Killing them in their beds without mercy. Killing everyone.

'I don't believe it,' a voice shouted. 'It's another trick, like the last time.'

'I saw them!' another voice shouted. 'Immish soldiers.'

'To the palace!' A third voice. 'Defend the city!' People began to move.

Nilesh looked at the faceless statue. Remembered the dead bodies piled in the Grey Square.

She followed the flow of the crowd down Moon and Sunlight. Through the Court of Evening Sorrows. Down the Street of Bones.

On the corner of Gold Street and the Street of Children a knife-fighter lay in the dust. Abandoned. As though the fighting had been cut off in the midst, before he had been killed. Before the gates to the House of Glass two men sat with wounds and bloody knives. 'The Immish!' they shouted hoarsely. 'Go back to your homes! It's too late! Too late!'

Lord Emmereth, thought Nilesh. Bilale. Oh, Bilale.

A troop of soldiers came towards them, down the Street of All Sorrows. The crowd stopped.

They were not Imperial soldiers. They were not armoured in shining gold.

Their armour was black. Thick, heavy corselets. Black helmets covering their faces, moulded into blank metal faces through which their eyes stared. They carried spears that ended in crescent hooks.

'The Immish,' the crowd whispered.

A couple of the spears were already stained dark with blood.

A soldier at the head of the troop strode forward. His helmet had a thick crest, like a horse's mane. He did not have a spear. Carried a drawn sword.

'People of Sorlost,' he shouted. 'Go back to your homes. The Immish Great Council has heard of your troubles. Murder. Treachery. Plague. The betrayal of your Temple to the Altrersyr demon king. And now the terrible death of your Emperor. The rightful Nithque, Lord Tardein, fearing for your safety, has appealed to the Immish Great Council for aid. And Immish has answered! We come to bring you and your children peace!'

Silence. The crowd shifted. The terrible spear hooks lowered behind the man with the crested helmet. Hooked blades reaching towards the crowd.

The man with the crested helmet said something in a different language to his soldiers. They took a step forward.

'Go back to your homes,' the man with the crested helmet went on. 'Your city is safe. The Imperial Palace and the Temple are guarded. The Nithque Lord Tardein will address you tomorrow. You must return home.'

The hooked blades beckoned like fingers.

The crowd murmured and shifted. Began to move back away.

Lord Emmereth is the Nithque, thought Nilesh.

I don't . . . I don't understand.

She remembered again conversations she had overheard between Bilale and Lady Amdelle. Lord Verneth, Lord Rhyl, Lord Tardein, Lord Emmereth. Treachery and betrayal. Everything going round and round. She went slowly back down the Street of All Sorrows. Down the Street of Gold. The knife-fighter still sat in the corner, clutching his wound. There was another troop of black-armoured soldiers in the Court of the Broken Knife. The man who had sat beneath the statue had gone. She went back to the Five Corners. Lay down in the storeroom with a chair pressed up against the door.

'Your city has fallen into great turmoil,' a voice shouted in the street. 'You have been betrayed and conspired against. But we come now to your aid.'

The Immish soldiers filed out through the city. Guards at the gates of the palace. Guards in the Great Temple, watching over the priestesses and Remys the new Imperial Presence. Guards in the Grey Square, in the Court of the Fountain, in the Court of the Broken Knife. Guards around the House of the East, the House of Flowers. Guards around the House of Breaking Waves where the true Nithque Lord Tardein tried to talk with an Immish general instead of weep for the death of his only son.

Six thousand men in black iron armour, black helmets that covered their faces like the priestesses' masks, crescent-shaped hook-bladed spears, fat stabbing swords. A mage in a silver robe. A representative of the Immish Great Council who dreamed of trade opportunities. A general in the Immish army who had once hanged the Telean nobility from a gateway after a company of mercenaries betrayed the city to his spears.

Sorlost. The Eternal, the Golden City. The most beautiful, the first, the last, the undying. The unconquered. The unconquerable.

The greatest of cities, that was old before Tarboran built her tombs, before the Godkings were even born. Its walls have never been breached: even Amrath himself dashed his armies to pieces against them to no avail and gave up in despair. Oh city of shit and sunlight! Oh city of dawn and the setting sun! So weak and defenceless and worn down. A dead man's dreaming. A useless heap of crumbled rock. The decaying heart of the decayed remnant of the richest empire the world had ever known.

Sold to the Immish by March Verneth may the God Great Tanis the Lord of Living and Dying blast his bones to ashes, and Eloise Verneth may the God Great Tanis the Lord of Living and Dying choke her lungs with gold dust, and Cammor Tardein may the God Great Tanis the Lord of Living and Dying run his veins with molten lead. Sold for gold and diamonds. Sold for fear and honour. Sold for hate. Sold for revenge.

Such precious things.

Orhan Emmereth is a prisoner in his study. He hears his wife and his son weeping through the walls. His sister is a prisoner in her bedroom. She beats on the door begging her husband to let her out. His lover lies a prisoner on his sickbed. He stirs in his sleep and calls Orhan's name.

'Traitor! Murderer! Monster! You did this! You brought this on us! I killed people for you! Because I believed in you! I'll see you and everything that's yours die in screaming pain! I swear!'

And how much will a man sacrifice, to make the world a better place?

PART SEVEN

THE PLACE OF

THE DEAD

Chapter Sixty-Five

Illyr did not, of course, fall to him in one battle, as Ith had done.

As Marith had said to Thalia, he didn't want it to. No mercy. No accepting their surrender. The descendants of the traitors who had defied Amrath. Abandoned Him, turned on Him, torn His watch towers and fortresses down. Killed any number of Marith's ancestors, saying they would have no more of demon-spawned kings. They wanted to fight for every scrap of ground he would rip from them? Then he'd fight them. Really fight them. Really make them suffer. Every village. Every field. Mageries and gods and magics, they'd throw at him, all the power that had destroyed his ancestors, and he'd show them.

The dragon looked to be even more fun than the shadows. His punishment on them. The way it killed things, the sheer power and weight in it, the glorious utter absurdity, 'a dragon killed them', 'my dragon killed them', 'I sent the dragon and it burned them all to ash'. It hated him, bucked beneath his control of it, spoke to him with pain begging to be let free. Loved him. Knew that in him, at last, it had found a thing more terrible than itself. It made him almost ashamed, sometimes. To have something that vast and terrifying bound to his control.

Osen kept suggesting he try to ride it. It didn't seem an entirely convincing idea.

'Too big.'

'Yes. Kiana said that to me this morning, too.'

They took the town of Thelkek two days after crossing the Nimenest into Illyr. Town: large village, really, low dark houses clustered around a meeting place with twin godstones, horses' skulls set up on poles around the wooden walls. Little worth taking, and most of the people had fled or been killed already. They rolled over it, pillaged its meagre store rooms for a feast day, set up the remaining inhabitants in a pile between the godstones, a pyramid of flopping, thrashing, weeping meat. Some of the men made victory offerings there: honey, beer, coins, blood. His grandfather must have come this way, from the look of the maps and thinking about the way the roads went. An Ithishman who claimed to have lived in Illyr said he could take them out to the site of a skirmish where Nevethyn had set up a marker to his dead.

'Did Amrath ever come here?' Marith asked the man.

'This is Amrath's own kingdom, My Lord King. Everywhere in Illyr, Amrath went.'

'Yes, well, obviously. But . . . did He come here? This particular place? Leave anything? Do anything?' An inscription, a statue, a pokey ruined backwater border post. After hurried discussion with a local girl one of the sarriss captains had taken a fancy to, a crack was found on the larger of the godstones made by a kick from Amrath's horse. Marith stood and contemplated it, awed.

'Too big,' said Osen.

'Shush. Don't ruin it.'

'What's that sound I hear? Could it be someone hurriedly hammering a crack in a stone?'

'Shush!'

Osen produced a wineflask from his belt and poured a libation over the crack, soaking a posy of flowers someone had left in offering beneath. '*Elenaneikth Ansikanderakane Amrakane*. This broken stone a holy relic of the passage of the World Conqueror, whose favour I invoke.' He grinned at Marith. 'Send for your horse and get it to give this a big hard old kick.'

The country opened up in beauty as they marched further into Illyr, harder and harsher than the Ithish forests or the wheat fields of Seneth, drawn out across the earth in fierce stark lines of green and black. It reminded Marith of the statue of Serelethe in the Amrath Chapel of Malth Elelane, the terrible, cruel beauty of the mother of Amrath's face. One could see why the Whites had seemed a new world of comfort to the grieving Eltheia. Grasses stretched thin over black soil, high fells like armour, narrow valleys running with silver water, sheer crags where only birds could reach. This country, Marith thought, this is what made me. Ruined by ancient battles, wild and empty, forcing his ancestors to wildness, until they had to call upon demons to help them survive. The beauty of the light on the grass pained him, shadows of clouds moving across the lines of the hilltops, the flash of a distant river, green slopes falling into black hollows, grey stone that gleamed in the sun. At night the sky was vast as thinking, an eternity of stars. For this, Serelethe had offered herself to the demons. For this, Amrath had been born. My kingdom, he thought. Mine. Marith Altrersyr, King Ruin, King of Death, King of Shadows, dragon kin, dragon killer, dragonlord. Amrath returned. If Illyr had been rich in wheat and wood and cattle, a wealthy land of great cities and ten times a thousand hulking meat-fed men, I would not be what I am.

Things were . . . easier, between himself and Thalia. The beauty of the country cheered her, she enjoyed riding again beside him at the head of the columns, enjoyed watching the world. The longer days pleased her, the long blue evening light. They stopped a few days to rest; they went out together alone, explored the country. He swore to her no more hatha. She smiled, knowing he lied but thanking him. Embraced him with a new fierceness to her. 'I love you,' she told him as they made love. 'I love you, Marith.' Her voice was strange, choked and savage. But she'd never said that she loved him as they made love before.

'I'm sorry,' he said to her.

'You should be.'

Ashamed. So sick with shame. Everything in you, you destroy, Marith.

But not her. Not her. Please.

'I'm sorry. Forgive me. Please.'

She rolled over, sat up with her hair shimmering around her. 'I should have told you, about meeting Landra Relast. Poor woman. I pitied her, Marith, that's all. She looked so broken, so cold. You destroyed her whole family, Marith. I thought I owed her that. Some little scrap that I could give her, at least stop her from freezing in the snow. Let her eat. Things she did not give to me. But I should have told you.'

And the gestmet, Thalia? The god that tried to kill me? Landra's friend? Should you have told me about that?

He said, 'I'm sorry about Tyrenae. I should not have done it.'

I don't regret it, he thought. Like my mother's body, Ti's body, it could not remain unburied to reproach me. Watch me. My heart was broken there.

Thalia took him into her arms. He heard her breath. The beating of her heart. Her heart was beating very fast.

'I know, Marith,' she said.

Alleen had a party for them that night in his tent, crowned them with bronze flowers more delicate and fragile than real living blooms. Osen and Alleen and Kiana and all, toasting them, smiling at them. There was a singer, a girl from the White Isles with a clear sweet voice. They both got very drunk, laughed together, Thalia kissed him and her eyes were heavy with lust. 'Get back to your tent, you two,' Alleen shouted at them. Their friends carried them there like a bride and bridegroom, a weaving procession of singing and torchlight.

'I forgive you,' she said the next morning. 'Now go away and let me sleep. Or stop the army marching. My head hurts too much to quarrel any more.'

'Lightweight. Do you need me to bring you a jewelled bucket to puke in?'

She groaned. 'And I said your divine blood had no importance.'

I think I understand, he thought sometimes, why my father did what he did. Killed my mother, my real mother. If indeed he did kill her. Why he married Elayne so soon after my mother's death.

'I know a very good hangover cure . . .' he said.

I'll give Alleen half my kingdom, he thought. For giving me this one happiness back.

Onwards. Dark hills rose around them, steep and jagged, yellow with gorse. Wild goats and wild horses, picking their way over steep crags. Strawberries grew in great profusion in the shelter of the rocks. Blackthorn trees laden with sloes. A waterfall tore through a hillside, plunged down into a valley that was white with human bones. The land was empty of people. The Illyians all gone and fled.

'Up there.' Yanis Stansel pointed to a high felltop, black against the sky. It was crested, at its very top, with a huge cairn. On two sides the curve of the rock fell away sharply, a natural rampart. Lower down the slope, the remains of what might once have been stone walls.

'What is it?' Marith's skin prickled. This was something of Amrath's. A fortress guarding the pass through towards the city of Ethalden. Walls built at His own command.

'The Watch Tower of Irulth Kelurel, My Lord King. You see, to the left, where the hill falls away, the walls on that outcrop of rock? One of the beacons Serelethe built to bring news of Amrath's victories, I think. And that cairn at the top . . . I think it must be the tomb of the magelord Nevet himself.'

Ah, gods . . . To see it! Actually to see it! To imagine the beacon relit, the walls raised, manned again with his banner flying proud at their top!

457

'Fetch the queen,' Marith said eagerly. 'We will ride up and see.'

They had to scramble the last bit on foot, so steep was the slope. Close to, the walls were enormous, blocks of stone taller than a man, unweathered, their sides as clean and sharp as the day they were cut. A spring flowing into a carved basin, what looked to be store houses, the remains of a gateway, its lintel carved with dragons gnawing at their own tails. Huge fire-blackened roof timbers, carved with faces and horses' heads.

'Nevet raised it with a song,' said Marith. 'He sang and the hills shattered and the tower was raised. Amrath lay here a night with Eltheia, when He brought her back in triumph as His bride. Nevet died here, killed by the traitor Imarayre who one of Amrath's own captains, when the people of Illyr rose up in rebellion at the end. Ah, gods, beloved! To see it! To stand here!'

At the very top the wind whipped Thalia's hair up, so that she seemed doubled in height. Their cloaks made a noise like wings. The cairn rose before them, a rough pile of white rocks. Marith put out his hand to touch it. It felt warm, like dry skin.

'Nevet . . .' Thalia was shivering, her shoulders hunched. 'I was always more afraid of Nevet than even Amrath, when I was a child.'

'Afraid?' But yes, he supposed, yes, she would have been afraid. The enemies of Sorlost.

'Mages' bodies are supposed to be incorruptible . . .' He traced his hand lovingly over the stones.

'No!'

'I've seen mages' corpses, beloved. All very much corrupted. In little crispy bits, indeed. One by a dragon's teeth and several more by my hand. Nevet's bare old dead bones. Don't fear.'

'He burned things,' she whispered. 'Nevet. Burned them with the power of his will. He destroyed the city of Elarne with a single word.' Her face was glowing, warm bronze light. Her light made the stones golden. Made dancing patterns on the grass.

She raised her arms, pointed to the sky. Cried out, 'Look! Look!' Fear and rapture in her face.

Marith turned. Knew what she was pointing at.

The dragon came down beside them. So fast: a tiny thing small as a hawk, rushing up suddenly so huge it filled the world. Landed in a swirl of air stirring up dust and pebbles. Its claws crashed against the hillside. Its breath scorched the ruined walls. It was indeed, Marith thought as he watched it, the most wondrous thing in all the world.

Thalia shook with fear beside him. He squeezed her hand. It's all right, beloved. I know what I'm doing. It's no danger to us, remember? It's just another thing of ours, like your jewels and my soldiers and my crown. Think of it rather as if it's a sealed jar of banefire. Dealt with correctly, it almost certainly won't explode.

The red scales shimmered before him. Long sinuous twists of the neck. The eyes turned from him to Thalia and back again. Eyes like shields. Eyes like stars. Eyes like staring up into the night. Falling upwards into the abyss. Falling down into the bottomless black sea. Cherry blossom falling white and pink like snow around him in triumph. Coloured fragments of mage glass falling falling falling red and blue and green and white. He thought: do dragons feel desire? Love? Pleasure? Need? Anything, aside from grief and joy at themselves?

'*Kel temen ysare genher kel Tiamenekil?*' What do you want, dragon?

The dragon cocked its head. Its teeth showed, yellow as old man's fingernails, crusted with shreds of meat. Abattoir smell. Rank disgust. It hissed out a cloud of dark smoke.

'*Kel temen ysare genher kel? Ekilet sasamenet!*' Answer me!

The dragon shifted. Its voice was softer than that of the dragon in the Sorlostian desert. A cool gentle babble of water, the green depths of a forest damp with rain. Birdsong, the chatter of insects, the drowsy low hum of bees. Beautiful. Sad. 'There was a village. A long morning flying north across the hills. A man stood up there, in the marketplace, rallied the people to him, called himself your enemy. Drew his sword. Promised them he would kill you.' A thrash of the tail, anger and hope. Like a child, Marith thought, it loved him beyond anything but yearned to be free of his love. So I loved my father, he thought. So I loved Carin and so perhaps I think Carin loved me.

Yes, he thought then. Dragons do feel desire, and love, and need.

'I killed him,' said the dragon. 'I killed every person in the village and for many miles around. Nothing lives. Nothing stands. Even the grass is gone. The soil is poisoned. For a hundred years, nothing that walks there will live.' The great head bowed, the eyes dulled to hot charcoals. 'Is this as you wanted, My Lord King?'

Marith said carefully, 'Yes. Yes, dragon. It is as I wanted.'

The dragon snorted. Hissed out smoke. *'Sekeken?'*

Why?

'There is no reason. I am your king. It is as I wanted. You do as I want.'

The dragon said, 'You outmatched my sister, in the deserts of the Sekemleth Empire. Broke her to you. She had watched that empire grow from a barren sand dune to a village to a dream. She had looked, once, upon the face of the Asekemlene Emperor, before he was bound in immortality, when he was a threadbare untested boastful young man. Now she is dumb and cannot think. You are Amrath. I do as you order me. My heart rejoices. But I do not know why I do this. And neither do you know why.'

'There is no reason,' Marith said again. 'It is what is. What I wish to do.'

The head turned again. Nostrils flaring. Scenting the air. The eyes closed, thinking. The tail thrashed.

'Amrakane neke yenkanen ka sekeken. Vyn gykanith enkanen.'

Amrath also did not know why. But your woman: she knows.

'Enkane. Ynkesisnen temet, Amrakane. Ke be temen gakare nen.'

She knows. She will tell you why, Amrath. If you dare to ask her.

'She is your queen.' The dragon's eyes looking at Thalia. The only thing in the world that resembled him. Understood what he was, how he might feel. The only thing able to judge him. Its huge broken-glass eyes. Looking at her. 'You do not look at her!' He squeezed Thalia's hand tighter. Sweaty trembling hot skin. Her nails dug into his fingers.

'*Nenakt*,' Thalia said. Leave. Go.

The dragon opened and closed its eyes again, thrashed its tail, sniffed at her. Its body shuddered, red scales moving changing colour, red-silver, red-golden, red-black. A great heat from its body, the smell of carrion and forge fires. Its wings beat and it was the sound of armies marching. Swords drawn, clashing together, cutting flesh and bone. Bronze spears striking iron armour. Cheering. Weeping. Ruin. Death. Its voice was cool as damp green forest trees.

'*Nenakt*,' Thalia said.

The dragon opened and closed its eyes again, thrashed its tail, sniffed at her. Its body shuddered. It leapt upwards, circling rushing up into the white sky. Its shadow filled the hillside. Then it was gone, tiny as a moth against the light of the sun.

Thalia said, 'Light the beacon. We will make camp here tonight. When we are victorious we will rebuild the walls of the watch tower. Raise up a palace on the ruins of Ethalden. Rule as King and Queen of Illyr and Ith and all of Irlast. Burn the world.' Her voice came choking. 'Come.'

Chapter Sixty-Six

An Illyian sneak assault in the dark that night. Marith woke to shouts and confusion. Flicker of lights and men's screams. Osen appeared in the tent doorway, a smudge of blood on his cheek.

'Nothing to worry about, just a handful of people wanting to commit suicide. Go back to sleep.' He rolled his eyes. 'I was nearly getting somewhere with Kiana, I swear, before they interrupted us.'

'Our losses?'

'A few soldiers down in the fighting. They cut the throats of two on watch duty. A third's alive but only just.'

Marith considered very briefly. 'Kill him.'

'I assumed you'd say that. He's only just alive because he's got the blunt end of a sarriss stuck three feet up his arse.'

'Lucky for you I didn't decide to spare him, then, isn't it?'

He sent the dragon out the next morning, to burn the villages along the road. A squad of horse under Kiana Sabryya to scout out what else might lie ahead. A couple of small walled towns fell easily to the dragon, barely requiring the soldiers' assistance. He let the dragon really loose itself on them. Stood and watched, awestruck, as it tore the buildings to dust. The place afterwards was a hole in the earth. A void, like the hole where an eye should be. Beautiful obscenity. A nothingness. The dragon bent at his feet and perhaps it did weep, for shame at what it had done or in grief it had come to an end. The only thing that understood how he might feel. In every way, truly, the Altrersyr were well named as dragon kin. He stroked its head and it purred with pleasure. Beautiful obscenity itself. Thalia kept well away from it. And perhaps indeed she might tell them why, if either he or it dared to ask.

A bigger town they took with little damage, ripping open the gates and killing the defenders, the dragon burning anyone trying to flee. The town didn't have much exactly in the way of three days' worth of looting: they went though it in maybe two hours, even then it was basically a bit of a forced jollity affair. But it wasn't long till Year's Heart, so Marith decided they'd stop there to celebrate. The feast day of Amrath's birth fell only a short while after, very close this year by good luck, so they could run the two together. Didn't know really where they'd be if they waited till the day itself, and it would be nice to do it vaguely properly, settled somewhere with walls and ceilings, not stuck in a tent. The town had itself been preparing for Year's Heart, of course, as had the villages around; it was not, perhaps, the most sophisticated of new year celebrations, but there was food and drink enough for a decent party (Osen Fiolt, praise his good and thoughtful heart, even produced not one, not two, but three vials of hatha for the two of them and Alleen Durith to share) and it was, Marith felt, particularly special. His first as king. His first with Thalia beside him. His first in Amrath's own kingdom. The local big man's house was fitted up as a lodging for him, they piled up a bonfire in the house's orchard, the town's gates were repaired and the walls strengthened so that a good number of the men could join in enjoying themselves. The men crowned Marith and Thalia with gold and silver and rubies and white flowers, dressed their helmets and spears with greenery, tied ribbons and bones and feathers to the branches of the town's trees.

Risky, Yanis Stansel kept muttering, to stay in one place for so long, let the enemy collect itself, being behind walls laid them open to a siege themselves, but, look, it was the feast of Amrath and the men deserved a bit of fun. The sky was brighter all night even than it was on the White Isles. Dry, clear air with a few wisps of high cloud that glowed golden in the sunset, glowed golden again scant hours later in the dawn. Too much light to see the stars, but the Fire Star shone. General consensus was that it was looking bigger and brighter than usual. 'The King's Star', the soldiers were beginning to call it. It seemed to outshine even the moon on the third night, when they celebrated Amrath's birth.

A couple of days to recover, yes, well, possibly maybe a couple of days longer than he'd originally intended (risky, Yanis Stansel kept muttering, to stay in one place for so long; take it up with Alleen, it's entirely his fault, he gave it to me, Marith muttered weakly back), then on again. They took two more towns in quick succession, marching along the banks of the river Laxartes that flowed down to meet the Haliakmon very near to the ruins of Ethalden itself. Three minor engagements with Illyian forces, two of which they won. They got further in Illyr than his grandfather. Further than any Altrersyr army had ever reached. The enemy fell back before them. The soldiers were in good cheer.

Then a body of Kiana's horse on scouting manoeuvres were cut up badly, the two survivors reporting mounted banefire archers, magery, a terrible panicking freezing sense of fear. Another scouting party was cut to ribbons behind them: one survivor, screaming with his face hanging off his skull. Behind them. Osen had the man killed, and the three soldiers who'd found him, and the four men who'd held him down when they tried to get him to say anything that made recognizable sense. The few scouts who did make it back reported the Illyians massing to the north. Difficult, somehow, to get any firm estimate of how many or exactly where. But smoke could be seen on the horizon. Dark thick columns of it, like fields burning, at night what must be fires off in the northern hills.

The next few days it rained heavily, hard heavy cold grey rain. Visibility was poor and they trudged along cautiously, sliding on muddy grass that sucked at their feet. Not as bad as the marshes in the Wastes had been, not even as bad as it often got on Sel or Third in winter in the hills, but somehow it felt worse. The rain sapped all the energy from the legs, got inside one's armour rubbing the skin raw. The Jaxertane rose, flooded its banks, looked to be becoming dangerous to cross. Marith pulled the columns under Yanis Stansel back across to his side of the river, keeping the troops close together in one long block. Safer, but the increased numbers slowed them, the ground was churned to mud up to men's knees, the carts floundered until a good number had to be left. The horses hated it, staggered along mired and snorting, a good number of them hurt their legs in the mud and had to be left as well.

All the stories about the endless Altrersyr failures. Soldiers who had recently been toasting Amrath returned on the feast of Amrath's birth day muttered lines from the *Death of Hilanis* and the *Death of Nevethlyn,* made signs against evil with their fingers when they thought their commanding officers weren't around. Thalia prayed at night to her cursed god.

The next day the sun came out. Marith had them go fast to press on. The valley of the Jaxertane was beginning to narrow, the hills rising nearer and higher and steeper. The valley now almost a gorge through the hills. He hadn't noticed yesterday, in the rain. They could have turned off up onto higher ground, where it was drier, where they wouldn't have been so pressed in. But they hadn't. He somehow hadn't noticed. Turning the long columns now would be difficult. Nasis Jaeartes had a column of light armed infantry up in the hills, flanking them on the left, Kiana Sabryya still had a troop of light horse across the river to their right. The maps showed the valley opening out onto a plain only a few hours at most ahead of them, before the land rose again towards the sea. The first columns could be there by evening easily, the rest by dawn at the worst. The benefit of the hills around them was that the enemy could not come down on them in any numbers. And of course he had the dragon. This was his rightful kingdom. The sun was shining. Things were just about fine.

He thought afterwards that his head had still been numbed perhaps by the after-effects of hatha, that the thing he should have seen that was so obvious did not occur to him until too late.

The valley did indeed widen out suddenly into a smooth plain, with the river bending away sharply to the west. More hills rose in the distance before them, high enough that their tops were shrouded in cloud. The evening sun flashed on the river, and on the armour of the men assembled in the plain. A thousand camp-fires like the stars of heaven, as the poets rightly said. Beautiful and bright and flickering and cruel as staring eyes.

The Illyians held the plain in front of him. Behind him was the narrow valley, churned to mud, filled with his soldiers marching up.

Silver lights danced in the sky overhead. The King's Star was hidden by clouds.

Chapter Sixty-Seven

'Burn them.'

The dragon bowed its head to Marith. Smoke curled from its mouth. Its eyes like mage glass. Cherry blossom. The sunlight dancing on rough water. Luminous sea creatures sliding through Carin's hands.

Never look into a dragon's eyes. Never. Look into a dragon's eyes and you lose your mind. It hurts. Hurts you. Marith stared back at it. The dragon blinked and turned its head away.

'Burn them, destroy them, tear them apart.'

The dragon hissed. Or laughed. Or wept. Lust shimmering off it. Oh yes, dragons did feel desire, and love, and want, and need.

'*Sekne, Ansikanderakesis.*' Yes, My Lord. Its soft green voice like the smell of summer trees.

Marith watched as it wheeled up into the sky. The setting sun caught it, lit it, it blazed red as the King's Star. It dived down like a thunderbolt just as the sun disappeared behind the western hills. He heard the howl of the fire from its mouth.

A silver light shot up from the Illyian camp to meet it. Mage fire, he thought, nothing of significance. Then the light reached it, enveloped it, the dragon struggling in a mesh of silver, bathed and covered in beams of light. Its fire choked out, he saw its wings beat frantically, the head and tail twist and writhe. It screamed.

Shadows tore from the sky. Rushed up to defend the dragon. The silver light took them. Like a mist rising from a river on a winter morning, or standing on a hilltop as the clouds came down.

The two armies watched mesmerized. Gods wrestling in the sky. A firebird of gold and silver rose up to the battle. Grappled with the shadows. A hawk catching geese on the wing, killing in the air. Gold feathers and fragments of shadow tumbling down. Crashing onto the Illyian army beneath but they did not move, stood staring, died staring where they stood. The night full of wonders. No moon, no stars, only gold and silver magic and the muffled jets of dragon fire.

Fighting. Fighting. A pageant of wonders. Gods dying ruined. Light and death and pain dying in the sky. Drifts of gold and silver. The dark formlessness of the shadows, faceless teeth and claws. Frantic wing beats, the dragon's body writhing. Muffled explosions of dragon fire. The most beautiful thing a man had ever seen. And silent. Slow and silent. So far away. Sparks from a bonfire. Fish moving beneath the skin of water. Nothing real.

A dragon can't die, thought Marith. A dragon is a marvel. An impossibility. Beyond death. A dragon can't die.

The dragon ripped free of its bindings. Screamed. Tore frantically across the sky. Wounds running the length of its body. It showered blood down on the Illyian army. Flew unsteadily, one wing ragged. Fire gushing out of its mouth and its belly. Screamed. Screamed. Screamed.

Wounded. Bleeding.

Dying.

You've killed a dragon, Marith. Dragon killer, you are. Of course they can die. Just mortal things. Life's an illusion. Everything dies. Even that, in the end. Even beauty. Everything.

And it was gone. A distant crash of fire from the hills far in the west.

Chapter Sixty-Eight

A very long silence. The whole world seemed to hold its breath, trying to understand what had happened. Marith stared dazedly at the empty sky.

The sun was rising. It bathed the plain soft pale warm pink. All the birds of Illyr began to sing.

Osen rode up beside him.

'What . . . What do you want us to do? Marith?'

Marith stirred himself. Do. What do we do? Yes. Do.

'Marith? My Lord King?'

Do. What do we do. He rubbed his eyes painfully. Hatha itch. Worse than it had been for . . . oh, days now. The severity of it suggested everything that had just happened couldn't have been a particularly horrible hatha dream.

'Marith! The men are standing exhausted and starving having just watched the enemy camped immediately in front of them destroy a dragon. They've been standing all night after marching all day. They haven't had anything to eat. We need at least to make camp.'

Do. What. Do. We. Do.

'Don't talk to me like that. I'm the king. You should be kneeling at my feet.'

Osen rubbed his own eyes. 'Gods, Marith! Stop it. I know you're the bloody king. Right now I'm trying to keep it that way.'

Looked bleakly at Osen. 'Are you? Why?'

'For gods' sakes, Marith! Just tell me what you want me to do?'

'Do . . .? Make camp, I suppose.' He looked across the plains at the Illyian army camped before them. A sea of horses and men and gods. Looked behind him, at the narrow river valley and the mud and the steep close hills. 'We can hardly pull back. Make camp, get a hot meal organized, prepare to meet them.' He rubbed his eyes again. Hatha. Ah, gods, half his kingdom for a few vials of hatha or a barrel of firewine. 'Get my tent put up. See that Thalia is comfortable. Leave me alone for a while. Keep Thalia away from me for a while as well.' I can't face seeing her, he thought.

Osen sighed. Rubbed at his eyes. Marith heard him shouting orders as he walked off.

Osen and Yanis between them got the army dug in at the mouth of the valley, the bulk of the troops on the flat with a ditch and palisade before them, Maen Bemann and Kiana Sabryya holding the heights to the east and west. They must not, must not be caught with the Illyians getting round outflanking them cutting them off in the hills overlooking the camp. Though scouts reported enemy horse in the hills a day or so behind them. Outflanking them. Cutting them off. In the hills overlooking the camp.

Smoke rose all day from the hills to the west where the dragon had gone; that evening they could see that the peak of one of the hills was burning. The pain of its dying gnawed in Marith's chest. Then in the night it rained again heavily, and the fire was put out.

The two armies sat facing each other. The Illyians manoeuvred in the plain, raced their horses, but did not approach.

Two days. Sitting staring at the Illyian army. It rained continually. The river broke its banks. The valley behind them was a marsh. A raid on the horse lines at night cost them twenty good horses. The gods alone knew how you killed twenty horses, silently, in the pouring rain, in the pitch black.

Gods, the soldiers muttered. Gods and magics. We're all going to die.

'I know where this place is, you know,' said Osen helpfully to Marith.

'*Dark its mountains,*
The wide green field where horses run.
The river is green and silver.
There all the world's ruin came.

'This is the Field of Shame, where the traitors first raised their standard to betray Amrath. "*They raised their voice loud to the heavens, the treacherous ones, the enemies of Amrath the Great. 'No more war! No more bloodshed! We will raise our children and live in peace!*" That's the plain ahead of us. It happened here.'

'Yes.'

'My tutor made me sweat over that section of the *Treachery of Illyr* for bloody weeks. Still have it off by heart. It's this place, I'm telling you. The Field of Shame.'

'I said yes. I know.'

Osen stopped. 'You know?'

'Of course I know. I've known since we got here. Since we left the Wastes, even, I think. It had to be here.' Sighed. 'Don't tell anyone.'

Osen sighed too. Rubbed his eyes. 'Gods. I wish you'd left us any of that hatha. Or the firewine. Or someone could just kick me hard in the head until I pass out. What effect does banefire have if you drink it, do you think? I'm not exactly the only one here who'll have read the *Treachery of Illyr*, Marith. Word will get round. An army stood here and swore it would destroy Amrath and all who followed Him. We're cursed and doomed. That's what they'll say.'

'That's what they're already saying.' Marith looked over at the Illyian campfires. 'That's what they've been saying about me for years, that I'm cursed and doomed. Putting money on it. You put money on it, in point of fact, I think.' He turned back to Osen. 'Banefire tastes absolutely disgusting and has absolutely no discernible effects whatsoever aside from taking the skin off the inside of your mouth and leaving you pissing blood for the best part of a week. Call the lords to my tent. It's time we ended this. Killed them. I'm fed up with sitting here in the rain.'

They met in the king's tent an hour later. Thalia sat in the corner, damp and miserable, suffering the beginnings of a cold. She felt sick, didn't want to eat. On top of everything else . . .

If she is harmed, Marith thought, if she is harmed, I'll kill every man, woman and child in Illyr, and every man, woman and child who marches in my army, and curse every man, woman and child left behind on the White Isles to rot and sterility and a long slow painful lonely death. Every child conceived on the Whites for a hundred years will die before it's born. The crops will wither in the fields. The woods will crumble to ashes. The clear sweet streams will run black. I swear.

Had sworn it once already, gazing up at her in fuddled adoration on the night of Amrath's birth day, after they had been enthroned as King and Queen of Illyr and All Irlast. Her eyes had paled and widened; she had run her fingers through his hair, stroked his face. Like he was a pretty child giving her a foolish gift. Then she'd laughed. 'I'd best not come to any harm then, had I?' she'd said.

Osen coughed. Maen Bemann was sitting down shaking rainwater from his cloak. The war council was assembled. Ten wet tired faces looking at their king to guide them. Yes. Down to business. Marith poured himself a drink and looked back. So here we all are back here again, sitting in a tent in the pissing rain wondering what the fuck to do next. Who's got enough courage this time to start things off?

Silence.

Come on then. Somebody. King Ruin led you to the Field of Shame and sat you down opposite the entire Illyian army. Somebody worth his position here needs to say something about that.

'We've been here three days now,' said Nasis Jaeartes at last. 'Nothing's happening. We could be sitting here for months.'

'They've got that . . . that thing,' said Lord Nymen. 'The dragon killer.'

Silence. Nobody wanted to think about it, whatever it was. Ignore it. Hope it goes away. Like a lump on a man's private parts. Lord Nymen swallowed. 'If we attack, we won't . . . That is . . . I . . .' Lord Nymen took a very deep breath. 'I can't see how we can hope to destroy them. Not with that thing. Sitting here is about the only thing we can do.'

'If we sit here long enough,' said Maen Bemann, 'the summer'll be over and we'll all freeze to fucking death.'

'Don't need to wait for summer to be over,' said Yanis Stansel. 'Not exactly a lot to eat around here.'

'We can eat the horses,' muttered Osen. 'The men, if they try to run away.'

'If we'd moved more quickly,' said Yanis, 'we could have been clear of the hills. Pushing the Illyians in their heartlands. Raiding villages where there's supplies and horses. Not stuck here in the most ill-fated cursed place in all Irlast. If we'd moved quickly. Not stayed so long in one place.'

Marith said irritably, 'You held us up as well, Yanis, you and the damn baggage, taking ages to catch up after we crossed the Nimenest.'

Osen's hand was on his sword hilt. He looked questioningly at Marith. You want me to do it now? his eyes said. Marith thought: oh, I'm tempted. Tempers all fraying, Yanis like a stone in his shoe. Stupid self-righteous cautious fool. But no. He tried as inconspicuously as possible to shake his head. This is, in fact, entirely your fault, Osen, he thought. Two days at least we lost thanks to you.

'They would have caught us anyway,' said Maen Bemann. The others looked at him. Shocked. Horrified. The scandal of a man speaking the truth to his king.

Maen Bemann said, 'They've killed every Altrersyr army that ever came here. We're no different. This is the Field of Shame. It destroyed Amrath. It'll destroy us. Cursed and doomed, we are.

473

Like every Altrersyr army in this treacherous god-cursed god-forsaking place.'

Osen slammed his fist into the table. 'This is the Army of Amrath! The army of King Ruin! The army of death! This is the Field of Shame where Amrath was betrayed? So we will avenge Amrath! Punish this country and its people! Wash the field clean with Illyian blood! We are the army of King Ruin! We will kill them all!'

Silence. A cup rolled off the table, knocked over by Osen's hand. The drip of wine on the floor of the tent.

'Oh, he's King Ruin, all right,' muttered Maen. 'King of dust and death.'

Silence. White terrified faces. A little noise like a laugh in Thalia's throat. The drip of wine on the floor of the tent.

Osen got up and walked over and stuck his sword into Maen's neck. Maen fell over and died. Osen sat back down again, wiping his sword on his cloak.

Marith got to his feet. 'You are the army of King Ruin. You will kill them all. We attack at first light tomorrow. I will give you your battle orders tonight. You are dismissed.'

They filed out, shaking. Thalia went with them, her body hunched. Marith sat down to review his battle plans.

Brief and uncomplicated. Took him all of ten heartbeats to review. Kill them all. Reclaim his kingdom.

Win.

Look at Maen lying there. A lump of meat. One sword stroke and just dead, just meat, nothing, just like that. Dead.

Of course he'd win.

Death always triumphs over life.

Chapter Sixty-Nine

And so in the grey dawn the Army of Amrath spread out over the Field of Shame to meet the Illyians, the traitors, the betrayers of the World Conqueror. The second great battle for Illyr, the greatest so far of Marith's battles, and the one upon which all else would rest. Thalia herself helped him don his armour, pinned his cloak with a brooch she had had made for him as a Year's Heart present, silver tendrils like flowers or water or her hair hanging loose, curling around a ruby almost black until the light struck it in just the right way and then it blazed blindingly bright perfect red. It had a flaw in it, a long dark scar running through it from end to end. If he twisted it in his hand, he could see the scar move. Alive. It made him think of dragon fire or the scars on Thalia's arm. Of something entombed and fighting to get out. She pinned it now to his blood-covered cloak. Flakes of dried blood stuck to her fingers. Her hands were trembling. The brooch stabbed her hand. Drew blood.

'Thalia! Are you afraid?'

She said, 'Not for you.'

'Promise me, you'll stay well back, this time. Keep out of it. Stay with your guards.'

'I wanted to see it close up. See what the men do. Dying for us.'

From outside the tent, someone, probably Osen, coughed.

'Now you've seen it. It's less confusing than it probably looks.'

It flashed across his mind that Carin would have been coming with him. Marching beside him to fight at his side. Would have to have been: he'd have been useless anywhere else where Marith couldn't keep an eye on him, he could never have trusted him with a command of his own. Next to him, cheek to cheek, licking blood from each other's kills from their lips.

Shook the thought away. Hadn't thought about Carin for a long time. Strange, to see him in his mind now so vividly.

She said, 'A lot of the men will die, won't they?'

'Probably. More than I'd like. Yes. My fault.' He said, 'I'll bring back a feather from the bird god for you to wear in your hair.'

She smiled. 'I want enough to make a cloak from. You go now. Poor Osen will cough himself to death if you don't.'

The Illyians had the better position. A very strong position. Their lines filled the plain, anchored at their left by thickly wooded hills, at their right by the deep waters of the Jaxertane, swollen from the rain. Marith could not therefore easily outflank them. They could form a solid wall and hold there steady, with his men breaking themselves against them like waves. The plain behind them was wide and gently rising, allowing if necessary an easy orderly retreat into the safety of the western hills. He had nowhere to go but back into the narrow river valley where the men would be penned like sheep. The sky above was filled with silver lights dancing. The gold and silver firebird god with its sharp shimmering metallic claws. Shadows gathered around Marith. Smaller. Weaker. Missing the dragon. Afraid.

'Hold them,' he commanded the shadows. 'No matter what comes. The things of power. The lights. They must be kept away from the men.' The shadows hissed obedience. Reluctant, but bound to his will.

The tragically unexpected death of Maen Bemann had necessitated a quick reordering of the senior command. Osen had the right wing, heavy-armoured swordsmen and a reserve of Ithish spearmen with poison-tipped trident spears. Yanis Stansel had the centre, the solid core of the sarriss. Kiana Sabryya had the light horse on the left wing, mounted swordsmen and her force of horse archers, interspersed with foot archers and two banefire trebuchets. On the far left, the small surviving troop of heavy cavalry, led by Marith himself.

'Hold,' he had ordered his captains. 'No matter what, hold the line. We cannot be pushed back. No matter what they do, we must not move back.' His lines glittering before him. Now he spurred his horse, raised his sword, shouted in a voice loud as trumpets, 'Amrath and the Altrersyr! This is my kingdom! The kingdom of Amrath! His very bones are waiting for us! Calling us to victory! Here, here on the Field of Shame we will conquer! Be avenged! In Amrath's own name, I promise it! For glory! For vengeance! For ruin! Death and all demons! Death! Death! Death!'

The Army of Amrath moved slowly forwards in the rain.

Chapter Seventy

Battle.

The armies thrashing together. At their centre, the heart of the fighting, like a forge, the two opposed ranks of sarriss. Smashing and grinding and holding. Dead men trampled underfoot. Kiana's horses charging the Illyian swordsmen. Crash of banefire trying to break the Illyian counter charge. Mounted archers wheeling and circling, never still, never stopping, rushing and shooting and moving like little darting high-flying birds. Marith, on the far left, on the banks of the fast flowing Jaxertane, waiting, breathless, his maimed left hand on Thalia's brooch. The sky was filled with fires, explosions brighter than the sunrise, flashes of darkness that made the air suddenly run cold. The shadows were just about holding. The silver lights squirmed around them trying to envelop them. The firebird god dived at his men and ripped at them with claws like hawks' talons. Banefire arrows flew over the battlefield. The light was blinding. But still his lines just about held.

His right hand itched on his sword hilt. Death and ruin! Soon. Oh, soon.

Kiana's charge had made a breach in the Illyian light armed infantry, pushed them back in confusion towards the hills. A good part of them cut up, cumbersome against the mounted archers

478

and then the fast mounted swordsmen coming at them in waves. Kiana pulled her troops together, reformed for another charge. The Illyian heavy cavalry charged to meet her, checked her and beat her back. She pushed again, the archers bringing down several of the Illyian horses. A burst of mage fire. Several of her horse archers went down.

'The mage!' a voice shrieking. 'Kill the mage!' An explosion of banefire. Green fire and white light. Another burst of mage fire. Another explosion of banefire. The mage went up in towers of green flame.

The sarriss lines wrestled each other. Stamp and creak of muscle. Shattered bronze spear points. Crack of wood breaking. Voices screaming orders, keeping the lines together, screaming at them to hold.

The shadows collapsed as the dragon had before the silver lights in the sky. Ripped into pieces. The few tattered remnants fled. Silver light exploded down over his army. Faces dissolving. Screaming. Beauty, wondrous to the eye. The firebird fell upon the shadows, consuming them. Still, heroically, his lines were just about holding. Voices screamed orders, moving to fill gaps emerging, howling at the men to stand firm. The right, the swordsmen under Osen, slowly beginning to be forced back. A shower of banefire struck the Illyian cavalry as they charged down Kiana's horse again. Bones went flying up burning. Lumps of metal that might have been swords. Osen's lines were moving backwards. Silver light melting over them. Dissolving them to nothing. Gaps, where man after man was torn down. Kiana charged again, her archers swerving off shooting high at the birds circling, Osen's lines still just about holding but being edged slowly slowly back.

The Illyians moving forward faster, confident, their gods and magics driving off the army of the demon. Gaps opening. Osen's men being forced back and back.

A clever man, Osen. Praise his good and thoughtful heart. Did exactly as he needed to without even needing to be told.

A gap opened too in the Illyian lines as they pressed eagerly forward.

Widened. Perfect ordered formations joyfully coming apart.

Marith charged at the head of his heavy cavalry.

The firebird saw him. Shot towards him.

As before, he killed it with one blow.

The sky roared. The silver lights came down at him. His charge punched through the Illyian right wing, skewed round, smashed into them again. The press at the centre suddenly slackened as the lines responded. The Ithish spears on Marith's right moved up for a charge. The pressures of the battle shifting, changing, shattered lines trying to reform themselves, all the powers of magic loosed on the battlefield pulled off from the soldiers and directed solely and entirely against him. Silver light crashing over him again and again and again.

The lights were . . . women? Beasts? Gods? Swirling patterns of branches with animal-like bodies and human heads. Dimly, striking at them, hacking off things like antlers only to see them grow again, formless twisting things of light, dimly he thought of the gestmet Landra had brought to his tent in the mountains. Fighting it, wrestling with it, struggling to keep himself. The smell of flowers and bread and muddy water. The taste of grass and rot and thick green forest leaves. Life things.

Laid about him with his sword, cutting into them. Each time they seemed to rise up around him taller and brighter than before. As vast as the sky and as tiny as insects, and he was with them, huge as they were, tiny as they were, moving, falling, flowing, fighting around and around and around. Through them, the ghost of the battle: he saw it, felt it in his mind, the ranks of his soldiers holding, pushing, killing, Osen rallying them onwards, Kiana taking his position leading another charge of the heavy cavalry, they might even be winning, the sarriss men pushing and the Illyian centre was broken, ah, but they went forward too eagerly, he could see it before it happened, breaking formation, the Illyian horse came

480

round to charge them, the line of spears wavered, he felt Nasis Jaeartes take a wound in the shoulder, stumble backwards, go down under a sword thrust, die. A flash of mage fire ripped towards Osen's lines. No, not Osen! Not Osen! Not after Carin! Tried to wade towards him, locked in the silver light embrace of his enemies the powers of life. Hacked and cut and tore at them and they enveloped him, surrounded him, kept him from his soldiers. Things that tormented Thalia, refused to leave her be, tried to hurt her to hurt him. Killing his soldiers. Punish them. Mage fire rolled over him. His skin felt dry and hot. He hacked and cut and tore at the lights and they were unharmed. Like trying to fight a rushing wave of water. Fighting the night sky or the bottomless sea.

The sky roared. Marith hacked at the gods fighting him. Death is stronger than living. Stronger than all the powers of life. One sword stroke and life is over. Ended, nothing, just like that. He hacked and cut and tore at them. His sword burned silver. Rainbows flickering around him. More and more shadows pouring out from a crack in the sky. The gods fighting him began dying. He slashed at them and they fell apart. Punish them. Death will always triumph over life.

Osen rallied the soldiers, screaming them on. They cheered him almost as they cheered Marith himself. The sword the Calien Mal blazing. The Eagle Blade, carved of eagles' bones. The sword dancing in Osen's hand. The Army of Amrath surged forward, trampling the Illyian traitors beneath them. Froth of blood, bodies tangled hacked up in pieces, astonishing beautiful perfect stink of shit and piss and death. Oh joy! Oh wonder! Kill and kill and kill! Marith screamed in jubilation. The gods of life fell broken before him. The soldiers of Illyr fell broken five, ten, twenty to a stroke. The paean rang out in a thousand voices. For Amrath! For death! For ruin! For the destruction of the world!

'Why we march and why we die,
And what life means . . . it's all a lie.
Death! Death! Death!'

Chapter Seventy-One

It was dusk before the Army of Amrath finally had the field secured properly, the few Illyian survivors penned in the mud by the river, a trophy of arms set up where the fighting had been fiercest, a bonfire of corpses smoking beneath it, burning brilliantly even despite the heavy rain. The tears of Illyr, the soldiers were calling the rainfall. The tears of Illyr, washing the Field of Shame clean.

'If I had my copy of the *Treachery of Illyr* with me,' said Osen, 'I'd chuck it onto that bonfire.'

'You should get the text carved into the hillside,' said Alleen Durith. 'With a big sign underneath saying "Avenged".'

Marith laughed. 'We'll have to rename the battleground. The Field of Vengeance.'

Osen said cheerfully,

'Dark its mountains,
The wide green field where horses run.
The river is green and silver.
There all the world's ruin came.
Still fits, no?'

A few hours' sleep. Should really celebrate with copious heavy drinking but gods they were all exhausted after the day. In the dawn the rain finally stopped, the sky clearing rosy pink. All the churned earth of the battlefield gleaming. Washed clean, indeed.

Marith cut the throats of five men and five horses beneath the victory mark.

They raised up one hundred of the surviving captives on poles beside the river. Another two hundred, shackled in pairs, followed along behind the Army of Amrath to help carry the baggage train. Their first job to strip the battlefield of arms and armour, sort all that was usable into piles. A rough tally of the dead suggested the Army of Amrath had lost perhaps one man in four. Or perhaps nearer one man in three. Cavalry losses in particular were atrocious, and they were very short of horses now. Made something of an effort to shovel up the bodies, but gave up when it became obvious just leaving them would in fact be slightly better for general morale. Mael Bemann and Nasis Jaeartes were buried with honours beneath a shared cairn.

The land grew still harsher. Everything burned. The soil was so thin anyway, very little would grow here, the horses gnawed at bitter scrubs and thistles, the men ate horses and dreamed of bread. The water tasted of rot. Godstones reared up through the skin of the landscape. Looked like graves. The men left offerings of blood and water and coin. Shuddered in fear, spat for luck. These were my people's gods, once, Marith tried to tell himself, as they rode past them. Thalia bent before them a couple of times to pray.

Three more skirmishes. They won one, drew one, lost one with a whole company of sarriss destroyed. Sneak attacks in the night, things clawing in the dark, invisible. The men screaming. Cutting their own throats. Ruined watch towers cresting the hills. Amrath's watch towers. Raised by Amrath's own command. 'There, the tower of Hekenae, where Serelethe spent a summer, when Amrath was a boy'. 'There, the fortress of Ilyryl, where Amrath drowned Lord Emrysis in a barrel of his soldiers' blood'. Ruined. Burned. Fallen tumbled stone. Another town to run through. Another skirmish: won it, but at high cost. Another scouting party came back cut to pieces. Reported through bloody broken mouths that they had reached the sea. Things were visible in the water, champing yellow teeth. No trees growing. No birds. No life.

The ruins of a fortress. Huge jagged towers lying shattered. Burned stone. Burned dead earth.

Ethalden.

Amrath's bones lay there. Unburied, scattered in the burned earth. The thought filled him with something between horror and joy and disbelief. What if he should find him? Look at Amrath's face? Where could he go, from that? 'Turn back', a tiny part of him whispered. Turn back.

To see Amrath's body. To see the ruined towers of Ethalden. To claim it all as his own.

Chapter Seventy-Two

'Here we are, then,' said Raeta. Her shoulder was all fat and swollen. Stinky. Rippled like mud as she moved. Made a squashy farty noise when she raised her arm too high. Tobias had got down on bended knee and begged her not to raise her arm too high. Her face was grey-green-white-purple. Her voice wheezed as she spoke. Dying: be a race to see who died first, him or her or all three of them. They were camped maybe three hours' walk from the walls of Ethalden.

'We'll be off at dawn,' said Tobias.

'At dawn. Why not tonight?'

'Because it's the Tower of Life and Death, the fortress of Amrath, and it therefore seems a jolly sensible idea not to walk there in the sodding dark. Yeah? And because I need a rest first.' I don't want to be walking there at all, Tobias thought. Been there once. Never wanted to go back. They could feel it, all of them. He could see it in them. The pressure of it. Haunting them. Every step they took now, they walked on sacred god cursed ground. Going to the ruins of Amrath's fortress to search for Amrath's skeletal remains and pull a ring with a demon imprisoned in it from His skeletal hand. The Tower of Life and Death. Naff as fuck and twice as terrifying.

'One day too late, I remember you screaming at me.'

'At dawn,' said Tobias. 'Dawn. Please.'

'At dawn. If you insist. But don't blame me.' Raeta said then, 'Tobias: I didn't magic you to come here. I didn't magic you to want to kill him.'

Dawn. They walked down through a narrow valley cutting between steep hills. A gash of moorland on the scorched black uplands of western Illyr, on the edge of the frigging world. The valley opened out into a huddle of burned-out houses. Some dead sheep. Three dead people. Tobias tried not to look at them and did and yet again swore off roast meat. Up above, on a hilltop, the ruins of a building. A watch tower. They felt it staring at them as they passed. The land rose again. Green barren walls closing. A stream of water trickling over boulders. Black rocks. White pale morning sky.

A beautiful place, oddly enough. The grass was soft underfoot. Mossy. A bare tree on the slope of the hillside thrust up against the white. The water sang as it fell. The curve of the hills like beasts sleeping. Rich, deep, warm green.

Maggots on a corpse, Tobias thought, looking at the landscape. That's what human life is. Maggots on a fucking corpse. Look at this place. It's beautiful. It's too good to have people walking in it, knowing what it is that people do.

'Not people,' said Raeta. 'Him.'

'They're following him,' said Tobias. 'They crowned him king.'

The hills dropped away suddenly to a broad river floodplain. Scrubby thorn trees, an outcrop of rock like a cairn, black mounds of ash. And noise, smoke smell, men smell. A salt wind. There, in front of them, the ruins of Ethalden, rearing golden out of the burned ground against the silver line of the sea.

A wound, it looked like. A world in the world. Pain.

It was vast. Bigger than Tobias remembered it. Like it had grown, since he last came here, like a tumour growing on a body, like a fungus growing on a tree. Dragon fire and ruin, and still it rose higher than mountains, squatted wide over the earth. Not a fortress

486

but a city. A kingdom. The air over it was empty of everything. The air shimmered. The air was very cold. Battlements. Gatehouses. Armouries. Marching grounds. Silver towers. White marble terraces. Walls of mage glass. Walls of gold. Walls of human bones. It stank of death and deathlust. Beat into the mind calling out to all who saw it to bow down in worship, rebuild it as the centre and heart and hearthstone of the world. Here, the broken stones screamed, here is the seat of the only true and real king. Here is power. Here is glory. Here is god. This is the only real place in the world.

Landra clapped her hands to her face in wonder. Began to weep.

The Illyian army was camped near to it, between the ruins and the river and the sea. The Illyian army now consisting of two men and a dog and a horse with three legs. They'd thrown up a palisade of thorn branches, in front of that a pathetic screen of wagons and farm carts. The thin line of the Jaxertane at least offered them some protection to the west. Silver lights shimmered in the sky around them. In the sea and in the river, things with teeth and clawed fingers stirred. Fight or die. Die fighting. Fight dying. Hold this last tiny stretch of ruined cursed ground. The shattered walls of Amrath's stronghold: we will not let you have it, the camp shouted. We will not let you return here to this place from which we destroyed you and drove you out.

The camp was in turmoil, figures running, shouting; looking down on them, Tobias could feel the fear rising off them, panicked voices calling men to order, frantic donning of armour, saddling of horses, preparations made.

A scream. The Army of Amrath was streaming down towards them. Marith himself was visible as a shining light like a diamond, galloping up and down the ranks. The red standard beside him snapped and shuddered. Dripped blood. Overhead, the shadows circled. Twisted their shapeless bodies, bared their teeth.

'So quickly,' said Raeta. 'He got here so quickly. I thought we'd have more time.'

Banefire rained down onto the Illyians. Little armoured figures shrieked and burned. The shadows poured in around the ruined towers. The stones of Ethalden seemed to sway.

The sea behind was a mass of thrashing limbs. Sea beasts. Sea monsters. Great white waves. Horse teeth gnashing. White foam hooves flailing out. Kicking madly at the shore. Desperate to reach him. Destroy him. Break his soldiers, as they had broken so many Altrersyr ships. The shadows flew out over the water and the waves rose up to try to drown them.

The waves broke back on themselves. White foam spraying, the waves swirling fighting thrashing round and round. A maelstrom building in the water, a whirlpool sucking at itself, pulling the sea beasts down. The water hissed up in steam. Waves crashed onto the shore reaching for the Illyian soldiers. Tiny stick limbs visibly flailing in their wake. Creatures in the water. Men and monsters together shattered. Smashed against the ruined walls of Ethalden, breaking against the stone.

Marith, Tobias remembered then, had had a weather hand with him in the White Isles. A man with power over the sea.

Bloody useless crossing a barren wasteland.

Bloody effective when your enemy's standing backs onto a beach.

The silver lights flickered in the sky. Banefire shooting out and down and skyward. Uncontrolled. Burning up Marith's own men. The shadows plunged at the Illyians. Golden god bird rushing to defend. Another circling, searching out something in Marith's ranks. The weather hand? Marith himself? A blast of white fire hit the front ranks of the Army of Amrath, tore men apart, devoured them.

The tiny figure of Marith, watching as his men fell dying. Tobias could swear, even from this distance, he gave a mildly irritated sort of shrug.

Marith raised his sword. Shouted. Sound like bronze gates slamming. The death scream of hope.

Another wave crashed into the back of the Illyian ranks.

The Army of Amrath charged the Illyians. Marith a shining diamond at their head.

Kill him, Tobias's mind screamed.

'Tobias,' said Raeta. 'You can go. Do it.'

'Maybe I magicked you to want to stay alive,' said Raeta. 'Do you think?'

The Illyian lines broke before the onslaught. Smeared and crushed. The Army of Amrath surged forwards. Every mind fixed. Only killing.

Kill them. Kill every single one of the sick poisonous vile bastards. I know what they are and what they feel, Tobias thought. They cannot be allowed to live.

Tobias found himself rushing down the hillside to join the Illyian soldiers. You can't run into this, some part of his mind screaming. No one in their right mind would run into this. Never go up against a drink- and drug-addled death-obsessed invulnerable demon. Old secret sellsword's wisdom, that. He drew his sword as he was running. The Army of Amrath! Destroy it. Wipe it out. Plague. Disease. Rabid ravening blind corrupting beast.

'Tobias!' Landra was howling behind him. 'Tobias! No. Please.'

He drew closer and closer to the line of battle. The ruined walls towering over him. A shadow blotting out the sun. Tobias threw himself into the fighting. Hacked and smashed at bronze clad soldiers. Shouted 'Marith! Marith!' as if the boy might hear him and come to fight him.

From a cloudless blue sky, it began to rain blood.

Chapter Seventy-Three

Landra stumbled two paces after Tobias. Stopped. Stared after him. Stared at the battle lines. She could feel Marith. Shining. He raised his sword again and the blade flashed. His voice cried out loud as the end of all things.

'Tobias!' Landra shouted desperately. 'Come back!'

'Leave him,' said Raeta.

'He'll be killed!'

Raeta said, 'Why else do you think he came?'

'He came to kill Marith.'

'He came to die, Landra. Die thinking he'd done something of use with himself. You, however, came wanting to live. So come with me. Down there. Now.'

They began to walk down the slope of the hill. Heat was rushing off the battlefield towards them. The air tasted of ashes and salt spray.

The ruins of Ethalden clawed at the sky before them. Here, Landra thought. The house of my ancestor Amrath. The house of my god. We have to go in there, she thought. Inside the walls. Through the battlefield.

Marith's soldiers were spreading out, heading for the fortress. She saw with a jolt people she knew in Marith's lines: Lord Stansel on his high square saddle, Lord Erith, Osen Fiolt waving his

490

sword. Their teeth were gritted, spittle dripped from their mouths, their faces yearned for blood. So many of them. They so far outnumbered the Illyian soldiers, as the dead outnumber those who now live.

If the Illyians had been wise, Landra thought, they would have dug themselves in behind the ruin's walls.

Crouching, shaking, they drew nearer. Ethalden's ruined towers shone in the sunlight. Running red as red rain began to fall. Shadows danced around the towers. It seemed to Landra that they were singing. The shadows and the ruins. Singing for joy.

The shadow of the towers fell on the Illyians fighting. Dark shadows. Cold. If the Illyians had been wise, Landra thought, they would have drawn up so that the ruins were not between them and the sun.

'Come,' hissed Raeta. Raeta's face was white as dying. Clutching her shoulder to keep her body from breaking apart. Shimmering fading away to nothing, a thousand faces staring through her face, teeth horns claws roots flowers wings. Crouched and shuffled. Moving on the wrong number of legs. They circled wide around behind the line of the fighting. Forced therefore to walk close to the sea and the shore. The water still churned, wrestling with itself. Great sea beasts that had once swallowed up whole war ships were dying in the pounding waves. On the shore there were bodies everywhere. Already rotting. The cursed ash earth of Ethalden reclaiming its own. The Illyian corpses were drowned and bloated. Seawater pouring itself down their throats. Dead sea beasts gasping for water. Suffocated. Fish-scale skins all cracked. The men of the White Isles were smiling. Honey-sweet pleasure in them as they died.

A man ran down over the beach in front of them. He was naked. Covered in blood. He was holding another man's severed head. Stopped, held up the head, kissed it. Set it down in the ashes, screamed 'Death!' Ran back off away from them. Threw himself at two men with swords coming the other way.

Rolling in the dirt. Stabbing. Clawing. Bare hands against metal blades.

491

Groan of pleasure as he died.

Landra turned her head away. Tried very hard not to be sick.

Tobias smashed at them. The Army of Amrath, curse them, damn them, shatter them to bits! Hammered with his sword blades, hacking, slicing, hitting, stabbing, take them down take them apart this disease on the world fucking ruin fucking death. Plague. Maggot things. Sick evil filth that didn't deserve to live.

The Army of Amrath wanted death? He'd give them death. Oh hell, yeah.

Sword in each hand. Never fought like that before. Crazy fighting. But way, way fun. Slaughter all of them. Stab them and bloody crush them to bloody bits. Filth and scum and pestilence. Sick fucks, all of them. Didn't deserve to live. Killing and killing and killing and gods he'd missed this. He was a soldier. He'd so missed fighting and killing things.

The Illyians smashed themselves against the Army of Amrath. The Army of Amrath smashed itself back. Men on both side groaning climaxing as they killed and died fighting. Glorious battle lust! Thrill of it rushing through Tobias's body. Panting in fervent killing sweat. Oh, it's wonderful! Oh, it's like nothing a man can imagine! And extra special this time in that it's being on the right bloody goodness and virtue side of things. Sword in each hand. Crazy fighting. But so much fun. Kill every single one of the sick poisonous vile bastards. The Army of Amrath! Destroy it. Wipe it out. Kill! Kill! Kill!

People think they care about living. But people, somewhere deep down, what they really care about is killing and death.

Landra stumbled through the back of the fighting. Four Illyian soldiers running passed with their faces on fire. Black as midnight now. Black clouds boiling. Red rain hissing on their burns.

A blast of white light hit the Illyian soldiers.

Gone.

Just suddenly not there any more.

You trained with a swordsmaster, Landra thought. You killed a man outside Skerneheh. Your father feasted men in his halls to keep them loyal to go to war for him. To kill for him. To die.

To do this.

'This way! Come on!'

She followed Raeta running. Raeta's body was shivering, changing. Throwing out branches and limbs. Raeta was vast like a giant. Raeta was limping barely able to walk. They almost fell over a group of soldiers, crouching in the shelter of a hollow to regroup. Marith's soldiers, from their red badges. Raeta flared up golden and the whole lot of them were dead. Like the Illyians. Just gone.

'This way! This way!' Raeta was frantic. Foam clung to her lips. The ruins loomed before them. To their left an explosion roared across the battlefield. A ringing following thousand-voiced scream.

Raeta screamed. Pointed. Horror. Broken, despairing, endless grief.

The dragon shot overhead spouting fire. Pus and maggots raining off its wings. Roared out in pain. Roared out in triumph. Flew out wide over the sea, bent its head and the sea boiled up white.

'It was dead,' Raeta whispered. 'It was dead.'

The dragon swept back over them. Overhead so close Landra could feel the heat of it. The rush of its wings. Dripping blood and pus from its belly. Her skin was burned where its blood fell. A jet of flame shot out upwards. Blood-red fire illuminating the boiling black sky.

'I really thought it was dead,' whispered Raeta.

Landra thought: fool.

'This way! This way!' They ran on across the battlefield. Had to shy away from a charging riderless horse. Landra's heart felt as though it was bursting. Couldn't go on. Couldn't go on. She almost fell, Raeta had to grab her hand to steady her. The ground shook like an earthquake. The dragon crashed downwards. Came down like nightfall on the battlefield beneath it. Shrieks. Crash of metal. Bronze and iron and bones melted, smashed, shattered beneath its weight. It rolled and howled. Another jet of fire shooting upwards from its mouth. The walls of the fortress shuddered. The dragon's mouth opened huge, feasted on the Illyian ranks.

'This way!' They stumbled forwards, running bent over, Raeta warded off a blood spattered swordsman with a blast of light.

The walls of Ethalden rose over them. They stopped gasping before the tumbled ruin of a vast gate.

Smashed, sliced, hacked, battered, hit, killed them. Kill the bastards! Sword in each hand. Blades dripping blood. Don't leave any of them living! They don't deserve to live! Swings and hits and misses and hits and cuts and kills them. A disease. They're a disease to be wiped out. Run and hit and kill and hit and miss and kill them.

An Illyian swordsman lined up beside Tobias. Limping barely walking his right arm useless, clutching a sword in his left hand. Mad rolling eyes in his corpse face. Bits of someone's brain matter dripping off him.

'We're holding them,' the swordsman gasped at him. 'We're doing it. We must. We can do this thing.'

A horseman charged the two of them. Tobias threw himself sideways. His body screaming. The Illyian swordsman went down under a sword blade. The Illyian swordsman's head rolled off and got trampled by a horse.

Hacked and slashed and spat and killed and injured. Kill them. Kill them. Kill them. Diseased plague things. Didn't deserve to live.

Maggots. Filth. Poison. Kill them.

Ah, gods. Ah, gods.

So much fun.

Landra staggered as she approached the gateway. The house of her ancestor, her god. The force of the fortress's power tore at her. Screaming at her. It beat against her, leering and hungry, filled with want and hate and need. She bent onto her knees, crawling, shaking, moaning in fear. One hand then another, trying to move. The stones of the gateway looking down at her. Such cruelty. Such hate. Such pain.

'Come on, Landra,' Raeta called to her.

'I can't . . . I can't . . . Eltheia . . . help me, be kind . . .'

'Don't say that name here! You can and you will.'

'I can't . . . please . . .'

'You can.' Raeta almost laughed at her. 'His death or our death. What are you going to do otherwise, sit waiting there until his coronation day?'

Landra dragged herself forward on her belly. Her face pressed on the burned ground. Worming her way forward, the ruins above her, remorseless, beating down. Lie here. Lie here and die. Even with her eyes closed she saw the stones shining. So slowly, crushed against the ground. Keep going. Keep going. Come on. Stretched out a hand and tried to pull herself along by her fingertips. The ruins rocked again, a shower of dust coming down on her. The stones of the gatehouse swayed. Keep going. Keep going. Come on. Dragging herself, her body screaming from the weight on it, her skin tearing on the ground. Keep going. Keep going. Come on. Come on. The ruins rocked. A roar. Screaming. I can't, she thought. I can't. The air howled around her. Amrath's house. Her ancestor. I can't go in here. I can't. He's there. Amrath. He's in there. His bones. His body. I can't. I can't.

Hacked and slashed and hit and missed and killed them. His whole body slick with blood.

'It's not their fault they're fighting for him,' Landra had said one night with the Army of Amrath's campfires off in the distance. Stumbled on a pit of still-living writhing chopped-up Illyian bodies that day. 'He orders them to do it. He's their king. He rules them. They follow him. It's not them we should be fighting. It's him.'

'They could say no,' Tobias had answered. 'They could put down their weapons. Walk off.'

'Could they?'

Hit and smashed and hacked with a sword in each hand and they fell dying. They could walk off. They could bloody walk off if they wanted to. They all knew what Marith was.

Hacked and killed and smashed and hit and missed and injured and killed.

Eyes gritted shut, seeing shadows. Rolling and twisting. Earth tearing her. Weak pathetic thing like a worm.

'Come on,' Raeta was begging her. 'Come on. Please, Landra.'

Distant voice. Like dreaming. I can't. I can't. I can't go on.

She dragged herself forwards. Hands pulling herself. Dragging herself with her fingers along the burned ash stone ground.

'Come on. Come on.'

The weight dropped away from her. Her eyes opened.

She was through the gateway. Inside the ruins of Ethalden.

The dragon crawled across the killing ground. Tearing the earth apart beneath it. Its blood consuming the stones beneath it. Pouring out fire. Killing everything it met. The sea boiled. Waves smashing the shoreline. Broken bones in their wake. Silver lights in the sky fading. Like stars as the dawn comes. Flickered out, slowly. Like a candle flame dying when the last living person leaves a death room. Fire and bronze and iron. Tobias killed and killed and killed and killed. Death. Murder. Carnage. Killing. Pleasure. Pain. Death. Love. Everything falling dying. Just ashes. Just dark. Dust. Bones. Blood. Bodies. Ruin.

Fun.

Hells, yeah.

You're enjoying it, aren't you?

Chapter Seventy-Four

The battle was winding up now. Been winding up since before it began. Last desperate stand of the Illyian people. Always knew it was going to end like this. Down to mopping up operations. The Army of Amrath making damned sure no one was still alive who might possibly otherwise be dead. Ensuring they squeezed every last drop of enjoyment out of it. The final conquest of Illyr. Might not get to really kill people again like this for, oh, weeks. Kind of like when you lick the last taste of something off your plate, it's that tasty. Don't want to lose a drop.

I said 'kind of', didn't I? Stop bloody looking at me like that.

Maggots on a corpse, thought Tobias. That's what people are. Maggots on a corpse. Life really is a pile of shit. Life's shit and unfair and pointless and hurts.

But it's better . . . He looked at the piles of bodies heaped up around him. Life's better than death.

So maybe you shouldn't have killed so many of them, he thought. Maybe?

A horseman ran past them, screaming. Both the man and the horse were on fire. A woman ran past them, screaming. Three men ran past them after her. The woman tripped and fell over someone's body part. The three men jumped on top of her. Swords went up. The woman shrieked. The men laughed. Started . . . doing things.

Tobias bent down and ripped a dark red badge off a dead soldier of Amrath. Tied it on himself.

I think it's fair to say we've lost.

Began to skirt towards the ruins. Find Raeta. Find Landra. Find . . . it. There's nothing left here, thought Tobias. Just the last desperate attempt to destroy him. Lie to myself that what's been unleashed here can be stopped if he dies.

If I hadn't . . . If Landra hadn't . . . If I'd . . .

If, if, if.

Any semblance of order was collapsing. The Army of Amrath, triumphant in its victory, dancing across the killing ground. A knot of Illyian prisoners rounded up and hacked to pieces. A knot of Illyians still fighting. A knot of Whites cavalry charging into them, still excitedly trying to trample them all to bits. Most of the Army of Amrath had given up fighting now, even. Running around drinking celebrating shouting 'Victory! Victory! Ruin! Death! Death! Death!' Even more low aspiration than the Sorlostians' 'Hooray, we survived past sunset!' as something to celebrate, really. Whoop whoop, look, some people were alive and now they're dead! Amazing achievement, hey, isn't it?

Some blokes rolled a big barrel of something past him, cheering. Trumpets sounding, drums beating out a victory chant. In the pockets where people were still fighting, quick glances: they've stopped fighting? They've started drinking already? Damnit, they could have waited for us! But wait, on the other hand, we're still killing people and they're not. Their loss.

Another explosion rocked the battlefield, almost knocked Tobias over. Winged clawed shadows flew off south over the line of the river. A troop of cavalry thundered in their wake.

Tobias began to steer round towards the walls of Ethalden. Passed a knot of White Isles soldiers looting a corpse. 'It's young Lory from Red Fields!' a man shouted as he turned over the body. 'Bastard diddled my cousin out of some money once over a pig. No idea he'd even joined up. Never ran into him out here when he was alive, and now here he is. Funny old world, isn't it?'

Passed a knot of White Isles soldier wailing over some big nob's battered body. Seemed genuinely upset big nob was dead. 'Lord Erith is going to fucking disembowel me,' a man shouted as he turned over the body. 'One perfectly understandable little mistake and his son's dead.'

Another man brought down his sword hard on the corpse's face. Up down up down up down. 'I know it was a mistake. Could have happened to anybody. So Lord Erith doesn't have to know the ins and outs of it, does he?'

Came to the walls of the fortress. Stopped. Maybe, thought Tobias, maybe I should just go up to those soldiers back there and ask them to kill me?

Gold walls. Huge. Solid gold. Studded with rubies. Winked and flashed and laughed and mocked and boiled with hate. Blank cold hard metal, and it looked like the most evil thing Tobias had ever seen. This is death. This is power. This is the house of the one true god. This is life and death.

Made the bronze walls of Sorlost look like the epitome of restrained good taste.

The walls were gold and rubies. And the gatehouse was human skulls. Each one had diamonds set where its eyes had been.

The blokes he'd fought beside today, they were going to look pretty good up there.

Soldiers were busy beside the ruins of the gateway, piling up a huge bonfire. Bodies writhing screaming shrieking as they burned. Men dancing naked and blood covered around it. Reek of drink and vomit and piss. Joyful shouts of 'Amrath! Amrath!' 'Avenged!' 'Victory! Victory!' 'Death and all demons!' 'Death! Death! Death!' A man dancing wrapped in what Tobias thought at first must be blood-red clothing. 'Amrath's banners!' he was shouting. 'Ben's banners, too!' A man dancing with a man's torso in his arms for a partner. A man dancing around a living man impaled on a sarriss. 'Victory! Victory!' 'Death and all demons!' 'Death! Death! Death!'

One of the soldiers noticed them looking. He had blood around his mouth. Tobias shouted, 'Victory to the *Ansikanderakesis*! Victory! Ruin and death!' Crossed his fingers desperately in the hope he wasn't about to die himself.

'Victory and death!' a maelstrom of voices shouted back. The diamonds winked in the firelight. All those shiny bald heads.

A woman ran up to him singing, hugging and kissing every man she met. She threw her arms around Tobias. 'Tobias! Hurrah! Glorious!'

Sweet Face. She kissed him. Ran off. Her amber necklace flashed in the firelight. Tobias walked through the ruins of the gates.

'This way. This way.'

Landra and Raeta walked in and out of the ruins. Throne rooms. Feasting chambers. Armouries. Dungeons. Tombs.

A wall of obsidian, higher than tree tops, wider than a man is tall. Cracked top to bottom like a sword blade. The edges of the crack still sharp as knives. A pool of blood at its base. A wall of mage glass, silver and shimmering, flickering with iridescent light. A doorway of green marble, with vast broken doors of green jade. The shattered pillars of a banqueting hall, column lintels carved in the shape of dragons' heads.

The whole place was an orgy of celebration. Drums beating, alcohol, roast meat. Bonfires of human bodies. Roaring choruses of *Why We March*.

'Never gets stale, does it, that ditty?' Raeta said. 'I swear, soon I'll be humming it in my sleep.'

Two men staggered towards them out of the ruined banqueting hall. Both already dead drunk from the look of them. One having to hold the other up.

Oh, gods. Landra and Raeta ducked behind a column. Froze. Landra's hands shook.

Osen Fiolt's voice: 'There you go, then . . . Oh, come on! You can't expect me to do that . . .? Yes, but I really don't care what Carin did . . . Okay! Okay. There you go.'

Landra's hands went to her knife hilt. Raeta touched her arm. Shook her head.

Osen Fiolt's voice: '"Death's Lieutenant", I heard some of the men calling me earlier, you know? "Death's Lieutenant", standing here holding King Ruin King of Dust and Shadows *Ansikanderakesis Amrakane* King of All Irlast's dick out so he can have a piss . . .'

Landra moved towards them. Raeta grabbed her arm and pulled her back.

Osen Fiolt's voice: 'Gods, watch it, you're pissing on your boot! That's better . . . Come on, then . . . No, look out! Gods, Marith . . . maybe you ought to think about stopping soon . . .? Okay, okay. Just try not to throw up on me again.'

Disappeared back into the forest of pillars, King Ruin King of Dust and Shadows *Ansikanderakesis Amrakane* King of All Irlast mumbling something about needing another drink.

But . . . but . . .

All Raeta's rotting animal faces sighed at Landra. 'It wouldn't work, Landra. Not bronze or iron. You know that. Come on. This way.'

They crept on through the ruins. Landra's heart pounding. But . . . but . . . They crept past soldiers drinking and celebrating. Piled up towers of Illyian corpses. Illyian prisoners tied up and tortured and still half alive. Soldiers decking the walls with banners of human skin.

Here and there a man stood staring at it. Perhaps amazed and astonished. Perhaps, some desperate lying hope whispered to Landra, perhaps horrified at what it was his companions did.

They crept on. On. On. On.

They stopped.

A shattered rib cage. A shattered skull case. The bones of an arm. The bones of a hand.

It was just lying there, in a jumble of fallen stonework. Just yellow old dry bare cold bone. Blind eye holes. Hole where the nose had been. White pearly teeth. Missing its lower jaw. A bronze helmet was lying beside it, red horse-hair plume still attached. It was still wearing the remains of battered, corroded bronze armour, marked with claw marks and the smoke of vast flames.

Just lying there.

Just a man who died and lay dead and unburied. A man who had no one left at the end to mourn for him.

It stank of hatred.

Landra fell to her knees.

'Amrath. My god. My Lord. My ancestor. World Conqueror. Demon Born. Dragon Kin. Greatest of all who ever lived.'

Thalia was standing over the skeleton, looking down at it. All the grief and guilt in the world on her beautiful face.

Chapter Seventy-Five

Tobias saw them. Came round the corner and saw. Landra. Raeta. Thalia. Amrath's bones.

Landra looked up and saw Tobias. His face, when he saw Thalia. His face, when he saw the bones.

'Thalia, girl . . .' Tobias said uncertainly. 'Thalia, girl . . .'

'You should just have left me alone,' said Thalia. Her voice cracked on the word 'alone'. She looked thinner. Older. The bones stood out on her neck and her wrists. A heavy necklace of diamonds tight around her throat. Like a collar, Landra thought. A collar for a slave. Or a dog. Thalia's hand moved to her stomach, her left arm, her stomach again.

'You're a fool, girl,' said Tobias. 'Endless number of times, I told you that.'

'I am the Queen of the White Isles and Ith and Illyr and Immier and the Wastes and the Bitter Sea. The Queen of All Irlast.'

'Worth it, is it?' said Tobias. 'All those lives, just so as you can say that? Really that good in bed, is he, your pretty faced King Vomit? Give you that necklace, did he, and that fancy shiny dress? I did warn you, Thalia, girl.'

'I am the Queen of the White Isles and Ith and Illyr and Immier and the Wastes and the Bitter Sea. The Queen of All

Irlast. My life is filled with wonders. Wonders and pleasures and power and love. The price of that . . . Why should I care?' Thalia's hand moving from her arm to her stomach to her necklace. 'You'd sell the world for far less than I have, Tobias. A handful of coins. A moment to pretend your life is worth living. That was your price.'

Tobias opened his mouth, and closed it, and made a dry croaking sound.

'Why must you still think,' said Thalia, 'that I am merely blinded by love for him?'

Raeta screamed something. Scream of hatred beyond human words. All her faces contorted with hatred. All her body lashing out, teeth, wings, horns, claws. Threw herself at Thalia. Knocked her crashing to the ground.

Men came running with their swords out. Thalia's guards? They charged at Raeta fighting with Thalia. Tobias was there meeting them. Four against one. Tobias was up against a pillar. Sword in one hand, sword in the other, defensive, just fighting fighting hopelessly to stay alive.

Golden light burst out from Thalia. Golden light swallowing up Raeta. Drowning her. Golden light warm and soft and comforting as the morning sun. Golden light like forge fires, wildfires, blazing parching sun in the desert, light with no shadows showing up every flaw and failure of a life.

Raeta shrieked. Pain in her voice beyond human language. Throwing out leaves and branches and claws and wings. The air smelled of fruit and flowers. Golden light ripping her burning her apart. Tobias up against a pillar fighting desperately defensively.

Her god's bones, lying in front of her. His empty staring skull. His ribs crushed where the dragon His brother had fought Him. A silver ring on the bones of His hand.

Landra bent forwards. Began to crawl.

* * *

Tobias was fighting, not even trying to injure them, not even trying to attack, just ward them off, just keep alive for one moment longer, just keep alive. Life's a pile of shit. Life's unfair and pointless and hurts. Life's a long slow painful way of dying. But I don't, I don't want to die. I don't want to die. A stab wound in his shoulder. A gash opening on his arm. Swords in both hands, and he's shaking so that the sword blades shake useless. Just stay alive. Just stay alive. Just stay alive. A gash opening on his face. His knees buckling. I don't want to die. I'm dying. I don't want to die. I want to stay alive.

Landra's hand closing over bone fragments. Dead and dry beneath her fingers. Her hands dried and mummified. Poisoned. Sucking the life out of her. She feels as though she is blinded. Clawing at them, unable to see, unable to feel. Blasphemy. Violation. This is god.

Raeta is dying. Tobias is dying. Tobias is trying to ward off sword blows with his raised arms.

The dry bones crumble beneath her fingers.

The ring slides off easily into her hand.

Tobias is fighting dying fighting dying fighting dying fighting dying fighting.

And then everything stops. The men killing him. Thalia killing Raeta. Everything.

Landra is standing there in front of them. Landra is holding a ring with a demon in it. The one thing Amrath Himself feared. The one thing that can destroy him.

Landra is holding a ring with a demon in it. And she can feel it. The hatred. The raging hunger. A thing of vengeance. A thing that seeks only and forever to kill.

Don't go looking for revenge, Ru had said.

Thalia is too beautiful to look at. Raeta is as huge as the stars. Tobias is dying. Landra is standing holding a ring with a demon in it in the dust of her god's burned dead bones.

Landra holds out the ring to Raeta.

'But it's worse,' Landra whispers. 'It's worse than he is.'

Raeta pulls the ring out of Landra's fingers. Tobias sees her face for a moment and she's so, so afraid.

'It's worse than he is,' Landra whispers.

'Yes,' said Raeta. 'But he has to be destroyed. No matter what. His death. That is all that matters here now. His death.'

Raeta burns up huge and bright and glowing, flowers and fruits and leaves and sweet fresh summer earth. The air roars like thunder.

The gabeleth breaks free.

White pale, like wood smoke. River mist. Strong and solid, the way mist is before the eyes. A man's shape, twisting. Man's long arms. Man's face.

Huge.

Shouts across the battle ground. Screams. Even cheers? But of course the Army of Amrath has seen demons and dragons. Whatever this is, it cannot be something to fear. White twisting thing rising, mouth opening, long arms reaching out. Blood marking its features. Eyes and mouth open wounds. Hands reaching out grasping. Maggot crawling fingers tracing over Landra's skin.

Huge. Towering over them. Raeta the life god lying broken at its feet.

Tobias screaming. Pissed himself in terror. He sees it. Knows it. Vengeance thing. Summoned up by the shedding of blood.

Landra crouches cowering. Maggot crawling fingers tracing over her. Pushing her downwards. Pain as it rips itself inside. My father's dead. My mother's dead. My sister's dead. My brother's dead.

No.

No. No. No.

Ah, gods, she thinks, what have I unleashed? What have I done?

Soldiers coming running. Blood-soaked armour. Blood-soaked faces. Blood-soaked minds. Drawing swords on it, shouting. Fall

506

before it, grovelling in the soil, eyes pressed down. Vengeance. Bloodshed. It consumes them. Destroys them. Vengeance thing.

What have I done? What have I done?

Soldiers coming running. Dressed in flayed human skin. Feasting and cheering victory. 'Death and ruin! Death and all demons! Death! Death! Death!' They do not know what they have been saying. Now they see the truth of it. Death. It destroys them. Tears them, rends them in agony, drags their hearts from their bodies, rips out eyes and tongues. Nothing, it makes them. Lumps of meat. Meat and blood and muck.

Always, for someone, the world is being ended. And this is vengeance. Ruin and death. Mindless dead despairing hate. Burn the world. Piss on the ashes. Life's an illusion. Life's filth and dying. Just death and death and death.

Marith coming stumbling towards it. Holding up his sword. Thinks he can kill it. Thinks it's the same as him.

Marith tries to hit it. His sword swings wide. White smoke mist fingers claw at him. Long blood scratch running down his arm.

Marith's sword bounces off it. Hacking, hacking. Marith swaying on his feet. Stabbing. Hitting. Staring in confusion. Helpless. White smoke mist body hits back at him.

Marith stumbling. Falling. Shouting out wordlessly. Still trying to swing his sword.

White smoke mist fingers close round him. Sinewed arm choking his throat.

All so silent. No sound. No smell. No feel. Thing that isn't a real thing. Smoke mist nothing. Crushing him.

He's dying! Landra's mind screaming. He's dying! He's almost dead!

Marith jerking, thrashing, down on the burned ground, smoke mist covering him.

Teeth opening through wound mouth. Teeth biting down.

Marith screams.

Shadows in the air, shrieking. Circling round and round. Shapeless. No wings, no hands, no face. Blind shadow clots hating the world. Plunge at it. Tear at it. Black shadows white smoke. Lightning crashing between them. Blast of black fire. Marith rolling screaming bloody on the ground. Marith's rolling around dying. Smoke mist hands crushing his beautiful white throat.

Crushing Marith. Destroying his soldiers. Bringing the stones of his fortress crashing down.

Vengeance! Vengeance! Vengeance for the dead!

Kill him! Kill him!

Warm white light. Lightbeams like the sunrise.

Brighter than anything. Brighter than living. Brighter than the sun.

Thalia raises her arms to the heavens.

Light pouring off her face.

The gabeleth shivers. Weak before her. Mist and cobwebs. Thing of hate and vengeance. Blood thing. Death thing.

Golden light. Golden shadows.

'Go,' Thalia says. She is shining with light.

So weak, the gabeleth. Weak, hate thing. Nothing thing. Death thing.

'Go.'

It howls at her. Claws at her.

She stands very still.

It cannot touch her.

Weak thing.

Nothing thing.

Gone.

Thalia shines triumphant. The mist clearing. The sky calming. The stars shine down on her. The Dragon's Mouth. The White Lady. The Dog.

The King's Star.

Shining.

Marith sits up. Bruised and battered. Coughing. Blood on his face. The starlight shines on Marith's silver crown.

Thalia helps him to his feet.

Thalia looks at Landra. Looks at Tobias.

Smiles.
Sighs.
Leads Marith away.
Tobias and Landra sit still and frozen.
Raeta lies there beside them dead.

Chapter Seventy-Six

The Army of Amrath lay down their swords and spears. Set to work to raise up the fortress of Ethalden greater and more beautiful than before. Its walls are gold and mage glass. Its towers rise gleaming in the sun. Its gates are carved of white marble. Its chambers are adorned with silk and fur and gems. Throne rooms, banqueting halls, pleasure gardens, crystal fountains, orchards that will soon be sweet with ripe fruit. A temple of gold. A temple of iron. A tomb of onyx. A spire of pearl and silver. Red banners caught high in the morning breeze.

On the feast day of Year's Renewal, with thick snow falling, the king returns to His home. He rides in through the main gateway and His people cheer Him. He smiles at them and His eyes shine with love. He stands in the throne room of His ancestor Amrath to be crowned. The clear ringing of silver trumpets. The peal of bells. The clash of bronze swords. The very stones themselves seem to sing. He raises His sword and it runs with white fire. The ruby in its hilt flashes brighter than the sun. His face is radiant. His voice trembles with happiness as He speaks.

'The king is returned to Ethalden! The glory of Ethalden is restored! The treachery of Illyr is avenged!'

A thousand thousand voices roar out in triumph, 'All hail Marith Altrersyr! King Ruin! King of Shadows! King of Dust! Amrath returned to us! Death! Death! Death!'

Chapter Seventy-Seven

Thalia Altrersyr Queen of Illyr. Queen of the White Isles and Ith and Illyr and Immier and the Wastes and the Bitter Sea. Queen of All Irlast. Eltheia come again.

I have seen so many wonders. I will see so many wonders still to come. I have a husband who loves me. A child is growing in my womb. I have made myself a life.

All human lives are built on others' suffering. Some die and some live.

I do not have to justify myself. To you or to anyone.

Acknowledgements

Once again, this book was only possible because of my agent, Ian Drury, and my editors Lily Cooper, Jack Renninson and Natasha Bardon at HarperVoyager and Brit Hvide at Orbit. Between them, they have changed my life. I cannot express my gratitude to them.

Similarly, all the writers, readers, bloggers and reviewers who have helped and supported me:

Christian Cameron, Michael R Fletcher, Mark Lawrence, Steve Poore, Joanna Hall, Adrian Tchaikovsky, Ben Galley, John Gwynne, Graham Austin King, Lucy Hounsom, Deborah A Wolf, Ed McDonald, RJ Barker . . . the list of authors whom I admire and am privileged to know is wonderfully long.

Adrian Collins and everyone at Grimdark Magazine.

Rob Matheny and Phil Overby at the Grim Tidings podcast.

Petros and everyone at BookNest.eu. Thanks to Petros, I've used my writing to raise funds for Medicines Sans Frontiers, which is a truly wonderful thing.

Leona Henry. Jinx Strange. Jo Fletcher. Michael Evans, Laura M Hughes, and Kareem Mahfouz at The Fantasy Hive. Robin Carter at Parmenion Books. Dean Clark at The Quill and Claw. Thomas James Clews. James Allen. The Second Apocalypse gang and everyone at GDWR. The Idle Woman.

John Scritchfield and Ashley Melanson. They won a competition, you know.

Allen Stroud and Karen Fishwick.

Russel Smith.

Helen Smith.

Everyone at my local Waterstones. The three sisters at Coffee Corner, and Janish who makes the best coffee I've ever tasted.

Sophie E Tallis, for the map.

Quint Von Cannon, for the pictures.

Julian, Gareth, Ronan and everyone else at PP, for being understanding.

Kate Buyers, Kate Dalton, Melanie Wright.

Judith Katz.

My family.

Everyone who read the first book. Gods and demons, I can't thank you all enough for buying the damn thing.